D0475149

35x 6|19

MURDER

in MONTMARTRE

MURDER
in MONTMARTRE

Cara Black

Published by
Soho Press, Inc.
853 Broadway
New York, NY 10003

Library of Congress Cataloging-in-Publication Data

Black, Cara, 1951–
Murder in Montmartre / Cara Black.
p. cm.
ISBN-10: 1-56947-410-9
ISBN-13: 978-1-56947-410-5
1. Leduc, Aimee (Fictitious character)–Fiction. 2. Women private
investigators–France–Paris–Fiction. 3. Montmartre (Paris, France)–
Fiction. 4. Terrorism–Prevent–Fiction. I. Title

PS3552.L297M798 2006
813'.54–dc22   2005050414

10 9 8 7 6 5 4 3

In memory of Guy Moquet and Marcel Rayman,
Resistance and Fichier Rouge member
and for the ghosts.

My deep thanks to Dot, Barbara, Heather and Jan, Dr. Terri Haddix, M.D., Mark Haddix, Dorothy Arkell, Carla Bach, Jean Satzer, Warren, Grace Loh, Don Cannon, Anton Rittu, and Stephen Scholer. In Paris: Alice B, Marie Colonna dePaoli for her knowledge of polyphony and her island, Corsica, Chantal Landi-Costerian, Chez Ammad, Espace Cyrnéa and Cintu, and Jon Henley. Heartfelt gratitude, appreciation and *bisés* to ma chère Anne-Françoise Delbegue, Cathy Etile of the Paris Police, Sarah Laurence Peltier for showing me Lamorlaye, Jean-Damien, Samir, Roger Trugnan, Resistance hero, Edwina, Gilles, Emma and Bus des Femmes, Madame and Monsieur Invisible, so named for security reasons. And always, always, James N. Frey, Linda Allen, Laura Hruska, my son Tate and to Jun.

Montmartre

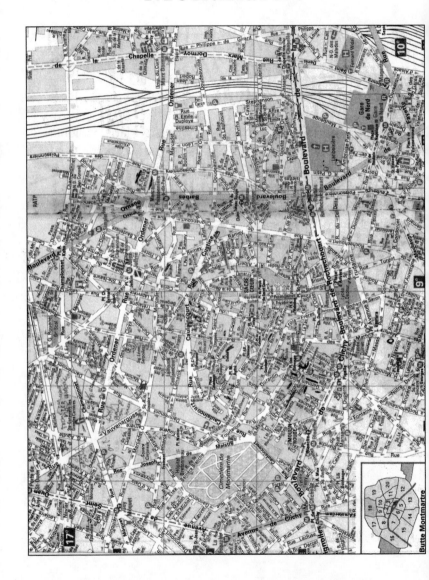

In Paris the past is ever present,
one can never escape it.

—Françoise Sagan

Paris 1995 January, a Monday Night

AIMÉE LEDUC'S HEELS SANK into the snow-crusted surface of the Paris street, quiet and deserted except for the whisper of ghosts. There were always ghosts, she thought, and they were even more poignant at this time of year: souls, wandering at night over the cobblestones, flitting through the dark paved courtyards, leaving exhalations of the past behind them.

The metallic edge to the winter air promised a storm. Below her, ice-veiled barges surrounded by escaping steam swayed on the surface of the slow-moving Seine. Quayside lights pricked the black water like so many stars. The hushed night noises, absorbed by the new-fallen snow, seemed planets away.

She hurried along the Ile St. Louis quai to her building, a relic of the seventeenth century, and mounted the steps, worn into grooves with the passage of time. Inside her cold apartment she met stale air and darkness. Disappointed, she hung her bag on the hook by the door. It was the third time this week Guy had been out at night, on call.

She heard a click, just audible. Alarmed, she switched on the light and called out, "Guy, is that you?"

He stood in the doorway facing her, his white evening shirtcollar unbuttoned, hands in his tuxedo jacket pockets, the expression in his gray eyes unreadable.

She gasped. Caught up in work, she'd forgotten the reception he was hosting as department head for Doctors Without Borders!

"Guy, forgive me but—"

"I was late for the reception," he interrupted. "When I reached the hospital there was an emergency waiting for me. I was four minutes away from my patient's losing his sight tonight. If I'd been there on time . . . but I waited for you."

A hot flush spread over her cheeks. "Work! I'm sorry, you should have gone ahead without me, I didn't think—"

"You know, at medical school they taught us to identify, isolate, and incise a malignancy," he said.

Her muscles tightened. A cold chill emanated from him.

"And to remove it before it spreads, engulfing the organs, choking the lymph systems."

"Guy, look, it goes both ways."

He headed to the bedroom, pausing in the doorway to say, "Which crisis this time, Aimée? The computer crashed, you were chasing an account that hasn't paid, you were lost on a hacking trail, or René left early and you had to cope?"

"Not bad. Three out of four, Guy." She wanted to feel the warmth of his surgeon's hands on her skin, his wonderful hands; his tapered fingers that had stroked her spine under the silk duvet last night.

A lost look crossed his face. Then it was gone. "It's not working, Aimée."

He opened the armoire and threw shirts into a duffel bag. He was serious.

"You'd flunk out of the navy," she said, blocking his path.

He stared at her. "What?"

"You jump ship at the first sign of rough water."

"We've had this argument before." He shook his head, looking down. "I wanted us to work."

"But it's not just me," she interrupted. "You're always on call, you go away for three weeks at a time to medical conferences!" She left out the holidays and Saint Sylvestre, New Year's Eve.

"I know." He looked away.

Stupid. Why had she said it? Never rely on a man. Or let them know that you do.

"Guy, I'll tattoo your schedule on my brain." She reached out and pulled him to her, enveloping herself in his arms. "Nothing ever felt like this before."

He traced his warm finger along her cheekbone. She closed her eyes, inhaling his lime vetiver scent. She felt something land in her pocket with a metallic sound.

"Here are your keys," Guy said.

"Let's work this out," she said, fighting her fear. Why had she ignored the warning signs?

"It's better this way, Aimée. For you and for me. I'm sorry." He grabbed the duffel bag, strode through the hall.

"But Guy . . ."

He was out the door before she could stop him.

Crushed, she ran to the window and pressed her nose against the cold glass as she watched him get into a taxi on the quay below. She heard the door slam and the taxi's tires churn away over the slush. Her eyes welled with tears. Two months of living together, trying to . . . he was the man who'd saved her eyesight, who had written poetry about her. . . . Now he was gone, just like that!

Relationships . . . she didn't get them. Shouldn't people take each other as they found them? She'd blown it. Again.

She sank onto the duvet, stunned, and grabbed the pillow. She found herself clutching one of his socks. She remembered lying in bed at sunrise as the blood orange sun peeked above their toes outside the window, how his long fingers brushed her thigh, the bowl of steaming café au lait he'd prepared resting next to the thick *Le Monde diplomatique* on the balcony awaiting Sunday morning reading. She remembered how his nose wrinkled when he laughed. She buried her face in the pillow. Punched it. Trying to shut out the hollow ache inside her.

A small wet tongue licked her ear. Miles Davis, her bichon frise, panted eagerly, carrying his leash. She heard his low whine.

"Just you and me now, Miles," she said.

A jade bangle, green and luminous, hung by the beveled mirror, on the birch branch where she kept her jewelry. It caught the gleam from the barge lights. It had been given to her by an old Vietnamese woman for good luck. She felt its cold smoothness as she slipped it onto her wrist, then pulled on a black down jacket, looped two wool scarves around her neck, and descended the drafty stairs, her heart leaden, to walk her dog.

A January night, and she felt as if she and Miles Davis were the only ones in Paris. Except for the ghosts.

She had lost her man.

A barge floated by with red Christmas lights still strung along the sides, framing the flat deck. A scratchy strain of a song accompanied by an accordion, reached her and she heard the lapping of wavelets.

Miles Davis wandered along, sniffing around the metal grille that surrounded the base of a leafless tree. She rubbed the jade but no reassuring warmth answered.

Her cell phone vibrated in her coat pocket. Guy?

"*Allô*," she said, hope in her voice.

"*Bibiche!*" She recognized Laure Rousseau's voice. Laure was the daughter of her father's first partner, and the endearment was the one she'd used since they were eight years old. "Come celebrate, Ouvrier's retiring. Remember him?"

Ouvrier was a horse-faced *flic* from her father's old Commissariat. She heard conversation and the pinging of a pinball machine in the background. A bar? Not her scene, with a bunch of old *flics* reminiscing and drinking, the type who'd joined the force before the earth's crust had cooled.

"I've got good news, *bibiche*. Don't I owe you a drink?"

"Sounds like you've already started."

"The seat next to me is warm," Laure said.

Aimée thought of her empty apartment filled with cold, stale air.

"Place Pigalle, you remember L'Oiseau?" Singing erupted in the background.

She'd prefer falling off a stool with Laure to drinking by herself at the corner bistro.

Aimée looked down. The snow crystals crunched below her feet. Miles Davis had finished; she could take him upstairs.

"I'll grab a taxi. See you in fifteen minutes."

THIS SLICE of Montmartre had witnessed several heydays. Before the turn of the century, Edgar Degas had discovered his models here among the *grisettes,* young women waiting for work amid the horse-drawn milk carts. Now the sex clubs and cut-rate North African shops contributed a different flavor. Still, pockets of cobbled lanes with two-story artists' ateliers dotted the route winding up to Sacré Coeur, which crowned the steep hill.

Aimée entered L'Oiseau through a haze of cigarette smoke and close, steamy air; the party was in full swing. Thank God she'd stuck on a second Nicorette patch in the taxi. Plainclothes *flics,* in their sixties and older, propped up the zinc bar and sat at the small round tables. She recognized several faces, men who'd worked with her father. They were more at home at a zinc bar than in their own kitchens. In this group, where she had once belonged, she now felt like an outsider.

Her godfather, Morbier, a commissaire, sat at the counter, his tweed elbow-patched jacket smelling of wet wool. She brightened, seeing a gold paper crown tilted on his salt-and-pepper hair, incongruous with his basset-hound drooping eyes and sagging cheeks. A half-eaten slice of Galette du Roi, Epiphany cake, and a small ceramic Santon charm sat in front of him.

Where was Guy? Forget it. She needed a drink.

"Now you're the king, eh, Morbier? Where's Laure?" she asked, motioning to the owner and helping herself to an almond-paste-filled tart. She took a sip from Morbier's glass, then another. "The same please, Jean."

She felt a tap on her shoulder and turned.

Laure Rousseau, grinning, stood framed against a yellowed Marseilles soccer-team poster that was peeling from the tobacco-stained walls. As always, her hand flicked across her mouth, a small self-conscious movement she made to hide the thin white line crossing her upper lip, the remnant of a cleft palate long since corrected by surgery.

"So, *bibiche*," Laure said, her brown eyes scanning Aimée, "you want to talk about the truck that ran you down?"

That obvious? Aimée choked and spilled her glass. Burgundy splattered on the zinc counter. Laure reached for a rag and wiped up the mess.

"That bad?" Laure asked again.

She nodded. "Guy's on call. Permanently on call."

"Aaah, the eye doctor. You've broken up?" Laure asked. "I'm sorry."

Aimée tapped her foot on the cracked brown tiled floor littered with sugar-cube wrappers and cigarette butts. "I blew it. But rather than go into it, maybe I should leave. I don't want to spoil the evening."

Laure put her arm around Aimée's shoulder. "Let's get rid of that long face. Tell me."

And Aimée did.

"He'll be back," Laure said.

"I'm not holding my breath. We're too different." Aimée picked up a new glass and threw back a shot. Men came and went, didn't they? There was always another one. With more wine, she'd convince herself of that and maybe get through the night.

"*Bibiche*." Laure hugged her. "You can have anyone in here, anytime. The trouble is they're all divorced, can't keep a relationship going for a minute, and are as old as your Papa and mine."

"As old as my father would have been," Aimée said. "It's been five years, Laure." The Place Vendôme explosion that had killed her father was now just a lost file in the Ministry, the one lead she'd had from Interpol . . . cold by now. She tried to shove these thoughts aside, too.

How familiar this smoky café-bar was. The kind where she and Laure had sat playing endless tic-tac-toe games, while their fathers worked weekend stakeouts.

She noticed the furrow in Laure's brow and that her friend kept tossing back her long straight brown hair nervously. The navy blue pantsuit hung on her.

"You've lost weight," Aimée said.

Laure averted her close-set brown eyes.

"I can't keep these dinosaurs in line," Laure said, a beat later. "At least the old-school types don't toss out sexual innuendos every five minutes and tease me like the new recruits at the Commissariat do. My life's on the line every day, just like theirs. When I leave in the morning, I don't know if I'll come back. Still, they think I'm fair game." *what*

"You're on patrol, just ~~want~~ you wanted," Aimée said, noticing the pin on Laure's lapel. "I'd offer congratulations, but you know how I feel about your patrolling."

Laure had left paperwork behind and was now assigned to active duty. Patrolling wasn't a job Aimée thought wise for her. They'd had endless discussions over it. Laure's need to prove herself—whether it arose from her complex over the harelip that had marred her appearance until the operation, or from her desire to match her father's decorated service—hadn't changed.

"Why must you put your life on the line?"

Again, that averted gaze, the hand motion brushing over her mouth.

Raucous laughter erupted from a knot of back-slapping gray-haired men, drowning Laure's reply. The well-lubricated crowd, conversing at a roar, competed with the pinging of the 1950's pinball machine.

"*Encore?*" Jean, the owner, asked, pointing to her glass.

Laure shook her head.

"Something bothering you, Laure?"

Laure jerked a thumb toward a man in his thirties with black slicked-back hair and a clipped mustache, who was crouched over the zinc counter. "My partner, Jacques Gagnard."

Aimée noticed Jacques's mouth twitch as he spoke into a cell phone while lighting a Gitanes cigarette. His hands shook, shook so much it took him two tries to light his cigarette.

Aimée had seen a lot of nervous *flics* in bars like this. The ex-military type who'd joined the police approaching middle age.

"Just divorced?"

"*Bien sûr*, got a new green Citroën and a girlfriend, the usual," Laure confirmed.

It must be nerve-racking to have a partner like that, Aimée thought. She took another sip, aware of the whispering and the pointed looks at Laure. Was there more to it?

"What's the buzz? You're up for promotion already?"

Laure took a deep breath and shook her head. Then she excused herself and joined Jacques.

Aimée downed her glassful, and had ordered another when she heard Laure's voice over the din. "The last time!" She saw Laure's flushed face. She was pounding her fist on the counter. The hush that fell over the bar was punctuated by the pinging of the pinball machine.

Aimée reached Laure's side just as Laure grabbed Jacques's drink. She seized Laure's hand before she could throw it.

"*Tiens*, Laure, what's the matter?"

Jacques's lips, which had been set in a thin line, formed a grin. "Having a partner's like being married, you know." He nudged Ouvrier, sitting next to him, wearing a Sunday-best pinstripe suit that Aimée knew he'd trotted out for the occasion. She'd only ever seen him in uniform until now. "Almost, eh, Ouvrier?"

Ouvrier's nervous laughter answered him. Others quickly joined in and amidst the tinkle of glasses conversations resumed.

"Time to go." Jacques stood up, placed a ten-franc note between the wet rings on the zinc bar, and shot Laure a look. "You coming or not?"

"She's having a conversation with me," Aimée said, her voice rising as she stepped closer to Jacques. "Aren't you off duty?"

"Since when is it your business?" he asked.

Before Aimée could answer, Laure tugged at her sleeve. "I'll be back in five minutes," she said in Aimée's ear. "I'm just going two blocks away."

Laure had a certain look in her eyes, the same look she'd had once when she'd given her report card to Aimée to hide.

The café owner waved away any payment and wiped the counter with a none-too-clean towel. "On the house," he said.

"Two blocks away? Jacques's a big boy, can't he handle it himself?" Aimée asked.

But Laure was already grabbing her coat from the rack. With her gloved hand she flashed five fingers at Aimée and followed Jacques through the door. Aimée watched them from the window as they talked. The next time she looked they'd crossed the street.

Monday Night

THE RED LIGHT FLICKERED on Jacques's grinning face, giving him a devilish look. He stood by the dirty snowdrift, buttoning his jacket.

"It's not funny, Jacques!" Laure said.

He shrugged and his expression changed to one he bestowed on puppies or assumed when he'd surrendered a seat to an old lady on the bus. "A shame to make such a scene, Laure."

"You know why!"

"Sweet, you're sweet, Laure. Quit worrying about my prescriptions. The clinic prescribes these pills to keep my back from tensing up."

His nervous twitches had grown more pronounced. And the cocktail of pills he'd just swallowed with his drink hadn't stopped them.

"Look, Jacques, it's my career, too. And this is my first patrol assignment."

"Who helped you, eh? Who talked the commissaire into overlooking your test results?"

She'd had low scores, it was true. She ignored the flashing neon Sexodrome sign that was casting red flashes onto his face as well as the large photos of semiclad women advertising the fading allure of Pigalle.

He flicked his cigarette into the gutter. Its orange tip sputtered and died in the gray slush. "I wanted you along, partner," he said. "In case."

"In case?" Surprise and a quick ripple of pride coursed through her. Yet nothing was simple with Jacques.

"Why do I feel you're going to do something stupid?"

"But I won't if you're with me. I'm meeting an informer. I'll play it right."

Like he'd played it right into divorce and pills?

The falling snow that had carpeted the street turned to slush under the buses but frosted the LE SEX LIVE 24/7 billboard above them like confectioner's sugar.

As he'd just reminded her, not only had Jacques recommended her, he'd taken her as a partner when no one else volunteered. He'd invited her for drinks after work and made her talk about her day; gotten her to laugh and bolstered her confidence. She *owed* Jacques.

"Who's this informer and why is meeting him tonight so important?" Laure asked.

"No questions. Trust me."

The new Citroën he made payments on and the hip flask he sipped from when he thought she wasn't looking bothered her. Jacques had a stellar record, but . . . his divorce had hit him hard.

"I know you're under pressure," she said. "You worry me. Before we go to the meet, let's talk it over."

Jacques beamed a smile at her. "I haven't asked you for anything, Laure. I need this."

"Like you need . . . ?"

"It's personal," Jacques said.

The rising wind gusted snow over their feet. "This informer's complicated."

"Doesn't vice handle informers these days?" Laure asked.

"Building trust and gaining an informer's confidence takes time. Little by little, laying the groundwork. I'm teaching you, remember? You with me, partner?"

Her reluctance wavered.

Jacques winked. "Like I said, five minutes and then we'll go back to L'Oiseau, OK?"

She ignored her misgivings as she pulled a wool cap over her thick brown hair, determined to discover what had made Jacques's upper lip glisten with perspiration, what had made him twitch.

Place Pigalle, deserted by pedestrians, lay behind them. Only the sex-club barkers who rubbed their arms while greeting the taxis pulling up in front of their doorways were still out. Jacques gestured to his parked Citroën.

"I thought we were only going two blocks?" she said.

"That's right," he said, "but we'll get there and back faster in this weather if we drive."

They passed the corner guitar store, a heavy-metal hangout in the daytime, in a quartier thick with instrument shops.

Turning into rue André Antoine, they rode by a small hotel. Fresh snow layered the mansard roofs of the white stone Haussmann–style buildings. A black-coated woman teetering in heels and fishnet stockings stood under a *lampadaire* in a doorway at the corner, then stepped back into the shadow.

Jacques parked at the curb where the street curved. He

pushed a button on a grillwork gate and it buzzed and the gate clicked open. Laure caught up with him as he strode across the small courtyard, her feet crunching on the ice. The building's upper floors and roof were wrapped in wooden scaffolding.

She stamped the snow from her feet, wishing she'd worn wool socks and different boots. Her gloves . . . she'd forgotten them in the car. Jacques hit the digicode and a door opened to a tattered red-carpeted hall.

"Wait here," Jacques said.

"In a freezing vestibule?"

He *was* going to do something stupid. Police procedure required that a pair keep together, not split up.

"We're a team, aren't we?"

Team? On the job they were. "We're off duty, remember?" she said. "How personal is this?"

"More than you know. But you can quit worrying. I know what I'm doing." He tugged his earlobe, a mannerism some women might find endearing. Grinned. Monsieur Charm was what they'd nicknamed him at the Commissariat.

"Tell me what's going on, Jacques."

"I just need some back up."

Was she reading this wrong? "So you want me to warn you in case some thug shows up?"

He put his fingers to his lips and winked. "Trust you to figure it out."

Jacques ran up the stairs. She listened as his footsteps stopped on the third landing.

Laure studied the names on the mailboxes uneasily. It didn't add up. A cold five minutes later she followed the red carpet up the creaking staircase. Three flights up, in a dim hallway filled with piles of wood and an old sink, cold drafts swirled against her face. An open door led into a dark apartment.

"Jacques? Quit playing games," she called out.

No answer. What had the fool done now?

She stepped into the apartment, into musty darkness, her footsteps echoing on the wood floor. It seemed vacant. From an open window, gusts of snow blew onto the floor. And then she heard a distant sound of breaking glass.

Alarmed, she unzipped her jacket and drew the gun she'd only fired previously on the shooting range. Her heart raced. Drugs! Was he on the take? No way in hell would she risk her badge for his dope habit. She peered out the window. No Jacques.

She climbed out onto the scaffold and navigated the slippery two-plank walkway gripping the stone building, her bare hands frigid.

"Laure . . ." Jacques's voice, the rest of his words, were lost in the wind.

A howling gust whipped across her face as she pulled herself up from the scaffolding and reached for the gray-blue tile edge of the slippery roof. A punch knocked her to her knees. The second blow cracked her head against the scaffold with a bright flash of light.

Monday Night

AIMÉE PEERED AGAIN AT her Tintin watch. Nearly eleven o'clock. "What's taking Laure so long?"

Morbier shrugged, taking a swig from his wineglass. "Better congratulate Ouvrier now, before he leaves."

Ouvrier stood near them, holding an open blue velvet box containing a glinting gold watch. "Thirty-five years of service."

She saw a wistful look on his long face.

"Congratulations, Ouvrier." Aimée nudged him. "How will you keep out of trouble now?"

"*Ma petite*, I've had enough trouble," he said, giving her a little smile.

Ouvrier, widowed, and estranged from his children, subject to flare-ups in winter from a knee injury in his rookie days, had been sidelined. A new generation of *flics* was taking over. She felt for him, aware of his scars, inside and out. For now, he had camaraderie but not much else to show for years of service besides the gold watch.

Where was Laure? Aimée stood and pulled on her coat. There was only one way to find out.

SHE CROSSED Place Pigalle toward the mounting zinc rooftops silhouetted against the moonlike dome of Sacré Coeur. Midway, in a frame shop, the white-coated long-haired owner nodded to her as he pulled the blinds down. But not before she saw the notice of an upcoming organic market below a Warhol-style silk-screen print of Che Guevara . . . black and red all over.

Montmartre embodied the bohemian spirit. In its past it had been the home of anarchist Communards and then of artists and writers for whom absinthe provided inspiration. Now it held a mix of small cafés and theatres that hosted poetry readings or a playwright testing a first act on patrons, and dance studios occupying ateliers that once boasted students like van Gogh.

Young Parisians treasured converted studios here, trading the trudge up the steep streets and flights of stairs for the view of the sweeping panorama below, just as Utrillo, Renoir, and Picasso once made their homes in cheap ateliers. This was where the Impressionists, Cubists, and Surrealists had painted. The tradition of the village, eccentric and stubborn, still remained.

There was no sign of Laure. Aimée turned the corner and saw a new Citroën at the curb under a No Parking–Tow Zone sign. Only a *flic* would dare. It was a nice chrome green Citroën, too. Jacques's? A glance through the half-frosted window revealed a crushed pill bottle on the floor by the clutch and blue gloves on the passenger seat. Laure's gloves.

Something smelled bad, as her father would have said.

A gate stood open. Fresh footsteps in the snow trailed across to a darkened building. She entered and crossed the courtyard, her heels slipping on the ice. Strains of music from the building opposite wafted through the courtyard, and patches of light came from a window. Another party?

Snow clumped in the building's half-opened door. Aimée walked inside into the dark foyer. A broken stained-glass window and water-stained doors met her gaze. There was a darkened concierge's loge on the right. Once plush and exclusive, she thought, now the building looked shabby.

"Laure?"

A gust of wind rattled the metal mailboxes. Wet footprints mounted the red-carpeted stairs.

She followed them to the third floor. Piles of lumber and paint cans sat under a skylight attesting to a renovation in progress. The apartment door stood open.

"Allô?"

No answer. She went inside, her footsteps echoing in a hallway. Beyond lay a dark, nearly empty series of rooms swallowed by shadows. What looked like a piano stood, ghostlike, covered by a sheet.

She shivered and backed up. In this bitter cold, half-empty apartment something felt very wrong. Metal clanged from outside where a construction scaffold was visible through the open salon window. Had Jacques and Laure, the idiots, gone out there? Snow blew in through the window, dusting a large armchair and wetting the carpet as it melted.

She stepped over the window ledge to the scaffold, which was barely illuminated by the dim light of the moon. Freezing wind and gusting snow flurries met her. Gloves, she needed gloves and a snowsuit!

At the shadowy scaffold's end, she could just make out a slanted mansard rooftop and behind it, a small flat area piled with rebar and bricks. Snow crusted the wooden slats over the windows; suffused moonlight showed a mesh of footprints.

She heard creaking and forced herself to traverse the scaffold, to look beyond the pepper-pot chimneys and zinc rooftops laced with snow stretching like steps down the hill of Montmartre. Taking small steps, Aimée edged toward the roof edge and tripped. Her arms flew out; icy slush brushed her cheeks. Then she saw Laure's sprawled body.

"Laure!" she cried.

A groan answered her.

"Laure, can you hear me?" she said, bending down. Her fingers located a weak pulse on her friend's neck.

She rooted in Laure's pockets for a police radio, couldn't find one, pulled out her cell phone, and tried to control her shaking hands to punch in 18, the emergency number for the police.

"Officer down, possibly two, 18 rue André Antoine, on the roof," she said. "Send backup, an ambulance. Hurry."

The Commissariat was nearby. Would they get here in time?

"Jacques," Laure moaned.

Dull thuds came from somewhere on the roof.

"Help him . . . hh . . . have to . . ."

Aimée tried to control her panic. Think, she had to think straight.

"Laure, backup's on the way. . . . What's going on?"

"Jacques . . . couldn't wait anymore, some informer. . . . He saved me . . . I . . . owe Jacques!"

If he had saved Laure's life . . . Aimée hesitated.

"You came up here after Jacques? Where is he?"

"Over there . . . take my gun. Help him!"

The last thing she wanted to do was deal with Jacques, or his informer. Sleet gusted and the rising wind took her breath away. Aimée felt for Laure's holster. It was empty.

Worried, she stood, took a few steps, and climbed onto the tiled rooftop, grabbing at the chimney to steady herself. She worked her way across the slick roof, the sleet blinding her. And then her legs buckled.

She landed on something bulky, inert. A body. Her gaze locked on its staring eyes. Jacques's eyes, his eyelashes flecked with snowflakes. Terror coursed through her as sirens wailed in the distance. She brushed the snow from her face and her hands came back covered with pink-red slush. Blood.

"Jacques!"

He blinked, the whites of his eyes showing. He was trying to tell her something. She checked his neck and found a weak pulse, the carotid artery.

She pulled herself to her knees, pinched his nose shut, checked his tongue, and started blowing air into his mouth. Her hands were so cold. None of the breath-and-pause sequences elicited a response from his blue lips.

"Can you hear me, Jacques? Can you talk?"

His mouth moved. She folded her hands, began quick, sharp thrusts to his chest. As Jacques tried to speak, a thin line of blood trailed from his mouth. She thrust harder now, counting and breathing. The air was stinging cold. Faster now, because while she panted and thrust, she felt him go limp. "Don't leave me now, Jacques!"

She didn't know how long her frozen, numb hands worked on Jacques. Finally, she heard footsteps on the scaffolding and the clang of metal. Chalk white beams blinded her.

"Take over . . . he's . . . respond . . ." She struggled, trying to get her breath.

She heard static from a police radio and the words "Move away from the gun!" And then she was flying into the wall, tackled, her head shoved into the snow. She couldn't breathe. Her hands were wrenched behind her, she heard the clink and felt the cold steel of handcuffs.

She fought, jerking her head, tried to move her legs. "What are you doing?" She spit out the ice that had been forced into her mouth.

More radio static, biting wind.

Catching her breath, she shouted, "Help him for God's sake."

A medic leaned over Jacques. She heard the words "crackling . . . subcutaneous emphysema wound seepage." A stark white beam of light showed the black-red bullet hole and the blood seeping from Jacques's chest.

"Too late," the medic said. "He's gone."

Her shoulders slumped.

"Backup's here, crime-scene unit's on the way," a hoarse voice shouted. When it was one of their own they made it a priority response. "Move her . . . careful."

She felt her arms lifted, hips shoved forward.

"I've seen it before," the hoarse voice said. "They shoot them, then try to save . . ."

"What do you mean? Check the roof," Aimée said, melting ice running down her face. "Someone attacked the officer on the scaffold. I heard noises and came up here and found her, then him."

"So you shot him with his own gun."

"You're wrong, I tried to save him!"

More footsteps and a portable halogen light illuminated Jacques's body slumped on the slanted rooftop between the chimney pots. His coat and pants pockets had been turned inside out. Clumped red matter spread across the snow. He'd been shot at close range, Aimée observed, horrified.

In the beam of the halogen light, Aimée saw a Manhurin F1 38 .357 Magnum nonautomatic, the standard police handgun, in a plastic bag laid down on the blue tarp. Jaques's gun or Laure's? Snowy sleet whipped by, sending flurries across the roof.

An officer, his crew cut sprinkled with snow, rolled up

Jacques's pants. "His gun's still strapped to his ankle. Yet this Manhurin's police issue."

"It must belong to the officer at the edge of the roof," Aimée said.

"And it just flew over here?" he asked.

She realized she'd better shut up and wait to explain to the investigating magistrate.

He leaned into his matchbox-sized monitor and spoke. "Bag the hands of the officer below and check for gunshot residue."

"You've got it all wrong," Aimée burst out, despite her resolve. "Jacques came up here alone to meet someone." She'd deduced that from what Laure had said.

"And bag this woman's, too," he said. "We'll send her down."

The wind rose again, whipping more snow into lacy flurries. Each breath stung. She wanted to wind her scarf over her mouth. The Level 3 weather warning had turned into a first-class storm. The plastic sheeting the crime-scene unit had raised whipped into shreds in the wind and blew away.

"Get another plastic sheet, quick!" a crime-scene technician shouted. "Now! Haven't seen a storm like this since 1969!"

A few members of the crime-scene unit unpacked their equipment on the coating of ice by the skylight, making a futile attempt to deal with the area.

"The light's changing every second!" said the photographer, pulling out his camera, his shoes crunching on the brittle snow. "Hurry up, I can't get a good light-meter reading!"

Aimée noted the interlacing footprints. Any evidence there might have been was now compromised.

"Take her downstairs," the officer said, an edge to his voice.

"I know my rights."

The officer waved her away.

From the edge of the roof, Aimée saw flakes swirling in flashlight beams and snow-carpeted rooftops stretching toward distant Gare du Nord. Across the courtyard, several lit windows appeared amid the yawning dark ones. Strains of bossa nova fluttered on the wind. That party in the adjoining building was still going on.

Down in the apartment, Laure crouched as a group of men with snow-dusted shoulders huddled about her, an anguished look on her pale face as the gloved technicians pressed double-sided adhesive tape over her fingers and palms. The wind blowing from the window snatched away their conversation but she overheard "Custody . . . at the Commissariat. . . ."

"*Bibiche!*"

Aimée froze. Laure's hair was matted and wet, a large knot welled on her temple, the white of one eye was discolored with blood. "Poor Jacques . . . who'll tell his ex-wife?" she asked as she tried to stand and slipped on the wet floor.

An officer steadied her. "Sorry, Laure, you know I have to do this and report anything you say," he said.

"Report what she says?" Aimée repeated, raising her voice to be heard over the wind. "Laure needs medical attention."

The *flic* turned to Aimée, irritated. "Who gave you permission to talk, Mademoiselle?"

"I'm a private detective."

"Then you should know better," he said, nodding his head at the man beside him. "Run this woman's ID. Why hasn't someone bagged *her* hands for gunshot residue?"

Edith Mésard, La Proc, the investigating magistrate, entered wearing a black cocktail dress under a fur stole. She stamped the snow from her heels. Procedure dictated that in dicey situations she arrive at the same time as the Brigade Criminelle. "*Désolé*, Madame La Proc," the *flic* said.

Aimée stepped forward.

Recognition dawned in Edith Mésard's eyes. "Mademoiselle Leduc." She sniffed, then frowned. "Light a match to your breath and the building would go up in flames."

Before Aimée could respond, La Proc cleared her throat. "Give me the details, Inspector. How does it come about that a *flic* shoots another *flic* on a slippery zinc-tiled roof in a snowstorm? Convince me."

"We found her weapon on the roof."

"Was it next to her?"

"The officer in question lay on the scaffolding below," he said, abashed. "Her gun lay next to Jacques . . . the victim."

"*Merde!*" La Proc said under her breath, pulling out tennis shoes from her Vuitton bag.

"What? Are you accusing Laure of shooting her partner?" Aimée said. "That's absurd."

"Or maybe *you* shot him, Mademoiselle?" said the inspector.

Panic coursed through her.

"Take her statement at the Commissariat!" Edith Mésard said, before climbing out the window.

The *flic* shoved Aimée forward and down the stairs.

The few bystanders in the narrow street—an old woman, her bathrobe flapping under her overcoat; a man with tired eyes in a blue-green bus driver's uniform—were illuminated by the blue rays of the revolving SAMU ambulance light. Morbier stood by an old parked Mercedes, its roof flattened under the weight of the snow. A tow-truck driver had hitched Jacques's green Citroën to his truck.

"They've got it all wrong, Morbier," Aimée called out.

"Move along, Mademoiselle," said the *flic*, pushing her toward the blue-and-white police van.

"Just a moment, Officer," Morbier said.

The officer raised his eyebrows, eyeing first Morbier and then Aimée's black leather pants, down jacket, and spiky hair.

Morbier flashed his ID. "Give me a moment."

"*Bien sûr*, Commissaire," the flic said, taken aback.

"What mess have you gotten yourself into this time, Leduc?" Morbier asked, his breath misting in the freezing air.

"You got that right, Morbier. A terrible mess." She gave him a brief account.

Morbier listened, pulling out a Montecristo cigarillo, cupping his hands, and lighting it with a wooden match. He puffed, sending acrid whiffs into Aimée's face, and tossed the match into the snow, where it went *thupt*. When she finished he shook his head and looked away, silently.

Why didn't he say anything? "Morbier, help me convince them. . . ."

"Might as well teach rocks to swim, Leduc. There's procedure. You know that. Do the drill. You're a suspect, shut your mouth."

"Shut my mouth?"

"Until you give your statement," he said. "Be smart."

She controlled her horror. Of course, he was right. She'd explain, diagram her route, show that Laure couldn't have killed Jacques.

"Laure wouldn't shoot her partner after practically the whole police force had seen them together in the café!"

Morbier flicked his ashes, they caught in the wind. "And witnessed their fight and your meddling," he said.

She'd forgotten about that public scene.

"You've got clout, Morbier," she said. "Use it."

For once, she hoped he'd listen to her.

The *flic* grabbed Aimée's elbow in an iron grip. "I'm sorry, Commissaire, the van's waiting."

"What a night for this to happen!" Morbier expelled his breath with a noise she recognized for what it was, resignation underlaid with the steel note of authority. A mode he'd perfected. Voices drifted from above them. Lights glowed from the building's roof.

Aimée noticed a black-leather-coated man, a pack on his back, standing in a doorway. He watched them intently, listening, as if gauging the situation. Could he have witnessed the shooting?

A battered Renault Twingo skidded to a halt beside the white morgue van. Several men jumped out, cameras in hand or on straps slung over their chests.

"The press! Excuse us, Commissaire; *allez-y*, Mademoiselle."

The *flic* bundled Aimée away before she could point out the possible witness to Morbier. He shoved her into the police van, handcuffed her wrists to the bar behind her like a criminal. She slipped on the floor, which had been salted to slow a prisoner's traction if he aimed to bolt. She felt each cobblestone as her spine jounced against the hard seat and the van headed, siren blaring, into the night.

Monday Night

AT THE BARK OF A GUN above him, Lucien Sarti had jumped and ducked into a blackened stone doorway. A reflex. Knots clenched his stomach; he wanted to melt into the stone.

He worried about crossfire. Relentless sleet pelted the buildings. Peering up the curving street, he saw no one else on the glistening icy surface. Then clumps of snow fell from a scaffolding above and crumbled on the cobblestones. He saw movement, heard thuds.

Lucien moved back deeper into the doorway, pulled his black leather coat tighter, waited. He brushed the snow from his curling black hair. Given his history, the best thing would be to leave. Run, get away. But his big chance lay a stone's throw off, just around the corner.

His luck!

The warren of nineteenth-century soot-stained buildings and twisted mounting streets reminded him of rue du Castagno in Bastia's old port. But instead of sun-baked stone, the sirocco whipping from Africa, and old women knitting on their stoops, the steep stairs ahead held clusters of new snow, gusts of wind, and prostitutes who'd stepped into the shadows.

He waited until he saw flickers of light and heard the wail like a cat in heat and then sirens. As he was about to run across the street, the door behind him was opened by an old man leading a Westie on a leash.

Think fast, he told himself.

"Pardon, I forgot the door code," he said to the old man. "My friends live on the second floor."

The old man nodded, a muffler wrapped high around his neck, and Lucien edged his way inside. He waited on the dank building's pitted stone staircase until the thumps in his heart subsided, until he heard cars pulling up and voices outside. He figured it would be easier now to blend into a crowd and cross the courtyard.

Since birth he had been taught to keep his mouth shut: *aqua in boca*. His *grand-mère* would indicate the need for silence by sliding her finger across her lips. He knew better than to get involved. He threaded his way past the police van to the gate and paused, listening. Snatches of conversation drifted on the sleeting wind. "Shooting on the rooftop" was all he could understand. No way could he get involved.

This city was filled with contradictions, unlike his native Corsica, where it was simple: all outsiders were viewed as a threat.

Satisfied that no one had noticed him in the flurry of activity, Lucien made his way across the snowdrifts in the courtyard to a jewel-like townhouse.

He opened the front door and mounted the staircase, passing several landings until an open door revealed a well-dressed crowd in the foyer. A party? He should have worn his new shirt. Conari had just told him to stop by for a brief meeting.

As a woman leaned toward an arriving couple to greet them, a scent of roses wafted from her. Familiar. Snowflakes danced outside the foyer window, catching the light and framing her tan, smooth back. Only one woman he'd ever known would wear something like that in this weather. But it couldn't be. And then he lost her in the crowd of newcomers.

"Lucien, so glad you're here." A voice, loud and welcoming, came from his host, broad-shouldered Félix Conari, who filled the doorway. Long charcoal gray hair curled behind his ears. His skin was Côte d'Azur bronzed, the all-year bronze of the wealthy. "Do come in; it's wonderful you made it."

"*Bonsoir*, Monsieur Conari, my pleasure." Lucien's hand picked at his coat pocket, a nervous habit.

"Welcome to our annual client party." Félix winked. "Impress with success, you know."

Lucien didn't, but he nodded.

Félix put an arm around him and escorted him inside the large apartment's reception rooms, which were high ceilinged and adorned by carved moldings, parquet flooring, and marble fireplaces. Lucien managed a smile, hoping his eyes didn't reveal his surprise. A mix of flat-chested, hollow-cheeked miniskirted models, advertising *médiathèques*, clad in head-to-toe black, and bourgeois matrons clad in Chanel hovered by the table, which was spread with hors d'oeuvres. The hum of conversation and the clink of glasses filled the air.

Right behind them a man entered and handed his overcoat to a waiter. "The police are blocking the backstreets; someone's been murdered on a roof," he announced with irritation. "It's a mess. I couldn't find a parking place!"

Someone murdered? Lucien concealed his shaking hands by putting them in his pockets. With his background, he had to steer clear of this.

"*Nom de Dieu!*" said Félix as a momentary hush filled the salon. "At least it seems under control." Félix guided Lucien toward the long white-linen-covered table. "Taste the foie gras and let's catch up in the study."

"*Merci*," Lucien said, conscious of Félix's practiced finesse as he was marshaled, with a well-loaded Limoges plate, to the study.

A fire crackled, illuminating minimalist furniture at odds with the ornate ceiling, wood-paneled walls, and curved windows. Old world meets avant-garde.

A man came out of the door of an adjoining bathroom, toweling his wet hair.

"Had to splash myself awake," he said, smiling.

"You're still working?" Félix pulled Lucien toward the man, who looked to be in his thirties. He wore a rumpled black suit and scuffed Adidas sneakers. His brown hair was pulled back in a ponytail. "Meet Yann, an associate. He does the brain work, I am just the brawn," Conari joked.

Yann grinned. "Not always." He shook Lucien's hand. "A pleasure."

Lucien felt a moist but strong grip. Then Yann shut down a laptop sitting on the desk. "I promised Félix to mingle and try to improve my social skills. Excuse me."

Lucien practiced his smile again. "You're so kind to invite me, Monsieur Conari."

"Call me Félix."

Lucien had sent Conari several tapes of his music. But Félix's invitation to come to his home to discuss them had surprised him. Lucien had no rent money in his pockets. A sleeping bag in the pantry of Anna's Corsican Communist resto, where he worked for food, was his bedroom now. He prayed this meeting would lead somewhere.

Lucien's cousin's great-aunt had married a distant relation of Félix Conari's. Félix wasn't even Corsican, but in Corsica family meant everything. Clan ties and family connections from the thirteenth century still governed the island. The code was strong. The basics still operated in Paris.

"Have your drink while you listen to my proposal." Félix gestured Lucien to a curved blond wood sculptural chair. "I'd like you to let me represent you and to introduce your work to the head of SOUNDWERX."

SOUNDWERX. The European recording giant! Lucien blinked in surprise.

"You have a unique sound, haute cool," Félix told him. "I want to help you."

It was an offer Lucien hadn't even dreamed of. He was almost afraid to believe it was real.

"You possess the gift, hard to define. As though you concoct words from the air and the stars sing. I'm saying it badly." A brief sadness crossed the face of this man in a designer suit. "My sister had it, too. She was so gifted, but she passed away." He looked down, rearranged some papers on his desk. "I couldn't help her, but I hope you will give me the chance to advance your career."

Lucien nodded, excited. So Félix understood his music and admired it, even if he wasn't Corsican. He explained, "My grandfather, father, and uncle sang polyphony, the seconda, bass, and terza, ninth-century poems in a cappella. At home, our saying is 'Three singers in harmony make an angel's voice.'" His heart raced; it always did when he spoke about his music. "Music filled our house. I build on the traditional foundation; I use it as a base and I go on to explore. I want to open our culture to the world."

The door opened, letting in the snare drum of a bossa nova and the murmurs of the crowd. Lucien turned. The woman he'd seen in the doorway entered the room. She'd thrown her head back, laughing. That long neck, curved, so familiar. Could it be? She wore a clinging coppery red dress; her straight black hair hit the middle of her bare back. She turned, her face caught in the light, and he recognized Marie-Dominique, his first woman. She still wore the scent of roses.

He froze. Four years . . .

"Aah, Lucien, meet my wife," Félix said. "Forgive me for not introducing you.

Marie-Dominique, Félix's wife?

He couldn't pull his eyes away. Marie-Dominique's gaze caught his as she inhaled briefly.

"Lucien," she breathed out. "I'm happy to meet you."

The world stopped. In Lucien's mind the cicadas were buzzing, their loud cacophony a wall of sound in the dry heat. The leaning pines sheltered by granite formations, the parched oleander, and withered, browning myrtle were all around them on the hill where he'd last seen her.

"Hasn't Félix shown you around? You look lost," she said.

Lost in the past, he thought. And pining for a future they'd never had.

"How long have you lived in Paris?" What he meant was how long had she been this sophisticated Parisienne, married to a wealthy man.

She looked down, curling a black strand of her hair around her finger. Just as he remembered her doing when she was thinking.

"Long enough," she said.

"Marie-Dominique," Félix said putting his arm around her, "find Lucien a seat at the table next to us. Persuade him to play something after dinner."

Lucien knew he should thank Félix for his hospitality and leave before he made the biggest mistake of his life. But Marie-Dominique's scent and his memories paralyzed him.

Amusement glimmered in Félix's eyes as he said, "Lucien, you'll let me help you?"

Lucien nodded, tongue-tied.

"As long as you're not involved in Corsican political causes or these Separatist groups. Are you?" Félix asked.

Should he reveal his past? But how could he tell the truth?

He was an unknown; he played in Corsican restaurants to eat. SOUNDWERX would make him.

"Félix, I'm just a musician!"

"Good. Monsieur Kouros of SOUNDWERX wants to meet you. He's a personal friend, Lucien," Félix said. "Connections are what count in this world. Forgive me if I assumed too much, but I've already given him my word that you'd sign an exclusive contract."

Lucien's mouth felt dry. Should he ask to read the contract, he wondered. Seeing Marie-Dominique while listening to Félix's proposal had his mind reeling.

Félix rubbed his chin between his thumb and forefinger. "You look unsure. After you meet Kouros you'll understand."

Out in the salon, Lucien's collar felt damp. He'd been perspiring. All about him, couples chatted, and everyone seemed to know one another. His awkwardness increased as he observed the well-dressed strangers surrounding him.

A waiter in a white coat stared at him. He had black eyes and an olive complexion that were at odds with his bleached-blond curly hair. A Corse, like himself, Lucien figured, trying to get by.

Lucien summoned a smile. "What village do you come from?" he asked, the question Corsicans always put to a fellow countryman. It was a way to pinpoint their place on the social map, to discover who their friends were, what power they had access to, or even if they were by chance related. Or, worst scenario, if they were involved in a complex vendetta against his clan, one that might have arisen from the defense of the honor of a twice-removed murdered cousin from the last century. These things had to be explored.

"Monsieur?" The waiter addressed him as if Lucien hadn't spoken. "Monsieur Conari said to tell you that dinner's served in the other salon." Then he edged closer and responded, "I'm from Bastia."

An *Italian*, as people from his rock-perched village would say. To them, all coastal people were descended from Italian fisherman. Even if their ancestors had reached Corsica five centuries earlier.

"And you?"

"Vescovatis," Lucien said.

A look of recognition flashed in the waiter's eye. Already Lucien was one up, hailing from a mountainous inland valley. A more pure Corsican.

Félix came up behind him, clapping him on the back, and flashed a big smile. "Listen, we'll sign the contract after dinner. You're going places, young man, I'll see to it."

Loud footsteps pounded across the parquet floor. And then Marie-Dominique's dress rustled, brushing his hand as she turned, searing his fingers with a touch as light as a leaf.

"Monsieur Conari," the waiter said. "The commissaire wants to speak with you."

"The commissaire? About what? We're having a party."

Several blue-uniformed policemen entered the crowded room.

Had the *flics* seen him, Lucien wondered, had someone identified him? The old man with the dog? *Nom de Dieu*, what if they connected him with the shooting! Or with the Corsican Separatists?

Foreboding flooded him. It felt like when he'd been little and the *mazzera*, the village shaman, had seen the spell cast on him by the evil eye. But no, this was not scientific; he was scientific and didn't believe in those things any longer.

"Monsieur Conari, you're the host?" said a brittle voice. Not waiting for a reply, it continued, "We're sorry for the inconvenience but a homicide's been committed across the courtyard. We need to speak with all your guests to find out if they noticed anything suspicious. We must check their papers. It's just a formality, of course."

AIMÉE TWISTED GUY'S RING back and forth on her middle finger. The cloudy moonstone in an antique setting reflected the sky's changing weather. Perfect for her, he'd said. She tried to think of something else. The Commissariat cubicle in which she sat being questioned felt glacial. Several overhead fluorescent panels had burned out, casting uneven stripes of light on the pitted linoleum.

Opposite her at the metal desk, a twenty-something *flic* with a razor-sharp jaw pecked with two fingers at the keys of a black typewriter. Didn't he have a computer?

"*Voilà*, Mademoiselle Leduc," he said, pulling the paper out of the roller. His cigarette smoldered in a filled ashtray. He leaned back in his swivel chair and eyed his large sports watch. "Read over your statement to see that it's correct. Then sign at the bottom."

She read the five-page statement twice, then nodded and signed. "Please attach this, too."

"What's that?" he asked, stifling a yawn.

"A diagram illustrating my statement," she said. So far she hadn't seen a computer. "I presume you will scan my statement and this diagram into a computer?"

"Curious type, aren't you?"

She heard the monotonous thrum of a printer from a back office. "Will you?"

"We know our job, Mademoiselle," he said. "Now if you'll come with me."

She shuddered. Good thing she'd made a copy of her diagram.

He escorted her across the foyer of the deserted Commissariat to a holding cell adjoining the dispatcher's room. It was more like a cage, she thought, with its steel bars, furnished only with a wooden slat of a bench. The *flic* unlocked her handcuffs and gestured her inside.

"Wait a minute, you haven't charged me. How long until—?"

"Sit back and relax," he interrupted and left.

The corners stank of old socks and other things she didn't want to think about. Across from her, flyers for a police-sponsored community marathon walk and bike security tips sat piled on the counter by the glass-paned reception cubicle.

She rubbed her hands, coarse from the lab soap they'd given her after the gunpowder residue test, and paced three steps across the small cage and back, hoping she wouldn't really have to stay here all night. So far she hadn't seen Laure.

She pictured the scaffold skirting the building's blue-tiled roof. The cape of snow, the angle of Jacques's body, his turned-out pockets, Laure's obvious concussion . . . but her mind kept going back to Jacques's gunshot wound. Had his killer been lying in wait? On a night like this, why had Jacques left a warm café and persuaded Laure to accompany him? Why had he ended up dead on the slanted zinc roof in a storm?

To play devil's advocate, if in fact Laure and Jacques had continued their argument, and Laure wanted to kill Jacques, easier and less damning ways existed. A blow rendering him unconscious, then a whack of his skull against stone bollards was one method. She'd read about it only last week in the daily *Le Parisien*. Or she could have tripped Jacques on the stairway leading up to Sacré Coeur. There were so many ways to stage an "accident."

Yet she'd found *Laure* unconscious from a blow! Surely, the lack of gunpowder residue on Laure's hands would establish her innocence. She hoped the *flics* had questioned the *mec* standing at the building gate. He might have seen something. . . .

A female officer, wearing a blue jumpsuit unlocked the cage, shaking Aimée out of her reverie.

"You're free to go," she said, handing Aimée a plastic bag containing her things.

Just like that? Morbier had put in a word, she figured. She hoped he'd done the same for Laure.

"Like a coffee?"

Grateful, Aimée nodded, accepting a cup of espresso. "*Merci*. What I'd really like now is to find Laure Rousseau."

The *flic* grinned. "And I'd like to find the man of my dreams. We can all hope, right? Try Hôpital Bichat."

THE SCUFFED walls and peeling linoleum of Hôpital Bichat needed refurbishing. Laure, her head bandaged, sat on gurney in the hall outside the triage area, accompanied by a tired-looking *flic*. ". . . speak with an attorney," Laure was saying. Her words were slurred.

"Officer, may I have a few words with Mademoiselle Rousseau?" Aimée asked.

"You're family?"

"She's my friend. Please!"

The *flic* adjusted his tie and then tapped his fingers against the metal gurney.

"*Bon*. I'll check with the Préfecture concerning the charge against her."

"What do you mean, charge? Check with La Proc. There's some mistake."

She saw his noncommittal expression. Then a flush rose from his neck to his cheeks. At least he had the decency to feel shame. After all, Laure was one of his own.

"Let me find out what's going on," he said.

"Where's the physician on call? Look at her. She needs immediate attention!"

"Bad timing. Several trucks collided on the Périphérique. She's next for intake."

Aimée saw the caked blood on Laure's temple, heard her labored breathing, and noted her dilated pupils. The classic symptoms of shock. The officer moved down the corridor, trying to find reception for his cell phone.

"This is all a formality, Laure," Aimée assured her. "There's a mix-up."

"Mix-up?" Laure's shoulders shook. Tears brimmed in her eyes. "The technicians found gunshot residue on my hands. I don't know what's going on."

Gunshot residue? Aimée was startled. "I don't understand." She had assumed Laure, too, would be cleared by the test. "There's got to be an explanation. When did you last fire your gun?"

"Maybe a month ago, *bibiche*, at the firing range, I think. I can't really remember," Laure said, her eyes glazing.

It didn't make sense. Then how could she have residue on her hands now?

"Tell me what happened after you left the bar." Aimée put her hand on Laure's shoulder. "Take it nice and slow."

Laure shook her head. "Jacques was acting strange. . . ." Her voice trailed off.

Aimée smelled the tang of the chemical used in GSR testing and saw Laure's fingertips, black from the fingerprint test. They hadn't even wiped her hands off.

"So you went along with him," she prompted.

"But I wondered . . ."

"What?" Aimée asked.

"His informer . . . Why would he meet an informer there?"

A meeting on a slippery roof on a frigid, snowy evening? Made no sense, Aimée concurred.

"It must have been a setup." Laure leaned against the wall and rubbed her temples, leaving black streaks. "My head, it hurts to think."

Aimée's eyes narrowed. "A set-up. How do you know?" Aimée asked.

"All I know is *I* didn't kill him." Laure's shoulders shook. "Jacques was the only one who gave me a chance. He took me under his wing. You can never return to the force if your partner's killed and you're . . . you're th-the suspect."

"We'll straighten this out, Laure, *reste tranquille*," Aimée said, even as she wondered what she could do.

A door slammed somewhere. The fluorescent lights flickered. Drunken voices shouted in the hall. An orderly ran down the green-tiled corridor, his footsteps echoing.

"You've got to help me," Laure said. "Everything's hazy, it's hard to remember."

Aimée feared they'd saddle Laure with an appointed attorney and conduct a minimal investigation. Or, more likely, just forward the inquiry to Internal Affairs, where police-appointed judges presided.

"They relish making an example of *flics* like me," Laure said.

The sad thing was, it was true.

But she had to reassure Laure. "It won't come to that, Laure. Like I said, there's been some mistake."

Laure stared at Aimée, her lip quivering. "Remember, we promised we'd always help each other out, *bibiche*," she said. Laure leaned against Aimée's shoulders, sobbing.

Aimée held her, remembering how Laure had always had to play catch-up, had been the butt of playground jokes before her cleft palate surgery, yet had dreamed of a career like that of her heroic, much decorated father. Unlike Aimée, who kept the *flics* at arm's length.

"I swear on Papa's grave, I didn't kill Jacques." Laure gripped Aimée's arm, then closed her eyes. "I'm dizzy, everything's spinning."

"Laure Rousseau, we're ready for you now," said a nurse.

About time, Aimée thought. "Looks like shock, a concussion," she said.

"Diagnosis is our job, Mademoiselle." The nurse wheeled the gurney toward a pair of white plastic curtains.

"How long will it take?"

"Intake and observation will take several hours."

The same *flic* walked past her. Aimée caught his arm. "I'll come back then to pick her up and take her home."

She recognized a "don't count on it look" in his eyes as he shook his head.

"Why not?"

"I don't have time to explain."

"Take my number, call me." She put her card in his hand.

He disappeared behind the curtains.

AIMÉE STOOD on the gray slush-filled pavement in front of the hospital. She had to do something. She couldn't stand the idea that Laure, still injured and in shock, would be arraigned at the Préfecture. There had to be evidence to clear her on the scaffold or the roof. There had to be some way out of this nightmare for Laure. She pulled out her cell phone with shaking hands and called her cousin Sebastian.

"*Allô* Sebastian," she said, eyeing the deserted taxi stop. "Can you pick me up in ten minutes?"

"For the pleasure of your company?" he said. "*Désolé*, but Stephanie's making a cassoulet."

Stephanie was his new girlfriend, he'd met her at a rave.

"Remember, you owe me?" Aimée replied.

Pause.

"It's payback time, Sebastian."

"Again?" She heard music in the background. "What do I need?"

"Gloves, climbing boots, the usual. Make sure the tool set's in your van."

"Breaking in like last time?"

"And you love it. Don't forget an extra set of gloves."

Sometimes you just had to help out a friend.

SEBASTIAN, WEARING tight orange jeans, an oversize Breton sweater, and a black knit hat pulled low but with the glint of his earring still showing, gunned his van up rue Custine. His over-six-foot frame was squeezed into the beat-up van he used for deliveries. Beside him, Aimée sat scanning the shuttered cheese shops, florists, and darkened cafés dotting the steep, twisting street. Once this had been a village high outside the walls of Paris. Parisians had flocked to the *butte*, "the mound," to dance at the *bal musettes*, to enjoy *la vie bohème* and to drink wine not subject to city taxes. Artists such as Modigliani and Seurat had followed, establishing ateliers in washhouses, before their paintings commanded higher prices. Then Montparnasse had beckoned.

"*Voilà*," she said, pointing to the gated building with leafless trees silhouetted against the lights of distant Pigalle.

The crime-scene unit and police vans were gone. Jacques's car, too. Sebastian parked by a fire hydrant Parisian style, which meant wedged into whatever space was open on the pavement.

"Bring the equipment, little cousin," she said. "Let's go."

Eighteen rue André Antoine, a white stone nineteenth-century building, faced others like it on a serpentine street. Gray netting camouflaged the upper floor and scaffolding of the roof, which adjoined the other buildings in the courtyard. A red-brown brick church wall partially occupied the rear of the courtyard, cutting off the view. She'd hoped to question the man who'd stood on the steps but he had not lingered. Only a crust of snow crisscrossed with footprints remained.

The wind had died down. From somewhere came the muted squeak of a creaking swing. The crime-scene unit must have left not long after she'd been evicted, evidenced by the light dusting of snow on the cars now parked where the police vans had been. Thank God, the architect Haussmann had been unable to swing the wrecking ball here. No one could tear these buildings down or the ground underneath would collapse. The earth was riddled with spaces and tunnels . . . like a Gruyère cheese, as the saying went. Aimée could never figure that out; Emmenthaler was the cheese with the holes. You received a certificate that the building was sound when you bought a place. But, as a friend had informed her, the latest geological calculations had been made circa 1876.

She rang the concierge's bell, unzipping her jacket to reveal the blue jumpsuit Sebastian had brought for her, and noted that there were no names inscribed above the upper floor's metal mailboxes. Several moments later, a sharp-eyed woman answered. She wore a man's large camel coat belted by a Dior chain, black rain boots, and had a cigarillo clamped between her thumb and forefinger.

"Don't tell me you forgot the body?" she said, exhaling acrid smoke in Aimée's direction.

Startled, Aimée clutched a workbag labeled Serrurie and leaned away from the smoke.

"I'm here to change the locks," Aimée said.

"But the locksmiths were already here."

Aimée stamped the ice from her boots on the mat. "To secure the windows and skylight access?"

"Far as I know."

"But we're doing the *rear* windows. They didn't finish." She jerked her hand toward Sebastian. "We had the parts back at the shop."

"What do you mean?"

Aimée thought fast, wishing the concierge would quit questioning her.

"*Tiens* . . . they didn't tell you . . . the rear windows need special locks?"

The concierge sighed. "The apartment's vacant. The upper floors are being remodeled."

"*Bon*, we'll go home," Aimée said, turning toward Sebastian. "You can explain to the commissaire why snow blew in through the windows to blanket the apartment like a rug. Squatters will love it then."

The woman glanced at her thumb, pushed the cuticle back. "The top floors have been empty for a month already." She shrugged. Another sign of the gentrification that was invading the area. "Be sure not to disturb the old coot on the first floor. He's furious as it is what with all the commotion," the concierge said. Her mouth turned down and she stabbed the cigarillo out in an empty flowerpot. Then she thrust a small key ring at Aimée. "That's the door key. I won't wait up for you."

"We'll see ourselves out," Aimée said, nodding to Sebastian, who shouldered the tool kit.

He followed her up the staircase, its worn red carpet held in place by bronze stair rods. The wrought-iron banister, an intricate pattern of acorns and leaves, spiraled up several floors. Once it had been exquisite, the latest style.

"Talk about a hike! What the hell can we find after all this time, Aimée?"

Sebastian's words mirrored her own doubts. Yet new evidence was vital. "If one listens, the scene will speak," she remembered her father saying. If there was any chance to prove Laure's innocence she had to find it.

"Put on your surgical gloves," she said, panting, wishing she hadn't gained that kilo over the holidays. She left the key in the door. "Rooftop first."

The snow flurries had subsided, melting onto the floor of the scaffolding. She and Sebastian pulled on woolen ski masks. Sebastian followed Aimée's lead and dropped to his knees. With luck, they might find something the police had missed.

"What are we looking for?" Sebastian asked.

"Wood splinters, blackened metal on the scaffold, a discarded lighter, cigarette butt, scraped tile . . . anything."

"Like in those shows on the *télé*?"

She nodded. She was doubtful but one never knew. The concierge had said the apartment had been vacant for a month. Was that why Jacques had arranged to meet his informer there?

The spires and roof of the church blocked the view of all but the adjoining roof and a dark neigboring building across the street. Witnesses, if any, would be few.

They crouched, moving silently to avoid detection from the adjoining apartments connected by the roof. One tall lighted window shone from across the courtyard. Below, from the construction site, came a pinprick glow like the tip of a lit cigarette. And then it disappeared. Into a hole in the earth? The remains of old quarries underlaid all of Montmartre. Gritting her teeth, she turned her gaze back to the roof.

For forty minutes, they crawled. They covered every centimeter of the scaffold, inspected chimney pots, stones, the windows and sills let into the mansard roof, and the small flat area of the zinc roof on top. Aimée's hands were wet with snow, sore from abrasion by pebbles and rough stucco. Disheartened, she leaned against the chimney.

"Find anything?" she said to Sebastian, who was leaning over the edge and combing the rain gutter.

He held up a fistful of sodden brown leaves. "Toss it or . . .?"

"Wait." She edged her way toward him, opening a plastic Baggie. "In here. What's that?"

"Just a twig, like these," he said indicating others clogging the gutter. "They need to clean this or . . ."

She pulled out a green stem. Smelled it. "Freshly broken, a geranium stem."

"My cousin, the botanist!" he said.

She gave him a wry smile. "A Calvados says there's a deck or window ledge nearby with pots of geraniums."

"Proving what?" he asked.

A few stars glittered under the thinning clouds, just over the dark line of roofs.

"I'm guessing. What if someone leaned out their window and saw the shooting."

"But, Aimée, people keep geraniums inside in this weather."

He made sense. A dead end?

Right now, it was all they had to go on.

"Give me a boost, I want to check."

Sebastian reached up the wall and tied the rope around the chimney bracer. Aimée tied the other end in a slip knot around her waist.

"Ready?" he asked, knitting his hands together and planting himself against the concrete. "On three."

"One-two-three."

Chill air and a dirt-encrusted skylight greeted Aimée as she reached the adjoining roof. She grabbed the roof edge, hoisted herself up further, and came face to face with a dormer window. Several pots of geraniums were visible within.

Now she knew where to start asking questions in the morning. But she'd found no evidence to indicate that anyone other than Laure had shot Jacques. Yet something . . . something had to exist.

"I'm coming down," she said, gripping the ledge caked with pigeon droppings by one hand, the other braced against the smooth wall.

"Sebastian, can you shine your penlight over here?"

"Gifts from the pigeon gods?"

As his thin beam illuminated the chimney pot, a light went on in a courtyard window opposite and they heard someone struggling with a window. "Quick, Sebastian. Time to go."

She felt him tug at the rope and her feet slipped on the slick ice.

"We've got company," he said, pointing below. "The *flics*."

Two cars had pulled up in the street, their blue lights casting a glow over the snow-laced courtyard. Had someone heard them and called the *flics*? She peered around the chimney, saw more rooftops and the pale moon's reflection glinting on more skylights, a few feet away.

"Grab the bag, come join me," Aimée said.

"You're kidding, right?"

"Hurry up. We can jimmy open a skylight."

She felt the rope tug.

"How many skylights do you see?" he asked.

"Three. Two side by side, then one some distance away."

"*Bon.* One of them must be over a hall. I'm right behind you."

She tucked the Baggie in her jumpsuit pocket, climbed, then gripped the chimney edge and let herself down on the other side.

Her feet scrabbled and she landed on all fours. And then she was sliding down the slick wet roof surface. Panic gripped her. Only the gutter ledge was between her and a drop of several stories. She grabbed and her hand caught the metal. She pulled herself up toward a rectangular flat area.

Sebastian landed behind her. By the time they reached the furthest skylight she was panting. The cold air hurt her lungs.

"Here," he said, handing her the pliers. "Work the skylight lock open."

She was startled to find that it was already broken. Sawtooth-edged shards of glass, knife sharp, jutted from the frame. Deftly, she eased her hand past them and grasped the lock from inside. Within seconds, with Sebastian's help, she'd lifted the skylight. She held onto the metal rim and let herself down, hoping her feet would find the ladder usually attached to the wall of a communal hallway, that she wasn't about to land in someone's bedroom.

Her toes hit ladder rungs, and she climbed down to a level surface, a musty carpet, wet with footprints. Odd.

"Quick, take the bag," said Sebastian, handing it down to

her. He made a perfect tiptoe landing and they found themselves in what appeared to be the entry of a sixth-floor *chambre de bonne*, a maid's room converted into an apartment.

"Look at the footprints."

"My feet aren't that big," he said, about to rub them out with his boot.

"Leave it, let's go," she told him.

They crept down the flights of creaking wooden stairs, past a glass entry door and into a covered courtyard area. Several doors fronted the coved stone alcove. Large green trash containers stood by a concierge's loge. Sebastian thumbed a button on the side wall and within the huge vaulted door a small door clicked open.

They found themselves outside on the street opposite their parking place. Lucky!

Back in the van, Sebastian switched on the ignition and turned on the heater.

"All that for a geranium twig! Satisfied?"

"In more ways than one," she said. "Think back to the broken glass, the open skylight."

He nodded, taking a curve, then gunning his engine as they climbed the steep street.

"We might have discovered an escape route."

Hot air shot from the floor vents, warming her frozen legs.

"Escape route?"

"The killer's escape route."

Later Monday Night

LUCIEN CLOSED HIS EYES. His mind flooded with childhood memories: his *grand-mère's* high-pitched funeral chant as his uncle's body lay stiff and waxen on the dining-room table. The women, all in black like a row of crows, wailing and the men pounding their rifle butts on the floor. The terrible rhythm had echoed off the stone walls. Sadness, borne on the dry wind, scented by the lavender and myrtle, had chilled him to the bone.

As long as he could remember, funerals had been *the* social gatherings in the village. Beyond it, the rutted road rimmed a turquoise sea whose waves beat upon the granite of abandoned Roman quarries. The stones were gouged as if the Romans had departed yesterday, not centuries ago.

That day, he and Marie-Dominique had taken to the mountain path, unseen, to escape the malaise clinging to the village, home of the old and infirm, like so many villages decimated by vendettas. They found the cave by a half-ruined shepherd's hut nestled in the crag of a sheer granite face where graphite and mica crystals caught the copper sun. Every moment was still imprinted in his mind. Marie-Dominique's long tanned legs ending in faded blue espadrilles. The fight her cousin Giano picked with him later in the bar, accusing him. . . .

"If you don't mind asking your guests to form a line, Monsieur Conari?" the commissaire was saying. "Each must show us a *carte d'identité*, and answer a few questions. Just a formality, of course."

With a start, Lucien opened his eyes. He was in Félix's salon and Marie-Dominique stood somewhere in the crowd, not nestled warmly beside him in the cave. He felt for his wallet, looked inside, and panicked. It held only his Carte Orange pass and a dirty cough drop. He'd forgotten his ID. By law, anyone without ID was subject to arrest. That law was rarely enforced. But for Corsicans like him, the *flics* exacted revenge for the Separatist threats and applied the rules strictly. In his village, men evaporated into the mountains when a police car rolled into view. That was what he wished he could do now.

And the contract Conari had spoken of? Later. Now he had to take cover someplace in this flat and think what to do. Lucien tugged at the waiter's sleeve as he passed. He had looked familiar. . . . "Compadre, where's the restroom?" Lucien asked.

The waiter gestured across the long room in the same direction as the *flics*.

"Any place closer?"

Understanding showed in the waiter's eyes. "Follow me."

He showed Lucien to a water closet by the kitchen.

By the time Lucien emerged from the bathroom, he'd decided to ask Félix to vouch for him. He was already late for his DJ gig.

But in the hall, Marie-Dominique blocked his way. "Something wrong, Lucien?"

Wrong? That she was married, that he couldn't take her warm brown shoulders in his arms? But he didn't say that. He searched for words.

"Marie-Dominique, seeing you again after all this time . . . there's so much to say." For four years he'd dreamed of her but his words came out flat and inadequate.

"Lucien, you still make music and that makes me happy." Her words hung in the air, full of the unspoken emotion.

A gardenia floated in a bowl of water on a table, a thin strand of diamonds around her wrist caught the light. Candles flickered, casting shadows on the moiré silk-patterned wallpaper above them. He longed to have time to watch her, to inhale the rose scent that surrounded her. The old thirties Tino Rossi song, "O! Corse, Ile d'Amour," looped in his mind; it was the tune that had been on the radio that afternoon.

"It had to happen this way," she said, as if reading his thoughts.

Startled, he clenched his hands into fists. "How can you say that? You know what we had, what I felt."

"My family was opposed." She looked away, her low voice

almost a whisper. "My father knows the Armata Corsa for what it is. Terrorism."

"When we all joined we were ignorant. But I never participated in any actions."

Fool! He'd been a fool to join with his drunken friends, hoping to free Corsica from French rule. Free? Not with middle-of-the-night bombings and the kidnappings for ransom, which the Armata Corsa used to buy guns. He shook his head, frustrated. He had to make her understand. "It's true. I never realized."

Marie-Dominique's eyes blazed. "Didn't realize the Armata Corsa was outlawed? After you left our island, the Armata Corsa plastered the walls with posters protesting the atrocities and with pictures of *you*."

"But I had nothing to do with it. I only went to one meeting."

"Your picture was on the posters," she said.

So that had been the reason his mother had put a ticket for the overnight ferry to Marseilles in his hands and insisted he leave that very night. "I won't lose another son," she'd said. Meaning neither to the vendetta, the gendarmes, or the evil eye cast by the *mazzera*, the sorceress crone who dwelled high up on the mountain. No one disputed the *mazzera*, least of all his long-suffering widowed mother, who was convinced the evil eye had marked him. Sardinian by birth, his mother was still referred to by his *grand-mère* as "the foreigner" after thirty-five years on the island. She had ignored his reluctance, overridden his arguments that fleeing would be taken as an admission of guilt.

He'd waited tables in the Marseilles *vieux* port, deejayed using a friend's cheap equipment, scraped by, and survived. A year later he'd moved to Paris. He'd bought turntables; it was a bare living.

"I wrote you letters explaining that I had to leave," he told Marie-Dominique. "But they all came back, unopened."

She looked away.

A *flic* in a blue uniform brushed by him, stopped, and took in Lucien's black denims and worn boots. "Follow me, we're questioning the staff in the kitchen," he said.

"But, Officer, he's our guest," Marie-Dominique told him.

The *flic* raised his eyebrows and shot a pointed look at Lucien. "Of course, Madame. Please, join us in the salon." He continued into the kitchen.

Lucien braced himself. Corsicans enjoyed "special treatment" during questioning at the Commissariat. Like his friend Bruno, who'd returned with a broken arm. The recent Separatist attacks had put the *flics* on edge. If they discovered he had no ID and lived on illegal, unreported wages from his DJ gigs, they'd take him in.

But if he left without signing the contract Conari had offered . . .

"I forgot my *carte d'identité*, Marie-Dominique." He glanced toward the salon. Félix stood with Yann in a knot of men, speaking with the commissaire. A loose line of guests had formed by the drinks table.

He edged closer to her, whispering. "Marie-Dominique, I can't talk to them right now."

Her eyes widened. "So you're still on the wanted list?"

"Show me a way to leave, please," he said. "Speak with Félix, tell him I'll sign the contract tomorrow."

"But what if—"

"No time to explain. Help me."

"Consistent, if nothing else. You're running away, Lucien. Again."

"It's not like that. Please, help me."

Marie-Dominique shook her head.

A door flush with the paneling was opened by one of the catering staff who was sweating as he carried a huge copper saucepan.

It must lead to the back stairs.

"Don't get Félix in trouble."

"Why would I do that?"

"You're still involved with the Separatists, aren't you? Still yearning to 'liberate' Corsica."

As far as he was concerned, if it hadn't happened in two thousand years, why now? She had him all wrong. Two hundred years ago, Pascal Paoli had taken power and, instead of making himself king as others had done, outlawed slavery, organized elections, and gave women the vote. Novel ideas for his time, for any time. Corsica had been a democracy briefly until Paoli was overthrown and its army destroyed. In 1768, Corsica was sold to the French for a million francs.

True, once he'd believed in a free Corsica and had joined the Armata Corsa. But when he saw the Mafia tactics of the faction-ridden group, he'd wanted nothing more to do with them.

"What you really mean is I don't belong here," Lucien said. "Not in your life, not in this chic milieu," he said, his hurt flaming into anger. He pounded his fist on the door. "But neither do you, Marie-Dominique. You've changed but I know you're still the same inside. I'm going. Tell Félix I'll contact him later."

He opened the concealed door, and shut it with a bang.

Tuesday Morning

AIMÉE LEANED AGAINST the slick tiled Metro wall, cell phone to her ear, and clicked off. Hôpital Bichat refused to give her any information about Laure. On top of that, the *flic* guarding her still hadn't called. Burnt rubber smells from the squealing train brakes filled the close air. She punched in another number.

"Brigade Criminelle," a voice said after ten rings.

"Last night, Officer Laure Rousseau was injured and taken to Hôpital Bichat; I'd like to know her status."

"Let me consult," said a brisk, no-nonsense voice.

In the background she heard footsteps slapping across the tile.

"*Allô?* Who's calling?" asked the voice.

"Aimée Leduc, a private detective."

"You'll need to inquire via the proper channels."

"Aren't I? I'm concerned. As I told you, she suffered an injury."

"She's in *garde à vue*," said the voice.

Already? It was not yet eight in the morning.

"Check with her lawyer," the voice said.

"Who's that?"

"A Maître Delambre is handling this case. That's all the information I have."

It sounded as if Laure had been given outside representation. Unusual in these circumstances. Good or bad? Surely, a good sign, Aimée thought, gaining hope. But how long would they keep Laure in a holding cell? She consulted the directory at the phone booth in the Metro, found the lawyer's number, and called him.

"Maître Delambre is in court until noon," said his answering machine.

"Please, have him call me, it's urgent, concerning Laure Rousseau," Aimée said and left her number.

Too bad she'd let René Friant, her partner in their agency, take the morning off. She could use his help now.

She pushed open the swinging doors of the Blanche Metro. All the way up the stairs crowded with winter-coated commuters she pictured Laure, disoriented, with her bloodshot eye, hunched over in a cell.

On the wide, shop-lined Boulevard de Clichy by the Moulin Rouge, its garish neon now dark, plumes of bus exhaust spiraled into the air. A straggling demonstration blocked the street as loudspeakers shouted, "Corsica for Corsicans!"

Waiting passengers stood on the pavement with that particular patience of Parisians, the collective shrug of acceptance reserved for slowdowns and strikes. Newspaper banners plastered across the kiosk read STRIKE IN CORSICAN CONTRACT DISPUTE. Another said ASSAULT ON ARMORED CURRENCY TRUCK LINKED TO ARMATA CORSA SEPARATISTS.

She saw a peeling poster on a stone wall bearing a call to action and the Armata Corsa Separatist trademark, the *tête de* Maure, a black face with white bandanna, in the corner.

The strident Separatist movements in Corsica took center stage these days, elbowing out Bretons demanding school instruction in Gaelic and ETA, Basque Nationalists, car bombings.

Right now, Aimée needed to speak with the person in the apartment with geraniums in a window box to discover if he or she had seen anything.

Above her, on rue André Antoine, the overcast Montmartre sky mirrored the blue-gray roof tiles. Like her heart, with Guy gone and Laure the subject of a police investigation.

Leafless plane trees bent in the wind. Steep streets wound up the *butte* of Montmartre. She stepped over puddles of melted snow. Tonight they would freeze and become slick. Tomorrow there would be articles in the paper about old people who'd fallen and broken their hips.

The gate to the upscale townhouse whose roof she and Sebastian had climbed over stood open for the garbage collectors. She scanned the cobbled courtyard, looking across to the adjoining townhouse roof and skylight. Several floors of iron-shuttered windows faced the enclave.

In this building, she figured most residents flew south for the winter to Nice or Monaco. They could afford to. She found the top-floor site of the geranium window box, a shutterless oval window.

She'd question all the inhabitants of the building, working her way up. In the entry, she hit the first button. There was no answering buzz. She stared at the numbers on the digicode plate.

From her bag she took a slab of plasticine, slapped it over the set of buttons, and peeled it back. Greasy fingermarks showed which five numbers and letters were most used. In less than five minutes, after she'd tried twenty combinations, the door clicked open.

Inside the building she climbed the wide marble steps, trailing her fingers over the wrought-iron railing. On the first floor, a young woman answered the door, a toddler on her hip and another crying in the background. Aimée saw suitcases and a car seat stacked inside the door.

"*Oui?*" the woman asked.

"Sorry to bother you but I'm a detective," Aimée said. "I'd like to question you about a homicide that occurred last night across the courtyard on the roof of the building undergoing renovation."

"What? I know nothing about it." The toddler pulled the strand of beads around the woman's neck and she winced. "*Non, chéri.*"

"Did you hear or see anything unusual at eleven o'clock last night?"

"You're kidding. My baby's teething. I can't keep my eyes open that late," she said, looking harried.

The toddler clung to his mother's neck, gnawing at her beads; the other child pounded a metal truck on the floor. "We were asleep. I put the children to bed at eight; half the time I fall asleep with them."

"There was a party in the building, maybe your husband noticed something."

"He passes out before I do," she said. "I'm sorry but I have to get the children ready."

"*Merci*," Aimée said. "Here's my card just in case."

"My husband's picking us up in five minutes. We're leaving for a month."

The woman stuffed Aimée's card in the pocket of her cardigan and closed the door. Aimée hoped the toddler wouldn't eat it.

She knocked on the doors of the two other apartments on the floor but no one answered. No answer from the other three apartments on the next floor either. On the third floor, an aproned housekeeper answered the door at the apartment where Aimée figured the party had taken place.

"*Bonjour*, I'd like to speak with the owner," she said.

"No one's here, I'm sorry. Monsieur Conari's at the office."

Even this early, the rich went to work.

Aimée showed her ID. "Perhaps you served at his party last night? I'd like to ask you some questions."

"Not me, I come to work in the morning," the woman said. "They use caterers for parties."

"Did you speak with Monsieur Conari this morning? Maybe he mentioned the homicide across the courtyard?"

The housekeeper dropped her dust rag. "They're never here when I get to work. Sorry." She picked the rag up and started to close the door.

"It's important," Aimée said. "Can you give me a number where I can reach Monsieur Conari?"

The housekeeper hesitated, rubbing her hands on her apron. "I never bother him at work, eh, but this—"

"*Oui*, it's *very* important," Aimée said.

The woman took the pen and paper Aimée handed her and wrote down a telephone number.

"*Merci*, I appreciate your help."

Aimée continued up the wide stairs. Her goal, the top flat, encompassed the entire floor. Here she had to find answers.

She heard low voices, music, a radio? She knocked several times. No answer. Then knocked again until she heard footsteps.

"*J'arrive*," said a voice.

The door creaked open. The middle-aged woman who opened the dark green door wore a flannel nightshirt and Nordic wool slipper socks, and was sipping something steaming and smelling of cinnamon.

"Forgive me," Aimée said. "I don't mean to disturb you—"

"No salespeople allowed in the building, I'm sorry," the woman interrupted in a nasal congested voice. "They shouldn't have let you in."

Aimée flashed her identification card. "I'm a detective, investigating a homicide in the building opposite you."

"Homicide?" The woman pushed her glasses onto her forehead and rubbed her eyes, which were a striking aqua blue. "I don't know what you're talking about. You'll need to excuse me, I'm sick."

This woman must have been at home last night. Aimée couldn't let her shut the door in her face. "Sorry to insist, but this will take just a moment. Probably you've answered these questions already," she said. She wanted to see the view from this woman's apartment. And there should be geraniums near a window facing the courtyard.

"What do you mean? No one's spoken to me," the woman told her. "What homicide?"

"Haven't the police questioned you yet?"

The woman shook her head.

Aimée wondered why not.

"Let me see your identification again, Mademoiselle."

Aimée handed over her PI license with its less than flattering photo: squinty eyes and pursed mouth.

"The pharmacy's late." The woman glanced at an old clock on the wall and handed the license back. "They were supposed to deliver my medicine by now."

"A man was murdered last night," Aimée said, wiping her wet boots on the mat. "I need to ask you some questions. May I come in?"

"It's nothing to do with me," the woman said, about to close the door.

"Let's talk inside," Aimée said.

"*Non*. I can't deal with questions," the woman replied.

"Just while you wait for the pharmacy delivery."

"*Non*," the woman said, alarmed. "I'm sick."

"But if we talk now, Madame—"

"I don't go out." The woman smothered a cough. "I won't go to the police station."

An agoraphobic? Aimée heard something in her voice, was it the trace of an accent?

"Madame, you don't need to go to the Commissariat," Aimée said. "I'm a private investigator, we'll talk right here. And I must see the view from your window."

The woman pulled out a wad of tissues from her pocket, reconsidered, and blew her nose. "All right, but just five minutes."

Aimée stepped inside the pale yellow hallway, eighteenth century by the look of it. A green plastic shopping cart was parked on the black-and-white diamond-patterned floor by a pair of worn snow boots. She expected a place dripping with antique chandeliers, but instead Art Deco sconces and Surrealist collages lined the walls. Several Man Ray silver-gelatin-print photographs hung over a gleaming Ruhlmann *secrétaire*. One appeared to be an original of *Violon d'Ingres*, the famous Surrealist image of Kiki, Man Ray's lover, in a turban, musical notes drawn on her bare back down her spine.

"Such a lovely apartment," Aimée said, aiming to get this woman to talk. "You've lived here a long time, Madame?"

"Zoe Tardou," the woman admitted, showing Aimée to a room furnished with sleek blond-wood Art Deco pieces and *moderne* thirties-style rugs. Black blankets hung at the floor-to-ceiling windows. Aimée's heart sank. How could Zoe Tardou have noticed movement on the roof with these blankets blocking the windows?

"Tardou, like the Surrealist?" Aimée asked to keep the conversation going.

"My stepfather," Zoe Tardou said, her mouth tightening.

No wonder she could afford this expensive apartment covering the entire floor. But from the way Zoe Tardou's mouth had compressed, Aimée figured she hadn't gotten along with her stepfather.

Zoe Tardou switched on the light, illuminating silver-framed black-and-white photos. Beachfront family scenes from the sixties and celebrity snapshots covered the baby grand piano. A late-model television sat in front of a damask-covered sofa. But an unlived-in feeling permeated the large room.

"You're an artist, too?"

"My mother was a Dadaist poet and did figure modeling," Zoe said.

One of the Surrealist muses?

Zoe Tardou took a deep swallow of her steaming drink. She beckoned Aimée to a small nook behind the sofa. "Medieval scholarship's my field."

Here a blond joined-wood desk piled with notebooks and books angled out from the wall. Well used. Above the desk, mounted on the wall, hung an ancient crucifix and framed manuscript pages bearing ornate gold lettering and ancient black script. Definitely at odds with the Deco-period furnishings.

The cold air in the darkened apartment began to chill Aimée. Didn't this woman ever turn on the heat?

"Were your windows open last night?"

"Always," she said. "The human body needs fresh air at night."

For a woman into health, she looked miserable.

"So, you would have heard the party below despite the storm?"

"I don't know the neighbors. I keep to myself."

"Mind if I take a look?" Aimée walked to the window and quickly pulled the blanket aside. The older woman's eyes blinked at the sudden light.

Directly across the courtyard lay the scaffolding under the roof of the corniced apartment where she'd discovered Jacques's body. The skylight on the roof level opposite glittered in the weak sunbeams from a sudden break in the clouds. She saw the path she'd taken with Sebastian, aghast at the steepness of the roof they'd climbed.

"Do you keep these blankets up at night?"

Aimée didn't remember seeing them.

"*Non.*" Madame Tardou blew her nose. "Look, if that's all you need to know I'd appreciate if you left."

But the woman might have noticed something after all, even if she didn't realize it.

"If you'll permit me to clarify a few things. Think back to eleven o'clock last night. Did you hear anything unusual on the roof, see any lights over there?" Aimée pointed at the apartment windows almost directly opposite.

"I did hear snippets of conversation," Madame Tardou replied. "At first I thought they were speaking Italian."

Italian? Excited, Aimée took a step closer. The woman reeked of eucalyptus oil.

"Do you speak Italian?"

"*Non.* And it must have been some drama on the *télé.* I was drifting in and out of sleep with this terrible cold."

"What made you think it was Italian?"

"We used to go there on holiday," she replied.

"What did they say?"

"Maybe it wasn't Italian."

"Please, it's important. Can you place the language?"

Zoe Tardou shook her head. "I know they talked about the stars and planets."

Had Zoe Tardou been dreaming after all?

"How could you tell?"

"Sirius, Orion, and Neptune, those names I could understand."

"Male or female voices?"

"Male voices. Two, at least. I remember, in the village people talked about the constellations," Zoe Tardou said, her gaze somewhere else, speaking as if to herself. "It didn't seem so odd." She shrugged. "Almost familiar. At least where I came from."

Curious, Aimée wondered how this tied in. If she didn't pursue the words of this strange woman she feared she'd regret it later.

"Where's that?"

"Near Lamorlaye."

Lamorlaye? Why did that sound so familiar? Her mind went back to the scratched yellow Menier chocolate tin always on her grandmother's counter, the words *fondé 1816* above the braids of the Menier girl with her basket filled with chocolate bars. And every summer afternoon her grandmother preparing her a *tartine et chocolat*, a thick slab of Menier chocolate laid between halves of a buttered baguette.

"Lamorlaye, that's near the Château Menier, the family that's famous for the chocolate."

Zoe Tardou sniffed and blew her nose. She sat down and rubbed her red-rimmed eyes.

"So you watched the stars at night?"

"Eh?" Zoe Tardou bristled defensively. "The orphanage bordered the observatory—" She stopped, covered her mouth with her tissue. Like a little girl caught telling tales out of school.

"What do you mean?"

"The countryside's full of glue sniffers," she said, her voice rising in anger. "I went back last year. The young riffraff lie around in train stations sniffing glue."

Glue sniffing? Where had that come from?

"Excuse me but—did you water your geraniums last night?" Aimée asked.

Madame Tardou started and dropped her tissue on the floor. "What if I did?"

"We think some men escaped across the rooftops and descended through your building's skylight. Did you see them while you were watering your plants?"

"It's not safe anywhere any longer."

Aimée paused. "Madame, did you hear any gunshots or see anyone?" she asked.

The woman shook her head. "The world's full of opportunists."

"I agree," Aimée said, trying to humor her before returning to her line of questioning. "But when you watered your geraniums, did you see men on the scaffold or any on the roof?

"I'm going to call the locksmith to get more chains and bolts installed."

Did Zoe Tardou fear retribution if she gave Aimée information? She seemed to be afraid of something.

"Please, Madame Tardou," Aimée said. "A man was murdered. We need your help in this investigation. Whatever you tell me will remain confidential."

Now the doorbell buzzed.

"Let me get that for you," Aimée said. Before the woman could protest, she answered the door, accepted a proffered package, and returned to find Zoe curled up in a chair.

"Here's your medication."

"I've told you all I know, I watered my geraniums, but I saw nothing. I don't feel well."

"Madame Tardou, your information may be important," Aimée said. "If you don't wish to cooperate with me, I'm sure investigators will insist on taking your statement at the Commissariat." A threat; she hoped it would work.

Zoe Tardou clutched her flannel nightshirt, pulling it tight around her. "Why question me, why not that *pute* on the street?"

Aimée didn't remember seeing a prostitute on the street. "What *pute?*"

"The one who hangs out around the corner. The old one, she's in the doorway all the time. Ask her."

"What does she look like?"

"You know the type, lots of costume jewelry. Now, if you'll excuse me, you must leave."

At least she had someone to look for now.

WITH RELUCTANT steps Aimée retraced the route she and Sebastian had taken. She pulled out her cheap compact Polaroid and took photos of the hall carpet, skylight, and the broken lock.

Outside, on narrow rue André Antoine, passersby scurried, late to work or school. She walked to the doorway of the building opposite. No prostitute. Disappointed, she tried Conari's number.

"Monsieur Conari's out of the office," his secretary said.

All the reasons she'd hated criminal investigative work came back to her. Half the time potential witnesses were out of town, or at the doctor's, or the hairdresser's, and tracking them down took days. Leads turned to dust. Evidence deteriorated.

But Laure needed help. Now.

"When do you expect him?"

Aimée heard phones ringing in the background.

"Try again later."

AIMÉE OPENED the frosted-glass-paned door of Leduc Detective, ran, and caught the phone on the second ring. Gray light worked its way through the open shutters into a zigzag pattern on the wood floor. She nodded to her partner. René's short arms were full as he loaded paper into the printer.

"*Allô?*" she answered the phone, at the same time grabbing the ground coffee beans.

"Mademoiselle Leduc? Maître Delambre here, Laure Rousseau's counsel," a high-pitched male voice said.

Thank God. But he sounded young, as if his voice hadn't changed yet.

"I'm between court sessions so I'll get to the point. We have reservations concerning your involvement in Laure Rousseau's case."

"Who's *we?*" Aimée said, catching her breath. "Laure asked for my help."

"The police investigation has been comprehensive and thorough," he said.

He not only sounded young, but as if he needed to show he was in control. She hit the button on the espresso machine, which grumbled to life.

"So comprehensive, Maître Delambre, that they haven't yet questioned the inhabitants of the building opposite or investigated a broken skylight?"

"That's the investigating unit's responsibility," he said. "And just how would you know this?"

"As I said, Laure asked for my help," she said. Better to explain and try to work with him. Not alienate him. "We're childhood friends; our fathers worked together in the police force."

"You have admirable intentions, I'm sure, but your involvement won't help the case or be looked on as anything but meddling."

In other words, back off.

"I'm a private investigator," she said, figuring it would be better not to mention that computer security was her field. "That's what I do. You don't even seem interested to learn that there may have been an eyewitness."

"Of course the police questioned all the people in the area," he said. "I'm sure they're aware of anything pertinent and will have it in their report."

"I'd like to see this report and discuss this further."

"As I told you—"

"Laure hired me and it's in her best interests that we work together," she said, stretching the truth. "But, naturally, it's your call."

Thick bitter steaming coffee dripped into the small white demitasse cup next to her.

"Meaning what, Mademoiselle Leduc?"

"Would you rather I turn over my findings to you or directly to La Proc?"

Pause. "I'll discuss this with my client," he said.

"Look, *I* found her concussed and injured. That should be in the report. Jacques's pockets were inside out, they'd been searched. Since the *flics* don't reveal information to outsiders, can you find out what the police report says?"

The shuffle of papers was her only answer.

"I'd like to visit Laure."

He took a breath. "It's questionable whether they'd allow you to see her."

"I'd need to get a pass and letter from you, wouldn't I?"

"Let me check into that."

Noncommittal, avoiding a flat no. But she wouldn't let it rest.

"I'd appreciate that and seeing the crime-scene report," she said. "Including the lab findings. I'm concerned about the gun residue Laure said they found on her hands. Of course, there's some mistake."

"Lab turnaround time is from six to eighteen hours," he interrupted.

"So you could have it by this afternoon," she said. "I'll call you later."

She hung up and plopped two brown-sugar lumps into her

espresso. A hot drop landed on her finger and she licked it. As she had feared, Laure had been assigned a lawyer from the bottom of the barrel.

René climbed into the orthopedic chair customized for his four-foot height. She noticed his new double-breasted suit and freshly manicured nails as he bit the glazed puff top off the religieuse, an eclairlike pastry. The shape had ancient origins and was supposed to resemble a famous convent deaconess from the fifteenth century.

"Like one?" René pushed the pastry box across the desk.

Why not? Did it matter anymore if she fit into that little black dress, a vintage Schiaparelli she'd discovered at a church sale?

"*Merci*," she said, walking to his terminal and exchanging the espresso for a coffee-cream-filled eclair. "Remember my friend Laure?"

René nodded; he'd met her the year before.

"She's in trouble."

"So I just heard," he said, wiping his mouth with a handkerchief. "Did she really hire you? You'll get a check?"

Aimée hesitated.

"I don't like this already," he said. "We do computer security, remember?"

He gestured to her desk, a pile of proposals by her laptop. "That should keep you busy."

"I owe her, René," she said. "She's been set up."

"And you know this for sure?" René stirred the espresso, his green eyes on the beige froth lining his demitasse cup. "It would be refreshing to get paid. Make for a nice change, Aimée."

"No argument there," she said.

If only their clients paid for their computer security on time! She perched on the edge of his desk. Walnut furniture oil, dense and heavy, stained her palms. He'd been cleaning again!

"Shooting her partner on a roof doesn't make sense, René."

"What do you actually know?" René's green eyes narrowed.

She sipped her espresso and explained what had happened.

"This sounds like an accident," René said. "Perhaps Laure tripped in the snow and her gun went off."

"Manhurins are designed to prevent that," she interrupted. "The *sécurité de shock* keeps the hammer from descending accidentally. Impossible."

René pulled his goatee. "Internal Affairs will conclude it was an accident, won't they?"

"René, I found her unconscious and Jacques shot. . . . His heart responded briefly, but it was too late."

She paused, shook her head, seeing the image of Jacques's snow-fringed eyelashes, his blood seeping onto the snow. She struggled with the feeling that he had tried to tell her something.

René stared. "I'm sorry, Aimée."

The steam heater sputtered, sending forth waves of heat that evaporated somewhere at the level of the high ceiling. She made herself continue. "Later, on the adjoining roof, Sebastian and I discovered a broken skylight and wet footprints on the rug underneath. That spelled escape to me."

"Escape?"

"The killer's escape. Then *flics* appeared and *we* beat a quick retreat over the roof."

René let out a sigh. "You promised to stop all that, didn't you? Let the *flics* handle it."

He sounded like Guy. But Guy wasn't around to say those words anymore. She combed her chipped copper lacquered fingernails through her spiky hair.

"Laure may face prison." She didn't like to think of the overcrowded eighteenth-century prison La Santé; the unheated cells and the reaction of the inmates when they discovered Laure was a *flic*. "I feel responsible."

"*Responsible?* Sorry to say it, but it sounds like Jacques brought this on himself."

"Laure has to keep trying to prove herself, to follow in her father's footsteps. Of course, she'd do whatever Jacques asked. Not like me."

"No one's like you, Aimée," René said, rolling his eyes. "Thank the Lord."

"René, Laure's the closest I'll ever have to a little sister. She's self-conscious, sensitive about her cleft palate. I know her; she'll break if she goes inside."

Break into little pieces.

Aimée sniffed, aware of a floral scent from somewhere in the office. "Anyway, I caught up. I did three-quarters of the proposals last night." And missed Guy's reception as a result.

"Morbier left you a message," René said, "something about keeping your paws clean. Maybe you owe him an apology."

"What can I do?"

"You're asking my advice?" René expressed mock horror. "It will cost you. Say you're sorry with flowers. He's a romantic."

"Are we talking about the same person?"

She surveyed the office. A jam jar with sprays of paperwhite narcissus sat on the printer stand, filling the air with fragrance. A harbinger of spring.

"Celebrating spring already? Or is this a special day?" she asked, trying to find out where they'd come from without asking outright. "What's the occasion? Good news?" She let her sentence dangle, hoping he'd say Guy had sent them.

"Pull up the Salys data," was his only reply as his fingers raced over the keyboard. "We need to draft a proposal. By noon."

Her heart thumped. Guy hadn't sent them.

The way René avoided answering, his appearance . . . that twisting feeling in her gut . . . could it be jealousy? Had he met someone? How could she be jealous? Why, it was wonderful René had been bitten by the bug! She watched him. It was all over his face. She should be happy for him, ecstatic. Why wasn't she? Just because Guy had left her didn't mean René couldn't find love.

"Who is she, partner?"

"Did I say that?"

She grinned. "You don't have to."

"There's work to check, lots of it."

"Better tell me," she said, adding more water to the narcissus. "Or I'll nag you until you do." She pulled out her chair and thumbed through the mail.

"I had a drink with someone after a full-moon party," he said.

"You mean you went to a rave?"

"That's for tonight," he said. "Eh, *voilà*."

René was full of surprises.

"What's her name?"

He mumbled something.

"Couldn't catch that."

"Magali. Now pull up the Salys account."

"I finished that proposal last night."

He stared at her.

"While you were out dancing. Makes a change, eh?"

Chastened, René sighed. "We just met. Now don't start with you and Guy wanting to—"

"Meet her? Don't worry."

She'd keep it to herself about Guy. No reason to burden René when he was so happy. Outside, melting ice spattered in silver droplets on the window overlooking rue du Louvre.

"René, I need help with a surveillance. I questioned a woman in an upper apartment overlooking the site where Jacques was shot. But there's a prostitute on the street across from her building whom I couldn't find."

His eyebrows shot up. "In case you haven't noticed, I'm meeting with the Salys account in half an hour. At least they pay on time."

And a nice fat account it was, too. "After that, please go on an assignment for Laure."

"*Me?*" René snorted. "Like I don't stand out in a crowd?"

"Find the *pute*. It's a village there. Those Montmartroise don't regard themselves as part of Paris. Besides, you're perfect."

"Reincarnate Toulouse-Lautrec and walk around with a palette of paints for the tourists?"

She smiled. "That's an idea."

"In this field, you use what you have, don't you?" he said half-seriously and paused, his fingers on the keyboard.

She leaned forward. "The building's under renovation; someone knew an upper-floor apartment was empty. Say the killer lured Jacques from this empty apartment, then took advantage of Laure's appearance to frame her. He knew the layout and escaped over the connecting roof. It's a theory."

"I've said it before: you have an overactive imagination. Put it to work on our new account with Salys."

He was right, of course. "I already have." She clicked on the keys and pulled up the Salys file on her laptop. "I submitted the proposal last night; they'll be ready for you."

She spread the rough diagram of the buildings and courtyard she'd made at the Commissariat across her desk. "I saw lights and heard music from a party there," she said, pointing to an apartment. "I'm trying to get ahold of the owner, a Monsieur Conari."

"The *flics* will question him."

"You can look for the prostitute after your meeting with Salys. Question her and whoever else you see go into any of the buildings next to or opposite the one where Jacques was shot. The clock's ticking. I'll concentrate on the one where the party was held."

"You really want me to go undercover?"

Was there a scintilla of interest in his voice?

"Haven't you always wanted to, partner?"

AIMÉE WORKED on some computer virus checks. Two hours later, her impatience took over and she called Maître Delambre again.

"I expect him any minute," his secretary told her.

She had to catch him before he left for another court session. She grabbed her leather coat. Without the police report, she was pedaling without wheels.

"Please tell him Aimée Leduc's en route to talk with him."

MAÎTRE DELAMBRE'S chambers were more impressive than his appearance. Wan, pale faced under wire-rimmed glasses and mouse brown hair, in his long black robes and white collar he looked barely twenty-five.

The vaulted wood ceiling and bookshelves lined with legal briefs and thick volumes of the penal code did little to allay her fears. The firm's letterhead on thick vellum sheets read Delambre et Fils. A family concern. Maybe Laure should request his father's help.

"Maître Delambre, I'm worried about Laure Rousseau," Aimée said.

"I haven't managed to speak with my client yet," he told her as she sat on a wingback chair. "How can I be certain that she hired you?"

Semantics, Aimée thought. She ignored the dubious ring of his words. "Have you received the crime-scene report?"

"I just reached the office," he said, annoyed. "I need to deal with a pile of messages. She's just one of several clients."

"And how many are facing possible imprisonment for shooting their partner?" Aimée asked. "Please, it's important. I'd appreciate it if you would check."

"Just a moment." He sorted a pile of papers, cleared his throat. "Let's see here." A pause, more shuffling of papers.

Outside on the quay, sleet battered the roof of a bus stuck in traffic. She heard his sharp intake of breath and turned.

"They've moved her. To the Hôtel Dieu, the CUSCO ward."

She gripped the arms of the chair. That was the public hospital's intensive-care criminal ward on Ile de la Cité!

"Has she been charged?"

"No charges have been filed yet. However, in such cases, that's the next step."

"Has her condition deteriorated?"

"Figure it out, Mademoiselle Leduc," he said. "You're the detective."

Aimée stifled a groan. "What information do you have?"

"She suffered a severe concussion," he said, consulting a message pad. "According to this, she's stable but they're monitoring her condition. That's all I know."

Laure in intensive care? Looming complications and the possibility of permanent damage raced through Aimée's mind. And representing her was a young lawyer who appeared to have just gotten his diploma.

"Please show me the dossier," she said.

With some reluctance, he slid it over the mahogany desk. At least he's trying to be accommodating, she thought.

Inside she saw the *procès verbal* consisting of Laure's statement, brief reports describing the crime scene, the weather conditions, and a description of the body, and a cursory pencil diagram of the roof. Even the statement she had made was included.

"Didn't a lab report accompany this?"

Maître Delambre shook his head.

"Odd. Laure told me the lab test had found gunpowder residue on her hands, although she hadn't fired her gun in a month."

She looked more closely. The scene-of-crime diagrammer had missed the angle of the roof at the scaffold, an aspect she'd only viewed from the chimney top. There was no mention of the broken skylight in the adjacent building. The police photos, clipped to the back of the report, showed only the immediate area around Jacques's corpse. "You have to demand a more thorough investigation of the roof."

"You're telling me how to do my job?"

She took a deep breath. How could she get him to act without revealing their rooftop exploits last night? "Not at all, Maître Delambre, but there was a Level 3 storm going on when the crime took place, impossible conditions. No doubt they missed something."

"See for yourself," he said.

She flipped through the addendum of partygoers interviewed in the courtyard building opposite. No one had seen, heard, or noticed anything. Had they interviewed that man she'd seen at the gate?

Was it due to time constraints that the crime-scene report for La Proc was so cursory? Laure was their only suspect; no other line of questioning had been pursued.

"I spoke with a woman on the upper floor of the building that adjoins the murder site," she said. "Last night she heard the voices of men on the roof, but no one had questioned her. And the skylight was broken in the hall of her building."

She handed him the Polaroids she'd taken. "You can see the broken glass in this hallway. Keep them."

"*Merci*. If it's relevant I'm sure the police will discover it," he said, hesitating for the first time. "Listen, there's another problem."

She looked up from the report. "What do you mean?"

"A Nathalie Gagnard has filed a civil suit against Laure," he said.

Aimée remembered Jacques's last name. "His wife?"

"Ex-wife. Charging Laure with murder."

Great.

"She's also complaining in an interview in tomorrow's edition of *Le Parisien*."

"Can't you stop the interview from appearing?"

She heard a clock chime in the background, measured and slow.

"Too late."

* * *

AIMÉE SHOWED her pass and authorization to the two young police guards at Hôtel Dieu. Instead of the trouble she expected, they waved her on to the hospital's criminal ward. Nurses scurried, their footsteps slapping on the chipped Art Nouveau tiles pleated by strips of the light coming through the window blinds. She usually avoided hospitals yet here she stood, in the second one in as many days.

And then she froze, confronted by a white-faced Laure who lay hooked up to machines dripping fluids through clear tubes. Monitors beeped. Rubbing alcohol and pine disinfectant smells clung in the corners.

Aimée's mind traveled back to an afternoon in the Jardin du Luxembourg under the sun-dappled trees, shadows dancing over the gravel. Her father and Georges, Laure's father, were reading the paper as they sat on the green slatted benches, partners who depended on each other when their lives were on the line, sharing a joke. The gurgle and spray of the fountain, so welcome in the humid heat. It had been two summers after her American mother had left them. Ten-year-old Laure had confided, in the playground, that she intended to follow her papa into police work.

The beep and click of the bedside machines brought Aimée back to the present. She made her legs move. Could Laure talk? Was she well enough?

"*Ça va?* How do you feel?" she asked, rubbing Laure's chilled fingers, careful to avoid the intravenous lines taped to her wrist and the top of her hand.

Laure's eyes fluttered open. Her pupils were dilated. Recognition slowly dawned in her face. "The report . . . you've read the report . . . that's why you're here, *bibiche?*"

"Laure, which report?"

"It's so cold. Where am I?" Laure asked, bewildered.

"In the hospital." Aimée pulled the blanket up to Laure's chin.

Laure's eyes wandered. "Why?"

Had the concussion wiped out her memory?

"Take it easy, Laure," she said. "Don't worry. Can you remember what happened?"

Laure tried to put her finger to her lips but missed. "It's . . . it's a secret."

Aimée's spine prickled. "Secret?"

"*Non,* I'm not supposed . . ." Laure tried to prop herself up on her elbow and slipped. With an exhausted sigh, she gave up and fell back, her matted brown hair fanning out on the pillow. "No . . . not right . . . the report."

"Jacques's report?"

Laure blinked, shook her head, and then grimaced in pain.

"You asked for my help, remember," said Aimée. "If you keep things from me, I can't help you. Even if you promised him to keep quiet, now it's all right to speak. You won't help him by keeping it inside."

Nothing could help Jacques now. Aimée hated pressing Laure while she was disoriented, but, with any luck, she might mention a sound, a detail, that would identify her attacker.

Aimée placed a small pot of hothouse violets next to the water carafe on Laure's bedside table. Say it with flowers—hadn't René recommended that for Morbier? "Too bad they don't have any fragrance."

"Violets in winter! *Merci.*"

En route, Aimée had spent an off-season fortune at the Marché aux Fleurs behind Hôtel Dieu. She'd asked the red-cheeked flower seller, a stout woman wearing layers of sweaters under her smock, how the flowers survived in such cold. "But the flowers like it here, Mademoiselle!" she'd answered.

Laure gave a weak smile. "So thoughtful. You always watch out for me."

"Laure, what do you remember?"

Pain crossed Laure's face. The thin white scar creasing her upper lip caught the light.

"My head's throbbing. It feels like it's full of cotton."

"Please try, Laure. Try to picture going up on the scaffolding and tell me what you heard."

Laure's hands balled into fists. But her eyes widened as though she remembered something.

"Stay calm, Laure," Aimée said, unfurling Laure's clenched fingers.

"So hard . . . yes, Jacques called me. Screaming. The men . . ."

Hadn't Zoe Tardou said *she'd* heard male voices? "You said he was meeting an informer."

Laure's eyes brightened. "He needed my back-up. Now I remember but . . . my head's throbbing."

"You saw these men?" Aimée leaned forward, gripped the metal bed rail. "You were set up! What did they look like?"

"I heard men's voices. That's all I remember."

"Raised in anger?"

Laure rubbed her head. "Can't they give me something to stop the pain?"

"Like an argument? Low or deep voices?"

"Not speaking French," she said. "I didn't understand them."

Zoe Tardou had said the same thing.

"What did it sound like?"

Laure closed her eyes.

"Try to think, Laure," she said. "What language did they speak?"

"I just remember the stale smell of sweat, a quick whiff from the rooftop," she said, her voice fading. "And thinking it was Jacques and he had to be scared. Maybe . . . I don't know . . . the way he called out."

A scared man because a deal had fallen through? Or was there something else?

"Were you afraid for Jacques? Did you feel that he needed help? Why did you enter the apartment, Laure?"

Tears streaked down her pale cheeks. "What else could I do? I couldn't even pass the exam . . . Jacques fixed it for me. . . ."

Her police exam, the one Laure had spent nights studying for? "Don't worry about that," Aimée said, wiping away the tears with a cloth, stroking Laure's arm.

If Laure had surprised the men meeting Jacques, they could have attacked her, taken her gun, and used it to shoot Jacques. But Aimée didn't see how to account for the gun residue on Laure's hands.

"Papa made me promise . . . not to tell you. . . ." Laure's voice trailed off.

"Not to tell me what?" Aimée demanded.

Georges had passed away several years earlier. Had the concussion returned her to the past, so she was reliving a memory? A feeling of foreboding filled Aimée.

"What do you mean, Laure?" She tried to avoid the exasperated tone she'd used with the younger Laure when she had tagged after Aimée and dogged her movements.

Laure's eyelids fluttered.

"That pile of Carambar, remember? I didn't tell you. I took them from the concierge."

Carambar, the candy caramels Aimée loved. Still did.

"He didn't mean to, Aimée. Neither of them did," Laure gasped in pain.

Aimée's spine stiffened. The way Laure spoke indicated that something more than stolen candy was on her mind.

"Who didn't mean to?"

"When we came home from school . . . that day I stole the Carambar . . . the envelope . . . on the concierge's table. Remember, I imitated her?"

The high-pitched beeps from one of the monitors alarmed Aimée.

"Laure, I don't understand."

"Your papa, the report saying your papa . . . *non*, I'm so confused. That happened much later. Some cover-up." She lay back. "With Ludovic . . . too tired."

Aimée felt a sickening lurch in her stomach. Laure's words indicated her father had gotten involved in something shady. A cover-up? With "Ludovic"?

"Mademoiselle, stand aside, please." Aimée felt arms pushing her out of the way and from the corner of her eye saw a team of white-coated staff rushing past her.

"Oxygen! Monitor her blood pressure," a doctor said. "Her pupils are blown."

"Sixty over forty," said the nurse.

"Looks like increased intercranial pressure—"

Aimée stumbled toward the nurses' station. The staff pulled a white curtain, its hooks jingling, around Laure's bed.

"Please, tell me what's happening."

"Complications," said a brisk nurse, grabbing a chart.

Complications. Did the nurse mean permanent damage? "Why has her condition worsened?"

"Only medical personnel are permitted here now. You must leave the ward."

"But my friend—"

"We'll handle this, call back later," the nurse said peremptorily, steering Aimée out.

Tuesday

AIMÉE STARED OVER THE melting, dirt-encrusted snowdrifts on the bank of the Seine, racked with worry and guilt. She'd pushed Laure, subjected her to critical stress. She would never forgive herself if the pressure of her questions had caused Laure permanent damage.

Laure's disjointed words spun in her mind. Old story, old news, about her father's corruption, she wanted to shout. Hadn't she proved he wasn't crooked? Yet a sliver of doubt remained. Had Laure some knowledge of a cover-up, something her father had gone along with? Ludovic . . . was he Ludovic Jubert? The one who'd been referred to by the Interpol agent in Clichy in connection with Aimée's father's death in the Place Vendôme? The gray-hued Seine, swirling by in eddies, provided no answers.

She had to set that aside, worry about it later, had to concentrate on Laure's predicament. She had to see the lab report for herself; she needed more facts to go on. She pulled out the list she'd copied of the partygoers the police had questioned, hoping the man she'd seen with the backpack was on it.

OF THE twenty names, she managed to reach eighteen by phone. The first, who identified himself as in "advertising," replied that he'd enjoyed the hors d'oeuvre table and the blonde he'd met. That was all he remembered. And it went downhill from there. A couple commented that with all the music they hadn't been able to have much conversation with anyone else. Two of the models indicated they'd been on their cell phones much of the time confirming their next day's bookings.

The catering-firm owner, a Monsieur Pivot, spoke for his staff. His caterers had slaved in a hot kitchen and hadn't had a break until the police arrived. Pivot was sure of that— "They'd be in trouble otherwise." The bossa nova quartet's guitarist confirmed that they had played until eleven-thirty, just before the police arrived. She left messages for the two others she'd been unable to reach and hoped for a call back.

Just before noon, sick of the phone, she changed into a wool pinstripe trouser suit, the warmest outfit in her armoire, outlined her eyes in kohl, and slipped on her coat. She had recalled where she'd seen Conari's name: on trucks all around Paris.

Half an hour later, she stood on avenue Junot at the Conari firm's address on the upscale side of Montmartre at the crest of the northwest slope. She entered a remodeled artist's atelier housing several architecture and construction firms. Conari's offices occupied an entire floor; the firm was prosperous if the building and its location were anything to go by.

"No appointment?" said the receptionist, with a perfunctory smile. She had short curly brown hair and good teeth. So good Aimée figured her paycheck had gone into them. "I'm sorry, Monsieur Conari's working on a deadline. It's impossible."

Aimée shifted in her high-heeled boots, wishing she'd worn her two-inch heels instead. "A homicide occurred in the apartment across from where he hosted a party last night. I have a few follow-up questions, routine, of course, that will take five minutes. Guaranteed. It's necessary to the investigation."

"But he's too busy—"

"Just ask him. He's been so cooperative already I hate to intrude, but I promise to take just five minutes of his time."

The receptionist hesitated, picked up the phone. "Monsieur Conari, there's a"—she glanced at Aimée's card, flashed her teeth again—"a Mademoiselle Leduc of Leduc Detective who insists she needs to speak with you."

The receptionist blinked. "Of course, Mademoiselle, go right in. Second door on the left."

Aimée's heels sank into the deep pile of the carpeted hallway whose walls were lined with abstract black-and-white paintings. She knocked on the door.

"*Entréz.*"

Floor-to-ceiling windows greeted her, a wall of glass giving a panoramic view of the rooftops below. What looked like several loft spaces had been combined into a large room with a cathedral-type glass ceiling that soared upward.

She focused on a middle-aged charcoal-haired man leaning over a drawing table, his shirtsleeves rolled up.

"Monsieur Félix Conari? I'm Aimée Leduc," she said. "Pardon me for disturbing you."

"Of course, no problem," he said, concern in his voice. "Please sit down."

He indicated a low-slung red leather chair that looked difficult to get out of.

"*Non, merci*, you're busy and I'll get to the point," she said, pulling out the list of partygoers from her bag. "Can you describe what happened at your party last night?"

Félix Conari rubbed his chin. "*Tiens*, let me think, the quartet played, my guests seemed entertained, the caterers kept stocking the bar and refilling the hors d'oeuvres trays, I made sure of that," he said, in a down-to-earth tone. "You see, the guests were clients, important to my firm. We were about to go in to dinner. Yes, that's right, and then the commissaire came."

"That's all you remember, Monsieur Conari?"

He expelled air from his mouth, shrugged. "*Oui*. But let me call Yann, he was there last night."

Conari hit an intercom button on his desk. She noted a Yann Marant on her list, one of the two she had not reached.

A moment later, a man in his thirties, wearing a rumpled black suit and Adidas track shoes, with long brown hair curling behind his ears, came in.

"My friend Yann Marant, a software engineer consulting with my firm," Conari introduced him. "Mademoiselle Leduc's a detective investigating the incident last night."

Aimée noted the telltale calluses on the edge of Yann Marant's palm. A systems analyst or programmer, she figured.

Yann smiled. A nice smile.

"Sorry to bother you, Monsieur Marant, but I understand you attended Monsieur Conari's party," Aimée said.

Yann nodded. "Do we need to identify someone in a lineup, a suspect? Is that why you're here?"

He watched too much *télé*. "Not quite yet," Aimée said.

"I want to help, but . . ." Marant shook his head. "I was preoccupied last night."

"You know these software engineers." Félix gave a small smile, slapping him on the back. "Code, numbers whirling in his mind all the time. It's hieroglyphics to me, but I pull him back to earth from time to time."

Aimée wondered if Marant was good. She and René used a consulting-systems analyst from time to time. They would need one if their proposals worked out, but since Marant had been hired by a successful outfit like Conari's she doubted he'd be in their price range.

"The commissaire told us very little," Yann said. "We're in the dark as to what happened."

Intelligence radiated from these men. They were not the type she could fob off with dumbed-down information.

"That's standard procedure, Monsieur. In investigations like this, the officers must gather all the facts before any hypothesis can be made. That's why I'm here, disturbing you," she said and smiled. "Monsieur Marant, try to think back to last night, just before eleven o'clock. Did you hear a loud noise or notice anything happening outside the window?"

He shrugged. "I worked in Félix's study. There are no windows. Then, Félix, your guest arrived, the musician? I lost track of time—"

"I take it the police questioned him," Aimée said. "His name?"

Félix Conari's hand clutched the slanted table's edge. "He's shy, that one, Lucien. A unique musician."

Aimée scanned the names. "There's no Lucien listed here. His last name?"

"Sarti. A Corsican DJ and musician. He mixes traditional polyphony and hip-hop."

No Lucien Sarti. Aimée thought of the timing and the man watching at the gate. "Does he have black hair and was he wearing a black leather jacket and carrying a backpack?"

Félix grinned. "That describes many of my guests. But, yes, he is tall, rail thin, and has black curly hair."

"How can I reach him?"

"Look, Mademoiselle, I don't want to get him involved in this."

"Of course not, but I need help, all the help I can get. I must speak with everyone. Can you give me his phone number?"

"Lucien's a musician, a free spirit," Conari said. "No phone. I contact him through a resto, Strago, and leave messages for him."

She wrote that down. "You mentioned your guests were clients," she said. "I'm curious as to how you know this musician, Lucien Sarti."

"Call it a middle-aged man's dream, but I'm planning to promote him," he said, with a small smile. "I have some connections in the recording industry. Music's close to my heart. But he disappeared before we actually signed the contract. Artists, you know!"

She wondered why this Lucien Sarti had disappeared before speaking to the police.

"Should Félix be concerned, Mademoiselle Leduc?" Yann asked. His ponytail poked out above his jacket collar. "I mean, has the *quartier* changed so much? Can I ask what happened?"

Marant asked a lot of questions. But then she would, too.

Félix nodded. "I've never seen such a police presence. This is Paris, not New York, where shootings are commonplace."

Read the papers, she wanted to say. But they might prove more helpful if she told them something. Word traveled in the *quartier* so even these busy urban professionals would hear, sooner or later.

"We're investigating a policeman's murder on the roof of the building adjoining yours. The storm hasn't helped," she said.

Two pairs of eyes watched her. "So anything that might come to your mind, a small detail—"

"You're a private detective, you said. Aren't the police in charge?"

Sharp. Didn't miss a thing. "I'm investigating on behalf of a client," she said. "Beyond that I can't say."

"Look, I want to be more helpful," Yann said. "How can I reach you if I remember anything?"

Aimée hid her disappointment at their lack of information. "I appreciate your time, *merci*," she said, handing them each her card.

STRAGO, ON the less fashionable and more working-class slope of Montmartre, was a storefront restaurant with a hammer and sickle on the old curling menu posted behind smudged glass. A handwritten sign in violet ink read FERMÉ. This side of the *quartier* hadn't changed much since Doisneau's black-and-white fifties photographs, she thought. Narrow cobbled streets wound up to the *butte*. The corner cafés and low buildings fronting rue Labat reminded Aimée of Edith Piaf's sad song of the rue Labat streetwalker who had lost her man. But, then, weren't they all sad?

Thoughts of Guy intruded. His scent, the way he ran his fingers through his hair. She pushed the sadness down; she had to find this musician.

At the vegetable shop under a green awning next door, Aimée asked the owner about Strago's hours.

"They open when they feel like it," he told her. "If you smell garlic, Anna's cooking."

She put a franc down and reached into the counter's glass canister for several Carambars. She unwrapped the yellow waxed paper, glanced at the joke printed inside, and popped the caramel into her mouth. "Ever seen Lucien Sarti, black hair, black leather jacket, who gets messages there?" she went on.

He shrugged. "When the weather's like this, I stay in the shop."

She handed him her card. "If you do, call me. I'd like to speak with him, Monsieur."

She wrote down Strago's phone number and belted her leather coat against the cold. Snow clumps in the plane tree branches melted into dripping lines that ran down the bare trunks. Snow, the rare times it occurred in Paris, never lasted long. The rising heat from the buildings took care of that. Like it had taken care of any evidence that the snow on the roof might have held.

She rooted in her worn Vuitton wallet. Found it. The card with Jubert's name that Pleyet from Interpol had given her when she'd dealt with him in the Clichy district. Her thoughts jumped to Laure's ramblings. For two months she'd searched for Jubert, the one link she'd found to her father's death in the Place Vendôme bombing. But he hadn't been at the address listed, or in the Ministry. It was as if the man had never existed.

Was Jubert the "Ludovic" Laure had mentioned? Was there another Ludovic in her father's past, a past of whispers, secrets, and shadows she'd only caught hints of. Morbier would know. She pulled out her cell phone.

"*Oui*," Morbier answered.

"May I buy you a late lunch?"

"You want to thank me?"

For what? she almost said, before she remembered he'd gotten her released from the Commissariat. She paused, looking down at the oily rainbow-slicked swirls reflecting the sky in a pewter puddle. A January sky.

"Or make it up to me for your atrocious manners, ruining Ouvrier's party and landing me in hot water with La Proc," he was saying.

"She's got it in for you, anyway," Aimée said. "But how—?

A diesel bus rumbled past her, drowning Morbier's response. Aimée felt for her gloves in her pocket.

"Le Rendez-vous des Chauffeurs in half an hour?" Morbier asked.

A taxi-driver haunt, with good food. That should sweeten the questions she had to ask.

* * *

MIRRORS LINED the walls, yellow-and-white-checked cloths covered the twelve tables in the resto, an aluminum meat slicer rested on the counter. The last diners finished a late lunch with a cheese course. Morbier sat on the camel-colored leather banquette, split and taped in places, worn by the repose of generations of taxi drivers. He was reading a newspaper.

"Nice choice, Morbier," she said, sitting down and hanging her bag on the back of her wooden chair. The hot, close air felt welcome after the brisk chill outside. Framed posters of the Montmartre vineyard *vendanges* hung above the mirrors. Background jazz played low on a radio as the owner wiped down the aging red formica counter through which patches of the original zinc were visible.

"Combines all facets of the Montmartre spirit: rustic, bohemian, and bon vivant," he said, setting down his paper. "But you're buying me lunch. What's your real reason?"

"René said you were a romantic," she said, pouring from the *pichet* of rosé, already on the table, into his wineglass. "And to thank you."

"If I didn't know you better," he said, his eyebrows knitting together, "I'd believe it, Leduc."

"Believe that Laure's in the Hôtel Dieu in intensive care," she said, spreading the napkin on her lap.

Morbier shook his head.

Should she tell him the rest?

"Laure heard men's voices from the roof," she said. "Speaking another language."

"You interrogated her, Leduc?"

"There's so little to go on, I had to ask questions," she said. "But I made her worse."

"Blaming yourself won't make her better. Look, we do it all the time."

"After I saw the police dossier at her lawyer's, nothing else looks good either."

She poured herself a glass of rosé.

Morbier touched the rim of his glass to hers. "À *la santé*. Clearing her is the lawyer's job, Leduc. Not yours."

He caught the owner's attention and pointed to the blackboard with the prix fixe menu chalked on it. "Two of those, *s'il vous plaît*."

"Of course, Commissaire," the man said, heading to the kitchen behind the small Dutch door, whose top half was open. From inside Aimée could hear chopping noises and the hiss of frying oil.

"You're a regular here, I see."

He gave a small smile, the jowly cheeks and bags under his eyes making him look more tired than ever.

"There's nothing more you can do, Leduc," he said, taking the rolled paper napkin and tucking the corner into his collar.

Aimée leaned forward. "Morbier, she didn't kill her partner. The techs made a mistake with respect to the gunshot residue. The lab report's not even prepared yet!"

"That's for the police to investigate."

"See what you can find out," she said. "When the report's filed, tell me."

"You know I don't have access to those investigations."

Didn't he?

She looked down, summoning her courage.

"At the hospital, Laure rambled a bit, obsessing about the past. She mentioned a report about Papa, hinting at some cover-up."

Morbier choked on his wine. Wiped his mouth with the napkin.

"Do you know anything about it, Morbier?"

"Live in the present, Leduc."

But in the brief unguarded look she'd seen on Morbier's face, she sensed he knew something.

"Does it have to do with when Papa and Georges were partners?"

"Laure's father?"

She nodded, took a piece of bread from the basket, tore off the crust, and chewed it.

"You were Papa's first partner, weren't you? What can you tell me about Georges?"

"Beats me."

"Your memory going, Morbier?" She leaned forward and brushed the crumbs aside.

"That and everything else. My retirement's around the corner."

For a man approaching retirement, he kept a tight schedule, working at the Commissariat and part-time at Brigade Criminelle as well. He'd never confided in her about his assignments.

"You know how Laure put her father on a pedestal. Help me understand what she meant by a report, some cover-up involving my father. There is some secret that's worrying her."

The owner set down two plates of fisherman's salad—potato and white fish and a sliced *saucisson sec* that she'd seen him unhook from its hanging place above the counter.

"That's in the past," he said. "Leave it alone."

There *was* something.

He cut the sausage into small pieces with his knife.

"Aaah, the owner's mother cures these herself," he said.

"Tell me, Morbier."

He sighed. "There's no secret. We all graduated from the academy together. You know that." He took a bite, then washed it down with rosé. "Then, like now, we worked in fours, two pairs. Beat the cobblestones together—"

"You, Georges, Papa, and who?" she interrupted.

Morbier set down his knife, rubbed his finger over his thumb, and looked at Aimée, an unreadable expression on his face.

She pulled out the old card. "Was it this man, Ludovic Jubert? A few months ago, an Interpol agent told me Jubert knew about the surveillance we did in Place Vendôme. If so, I want to talk to him."

He scratched a wooden kitchen match on the table leg and lit a Montecristo cigarillo. He took several deep puffs and leaned back, silent.

"Where is Jubert?" she asked.

"How do I know?"

"But you can find out."

The owner stood by the table and asked. "The sausage, it's not good?"

"Lost my appetite, Philippe," Morbier said. "Bring us an espresso and the check, please."

She wouldn't let Morbier off so easily. Plumes of acrid smoke rose from his cigarillo. She tried not to inhale them. Yesterday she'd thrown away the pack of Gauloises she'd hidden from Guy.

"Would you find him for me?" She took another sip of wine, thinking. "When you and Papa worked in the Marais together, where was Georges?"

"Kicked upstairs. Driven, he was."

"And Jubert?"

Pause. "Retired now, most likely."

"Retired? Then what did Laure mean?" She took a deep breath.

"She's injured, isn't she? Making no sense. Listen, I'll say it again, I live in the here and now. So should you." He ground out his cigarillo. "And some more words of advice."

Morbier was good at that.

"Let Laure's lawyer handle the matter. Don't step on the investigators' toes. They don't like it."

"How can I find Ludovic Jubert?" Aimée repeated.

Morbier stood and took his scarf and overcoat from the rack. He picked up the espresso cup, drank from it, and threw some francs on the tablecloth. "Tried the phone book?"

He took a step toward the door.

She reached for Morbier's hand and gripped his thick fingers with their nicotine-stained, ridged nails. He tried to pull his hand away but she held tight.

"Morbier, there's a saying 'To continue a journey one must put the ghosts to rest.'"

A faraway look came into Morbier's eyes. "That's a hard order to fill, Leduc," he said, in a voice so low she almost didn't catch it. "One can spend a lifetime trying."

He wrapped his muffler around his neck and was gone. A cold draft of air hit her as the door slammed. His newspaper had fallen to the floor. She picked it up, glancing at it while pulling out her wallet. Morbier's distinctive slanted handwriting caught her eye. "The Corsican arms investigation report six years ago that traced links to the Paris Préfecture, which caused furor in the Ministry of Interior, has resurfaced. Spokesmen for the Ministry decline comment," she read. He'd written the letters JC beside the article, in the margin, heavily underlined.

"He's like that these days," the owner said, bringing her change and retying the apron around his waist. He shot Aimée a knowing look. "You should try to make him happy, Mademoiselle."

JC . . . JEAN-CLAUDE . . . Jean-Claude Leduc, her father? Or was she reading too much into Morbier's doodles? Six years ago he'd run Leduc Detective while she was in her first year of medical school, helping him out occasionally.

Then, on a weekend surveillance at the Place Vendôme, there had been an explosion and her father had been killed. She still didn't know who to blame but she had to keep trying to find out who as responsible, even if putting the ghosts to rest, as Morbier said, was hard to do. She folded the newspaper and put it in her bag.

She caught the bus on Boulevard Magenta, trying the Hôtel Dieu twice on her cell phone to inquire as to Laure's condition. Both times a message machine answered. Frustrated, she could only leave her number.

From the bus window, she saw the St. Vincent de Paul's vans parked where they were setting up the soup kitchen near Gare de l'Est. A line of men was already forming for the evening handout.

She'd been lucky that food had always been on the table. It had not been easy for her father, she imagined. She remembered her excitement and the wonder in Laure's eyes as their fathers cooked crêpes for them for La Chandeleur, the feast of Candlemas on February second. This coming weekend. They'd observed the tradition of flipping crêpes with a coin in hand to make one's wish come true. She'd wished for her mother to come back. Georges had been the only one to flip without breaking the crêpe.

On the bus sat an old man with his dog in a basket; a teenager wearing headphones and nodding to his own beat; a silk-scarfed woman reading Balzac, rubbing shoulders with a cornrowed mother, her coat covering a bright, flowing African *boubou*, a stroller at her side. Faces of Montmartre from the other side of the hill, away from the tourists and Sacré Coeur, where affordable apartments adjoined the African Goutte d'Or *quartier*.

Her ˌthoughts turned to Jacques's ex-wife, Nathalie. She dreaded an interview with the woman who'd already filed a lawsuit against Laure. But it was all she had left to go on.

* * *

AIMÉE STOOD in front of Nathalie Gagnard's work address, 22 rue de Douai, a Second Empire mansion. The building stood on the corner of the rue Duperré, a street of white stone buildings with shuttered windows and balconies bordered by black iron grilles. A one-way street, lined with parked motor scooters and a car with an AUTO-ÉCOLE sign on top. Across from her in a nearby café's window, a leftover lumpy St. Nicolas figure still lugged presents. A mobile phone store and several *immobiliers*, real estate agents, indicated this was an upscale slice of the quartier below Place Pigalle.

Aimée skirted an open hole in the pavement, blocked off by plastic orange webbing, revealing the sediment and rock below. It brought back her geology teacher's rhapsodies describing the nuanced aroma of schist, the gypsum and stone layered under the streets. To Aimée, limestone or shale, it all smelled the same. This *quartier* had been built over an ancient lepers' cemetery, he'd told them. She doubted the residents would be happy to know what lay moldering underneath their feet.

Fluttering cloth banners across the front of the building advertised *espace*, space available for events. She entered the foyer, reached by a marble staircase beneath a hexagonal wooden fretwork of inlaid lights. Somehow she'd have to get Nathalie Gagnard to talk.

Gilt chairs were turned upside down on tables in the high-ceilinged salon. Aimée almost tripped over a waiter sitting on the parquet floor, his eyes closed, rubbing his stockinged feet. As she neared the reception desk, she saw a gaunt-faced woman in her midthirties, with black wispy hair and gold hoop earrings, wearing a white shirt, black skirt, and sensible low heels, stacking brochures on the zinc bar.

"*Bonjour*, we do private receptions, wedding parties." The woman smiled, coughed, and covered her mouth. Her voice was low and grating, a smoker's voice. "Here's a brochure. Perhaps you're interested in having an event?"

Aimée returned the smile and pulled out her card.

"I'd like to speak with Nathalie Gagnard," she said before the woman could launch further into her sales pitch.

The woman's eyes narrowed, taking in Aimée's navy pin-striped trouser suit, pointed boots, and leather backpack.

"Regarding?" Her charm evaporated.

"A police matter. Does she work . . . ?"

"You're investigating my ex-husband's murder?" The woman's grip on Aimée's card tightened.

Aimée inhaled, determined to try a tactful approach, a skill René often told her she needed to practice.

"So you're Madame Gagnard?" Aimée said. "Please spare me a few moments to clear up some points in the investigation."

"About time." Nathalie Gagnard looked at her watch. She straightened the brochures. "I'm done. Take a seat over there," she said, her voice clipped as she pointed to a smaller room lined with carved wood *boiserie*.

Aimée heard Nathalie give instructions to the waiter concerning wineglasses. Sculpted cherubs and a frieze beneath a ceiling mural surrounded her in an eclectic mixture. Stone sculptured caryatids of women held up the ceiling; gold and painted glass panels framed the outer salon. It was a nineteenth-century potpourri.

The thick expensive brochure proclaimed that here Bizet composed his opera *Carmen*, and his wife held salons attended by Proust and Henri de Toulouse-Lautrec, a neighbor across the street. Later, Aimée read, the mansion had become a working-class *bouillon* canteen; later still, a bordello, until they were outlawed; and most recently, a post office.

"Cornered the bitch, have you?" Nathalie said, sitting down, pulling out a gold-filter-tipped cigarette, and flicking the flame of a plastic lighter.

More than hostile, she was vindictive.

Nathalie took a deep drag, then exhaled a plume of smoke and leaned forward in her chair. "I swear, she went after Jacques like a cat in heat the minute he was nice to her. Can you imagine? Jacques would give the shirt off his back to help someone."

Even if the shirt belonged to someone else, Aimée wondered? From what she'd gathered, Jacques could make an omelet without eggs, a real *débrouillard*—what some people called a wheeler-dealer.

"I'm not sure I understand."

"That harelip, the whiner," Nathalie said, tapping her ash into a white porcelain ashtray.

Cruel, too. But much as she'd like to slap the woman, it wouldn't help her.

"You're referring to Laure Rousseau?" she said, determined to keep her emotions in check and probe deeper into Jacques's life.

"The murderer. So jealous . . ."

Rolling a boulder uphill would be easier than talking to Nathalie.

"Help me to understand this," Aimée said, curious about the Gagnard woman's delusions. "According to the file, their professional relationship worked well. Why do you suspect her?"

"Who else? Despite her, Jacques and I were getting back together." Nathalie's shoulders heaved and she covered her eyes, sobbing. The smoke spiraled into Aimée's face.

Surprised, Aimée ground out the cigarette, pulled out a tissue, and passed it to Nathalie.

"She'll pay, the bitch," Nathalie interrupted, blotting the tears on her cheeks.

"From what I gather," Aimée said, reining herself in with effort, "your divorce was finalized a few months ago."

"Where's justice, that's what I want to know."

"Justice. That's what we want," Aimée agreed. "But we have to dig, find the evidence, put the pieces together, and nail the perpetrator. Procedure dictates questioning and investigating every aspect to get a complete picture. Going to the newspaper doesn't further your cause, Nathalie, does it?"

"At least it gets attention." Nathalie reblotted her eyes, careful not to smudge her mascara. Suspicious now, she asked, "Who do you work for?"

"Nathalie, what if there's an accomplice? Others may be involved."

Nathalie stuffed the tissue into her purse. "I asked who you worked for."

"I'm investigating on Maître Delambre's behalf," Aimée said. She figured Nathalie wouldn't know which side he represented. At least not yet. She pulled out her cryptography notebook. Pretended to consult it, flipped through some pages, then stared at Nathalie's face, disappointed at the firm set of her mouth.

"The report indicates your former husband saw other women," Aimée said, thinking of Laure's comment about a girlfriend. A new tactic might loosen her lips. "We believe he was meeting an informer that night. A woman."

"You don't understand. Jacques respected women," Nathalie said, as though stating a simple fact. "He treated them well. But *she* took it the other way."

"I'm curious, looking at the logic of that evening," Aimée said, hoping her voice sounded reasonable. "From the suspect's viewpoint, it wouldn't make much sense to murder Jacques since everyone saw them leave the café together!"

Nathalie's eyes hardened into slits. "Do your job. Nail her."

"Was Jacques under pressure? Bills? The job? Did he mention people he owed money to?"

Nathalie stood. "I have an appointment."

"Nathalie, La Proc demands proof. Facts. When did you last see Jacques?"

"I set a place for him at dinner on the eve of Noël but at the last minute he had to work." Her brow creased as she combed her memory.

"That was a few weeks ago. Nothing more recent?"

Nathalie shook her head, hurt pooling in her eyes.

For a moment, Aimée pitied her. Guy had bought a Christmas tree and together they'd strung the lights on the tree and on Miles Davis, too, finally falling asleep in each other's arms at dawn.

Snap out of it, she told herself. Get down to business. Think. Did Jacques have mistresses whom he supported? Was he trying to maintain a lifestyle beyond his reach? She'd seen it happen to her father's colleagues.

"Jacques was making monthly car payments according to the report," Aimée said. She remembered seeing the tow truck hooking the Citroën. "What happened to his car?"

"I can't make the payments," Nathalie said. "I've returned it."

"Did you divorce him because of his spending?"

Nathalie leaned forward. "Just between you and me, things *were* tight. We divorced and declared bankruptcy to save our assets, but we were still together. How plain must I make it? The woman killed him out of jealousy. But she won't get away with it, I won't let her."

Aimée felt sorry for Nathalie, desperate to revenge her unhappiness somehow. But her accusations damaged Laure, who was surely innocent.

"The Brigade Criminelle will investigate and find the criminal."

"Wake up," Nathalie said, rising and pushing back in her chair so that it scraped on the wood floor. "The old-boy network didn't want her father's name dragged in the mud. But no one will cover up for her."

"Yet, Jacques took her as a partner—"

"Like I said," Nathalie interrupted, "he liked to help people."

Something struck Aimée as wrong.

"I'm late." Nathalie looped a tangerine kerchief around her neck, reached for her coat, and walked out of the building.

Aimée followed her to the low-slung Renault Mégane with the AUTO-ÉCOLE plastic box on top parked outside. Wind whipped down the street, bringing the smell of wet, sodden leaves.

"You own a driving school?"

"We only kept this," Nathalie said, unlocking the door. Her sigh indicated she'd known a better life. "Before the divorce we had a fleet of six cars, eh. I'm not the type to sit at home so I was involved in the business."

So the divorce had saved what was left of their business. Again she wondered if Jacques had grown too accustomed to the finer things. *Flics* often moonlighted, doing security to supplement their salary.

"Did Jacques work security?"

Nathalie's mouth formed a moue of distaste. "Consultant," she said. "He did consulting."

The rain-swept pavement mirrored the dull gray clouds. The number seventy-four bus shot out diesel exhaust as it gunned by.

"With his skills, of course," Aimée said. So both of them had held two jobs, working hard. Yet Nathalie had stiffened when she'd asked about Jacques's past.

Nathalie opened the car door.

"I need to verify this," Aimée said. "Can you remember the company for whom or the location where he consulted?"

"He knew Montmartre, he had contacts here. Sometimes he took private jobs, you know, for VIPs."

"Who could I talk to who might know about this sideline?"

"I didn't get involved."

Why wouldn't this woman talk?

"Try to remember, Nathalie. A name?"

"Look, *she* murdered Jacques, how does it matter?"

"Everything's important," Aimée said, trying to appeal to

the woman's pride. "Let me stress that if all the facts don't come to light now, they could be used later to prevent a conviction, to let the killer go free. As a *flic*'s wife, you know that."

Nathalie blinked, threw her purse in the passenger seat. "He talked about Zette sometimes, an old boxer who runs a bar. On rue Houdon."

CLUB CHEVALIER, the bar on rue Houdon, had seen better days. And they had passed several decades ago, Aimée figured. The dark bar was lined with plastic-covered banquettes and decorative columns, their plaster bases now heavily gouged. A large woman with blonde hair, a pink apron around her girth, vacuumed the matching once-pink carpet. What VIPs did they serve here, Aimée wondered?

"Pardon, Madame, may I speak with Zette?"

"Eh, we're not open."

"Is Zette here?"

The woman sighed and switched off the vacuum. An artificial-stone water fountain gurgled in the corner, green fungi grew on the lip of the shell-like basin. Several game machines blinked red and blue in the corner, the kind that used to have slots but now were computerized. A radio blared out the results of the horse races from somewhere in the back.

"Who wants to know?" the woman said, her hand on her hip.

Aimée grinned. "Jacques's friend sent me."

"Not that business again?"

Have the police been here, too, Aimée wondered. "I need to talk with him."

The woman shouted, "Zette!"

No answer. Just the excited voice announcing the race winners: "Fleur-de-Lys by a head, Tricolor a close second, and Sarabande makes it third!"

Aimée heard the clink of a glass and someone slapping papers down.

"Zette!"

"Leave me in peace, woman!"

"Someone to see you," the woman said.

Aimée heard a muttered "*Merde.*"

A balding gray-haired man poked his head around the door in the back of the small bar. He had several gold teeth, a crooked nose, and a white scar splitting his right eyebrow, giving him a perpetually questioning look.

"Will talking to you make me happy, Mademoiselle?"

"How about a drink and we'll find out."

"Aaah, such possibilities!" He scratched his neck, gave her the once-over, and raised his other eyebrow. "But I can smell a *flic* from way off," he said, with a wide smile. "Have your boss call me. I deal with the commissaire. Show me some respect, eh, Mademoiselle."

Respect? Who gained respect that way? The woman, a bored look on her face, pulled the vacuum cleaner into the back.

"I'm not a *flic*, but my father was."

"So you say. Where?"

"Commissariat in the fourth arrondissement before he joined my grandfather at the detective agency that I run now."

"Aaah, so you know Ouvrier?"

He was testing her.

"I went to his retirement party last night, around the corner."

"Me, too," he said. "I didn't see you."

"The tail end," Aimée said, edging toward the bar. "I'd never seen him out of uniform but he looked sharp in a pin-stripe suit, eh?"

"That's a fact," he said. "I left early, had to man the bar here. Knowing Ouvrier, next time he wears it will be his funeral."

Pause. From the silence, she figured Zette hadn't heard about what had happened to Jacques.

"Mademoiselle, I didn't catch your name, or your father's," Zette said.

Not only careful and street-wise, he'd let her know he was well connected at the Commissariat. As a smart club owner should be, but it bothered her.

"Jean-Claude Leduc," she said. "Aimée Leduc, here's my card." She set it on the wet, glass-ringed counter.

He turned her card over in his hand. "A woman PI?"

She nodded. "Computer security."

Had he known her father? "Does the name Leduc sound familiar?"

"I know a lot of people. So tell me what you really want to talk about."

Aimée realized she'd passed muster, set twenty francs on the none-too-clean counter, and smiled. "Bet you're thirsty."

Wine would make this dance with Zette more palatable. Or so she hoped.

"I've got a nice little Corsican red that sings in the gullet." He reached for an unmarked bottle and two wineglasses and set them in front of her. "It's never too early for me."

She noticed his loaf of a body, a bit gone to fat, but biceps bulged under the tight red soccer shirt. He must work out. An old prizefighter with the scars to prove it.

"Young ladies don't visit me much anymore," he said, pouring the garnet red liquid.

Zette's attempt at charm? She took a sip. Plump, fruity, and smooth on the way down. Not bad.

On the bar wall hung a framed newspaper sport section headlined ZETTE KO'S TERRANCE THE MAD MOROCCAN.

"So you're that Zette? My father went to your matches at the Hippodrome."

She stretched the truth. He'd won complimentary championship tickets from the Commissariat once. A worn-around-the-edges retired prizefighter might soak up the flattery.

Zette shrugged as though used to this.

"Boxing gave you a good living, eh?"

"All this." He took a long sip and gestured around the bar. "And a VIP security service with Jacques Gagnard, *non?*"

"You've got it wrong," Zette said without skipping a beat and drained his glass. Poured another and topped up hers. She took another swig.

"How's that, Zette?" she said. "You worked with Jacques, didn't you?"

"So that's who you want to talk about," he said, staring at her. "Something's happened to him, hasn't it?"

She hesitated to give him the bad news. "I'm sorry."

"Sorry, what do you mean?"

She paused, her index finger tracing the rim of the glass. "He was shot and killed on a rooftop. On the next street."

Zette's fists balled. He shook his head. "But I saw him last night! *Nom de Dieu*, he was at the bar, I bought him a drink, we talked—"

"Everyone did. We're all shocked. He was off duty, too, when it happened."

Zette's face clouded with sadness and he poured more wine. Was there more behind that look?

"To Jacques, a good *mec*."

They raised their glasses.

"Who found him?"

"That's the thing, Zette; I did."

Zette made the sign of the cross with his big knuckled hands. "I still can't believe it."

"What did Jacques talk about, do you remember?" Aimée asked. "Was he nervous, was he acting any way unusual?"

Zette rubbed his jaw. "How did you get my name?"

She controlled her frustration. "Nathalie, his ex-wife, said he worked for you."

"Work? More like he did me a favor from time to time. My VIPs like protection."

What celebrities called Club Chevalier their hangout?

"By VIPs, you mean who?"

"Tino Rossi sat on the stool you're sitting on," he said, with a proud look on his mug.

Tino Rossi, a Corsican singer popular with the over-sixty crowd? She tried to look impressed. "Wasn't he before Jacques's time?"

"My guests want to keep a low profile, they want discretion," he said. "They like to sample Montmartre without their goons, and to be escorted by a local."

An escort service? She looked around the club, saw the frayed postcards of Ajaccio on the smudged mirror. Of course, this was a *Corsican* bar, why hadn't she picked up on that? Instead of Jacques squiring provincial businessmen to the hooker clubs, could it have been Corsican gang leaders who wanted protection without their "goons"?

"I see. You're Corsican, Zette?"

He flashed his gold teeth. "At one time we ran the *quartier*. The golden days. Pepé *le grand* was rubbed out right in front of my place, and Ange Testo ran the big *brasserie* on Place Pigalle. It was a *wehrmachetspeiselokal*, German soldiers' canteen, during the war. Those bathrooms were a mess, all graffitied with swastikas, things you don't want to know. In the end Ange just wallpapered it over." He shrugged. "We Corse had a code of honor, still do. But now, I'm the only one left."

She nodded and drank her wine. Code of honor? More like the code of silence. Talk and one talked no more.

She envisioned the postwar days of *zazous* wearing big zoot suits and flashing money, the jazz clubs and strip bars, when the Moulin Rouge was considered high class.

"Zette, tell me about the last job Jacques did for you."

"Like I said, now and then he did favors for me."

"*Bon*. What favor did he do for you?"

"Like I said, some escorting."

Getting a Corsican to talk was hard work.

A broad-shouldered young man wearing a leather jacket,

wool cap low over his forehead, and jangling what sounded like coins in his pocket, entered. Zette glanced up. Instead of telling him the bar was closed, as Aimée expected, he nodded at the young man who'd gone over to a game machine. If she hadn't been studying Zette in the mirror behind the bar she would have missed what came next. The flick of his wrist under the counter, the slight whirring sound, and the brighter red glare of the game machine reflected in the mirror.

And then she knew! It was a fixed machine, regulated by a switch under the counter! Pigalle and Montmartre bars had once been notorious for them. Placed among the legitimate game machines, one, resembling all the others, would be rigged. Inside was a device, a Sicilian specialty. The owner kept a tab of wins and losses and paid out or collected. If the player didn't honor his tab, he never played the machines in Montmartre, or anywhere, again.

"Look, Mademoiselle, I'm busy. Time for me to open up. Jacques, rest his soul, hadn't done a favor for me in months."

He wanted her to leave so he could carry on with his crooked machine unobserved.

She gave him a look, understanding in her eyes. "But I want to find Jacques's killer. If you're his friend, you'd want to help me."

"Mademoiselle, stick to your own concerns."

She resented the brush-off. "I'm not interested in your business here. The rigged machines." She gave a pointed look at his hands resting on the glass-ringed counter. A look to say she held something over him now. Or was he protected by the police, as he'd implied? Did they let him operate in return for information? Did he inform? That could be messy. But she didn't care. There had to be something beneath the surface here. And it might have gotten Jacques murdered and backfired on Laure.

She tried a hunch. "Jacques owed money, didn't he? To

you, and he had to work it off. Repay you with your favors to your clients."

"I don't know what you're talking about," Zette said. He took the wine bottle, set it back on the shelf, put the wineglasses in the sink, and grabbed a towel.

"I think you do," she said. She paused. The *pings* of the game machine filled the empty bar. Rows of cherries and bananas whirled behind the young man's shoulder. "And who might have wanted him dead."

"That's a big leap," Zette said, his voice even. Unconcerned. "And here I thought you were being friendly, buying me a drink."

He must be protected. Well protected. Maybe he paid off the Commissariat big time for his crooked machines. She gripped her bag. A new thought occurred to her. Had he been paying off Jacques?

"Help me here, Zette," she said, in a conciliatory voice. "Why do you think Jacques was killed?"

"I have no idea."

He swiped the towel across the counter, rubbing the water rings into blurred spots on the zinc. Try some cleanser, she wanted to say.

Instead she leaned forward, planting her elbows on the counter. "Your turf's Montmartre. Don't tell me ideas aren't going through your mind about who had a reason to off Jacques. Wasn't this his beat, his turf, too?"

Several men walked in through the door. Some wore wind-breakers or tracksuits. Dark, hollow eyed, the kind of men who hung around Pigalle Metro station, picking up odd jobs, helping movers or unloading trucks. Not legal, but better than begging. Some did that, too. A sinking feeling came over her as she realized that all the money they earned ended up in Zette's machines.

Annoyance shone in Zette's eyes. Good. If she badgered him enough he'd give her something to get her to leave.

She put her bag on the counter, careful to avoid the wet

spots, to show Zette she wouldn't budge until he talked. "Who might have killed him, Zette?"

He didn't like that, she could tell. Silently, he glanced at his watch, then looked out the fogged-up window.

"I've got time for a nice long conversation," she said. "I can wait."

Zette leaned forward. "You've heard of the vendetta?" he said, his voice lowered.

Surprised, Aimée nodded.

"Vendetta?" she repeated, in a loud voice.

That bothered Zette and she felt the eyes of the men on her back. "Jacques wasn't Corsican—"

"His mother was. That's why I helped him. Now, if you don't mind, Mademoiselle, I'll escort you to the door."

OUT IN windswept Place Pigalle, she stared at the dry fountain. All but the Saint Sulpice and Jardin du Luxembourg fountains were kept dry in winter to avoid freezing. Gambling, a vendetta? She knew a large percentage of the police force was Corsican. Still in the dark but full of new questions, she headed to the Metro.

Tuesday Afternoon

LUCIEN PAUSED BY THE industrial stove. Steam rose from copper pans, the high blue flame licking the blackened edges. He stepped over gunnysacks of red potatoes and cardboard boxes half-filled with carrots lining the clapboard-sided kitchen of Strago. Above them hung Lenin's stern-jawed photo and thirties Moscow State Theatre posters with their bold Constructivist geometric designs.

Anna had run this Communist Corsican restaurant for years, letting him sleep in the back room when times were rough, as they had been recently. She read manifestos to him while she fried onions or cured *prisuttu* ham.

"Lucien, some *mecs* were nosing around here." Anna, stout and with graying hair, stirred the pot of *ziminu* spicy fish stew on the iron stove as she spoke. "Good thing I'd sent Bruno next door to the *marché* for eggplant."

Lucien's hand clenched in his pocket. His eyes rested on his *cetera*, the sixteen-string lute-like instrument in his open bag next to the compact sound mixer he'd packed for DJing later. Should he grab it and run, forget his clothes stored in the pantry?

"Looking for anyone in particular?" he asked.

"You tell me," Anna said, tasting from a wooden spoon. She grabbed a handful of chopped garlic, tossed it in.

Calm down, he had to calm down. Not overreact.

"Some detective asked the vegetable seller about you," Anna said. "Those capitalist lackeys always harass those who protest!"

The *flics*, now a detective!

"What do you mean? Who's looking for me?"

"Stay somewhere else for a few days," Anna said, her mouth turned down in a disapproving frown. "I don't want to know where, don't want to hear about it. At my age, I have all the excitement I need."

It was a frigid evening and Lucien had counted on waiting tables, on earning some tips and a bowl of that hot stew.

"*Mecs*? Who?"

Anna ladled out a heaping bowlful of fish stew and handed it to him. "Looked like rent-a-thugs. *Zut alors*, I don't want to know what you do."

"*Merci,* I play music, that's what I do," he said, running his hand over his worn *cetera* case.

"Far as I'm concerned, you're as political as an ant," she said. "But I never give up hope that soon Corsica will be free and run by true Socialists. Egalitarian. No more medieval fiefdoms, but an agriculture system that works."

His people, a proud people, were driven by the fierce love of their land and a stubborn desire to live as they had since time immemorial. The Genovese and French had erected columns and towers and thought they ruled the island. But the real Corsica, then as now, was governed by familial clans, bound by tribal ties and by obligations granted and repaid. That had never changed.

Anna had been away from Corsica too long. She liked to forget the unchanging *clannisme* that was at odds with her Socialism. Yet, appreciating her help, he couldn't point this out to her. Words were not his métier. When he played music his fingers found the way to express his thoughts, layering the sound with jazz, lacing in harmonic polyphony. Plucking his *cetera*, he could give ancient threshing songs an electronic beat. Let Félix call it world music or whatever he liked. He gave voice to the breath of rosemary-scented air hovering over sun-warmed limestone, to a chapel bell echoing off the granite mountains. He played the poetry of everyday life: a woman sweeping, the gaiety of feast days, the backbreaking toil on the hard earth, a code of honor despite years of oppression and now this new invasion by land-gutting developers.

His music said that; he couldn't. Lucien spooned up the last bite of the stew and buttoned his leather coat.

"If Félix Conari calls—"

"I didn't see you," she replied.

"*Non*, Anna, he's offered me a contract," Lucien told her. "Now my music will get heard."

"A bourgeois corporate pig who will take advantage of you, more like," she said. "Stay true to the voice inside you, Lucien."

She was wrong. Félix appreciated his music. The only other display of interest had come from the ethnic music festival at Chatelet.

"Your eyes give you away, Lucien," Anna said, shaking her head. "They're the doors to your soul. Don't jump at the first offer you get."

He grabbed the nub of a baguette from the day-old bread bag, stuck it in his pocket, and bid Anna *au revoir*. Outside on the street, he crumbled the hard bread and scattered crumbs to the gray-and-white feathered pigeons on the cracked pavement. They looked as cold and hungry as he'd felt.

He caught the bus to Place Pigalle, passed the Bistrot du Curé next to the Sexodrome, run by a priest for street people who needed a warm meal, and walked up the steep street into Montmartre. He had to get ready for his DJ gig, then sign the contract with Félix.

The club, formerly a bathhouse, was locked. The thirties sign of now-rusted neon reading *Pigalle Bains Douches* protruded from the white-tiled wall. He paced in front of the door, the light crust of snow crunching under his worn boots, wondering why a detective was looking for him and wishing more than five public baths remained in Paris. He'd like to warm up, get the chill out of his bones.

"You're late," said Pascal, the owner of the club, meeting him at the door.

So was he, Lucien wanted to say.

Pascal, all in black, pulled a key chain from his suede jacket and unlocked the wooden door. He switched on the lights illuminating the tiled walls, red-and-silver-velvet-wallpapered bar cove, faux-zebra-skin seat covers, and gilt-framed mirrors. The decor exuded a faint air of bordello.

"I'll set up," Lucien said, pulling out his compact turntable.

"You spin lounge, followed by acid jazz, and then the playwright reads," said Pascal, a gruff, no-nonsense Auvergnat, who watched every centime and ran a tight ship, like most *bougnats*, who had migrated from the Auvergne countryside at the turn of the century. They still operated a good number of cafés. Pascal consulted a ledger on the counter. "A *mec's* been looking for you."

Here, *too*? Lucien kept his hand steady. "The *mec* have a name?"

Pascal ran his finger over the ledger. "A foreign type, maybe Corsican, with bleached-blond hair."

The waiter from Bastia who had served at Félix's? Good news! Then Félix was still anxious to sign the contract.

Lucien connected the turntable and his equipment in a hurry. "May I use your phone?"

"Make it quick," Pascal said. Paused. "No trouble, eh? I don't want any trouble here."

Little did Pascal know that once he signed the contract, he'd be out of here so fast.

"Can't I have friends, Pascal?"

"Friends like that?"

Lucien left it alone, ignoring his barbed question. "*Allô*, Félix?" he said into the telephone.

"My boy, you disappeared last night," Félix said.

Hadn't Marie-Dominique explained? But why should she mention an inconvenient old lover who'd appeared, then disappeared.

"Things got sticky, Félix. I didn't have ID. . . ."

"Make it up to me, eh? Stop by my home and sign the contract before you go to the theatre. Kouros, from SOUNDWERX, will come to hear your show tonight."

LUCIEN DESCENDED the ice-crusted staircase from Place des Abbesses with eager steps on his way to sign Félix's contract. He pulled his collar up against the wind and that's when he saw the *flic* on the corner of rue Veron. The flare of a match illuminated the face of the man he'd seen questioning partygoers last night. The *flic* was only a few feet away. Lucien ducked into a doorway. Above him, a carved plaque stated, "1872, site of the first free theatre" and he realized he stood under a nude reclining female reading a book sculpted in the stone portal.

"No sign of him. Not yet," the _flic_ said into his phone. "Copy me on the bomb alert."

Were they looking for _him_? Some _mecs_, a detective, and now the _flics_? When a couple passed arm in arm under the globed light, he hurried behind them back up the steps. At Place des Abbesses, outside a bookshop, he saw the headlines in _France Soir_: CORSICAN BOMB THREATS—ARMATA CORSA SEPARATIST RING ROUNDED UP.

Again?

He bought a paper and scanned the article. "Reports of bombing threats in Ajaccio and on the French mainland have sparked heightened security by the DPJ. Several Paris targets have been named by the Armata Corsa. . . ."

He shuddered. "Find and round up the Corsicans" time. If he signed the contract, would it give him credibility? But he couldn't tell Félix his problems, at least until he in turn had signed. He'd avoid Marie-Dominique, sure she would do the same, unable to face her disdain or his feelings for her. At a phone cabin, he inserted a calling card with ten francs left on it. Félix's answering machine responded.

"Félix, something's come up. I'm sorry but please meet me at the theatre with the contract" was the message he left.

Lucien hurried into the dusk, avoiding the green street sweepers' spray on the cobbles.

Tuesday Afternoon

RENÉ SHIFTED ON THE wet cobblestones. Thank God he'd worn his thermal underwear and several layers under the painter's smock. So far he'd seen no prostitute or anyone else in or around the building.

He shouldn't have followed through on his big idea. What a joke. He'd just wasted an afternoon.

Had he really believed he could pull this off? Feeling sheepish, he'd hidden his online PI class from Aimée. If he kept at it, in a year or more he'd have enough credits to earn a PI license. The difficulty had been the undercover work required for field research credit. This had seemed to be a golden opportunity.

But a freezing afternoon spent with no result . . . . Delusional, that's what he was. No one his size could do undercover surveillance. After all this effort, it rankled. He'd worked a deal with an acting troupe, rented a costume—all in all a costly project just so he could stand outside in the cold. He felt like an idiot, but without the costume to impersonate Henri de Toulouse-Lautrec, the crippled artist famous for sketching Montmartre nightlife, he'd never have fit into the neighborhood.

One of the actors pumped an accordion, his fingers racing over the keys. A tall thin woman with bright red hair piled on her head 1890s style, black skirt and ruffled pantaloons à la Jane Avril from a Moulin Rouge poster, did the cancan on the slick pavement. A cluster of small schoolchildren divided their attention between her and René. *Le vieux* Paris! Something they'd heard of in between bouts of video games. Most stole glances at the fun fair carousel being set up near the Metro exit.

A pale-faced boy close to René's height nudged him. "Can I see?"

René showed him a prepared pastel, a print of one Henri de Toulouse-Lautrec had done while studying in an atelier nearby. Now the atelier was part bathroom-fixture warehouse and part dance studio.

He'd heard the teacher identify the group. They were from the local *école primaire* around the corner and he figured the boy must live nearby. This was René's first chance to question someone and it turned out to be a little *poulbot*, a pint-sized Montmartrois with too-short jacket sleeves revealing a dirty shirt beneath.

"You live on the square?" René asked.

The boy shook his head. "Over there." He pointed to a building down the steps from the Abbesses. "But we've lived lots of places."

René's interest heightened. Establish rapport, wasn't that what the detective manuals said? "You mean the building with scaffolding?"

The building where Jacques had been shot.

"Across the street, on the top floor," the boy said. "I pull my book bag up by a rope."

René controlled his excitement.

"I move a lot, too," said René. Toulouse-Lautrec had lived all over Montmartre, his landlords kicking him out when he'd been too drunk to pay his rent bill.

From a wax-paper bag in his pocket, René pulled a *villageoise*, Montmartre's brioche-type specialty. The small boy sniffed and looked with longing at what René held.

"Like one?"

"We're not supposed to accept food from strangers," he said.

"Of course, but I'm Toulouse-Lautrec." René winked. "You know me, eh?"

The boy nodded. René put the warm pastry bag in the boy's cold hands.

"*Voilà.*" René nodded. "Share them with friends."

The boy shook his head. "We haven't been there long. But I know the concierge; I help him with jobs."

A loner? René noticed now the boy kept apart from the others crowding around the teacher.

"Jobs, like what?"

"I carried his hammer when he fixed the gutter."

The gutter bordering the roof? René remembered the layout Aimée had described. Had the *boy* seen something?

"So your apartment looks out onto the roof with the scaffolding?"

The boy nodded.

"Dangerous, *non*. Climbing at that height for a little boy!"

"Easy," he said. "Maman says I climb like a monkey."

"Even for someone with short legs, like me?"

The boy's eyes sparkled for the first time. "You can see everything from up there. The roofs, the Tour Eiffel, even people cooking and getting undressed!"

A lonely, mischievous boy who watched life from the rooftop? René thought fast.

"But you couldn't have seen those men on the roof with the scaffolding last night. You must have been in bed."

"I go to bed when I want!" The boy pointed again to the pastel René held. "She looks sad," he said, his mouth full. "Like Maman looks," he went on, brushing his hair from his eyes. He had no gloves.

René looked for the teacher. She stood surrounded by a group of bundled-up children, explaining how the accordion music came from ivory keys and a sound box.

"What happened to your legs? Why didn't they grow?" The boy licked the crumbs from his chapped lips.

René had asked the same question when he'd realized he'd never grow like other children and would always have to reach up for door handles, get on his tiptoes to grasp a boiling kettle, hike himself up to sit on a chair from which his legs always dangled.

"When I was young, something happened and my legs never caught up with my body," René said.

"Sometimes things shouldn't catch up, my maman says, or we'd be in the street."

René wanted to steer this conversation back to the roof. But he didn't feel much like a detective, questioning a little boy who looked as though he wore the clothes he'd slept in. Still, he had to try.

"So you didn't see what happened last night, you were asleep."

"*Mais non,* I heard a shot, saw a flash like on the *télé.* Then another flash. Maman got mad, said I shouldn't talk about it."

Then the boy clapped his hand over his mouth.

Two flashes. Did that mean two shots?

"You're sure?"

He nodded.

Had the boy witnessed the murder?

"Back to school, children," the teacher said, gathering the group. "Paul, *allez-y!* Thank Monsieur Toulouse-Lautrec for his help. I'm sure you gathered a lot of information for your report."

The boy stiffened. René saw the fear in his eyes. What should he do? He slipped a Toulouse-Lautrec guide into Paul's hand and grinned at the teacher.

A look of relief flooded Paul's pale face. René waved good-bye, pulled out his phone, and called Aimée.

"I found a witness," he said.

"Good job!" she said. "So you did some poking around."

René heard pride in her voice. He'd never tell her about this foolish costume.

"Can you get this person to come forward and testify?" Aimée asked.

René hesitated. "There's a catch. Paul's maybe nine years old. He lives across from the murder site. He said he saw two flashes on the roof."

"Two, you're sure?"

"That's what he said. He was with a school group. He's doing a report on Toulouse-Lautrec."

Pause.

"You mean you . . ." Pause.

Why had he admitted that?

"Bet he could use some homework help," she said.

"But, Aimée—"

"I'm sure you can handle it, René. Talk to his mother. I've got other fish to fry at the Préfecture."

RENÉ SPENT the next freezing hour shifting from foot to foot on the cobblestones, keeping watch on the building and avoiding the tourists. The only people he saw enter the building were a team from EDF, Electricité de France, two men who spent ten minutes inside and then left.

As dusk fell, shading the buildings, René trudged up the long staircase of Paul's house armed with more warm pastries. Up six flights of worn wooden steps, the smells of fried onions and garlic permeating the stairwell. It was an old building with a WC shared by two floors on alternate landings.

His hip ached and he wished for an elevator, even one like the wire-framed, grunting affair at their office. He'd speak with Paul's mother first; he'd have to overcome Paul's fear in order to coax him to elaborate on what he'd seen.

René knocked on the first door. No answer. The second was answered by a toothless old man bundled in sweaters.

"Try next door," the old man said, his gums working.

At the third, he heard reggae music. He knocked. The music lowered and the door scraped open. He saw a dark, low-ceilinged room with beaded curtains partitioning off a galley kitchen.

"*Oui?*" said Paul, halfway behind the door.

"Remember me?" René smiled.

Paul's large brown eyes blinked. "Maman's sleeping."

Too bad, he would have liked to speak with her.

René handed Paul the bag of pastries. "I can't stay long but I forgot to tell you about my accident and why I painted horses. See?" René pulled out the book he'd bought at a shop on Place des Abbesses. He flipped open to the page of Toulouse-Lautrec's early sketches.

"Beautiful . . . they look like they're breathing."

René agreed. The rounded flanks and flared nostrils brought the racehorses to life.

"Let's look at it on the roof."

Paul shook his head. "Why?"

"Didn't you say it was easy to go there?"

Reluctance gave way to a mischievous look in his eyes. He opened the door wider. "Shhh!" Bottles clinked behind him, one crashed to the floor.

"Let's go," René said.

René followed Paul to the skylight at the end of the hall, helped him take down the ladder, and together they steadied it.

"After you," René said, groaning inwardly.

Paul climbed the ladder, popped open the skylight. "The lock's simple, I can open it myself. The concierge showed me how."

A lonely boy with a roof for a playground? The darkening view, an expanse of jagged rooftops framing the Paris skyline, made the aching climb worth it. He dealt with heights every day, knew how to balance the awkwardness of his ill-proportioned body and, when climbing, to look up, to concentrate on his goal. He followed a nimble Paul, climbing the rusted iron rungs protruding from the cement wall.

René trained his binoculars, hanging from a strap around his neck, on the scaffolding. He took a *Paris Match* magazine from his pocket, set it on the damp ledge, and sat.

"My teacher says you're an actor," Paul said. "You act like Monsieur Toulouse-Lautrec so we can understand his work."

"She's right." René nodded. "I was going to tell you."

"Tell me about the horses," Paul said.

And René told him how Toulouse-Lautrec had fallen from a horse. Due to genetic weakness resulting from family intermarriages, his bones had been too weak to knit together. "His father, the *comte*, had stables of racing horses, heavy-footed Clydesdales for work, and even ponies for visiting children. All that summer after the accident, Toulouse-Lautrec sat in a special wicker wheelchair and drew them. They were his friends. His only friends."

René opened the book, and, together, using his pen flashlight, they leafed through the pages.

"Why don't you try, Paul?"

René passed him a tin of pastel chalks and a sketchpad.

"Horses?"

"Draw the roofline, that's what's familiar, *non*? You could start with the gray . . . try the blue one to shade in the building, smudge it . . . see?"

René wiped his thumb across the line. "Give it depth, suggest . . ."

"Can I use that in the report for my teacher?"

"Why not? And the drawing, too. She'd like that. It shows you are resourceful."

Paul nodded, his hands busy. Ten cold minutes later, he looked up. "You mean like this?"

René looked. The bold gray lines depicting the building were quite skillful. "You're a born artist, Paul. Good job!"

A wide smile split Paul's face. René realized it was the first time he'd seen the boy's teeth. Didn't his mother ever praise him?

"I see *this* every day, like Toulouse-Lautrec saw his horses every day."

René grinned. "Of course, draw what you know. But you must work at it. He did. Every day."

Paul nodded.

And then René noticed a half-open plastic bag in which model airplanes were just visible. Expensive ones.

"They're mine," Paul said, following his gaze.

"Eh, why do you keep them up here?"

"My friend gave them to me!" Paul's lip quivered.

René doubted that. "Look, it's not my business—"

"None of your business. You're wrong," Paul interrupted.

"Correct, none of my business. I once stole car magazines. The shop owner caught me. Told me if I ever did that again he'd take me to the Commissariat." René shifted on the tiled roof. "I know you didn't *steal* them but things can be returned in a quiet way with no one the wiser. I mean if your friend had taken them, of course."

"He's a good friend."

"Good friends need help." René winked, thinking it best to plant the seed and change the subject. "But I still don't understand how you could have seen those flashes from here," René said. "You didn't have binoculars, did you?"

"Of course I could see. They were right there."

"You must have good eyes. How many?"

"Two flashes."

René shook his head. "Impossible."

"There were two men arguing," Paul said, his voice serious. "Then another man came, they were nice, and then . . ."

"What?"

Paul looked away. "My *maman* told me not to talk about it. She said it could get us in trouble. And we have all the trouble we need. She hates the *flics*."

So that was it.

"She's not alone in that, Paul. But I know someone who's a private detective. She can do things and not get people in trouble."

"Like what?"

René leaned forward. "I'd have to tell her what you saw. Exactly. But she can make anonymous calls and investigate without anyone knowing. That's what she does best; she's a computer detective. No one will know."

Paul's mouth dropped.

"A computer detective?"

René nodded, stuffing his gloved hands in his pockets. Lights twinkled beyond the dark outlines of the roofs stretching before them.

"No one will know?"

"I promise."

AIMÉE'S CONNECTION at the *police judiciare*, Léo Frot, had moved to the Finance Ministry. And he wouldn't return her calls. So she had to take a chance and try to access STIC, *Système de Traitment de l'Information Fichier Central*, the intranet police computer system; she would have to move fast and find Laure's file.

From her vantage point, a table in the back of a bistro filled with early diners, she observed the crowd. This was a haunt of men and a few women wearing the badge of the DTI, *Direction des Transmissions Informatiques*, the computer division that was located across the street at 7, rue Nélaton where the DST, *Direction de la Surveillance du Territoire* was housed. They wore street clothes, no uniforms. A plastic holder was clipped to each jacket bearing an ID card with the blue Ministry crest and the employee's name. Such a card would be simple to duplicate and would get her past the entry guards. Once inside she'd have to do some "social engineering," as René called it. Faking it expressed it better. The graveyard shift, when there was minimal staff, would be the best time to try.

She finished the dregs of her espresso, paid, and fetched her coat from the rack. It hung under all the others, as she'd planned, since she'd arrived early. By the time she found it, she had memorized the badge of one Simone Teil, #3867 Dept AL4A, clipped to a black raincoat whose owner sat at a nearby table. She drew a sketch of the badge crest and design on the white paper tablecloth. Now she put that piece of paper in her pocket and left.

JUST BEFORE MIDNIGHT, AIMÉE flashed her plastic laminated ID at the pair of guards behind the tan-and-turquoise reception counter at the DTI. There was a faded, scuffed feeling to this seventies-era building. Even the curling emergency-exit plan taped to the wall had seen better days.

Several men passed through the turnstile and signed out. The guard barely glanced at her badge. "Back again, Mademoiselle Teil?" His partner sat with his eyes glued to the video monitors.

Aimée nodded, keeping her head down, the black-brimmed hat and turned-up coat collar on her neck, hiding most of her face as she scanned the log. Simone Teil's angular signature was distinctive and easy to copy. She signed in. "My report's due in the morning." She sighed. "You know how that goes!"

"No rest for the wicked, eh?" the guard said, his eyes darting over her.

Little did he know.

"*Merci.*" She shouldered her bag, edged toward the turnstile, and inserted her card. The machine beeped and the metal bars locked, barring her entry. Her hands trembled.

She took the card and made a show of rubbing it. "The magnetic tape's worn. Can you let me in?"

"Worn? But those are the new cards, issued last week!" the guard said.

Great. And her luck to get a talkative guard.

"Go figure," she said. "Must have gotten scratched in my purse."

"Odd. They designed them to avoid that."

"Why don't you pass me in?"

"Your card should work."

"Of course, it should! I'll get it taken care of tomorrow. But just this once?"

He hesitated, looked at his watch. "I'm off in a few minutes."

She rubbed her head. "The chief himself called me and insisted I come back."

"Time to tally the end-of-shift report, Fabius," said the guard by the video monitors.

He shrugged and took a card from his pocket. She edged into the turnstile.

"You're sure it doesn't work?" Fabius asked. "I just checked the card assignments."

"Eh?"

"Swipe it once more."

Think fast.

"My nail file," she said, pretending to swipe her card. "That's what scratched it up!"

The turnstiles clicked. Thank God he was going off duty. Somehow she'd figure a way to get out. But poor Simone Teil would get a questionnaire next time.

Now the hardest part. Logging on with someone else's password.

On the fifth floor, as she passed a large photo of President Mitterrand adorning the drab corridor, bile rose in her stomach. She felt a sickening lurch, ran into the restroom, and threw up. Mostly espresso, leaving an acrid bitter aftertaste.

Nerves. Infiltrating the heart of the police nerve center was the most audacious thing she'd ever done. She'd never attempted anything like this on her own. To break into STIC, the interior police file system, what nerve!

Flirt, bluff, maneuver . . . she could do this. Had to do this. Too bad René wasn't here. No system was impenetrable, he always said. The perfect crime was the undetected crime.

She took off her hat, splashed water on her face, cleaned her mouth, and popped some cassis-flavored gum. Think. Prepare.

She opened her oversized leather bag, took out her femme arsenal, thickened her mascara, rouged her cheeks to give color to her paler-than-usual complexion, and outlined her thin lips in red. Carmine red. Her short hair she gelled into wispy spikes. Looking into the soap-splashed, dull mirror she reconsidered. *Non,* too recognizable. She pulled a blonde shag-style wig out of her bag, combed it with her fingers, and put on blue-tinted John Lennon-style spectacles. Then she said a little prayer as she strode into the large fluorescent lighted room containing fifteen or so metal desks with computer terminals.

"*Bon.* Better be the right terminal," she muttered, setting her bag down at the first one with a loud thump.

A few heads looked up. She booted up the computer.

"*Merde!* I've been having this trouble all day. Anyone else get stuck logging on?" she asked.

Several of the men shook their heads, bent over their terminals. One, his plump face mirrored in the screen, grinned.

"New?" he asked.

"Can you believe it, they assigned me to a special branch this afternoon, then switched me here tonight for a case La Proc is determined she'll put on the docket tomorrow?"

"These things happen," he said, sipping from a stained brown espresso cup.

Aimée's stomach turned as she tried to ignore the smell of espresso. The papers piled on his desk were addressed NIGHT SUPERVISOR. If anyone could help, he could.

"It's for the Antecédents Judiciares . . . but it's happening again . . . the stupid system won't let me log on!" She pulled out a pack of Marie Lu butter biscuits, the children's comfort food. He looked the type. "Like one?"

"*Merci,*" he said. "Have you tried Système D?"

Did he mean what she thought he meant? Système D, the term everyone used to wangle a way around bureaucracy: cir-

cumvent forms for the notary, hedge the real estate require-
ments or the school registration regulations.

She perched on his metal desk, flicked some crumbs off her
leather miniskirt, and crossed her black-lace-stockinged legs.

"Why don't you show me?"

"How long is your shift?"

She wanted to scratch her scalp under the hot, itchy wig.

"Depends how long it takes." She sighed and leaned closer.

"Like to watch the sunrise over the Seine?"

Startled, she looked away. That was Guy's favorite pastime,
one they shared together. The thought of his gray eyes and
long tapered fingers passed before her. She pushed him out of
her mind.

"I can't plan that far ahead, I've got so much to do, Gérard,"
she said, noting the name after his title. "I'm Simone."

"Let me see if I can help." He grinned, a nice smile despite
his pockmarked round face. "What's the first log-in problem
you have?"

"The system refuses to accept my password."

Gérard clicked *Save*, closing the file he was working on. He
swiveled his chair to the next terminal.

"Try this." Within a minute he'd logged her on and navigated to the records section. "We go in like this. It confuses a
lot of the newbies."

She nodded, absorbed his instructions, and pushed the spectacles up on her forehead. He'd bypassed two of the tedious
steps. And he was fast.

"Cases pending. Cases before the Tribunal," he said. "See,
cases about to be arraigned. Enter the dossier number here."

"Like this?"

She moved next to him, her leg brushing his, and typed in
Laure's dossier number that she'd memorized from Maître
Delambre's file.

"*Voilà! Merci*, that's great."

"Gérard," said a young man two rows over. "Earn your pay. Give me the authorization code on this mess!"

She now had access to Laure's file but that wasn't all she'd come for. She had to think fast before he left. "The files from the sixties and seventies. Still kept on paper?"

He shrugged. "Of course."

"*Non*, pardon Gérard," she said with big smile, eager to cover up her faux pas. "I mean personnel. The *flics*' assignments. They want me to go in depth into someone's record."

He moved the cursor up to archives.

"The system will say special clearance needed," he told her, glancing at her badge. "But with your clearance it's allowed if you go in the back door."

Nice new added feature!

"Back door?"

He reminded her of a bear: brown fuzz on his scalp, the round face, and barrel-shaped chest.

"Use my nickname here." He typed in *ours*: bear. So she hadn't been the first to notice it.

Too bad she couldn't e-mail Laure's dossier, newly swollen, direct to Leduc Detective. She'd have to copy what she found onto the disc she'd brought with her.

Aimée scanned the police interviews and the crime-scene findings in Laure's file. Only one had been included in the file the lawyer had shown her. Sloppy policework, or a cover-up?

She inserted her blank disc. The Manhurin .32 PP, the police weapon licensed by Walther and manufactured in France, had, she remembered, the characteristic six-groove rifling, and its accuracy was up to fifty meters. At least that's what her father had claimed: accurate and heavy. She'd study the ballistics findings and other reports later. Right now all she need do was copy them to the disc.

After two attempts, she accessed the older personnel files.

The most recent for Ludovic Jubert were dated 1969. What about the rest of his career? Where was he now? She had to work faster. Gérard, helpful as he appeared, could check and ask her some difficult questions, like why "Simone" was working on these reports.

All the later data had been pulled. The few documents in Jubert's file were standard reports covering his police academy graduation, first assignments, and some sparse information ending in 1969. Had these been left in by mistake? The documents listed Jubert, Morbier, Georges Rousseau, and her father as a team working in Montmartre.

So he had worked with her father!

And then something caught her eye. Jubert had worked a special detail, the game-machine detail, in Montmartre. A café owner would buy a fixed machine for ten thousand francs and make fifty thousand francs a month from each. Like the ones she'd seen in Zette's bar. The special investigative section policed gaming and the 147 legal casinos in France. MI— Ministry of the Interior—was stamped on the top of the pages describing the investigation.

The fluorescent light bothered her eyes, the metal surface of the desk was stained with brown coffee rings, and the buttery smell of Marie Lu biscuits made her want to heave again.

"Seems you've found your way around," Gérard said over her shoulder.

She gritted her teeth and nodded. "Funny, haven't found the rest of this man's dossier."

Gérard rubbed the worn elbow patch on his blue regulation police sweater. Most of the computer technicians, even though they were police, wore street clothes. Was he a wannabe action man?

"Aaah, one of those!"

"What do you mean, Gérard?"

He rolled his eyes. "Hands off."

Jubert was protected. By whom and why?

Only a few men still worked at their computers now; the others had drifted out to the espresso machine. Smoke curled from the hall.

"Break time," he said.

She didn't want to leave. "*Bon.*" She stretched, did some head rolls. "I've got to finish this." She yawned. "Who is he anyway?"

Surprise painted Gérard's plump face. "The boss?"

Stupid. Why hadn't she put it together? She had known that Jubert was high up. She tried to recover.

"Oh *that* one," she said, injecting a bored tone into her voice.

Gerard grinned. "You're a techie, right?"

"Names don't mean much to me. Ministry types, well, they're not part of my world. My *quartier*'s Montmartre, the unchic side. Looks like he started there," she said as if it was an afterthought.

"Maybe, but he's moved up in the world. More like rue des Saussaies now."

That was where the head of the Ministry of the Interior had his office. An inquiry by the Préfecture de Police was accessible to the Ministry. She knew that much. Both branches could access the STIC files.

"You're with IGS, *n'est-ce pas?*" Gérard whispered and leaned closer.

Inspection Génerale des Services—Internal Affairs.

"Did I say that?"

"You don't have to." He grinned. "Just remember how I'm helping you, eh?"

"Of course, Gérard." She returned the smile. How long could she keep up this charade? She ought to leave but first she wanted to find out as much as possible.

"What about these men? Both deceased, Leduc and Rousseau?" She tried not to flinch when she said it.

Gérard hit the control key and F1.

Rousseau's file filled the screen. "*Voilà.* Come have a coffee when you finish."

Where was the secret Laure had alluded to and felt guilty about? It didn't jump out at her. What about Morbier's scrawl on his newspaper about a report six years ago dealing with a Corsican arms investigation? All she could find in his file documented Rousseau's rapid rise in the Commissariat after a successful gaming investigation on rue Houdon, at a Club Chevalier.

Zette's club!

Montmartre again. She copied it to the disc, controlled her shaking fingers, and typed in her father's name, Jean-Claude Leduc.

And then she saw the grainy photo, one of a young Morbier, Rousseau, another man, and her papa all in uniform, smiling on the steps by Marché Saint Pierre, the textile market, Sacré Coeur in the background. The fourth man—who, she figured, was Jubert—was her father's height and had small eyes and a prominent nose. His hands were in his pockets. All young, with expectant grins on their faces, their lives before them. What had happened? She choked back a sob.

"Simone, Simone . . ."

She realized Gérard was calling her from the hallway.

She wiped her eyes. The words jerked her back to the present. "*Oui, j'arrive.*" She dragged the file to the disc, copied it, and thrust her coat inside her bag.

She hit *Quit* and grabbed the disc as it whirred out, stuck it safely inside her blouse, then joined Gérard.

"*Une débâcle!*" one of the techies was saying. "Just like that, the network froze."

"You remember that, eh, Simone? Last week . . ."

Gérard was getting too friendly or too inquisitive. Testing her? Time to get out.

"Don't remind me," she groaned, interrupting him as he

offered her a small plastic cup of steaming espresso. From the vending machine. Awful stuff! She pitied these *mecs*.

"*Un moment*, eh. I've got to pee," she said with a big smile. "I'll be right back."

She rounded the corner, her bag hitched over her shoulder, and ducked into the women's restroom, then peeked into the corridor. Deserted. She slipped out, ran down the hall, and to the door marked STAIRS. She shut the door so it closed without a click, then raced down the five flights. Still in the enclosed stairwell, she took off her wig and glasses, pulled on her coat and hat, adjusted the brim low to hide her face, and stepped into the main foyer. The turnstile lay just ahead and she almost breathed a sigh of relief.

"Monsieur, my card won't work. Pass me through, eh?" she said to the new guard as she made a show of wringing her hands at the turnstile.

The phone rang. The red light lit up. The inter-building line? Gérard?

The guard glanced at the switchboard. Only one on duty. He hesitated.

"Please, Monsieur, eh, my taxi's waiting!"

She heard a buzz, the turnstile arms grated forward, and she shoved her way out.

"*Merci!* I have to hurry, hope the taxi hasn't taken off."

"Mademoiselle, wait—"

He reached for the phone as she ran past the sign-out log and through the glass doors. She didn't stop running until she'd made it into the dimly lit bistro restroom across the street. Her lungs heaved and she couldn't stop shaking. Ten minutes later she'd wiped off her red lipstick, applied an orange bisque, turned the reversible black coat inside out to its tan side, pulled black tights over her stockings, and changed her boots to Christian Louboutin red-soled pumps, a flea-market find.

Thank God the bistro was crowded. She sidled her way to the counter, more relieved than she'd felt in hours, and ordered a *perroquet*, pastis with mint syrup, named for the colors of a parrot, and watched the front of the DTI building.

A car pulled up, an unmarked *flic* car by the look of it. *Mon Dieu!* Several men joined the two men who'd stepped out onto the wet pavement. The guard appeared. He was probably telling them about her supposed taxi. With trembling fingers she punched in René's number on her cell phone.

"*Allô*, René," she said. "I need a ride."

"No taxis around?" he asked.

One of the officers looked around and jerked his thumb across the street toward the bistro. Her shoulders tensed. They'd question the man behind the counter.

"You could say that," she whispered into the phone. "I'll be waiting at the Vel d'Hiv."

She placed ten francs on the counter and made it out of the bistro door before the *flics* crossed the street. At a brisk pace, her head lowered, she walked down rue Nélaton and turned right down the next cobbled street. Breaking into a run, she made it to quay de Grenelle. Panting, she faced the needle-shaped tree-lined island allée des Cygnes, at one end of which was the original, but smaller Statue of Liberty. At the other was the Metro, rumbling over metal-strutted Bir-Hakeim Bridge. Double swaths of planted shrubs bordered the Seine here.

She didn't stop until she reached a small grove bathed in the glow from a yellow streetlight. Kneeling under the bushes, she caught her breath. Sirens wailed on her right. She saw the blue flash of a police car's light against the stone buildings. Why couldn't René hurry up?

Damp red rose petals and the smell of earth stuck to her hand. Flat stones embedded in the ground, gravelike, held scattered bunches of flowers. She shuddered. This was once a bicycle-racing vélodrome where Jews, rounded up in July 1942, were held. Now the Vel d'Hiver was a memorial garden adjoining the DST.

Messages had been placed under the stones: "For Maman, I never had the chance to say goodbye and tell you how I love you. I pray you are in the stars shining above."

Her own mother, an American radical activist, had left them when she was eight, without saying goodbye. The pain never went away, but she'd tried to move on. Sadness vied with her apprehension that René would be too late.

Her cell phone vibrated.

"René?"

"What have you done now? There are *flics* crawling everywhere; foot patrols, cars. They're stopping taxis."

"Well—"

"*Non.* Don't tell me. Where are you?"

She looked through the bushes. "I can see your car. Park on quay Branly facing the monument. Open the trunk like you're looking for something. Be sure you get your brake lights even with the chestnut tree, the big one. See it?"

René's Citroën edged along the street and parked by the tree. He got out, wearing a painter's smock, and unlocked his trunk. Under the street lamps, his resemblance to Toulouse-Lautrec was uncanny. He pulled out a tool set and placed it on the glistening pavement. A blue-and-white police car prowling the quay paused. She crouched, gripping the branches, her heart pounding. Then it drove on.

Her heels sank into the dirt as she made her way from the memorial to the quay. René pulled out a blanket, shook it, folded it laboriously to shield Aimée from the view of another cruising *flic* car. She held her breath until it passed and then ran, keeping low, and barreled into the trunk.

"Hope you cleaned up your tracks," René muttered, putting his toolbox back, then shutting the trunk. He'd spread blan-

kets over the tire jack, yet it dug into her spine. Still it beat
riding in a *flic*'s car in handcuffs.

All the way back, wedged in René's trunk, her mind spun.
Had she remembered everything? Kept her head covered and
down when she was within the security camera's range?
Wiped all her prints off the keyboard, the bathroom faucet,
and door handles? Worn gloves in the elevator and not
touched the stair railing? Yes . . . her heart skipped. The
Marie Lu foil biscuit packet. Gérard had finished the biscuits,
wadded the wrapping, and thrown it in the trash bin by his
terminal.

With Gérard's help they'd soon discover the files she'd
copied, but she'd stolen nothing, destroyed nothing. Like a
courteous hacker, she'd cracked the system but wreaked no
havoc. All she'd done was level the playing field in Laure's
investigation. At least for now. If she gave the files she'd
copied to Maître Delambre, how could the *flics* complain? The
information was already in their files. They'd be caught concealing evidence from the defense.

Maybe she could shake Jubert from his lair. Now at least she
knew what he looked like, albeit as a young man, and she'd
found out that at one time he'd worked in the Ministry of
Interior. If Gérard had steered her right, even on rue des
Saussaies. A place she doubted she could crack with dynamite.

BACK AT her apartment, she banked the fire in her salon
while René hung up his painting smock. Crackling flames cast
shadows onto the tall ceiling. Miles Davis was curled on the
rug. At least the contractor had given her a working fireplace.
The kitchen and bathrooms, their gaping-open walls revealing
ancient electrical wiring, were another story.

"You first, Monsieur Toulouse-Lautrec," she said. "What
have you found out?"

He stuck his short arms into a wool cardigan, buttoned it,

and joined her, cross-legged, on a sheepskin rug on the parquet floor. She passed him a hot buttered rum, and he closed his eyes and inhaled. The fire's warmth heated a small area, never penetrating to the cold corners.

"Much warmer than the roof. That's where I was when you called. Pretty quick, eh!"

From the eighteenth! René was a speed demon behind the wheel. "You, on a roof?"

"You're not the only one, you know," he said. "A fantastic view despite the ice. Right across from the building where Jacques bought it."

She swallowed the wrong way. Choked. He amazed her all the time.

"Eh, Monsieur Toulouse-Lautrec, what did your eyewitness see?"

"Paul's nine years old, shoplifts, and promised his mother not to tell about the two flashes he saw on the roof."

"Two shots? Hold on, then the ballistics report should indicate two bullets. *Un moment.*" She pulled out the disc from her shirt, pulled the laptop from her desk, and booted up. "Let's see, the ballistics report should clarify it."

René's jaw dropped. "This information . . . did you . . .?"

"I thought you didn't want to know," she said, inserting the disc. "That intranet system gave me a headache. But as you always say, no system's impenetrable. And I had a little help. Until the *mec* ate my biscuits and woke up."

"You've done it now, Aimée," René said. "They won't stop till they find you. Breaking into—"

"They don't know who I am." She kept telling herself that, praying that her fingerprints wouldn't be found. And that she'd never run into Gérard on the street. But even if she did, how would he recognize her?

"Look at this." She clicked on Laure's dossier. The screen filled with the files, arranged by unit. "Strikes me as funny that only one of these was furnished to her lawyer."

"Check the entry date and time," René said, rubbing his arms. "More might have been entered after her lawyer received his information."

She checked. "These were entered several hours before I met Maître Delambre. What's going on?"

"A police cover-up?" René said.

She opened the ballistics file and read it. "One bullet was recovered from the corpse. From Laure's Manhurin," she summarized.

Great.

But if Paul had seen another flash . . .

"You're sure he really saw something, René?"

"Paul has an eye for detail," René said. "I don't think he'd make it up. He has no reason to."

It was the only hope she had. "Say there were two guns. If Paul saw two flashes—"

"And heard only one shot," René interrupted.

She stared at René. "I'd say the other gun had a silencer."

René rubbed his wide forehead. "That's what it means?"

"Stands to reason."

"How would the bad guys know Laure was down below?"

"Good question." She watched the fire, trying to make sense of what Paul had observed.

"If they planned to shoot Jacques and he boasted he had backup—" she ventured.

"Would he do that?" René interrupted. "Show his ace in the hole like that?"

"True," she said and thought. "Think of it from their point of view. What if, from the roof, they saw Laure accompany Jacques across the courtyard. Let's assume they took advantage of an opportunity to implicate Laure by using her gun and leaving gunshot residue on her hands."

"Maybe," René said. "That's plausible. But why kill Jacques in the first place?"

"I'm working on that. Blackmail? Bribery?" She shook her head and stared at the fire. Did Zette's gambling machines fit in this?

"What about other witnesses?" René asked.

"The partygoers saw nothing. Félix Conari, the host, and Yann Marant, his systems analyst, mentioned a musician, Lucien Sarti. So far, I haven't been able to find him. That old lady, Zoe Tardou, on the top floor across the way acted secretive but she's an odd bird." Such a strange woman. She filed away the thought that she should question Madame Tardou again.

"Did Paul see anything else?" she asked.

René shook his head.

They didn't have much.

"We have to get Paul to give a statement to Laure's attorney."

"His mother drinks, he shoplifts." René told her.

She shrugged.

"First thing tomorrow, I'll give the files to the lawyer and I'll explain what Paul saw," she said. "This lawyer needs all the help he can get."

"Will you explain that you entered the DTI and tunneled into the intranet system?" René shook his head.

"Not in so many words," she said. "But if the lawyer has this information, what can they do? Accuse him of illegally obtaining the documents they were mandated by law to furnish him?"

René's cell phone beeped in his pocket.

"*Oui?*" he answered, a smile on his face. He took the call in the kitchen. Miles Davis growled.

"We can't be jealous, Miles," Aimée said, ruffling his neck. René demonstrated classic symptoms of a *coup de foudre*, love at first sight.

"Off to a rave?" she asked, on René's return.

"The rave sputtered and died." René pulled on his coat, slipped his fingers into fleece-lined gloves.

She didn't want to ask him why he was leaving instead of staying to pore over the files with her.

"I'm meeting her for a drink. Guy should be back soon, right?"

Aimée knew if she told him the truth and asked him to stay, he would. But that would be selfish. René deserved to love someone.

She nodded.

"E-mail me the ballistics report. I'd like to check something."

"Like what?" She stood, excited.

"Just an idea. If there was a second shot, wouldn't there be a bullet somewhere?"

"You're a walking genius, René."

SHE GRIPPED the velvet curtains at her window, watched René emerge from the shadows onto the quay, and enter his Citroën. Below, the Seine flowed black and inklike. An ice-flecked barge glided by, its blue-lighted captain's cabin and red running lights reflecting on the water.

She put another log on the fire, thinking of Laure's father policing Zette's bar and the illegal gaming machines. Why would an old gaming investigation matter now? Did it? Then Jacques had worked with him. Zette had ties to the Commissariat. Was she right in guessing that he was an informer? Tomorrow she'd probe deeper.

Thin beams of moonlight slanted across the parquet floor. Her mind drifted to when she was nine, Paul's age, and to the policeman's ball she'd attended with her father. He'd escorted her to the rented hall in the tile manufacturer's on Canal Saint Martin. Couples glided across the polished wood floor surrounded by tables bearing white tablecloths, silver-plated breadbaskets, and gleaming candles.

"Papa, I want to dance."

"*Ma princesse*, this isn't your ballet class," he'd said, affectionately. "They're waltzing."

"I know." She'd smoothed down her velvet party dress, several centimeters shorter than when she'd worn it the year before. "Dance with me, Papa?"

Was it Morbier or someone else at the round table who'd

nudged him? "Go on, Jean-Claude. Bad manners not to dance with your little *princesse*."

"*Mais*, it's been years—"

"Please, Papa!"

An odd look had crossed his face. He took her arm, escorted her to the edge of the dance floor, a serious set to his mouth. "We'll make a little square, eh? Like this: side, back, side, and front. Follow me."

Her legs tangled with his right away. He gripped her back. "Try again."

More frustration as he stepped on her toe.

"Aimée, let's give this up."

Shame bubbled up inside her and her face reddened.

"Papa, you said I can do anything if I try hard enough. Why can't I dance like a big girl?"

"You know, I haven't danced with anyone since your mother."

"*Maman?*"

She couldn't read his expression. He never talked about her mother. Refused to.

"*Et alors*, stand on my feet. Remember, we make a little box, one . . . two . . . three . . . one . . . two . . . three."

She remembered her father's black polished shoes, hard under her small feet, how he gripped her and whirled her around the dance floor. And the feeling she'd never forgotten of moving with the music, safe in his arms.

She'd never stop loving him, but she had to *know*. The hard part was going to be reading his dossier. Would she find evidence of a cover-up, extortion, bribes? She could delete the dossier before reading it and never know.

She joined Miles Davis on the rug by the crackling fire and took a deep breath. Then she scrolled to the file entitled Jean-Claude Leduc and clicked on it. She closed her eyes, took a deep breath, and opened it.

Empty. The file had been erased.

LUCIEN BOWED TO THE applause of the small crowd. He'd seen Félix deep in conversation with a white-haired man. No Marie-Dominique. He knew she wouldn't come, but the curve of her tan back, the green flecks in her eyes, invaded his thoughts.

Never get between the fingernail and the flesh, his *grand-mère* would say when she wanted him to mind his own business. Marie-Dominique had indicated loud and clear that he was an inconvenience in her life.

He fanned himself with a program in the close air, picked up his *cetera* and case. The next act was a magician who grinned as he set a black velvet box on the stage.

"Marvelous!" Félix said, coming up and clapping him on the back. "You capture a Mediterranean spirit with this Euro-hop rhythm; I couldn't stop tapping my feet. Neither could Monsieur Kouros."

Kouros was the short white-haired man wearing thick black-framed glasses. He resembled the Greek millionaire Ari Onassis. Kouros, the head of SOUNDWERX. A giant in the recording industry, despite his unassuming exterior. He was rumored to be hands-on all the way.

"*Bonsoir*, Monsieur Kouros, I'm honored to meet you."

"We want an exclusive young man," Kouros said. "Your music defies labels. Everyone, even jazz aficionados, will love it. Montreux, San Marino—I'll book you in all the music festivals, put you on the circuit."

SOUNDWERX never followed trends, it created them. Kouros discovered talent and made careers.

"How generous. Thank you, Monsieur."

"People want this. Ageless yet new, hip and still classical. Your music builds on traditions but it goes beyond borders."

All he knew was that when he picked up the *cetera*, harmonized with his recorded tracks, and found the right hip-hop beat, it poured out of him, he couldn't stop. His fingers found the truth on the strings.

"You'll get him studio time tomorrow, Félix? Work with the tracks he has, add some new ones?"

Félix beamed. "As soon as we take care of the contract, eh, Lucien? Just your signature and then a CD as soon as we can press it, *oui*, Monsieur Kouros?"

Félix put his arm around Lucien, squeezed him, as if to say, it's a done deal. Lucien wished he hadn't spent all last night thinking of this man's wife.

"Everyone's political these days," Kouros said. His smile was at odds with the steely glint in his eyes. Or was that the glare on his glasses? "It gives an edge to the lyrics, but I must be sure you have no connections with these Separatist extremist groups, eh? These bombings. Terrible."

Lucien's knuckles, gripping his *cetera*, whitened. "My life's music, Monsieur Kouros."

"Just needed to clarify, young man." He reached for Lucien's other hand, shook it with a strong grip, and folded it in both of his. "This is the way I seal a contract." He pumped Lucien's hand harder. "Old style. It works for me."

"We'll just sign the contracts at my office," Felix said.

"It's already done as far as I'm concerned. Send it to my administrator," Kouros told him before barreling through the crowd behind the red plush theatre seats with surprising agility. They followed as he rushed outside and turned. "A true pleasure to hear you. Excuse me, other commitments." He climbed into his limo.

Standing on the wet street, feeling as if he'd been swept up in a whirlwind, Lucien hugged Félix. He wanted to jump in the air and kiss the first woman he saw. He looked around for a likely candidate.

"Félix, I can't thank you enough."

"Lucien." Félix's tone had changed. "We did background checks, you know; it's standard procedure these days."

Lucien froze.

"For everyone." Félix spread his arms in a what-can-you-do gesture. "We even run them on the cleaning staff. Go figure."

Had he found out about his involvement with Marie-Dominique?

"This Armata Corsa group."

"I'm not a Separatist, Félix," Lucien interrupted. If anything, he was a lover, not a fighter. "Politics isn't my interest."

"Then how do you explain your membership?"

Had Marie-Dominique told him, after all? Or was it in some police file? He had to allay Félix's suspicions.

"The truth? Years ago, in drunken camaraderie with my friends, I joined. We went to one meeting. Total."

Félix shifted; his elongated shadow in the light of the tall green metal *lampadaire* stretched across the street.

"Marie-Dominique said you had no papers," Félix said. "Why didn't you tell me? And then you disappeared from my house when the police came."

"I have a *carte d'identité*, but I forgot it. I wanted to explain but with the *flics* . . . you know how they treat Corsicans, Félix." He took a deep breath. "Every time Separatists make the headlines, the *flics* beef up security and round up types like me on the street to make themselves look efficient." He paused; Félix lived in another stratosphere. Could he have any idea? "This has nothing to do with me. The bombings, the vendetta, all that violence, that's why I *left* Corsica."

Part of the reason. The other part being his picture, among others, plastered on every telephone pole and peeling stucco café wall on the island.

Félix's brow furrowed. "A detective asked about you."

Lucien controlled a shudder. The *flics* outside Félix's gate and now a detective. The same one snooping at the vegetable shop next door to Strago?

"That makes no sense."

"Innocent people don't run away."

"You lead a protected life, Félix," Lucien said.

Félix shook his head, put his arm around Lucien's shoulders, and they walked down the steep street. "Not always, Lucien. I was born on the wrong side of the blanket, you know that saying, eh?"

Illegitimate.

"We lived in one room. Everything I have now, I worked for."

"My songs are all I have," Lucien said. "You have my word, trust me."

In Félix's study he signed the contract, signed away his rights to his songs, and prayed he'd done the right thing. The Corsican saying, "Bad things never happen alone," echoed in his mind. Down the road of life, he'd pay for it. One always paid.

He peered outside Félix's gate. No *flics*. At least he had the contract. Halfway up the dark stairs to Place des Abbesses he heard a snatch of song, low and echoing off the dripping stone walls. He stopped. Listened. A woman's voice from somewhere in a song about the fragrant maquis smells drifting across a baby's cradle.

Wednesday Morning

"YOU'RE LOOKING FOR ZETTE?" said the blonde woman to Aimée in the rue Houdon bar. She shook her lacquered blonde bouffant hairdo. "Not here. His day off."

A pity. Aimée had counted on probing and getting answers. Next, dropping off the computer files she'd copied at Maître Delambre's office, and then visiting Laure.

"Where can I find him?"

"Sleeping it off," the blonde woman said, tying an apron around her waist, about to turn on the vacuum cleaner.

"And that would be where?"

The woman stared. "You were here the other day."

Aimée nodded; she had to dispel the woman's suspicion. "Zette's an old colleague of my godfather's," she said, hoping it sounded plausible. "I wanted to show him a photo."

The woman's eyes narrowed. She switched on the vacuum. It wheezed as it sucked up grit from the floor. "Come back tomorrow."

Aimée peered at the counter, which bore wet ring marks and a filled ashtray. Below the counter sat a pile of stapled invoices addressed to Z. Cavalotti. She couldn't read the rest.

"Does he work from home?"

The blonde woman's mouth tightened in a thin smile.

"In a manner of speaking, eh. I think he does the accounts at his place," she said, turning to the vacuum cleaner. "If that's all . . ."

"I'll come back, *merci*."

Aimée left, pulled her coat tighter, and sidestepped across the slush. Five minutes later she'd found a Z. Cavalotti in the phone book, listed on rue Ronsard. Time to pay a visit chez Zette.

She climbed up the street, made a right downhill, then another right, and a left into Place Charles Dullin. *Camion-nettes,* small delivery trucks, their doors open, lined the bare-branched, tree-filled square. Posters advertised a current adaptation of Racine's *Phèdre* at the nineteenth-century the-atre at the rear of the square. *Phèdre* played in Paris all the time, either a classical performance or an avant-garde one like this version, with an African tribal motif. The timeless Greek tragedy of a woman in love with her stepson still filled the seats.

Beyond the iron-and-glass-roofed Marché Saint Pierre, a stone-and-brick wall bordered a Neolithic mound and wound its way upward. She climbed the steep flight of stairs with double rails in the middle, so typical of Montmartre, and found Zette's address, a white stone building tilting into the hill like so many others. His, unlike them, however, had weeds in the concrete cracks, worn stucco walls, and peeling pale blue shutters.

The wooden front door lay open to a courtyard with ivy-covered walls. She peered at the mailboxes, found the name Zette Cavalotti, and trudged up a spiral staircase to the first floor. She stopped at a warped wooden landing that creaked beneath her feet; before the door was a woven mat and a sign CHAT LUNATIQUE! So, Zette had a crazy cat. She knocked on the door and it opened. Her hand paused in midair.

"Monsier Zette?"

No answer. Apprehensive, she stepped inside the sparse, chilly apartment. It was neat and orderly. She shivered at the freezing blast from the open window. Framed newspaper arti-cles and photos lined the walls showing Zette, "The Corsican Magnifico," defeating Terrance, "The Blue-Eyed Mad Moroccan," for the championship. He'd had quite a career. Tracksuits and sweatshirts were hung from nails in the wall around the otherwise neat room. Hadn't Zette heard of hang-ers or *armoires*? A hot plate sat on a thin wooden counter next to bottles of mineral water.

"*Allô?*"

No answer. Where was he?

A poster of "Corsica, Isle of Beauty" hung over the sofa, which he used for a bed, she figured from the piled blankets.

She poked around. Just the remnants of a glory-filled boxing career long over. A late-model Moulinex washing machine hummed. A matchstick was wedged into the wash-cycle panel.

Was that the only way it worked? Judging by the heat radiating from the washer, it had been on for hours. A plastic basket with dirty sweats and an empty lemon-scented Ariel detergent box lay on top of a table together with bottles and vitamins, protein powder. Had he run out to buy laundry detergent and left the door open?

She leaned against the machine to wait for him. Tapped her heeled boots on the wooden floor. She heard a faint meow, noticed a closed door.

"Monsieur Zette?"

The meowing grew louder. She knocked. Waited, then opened it. A small room with barbells and weights filling the corner. Looked like he still trained.

She felt fur rub her legs as a black cat with yellow eyes passed her. Zette could have stopped for a *verre* at a local café. She looked at her watch. Better to wait for him downstairs, outside.

The black cat padded beside her on the staircase, then continued out to the courtyard. Had Zette stopped to chat to a neighbor? She followed the cat, who stopped by a wooden water-stained door, an old WC in the rear of the courtyard.

"*Allô?*"

The sweetish cloying smell of cheap detergent wafted from Zette's window. The cat meowed louder, claws scratching on the wood.

Curious, she pulled the door handle, felt its heaviness as it creaked open. Mold and damp mingled with the detergent aroma. Her arm brushed something and she turned. Zette's arms hung and his feet dangled, his collar was stuck on a hook in the door. She gasped and stepped back onto the cat's tail. He screeched and bolted. Zette's throat was slit from ear to ear in a red smear, and his long blackish tongue had been pulled out through the hole. A Sicilian necktie. Grotesque.

Covering her nose and mouth with her sleeve, she forced

herself to look at Zette's body suspended from the door hook; the whites of his eyes were visible in the slants of light. The murderer had seen to it that Zette would talk no more. Vendetta-style. A toad of a man but he didn't deserve to end like this, whatever he'd done. No one did.

Clotted black-red blood trailed down his chest. A thin cape of ice sparkled over his sagging shoulders. His red tracksuit jacket was ripped where he'd been hung from the door hook. Whoever did this hadn't meant him to be found for a while. Or for his dirty sweats heaped in the basket to be washed. Ever.

She backed out, shaking. The strains of a harmonica wheezed from a children's television show blaring somewhere above. She ran from the building, trying to get the smell out of her nose.

Around the corner, she found a phone cabin. She didn't want to use her cell phone because it could be traced. She dialed 18 for the police.

"Sixty-eight rue Ronsard," she said, catching her breath. "The courtyard WC, something smells bad. An old man went down there and we're worried."

"Name please, caller. We need to verify your identity and your location."

She hung up. Took a deep breath. Tried to still her shaking hands.

Jacques murdered and now Zette, too, a Corsican tied to illegal gaming, with police connections. What did it mean?

She hitched her bag onto her shoulder and turned, about to push open the door of the telephone cabin, and found herself facing the side steps up to Sacré Coeur.

Then she remembered something.

She rifled through her bag, found the photo she'd printed out from Jubert's file, the one she'd planned on asking Zette about. She stared at it closely.

Those were the same steps in the photo. Overgrown with

ivy now, but it was the same place. These were the steps on which her father, Morbier, Rousseau, and Ludovic Jubert had stood years before. They had been facing Zette's building. If Zette had known her father, why hadn't he said so?

Two broad-shouldered men in down jackets and blue denims stood in front of the phone cabin. She didn't like the way they crowded the door. She had to think fast. She shoved the door open.

"What's your hurry?" said the taller *mec*, who wore dark glasses and a black wool cap.

"Do I know you?"

He grinned, showing a mouthful of yellow teeth. "Not yet. What were you doing up there?"

He jerked his thumb toward Zette's building.

"You've mistaken me for someone else," she said, edging past him.

He kept pace with her. The other *mec* hemmed her in on the other side. "You're out of your league, Mademoiselle."

"I don't understand." Panicked, she waved to a man bent against the whipping wind in the otherwise deserted street. She called, "Pierre . . . wait!" But the man kept going.

With a quick step she dodged past them and headed down the hill. She felt the men's eyes on her back as she hurried on the wet pavement, heard their steps behind her. Their footsteps were faster now. Why weren't there any other people on the street? Who were these *mecs*?

She quickened her step. Whoever they were they could gang up on her, shove her into a doorway, and . . . imagining the possibilities, she broke into a run.

The street forked at Marché Saint Pierre. The Art Nouveau metal struts of the red-brick market were frosted with ice. A dull silver overcast sky threatened rain, then opened. She ran into an alley filled with fabric shops. Rain pelted the canvas awnings. Underneath them, bolts of toile, bright Provençal designs, and gauzy chiffon reminded her of a bazaar. Every hue, texture, and width imaginable was on display. Glancing behind her, she saw the *mecs*. Ahead the alley came to a dead end.

Frantic, she looked around for shoppers to hide amongst. Usually this area hummed with activity. Where was everyone? Chased indoors by the bitter cold?

Cornered in the fabric market! There had to be a way out.

She rounded the corner. A street-level chute used to deliver bolts of fabric to the basement stood flush with the pavement. She hunkered down in the cold iron chute and gripped the sides.

"Mademoiselle, that's for deliveries. You can't go down there!" a deliveryman shouted from the shelter of his van.

Like hell she couldn't.

She slid down the chute before the *mecs* saw her, landing on rolls of fabric in a vaulted white-plaster-walled cellar. The strong musky scent of silk fiber made her nose itch. And sneeze.

"Eh, Alphonse, that you?" said a man's voice from behind the piles of dictionary-sized spools of thread. "You filled the last order, what's the matter?"

Quick. She had to escape before this man investigated. Navigate this underground honeycombed by tunnels, riddled with caverns. She edged her way into the shadows, walking fast, following a trail through the piled rolls of shining silk.

"Alphonse?"

She kept going, blinking in the darkness, wondering where this led. Rounding a curve, she saw steps, and mounted a spiral metal staircase. Opening the door, she found herself standing behind a glass counter heaped with bolts of cloth. What now? Then she ducked, as a man with a tape measure hanging from his shoulder appeared. Her cell phone fell and she heard the resounding crack of the antenna. She grabbed the phone and, shaking, crawled through several aisles until she saw a pair of brown loafers in front of her. A magenta gauze cloud billowed over her and she sneezed again.

"Mademoiselle?"

She got to her feet, the swag of magenta tenting her head.

"My cell phone . . . I dropped my cell phone," she said to the surprised face of a gray-haired clerk. "Excuse me."

She'd emerged into the shop next door to the one with the chute and realized that these stores connected in their basements. Through the window, she saw the *mecs* waiting in front of the other store. She controlled her trembling. Somehow she had to find a way out, avoiding them. She made her way through the almost empty store, pretending to study the tables spilling over with fabrics, one eye on the *mecs* outside. A stroller blocked her way in the cramped aisle. The lone shopper, a mother, lugged a large shopping bag and urged her red-cheeked toddler to get inside the stroller. Aimée had an idea.

She smiled. "Would you like some help? I'm leaving, too."

"Why, *merci*," the woman said.

Aimée leaned down to the child by the stroller. "What about a ride in this, eh?" She lifted the child inside. "*Voilá*. Let me push the stroller; it will make it easier for you."

"I appreciate it," the woman said, "my bag's heavy."

Aimée pushed the stroller out the street door, walking with her head down next to the child's mother until she paused to look in a shop window. Then Aimée hit the stroller brake with her toe and ran off.

Wednesday Afternoon

RENÉ LEANED FORWARD IN his orthopedic chair, staring at their computer screens. On the first, he updated and audited the database-registry settings and user-account configurations, something he could do in a half-sleep. On the other computer, he studied a display of the magnified six-groove rifling and RH twist of the bullet from a Manhurin .32 PP. He scanned the specifications text, wishing he could understand it: a 3.35 barrel length, operating as a direct blowback, double- or single-action semiautomatic pistol, it had a spring/momentum locking system that could take an eight-round box magazine with front blade and dovetailed rear sight. So, in human terms, what did that mean, René wondered. His phone rang and he jumped, knocking a batch of printouts to the floor.

"*Allô?*"

"Find anything interesting in the ballistics, René?" Aimée asked.

He heard something in Aimée's voice; the words seemed to catch in her throat.

"Like I'm an expert?" he said. "Hold on a moment." He put on a headset, hit the lever lowering his chair, and bent down to gather the papers. The pain in his hip flared and he winced.

"Didn't you tell me you wanted to examine the ballistics report and check on something?"

The bleep of a truck backing up came over the line.

"I e-mailed the file to you," she said.

"I got it. But the autopsy report is not in Laure's dossier," René said, setting the papers on his desk. "So it's impossible to compare."

"Compare what? You noticed something, didn't you, René?"

Notice? More like a lurking question. Could be off the track but . . . "It's just a question that bothered me."

He readjusted the height of his chair and sat.

"Come on, René!"

"Haven't you wondered why these men used Laure's gun, if they did?" He pulled his goatee, studying the laptop screen.

"All night long," she said.

"Well, I was thinking, too, after what you said last night. If they saw Jacques had brought backup, and lured him to the roof—"

"*Alors*, René," she said, an impatient edge to her voice.

"If, as little Paul claims, he saw two flashes on the roof, what about the other bullet?" It was an obvious question, he realized. "In your diagram of the rooftop, the area seemed partially enclosed. It could be in the chimney, or the walls."

"Good point," she said.

"Meanwhile, I'm updating our new accounts," he said, placing a hot-water bottle against his hip. Heat eased the pain of his hip dysplasia, which increased in the damp cold. "Someone's got to work here."

Pause.

"René: Zette, the bar owner."

"The one Jacques moonlighted for?" he interrupted.

"I just found him, René, garroted. Vendetta-style, with a Sicilian necktie."

He took a deep breath. No wonder she sounded on edge. Things were going from bad to worse.

"Then *mecs* chased me through Marché Saint Pierre."

"What?" René clutched the water bottle and listened as she told him.

"What if Zette was the victim of a vendetta, Aimée? Let the *flics* handle it."

"Or someone made it look like that," she said. "Zette knew something."

From her tone he knew she wouldn't give up. Not yet. He shivered. "If they were on the lookout, you gave them an eyeful."

"I'm giving Laure's file to Maître Delambre," she said.

"Aimée, be careful. Watch yourself."

"I will. And you've got to arrange for Paul to see him."

AIMÉE PACED back and forth in Maître Delambre's oak-paneled reception foyer, waiting. The fusty paper smell kept her company. The young receptionist, wearing a string of pearls and a blue sweater set, worked on a computer, ignoring her.

She'd taken two taxis and the Metro to the lawyer's, to make sure no one followed her. Zette's murder had convinced her this was part of something bigger.

Had René hit on something? René viewed things from different angles, tried odd equations. Like a good computer hacker.

Maître Delambre rushed in, his white-collared black robe trailing. "You said you had some reports? Just leave them. I'll go over them tonight, at home."

"We need to discuss them," Aimée began.

"Look, I'm late and I can't talk." He unbuttoned his robe, hung it on a wooden coatrack. "Catherine," he said, turning to his receptionist. "Cancel my next two appointments."

"Maître Delambre," Aimée said, trying to control her voice so as not to show her rising anger. "It's vital. This can't wait."

"It has to," he said. His face looked paler than usual. A strange rose pattern mottled his jowl. "The dentist has to finish the extraction and take out the tooth slivers he 'overlooked' last week. Otherwise it will abscess and he'll have to lance my jawbone."

Aimée grabbed her coat. "I'll go with you."

IN THE overheated taxi, she punched in the Hôtel Dieu's number. "Please, can you identify yourself and inquire about Laure's condition?"

Maître Delambre waved the phone away.

"They won't talk to me," she said. "Something's very wrong with Laure. Please ask. That's all; then you can sit back and—"

"She's in a coma."

"What?" Fear prickled her spine. Laure, comatose!

"The message reached me in court this morning," he said. "She's stable but nonresponsive."

The taxi sped along the quay. Aimée eyed the rising waters of the gray-green Seine, white wavelets lapped against the weathered stone. Things had become murkier like the water below them.

"Zette, the bar owner Jacques Gagnard worked for, was murdered in Montmartre," she told the young lawyer.

"Murdered?"

She explained finding Zette and her suspicions.

"Mademoiselle Leduc, you're convinced of something I'm not sure even connects."

"Convinced? The very day after I question him, Zette's killed. I call that a connection. A big one."

Maître Delambre clutched his jaw in pain.

"Don't you have the autopsy report yet?" she asked him

"Somewhere . . . here in my briefcase," he said.

She wanted to yank the case from his lap and open it. Yet she realized his head would be clearer now than it would be after he was treated by the dentist, and she had to show him the files she'd printed out from the DTI disc. "These reports weren't included in Laure's file. You should be aware—"

"What reports?" He winced and clutched his jaw again.

"The detailed crime-scene investigators' report, the—"

"How did you get them?"

She handed him a Doliprane and fished a bottle of Vichy water from her bag. He hesitated, then popped the pain-killer and uncapped the water bottle.

"By law they should be in the file you received," she said. "They can't really refuse to acknowledge them, can they?"

He shook his head as a spasm of pain crossed his face.

"Now you can deal from an equal position, at least, for the moment."

"I can't accept these," he said. "It would be unethical. I can't afford to."

"You can't afford *not* to. After all, it was their duty to furnish you with these reports."

He sat back against the taxi seat, closing his eyes. "Are you insinuating they left these out on purpose?"

"You're the lawyer," she said. "Aren't the police required to furnish you with all pertinent documents relating to your client?"

The taxi halted in Nouvelle Athenes in front of a soot-stained *hôtel particulier* now occupied by offices, opposite the building where George Sand and her lover, Chopin, had lived, on the slope below Montmartre. Now the eighteenth-century mansions housed government ministries, corporations, actors wealthy enough to remodel. Or they crumbled away in decayed splendor, awaiting developers.

"You've put me in a difficult position."

Of course she had. However, ethics dictated he act in the interests of his client. How could he ignore the reports now that she'd thrust them in his face?

"But I can't take these if you obtained them under false pretenses. A simple case shouldn't turn me into the Préfecture's enemy."

"*D'accord*," she agreed. "Who says I gave them to you? They could have just turned up on your doorstep. For all intents and purposes, they have. You present these files. They can't very well deny them. The files contain the officers' names, required filing date, and case number." She went on. "Besides, they already know the information's been copied." She bit her tongue to stop herself from adding that he'd be a fool not to use it.

"By someone . . . like you?"

She shook her head.

"I realize these files come from the police intranet system," he said, his eyes narrowed.

"STIC, to be precise."

He handed the taxi driver twenty francs and opened the door to a wall of cold air. "I have to think it over."

Rain pelted down on them as she ran after him.

THE WHIR of the dental drill drowned out most of Delambre's moans in the next room. Aimée gave a small smile to the white-clad dental technician who held a tray of surgical instruments.

"Valérie, I need the clamps!" said a deep voice from the open office door.

Valérie disappeared into the office, accompanied by a whiff of mint fluoride, and shut the door. Aimée hated waiting. Maître Delambre's damp raincoat hung from the coatrack by the receptionist's desk; his briefcase stood on the floor under it.

The receptionist sat with her head turned away, talking on the phone. To her boyfriend, from the sound of the conversation and giggles.

Aimée picked up a magazine, thumbed it open, and slid her leg toward the briefcase, hooked her foot around it, and drew it to her.

She unclasped the briefcase, found Laure's file, and stuck it between the pages of her magazine to study.

Autopsies, as her pathologist friend Serge often said, showed the road map of death. Atherosclerosis, sky-high blood pressure, a wearied heart pumping into arteries constricted by plaque. And the path of a bullet ripping tissue, slicing organs and muscle, too. A good pathologist, like Serge, was like a detective, listening to what the body told him as he probed, weighed, and examined organs, to reveal their secrets.

The autopsy on the body of Jacques Gagnard, dated Wednesday morning, stated, "Exsanguination due to gunshot wound to left lung and heart. Entrance wound on the left side of the chest. The bullet was recovered in right pleural cavity."

The image of Jacques on the snow-topped roof passed in front of her. She didn't like the man or his manipulation of Laure but she'd wanted to save him. Would have . . . no, not with part of his lung and his heart impacted. His eyes. They'd widened for a brief second and his lips had moved as though he wanted to say something. She finished reading the report, disappointed at the scant findings.

There was no mention of a second bullet. She sat back on the waiting-room bench to think. Could Jacques have been working undercover? Were the police protecting their own? Would her efforts somehow compromise an ongoing investigation? She was clutching at straws and her grip was slipping.

Wednesday Evening

"BIG POUT THIS TIME, Marie-Dominique," said the long-haired photographer, clicking the Hasselblad. "Show me big lips!"

Her mouth hurt after two hours of thrusting out her Bardot bee-stung lips. His cigarette was burning in the overflowing ashtray. The Gauloise tang hovered thick in the air. The *slick-slack* of hangers skeeting over the metal rack raised goose bumps on her arms.

"That's it . . . more! Let me see those cheekbones."

The techno beat pounded in the antiseptic whitewashed two-story studio, a former dairy reincarnated into l'Industrielle, the cow stalls now home to chrome banks of digital equipment.

"Lean more . . . good!"

Marie-Dominique did the model slouch, multiple black layers rising over her nonexistent hips, rubbing her diamond navel ring. She tried to look bored. Not hard, tottering on stiletto sneakers, the laces tied over fishnet stockings. She baked under the klieg lights in her midriff-baring black turtleneck sweater plus a jean jacket worn under a black leather biker jacket.

"*Nom de Dieu* . . . she's shining . . . *powder!*"

The makeup artist, his hair in short blond braided tufts, rushed to daub Marie-Dominique's forehead with matte powder.

"His girlfriend threw him out," he said in a low voice to Marie-Dominique. "He's camping out in back here. Me, I'd never live on the ground floor. Too dark, too noisy, too many break-ins." He redefined Marie-Dominique's lips with a chocolate brown pencil.

"The light's gone. Impossible!" The photographer ground out his cigarette with his heel. Lit another. "That's it for tonight."

"What about the Vénus de Vinyle shoot?" someone asked.

In response, the photographer turned the techno up louder. Relieved to finish sooner than her booking time, Marie-Dominique hung up the outfit and left her makeup on. Félix would like that, get a kick out of it. Sometimes she thought all he noticed about her was whether or not she'd had a pedicure.

Back in their apartment, along with the faded gardenia scent in the dark hallway, lay a note from Félix. "Another crisis. Off to Ajaccio. Back tomorrow."

He spent more time with hard hats, union stewards, and ministry officials than he did at home, apart from holding catered parties to entertain clients and grease his connections. No intimate dinners with friends. Their social circle consisted of his business partners and clients.

Another long winter evening alone. Thoughts of Lucien kept coming back to her, his music, the way his hair curled around his ears. His stubborn streak.

She sighed, taking off her boots and stockings, reveling in the smooth texture of the Aubusson carpet, scrunching it between her toes. Until she was six years old she hadn't owned a pair of shoes. Hadn't needed to.

Félix didn't understood her loathing of the runway, the numbing club scene where models' careers were built based on where and with whom they were seen. Her colleagues subsisted on injections, all kinds; she'd rather chew on a hunk of brown-crusted bread and cured olives. Olives from her family's olive mill. Her mind went back to the bitter olive essence ground by the granite grinding wheel, the dripping amber oil in the shadowed stillness, and the slow scrape of stone against stone. The path circling it worn by generations of mules. Cool, despite the relentless heat outside. The whir of bees hovering in the rosemary climbing the walls of the stone mill. Where Lucien had helped her father every summer until . . . that day.

Marie-Dominique shoved the image away. At least here she wasn't the object of constant scrutiny in an isolated hamlet with its archaic code of honor, presided over by a village chief whose other job was running a corner grocery. Paris might be gray, people living on top of one another, yet here the corner *café-tabac* owner knew her name but not her history. In short, she was free. Until Lucien walked back into her life.

In the huge gourmet kitchen where she never cooked, she tore off a hunk of baguette and smeared a Corsican *brébi* goat cheese over it, imagining the look of horror the high-strung photographer would give her if he knew. "Salt! You'll plump up. Diuretics work too slowly, do something immediately." She'd heard him say this to a beanpole-figured young girl who'd obediently gone and thrown up in the bathroom.

A voice came from Félix's study. Félix! Had his plans changed? Eager, she opened the door to surprise him and then stared.

Petru, Félix's factotum, sprawled over the armchair facing

the window, murmuring into Félix's private phone. The way Petru took over in Félix's absence irritated her. When Félix had hired him this year, she'd nicknamed him "the body-guard". His hair was black today. Yesterday it had been white blond; he dyed it more often than the stylists she worked with.

". . . of course, Lucien's implicated," Petru said, with a low laugh.

Implicated? She caught her breath, tugged the smooth brass doorknob back, and put her head to the crack between the door and the wall. What she heard startled her.

"The *flics* arrest him at the studio," he was saying.

Will arrest him or he had been arrested? Who was being discussed? Lucien? He'd denied being political. But was he telling the truth?

"Armata Corsa pamphlets, the works."

Just as she'd thought. Lucien was with the Armata Corsa. The liar!

"Everything's arranged. I put them there myself."

Her heart dropped. No wonder his conversation had sounded ambiguous. Petru was sabotaging Lucien.

"In less than an hour," he said. Then he turned toward the bookcase.

She couldn't hear the rest. She was about to storm in and confront Petru but she realized that bursting in wouldn't help Lucien in time if evidence had been planted already. She had to warn him. Thwart Petru's plans. But how?

Corsicans betrayed each other but never to an outsider. Unless . . . she looked at her Patek Philippe watch, Félix's wedding gift. She ran to the hallway, grabbed her shoes and coat. Out in the street, she called Félix. Busy.

She left him a message. Her hands trembled as she pushed the numbers. It was happening all over again.

"MADEMOISELLE ROUSSEAU'S condition remains unchanged," said Dr. Huissard from Hôtel Dieu in a harried voice.

It had taken Aimée twenty minutes on the phone persuading a liaison at the Préfecture to give her authorization and another twenty being switched around departments at the hospital before she was able to reach the doctor who was treating Laure.

"She's young, that's in her favor," Dr. Huissard said. "We're running tests. She'll have a CT scan this evening. For now, that's all we can do."

"Please don't think I'm telling you how to do your job, Doctor, but your service provides basic care," she said, aiming to be tactful. "Can't you transfer her to another more specialized ward in the hospital?"

Should she ask Guy to put in a word of recommendation? Despite his surgical excision of their relationship, she could call him. Perhaps he could help somehow. For Laure she would beg.

"Doctor, I know an eye surgeon."

"No outside specialists, they don't allow it. She's being treated by the specialists here."

"Her condition's deteriorating, as I understand, or it may. Why won't—?"

"I shouldn't say this." She heard the doctor sigh. "I've already requested that Neurology take over. Right now, they're overcrowded. As soon as a bed's free, she's next on the list for a neurology consult. She could be moved within the hour or later this evening."

"May I see her?"

"No visitors. She's in critical condition. We're not equipped, as you know, in the criminal ward."

"How soon could she—?"

"Mademoiselle, I promise you she's next on the list," Dr. Huissard said, his voice not unkind. "I need to get back to my rounds."

"*Merci*, I appreciate all your efforts, Doctor," Aimée said.

She opened the shoebox-sized refrigerator under the kitchen counter. On the shelf with the bottle of champagne and yogurt past the due date was a white wax-paper packet of butchers' scraps.

"Miles, *à table*," she said, putting the scraps into his chipped Limoges bowl.

Miles appeared with what looked like a rag in his mouth.

"What did you find this time?"

He dropped it on the floor, licked her leg, then bent over his bowl.

She picked it up. Guy's washcloth. She caught the clinging scent of his vetiver soap.

"I miss him, too." Her lip trembled.

Miles Davis looked up from the rim of his bowl, his head cocked to the side. Sometimes she'd swear he could understand.

She turned on her radio, a 1960s aqua rectangle with a JOHNNY HALLYDAY LIVE AT THE OLYMPIA! sticker she'd found on the street. She turned to a talk-radio station. But the callers complaining about their apartment neighbor's cat or the higher tax on cigarettes didn't drown out her thoughts of Guy.

On the next station was an interview with the breathy, vaguely sexy voice of Madame Claude, notorious for her exclusive *maison close* that had hosted an elite ministerial clientele in the seventies. Now Madame Claude peddled her memoirs instead of high-priced girls.

She switched the channel to Macha Meryl's show on RTL, the *intime* hour for the lost, the lovelorn. For years, Macha, a brusque therapist, had dispensed advice on late-night radio of the tough-love variety, often to the rejected, loveless callers. To the pathetic like her.

"Caller, *c'est simple*," Macha said, "a man leaves for two reasons: another woman, or the woman he thought he loved isn't whom he thought. *Et voilà*, it's not rocket science. My advice for when a man leaves? Shut the door behind him."

The husky cigarette-laced voice had gotten that part right. Get on with one's life!

Aimée put Guy's washcloth and the moonstone ring inside an envelope and addressed it to him at the hospital. She wished she didn't long to hear his voice one more time. One last time. Could she make an excuse and ask him for a referral for Laure?

Non, dumb. Don't call, she told herself.

A moment later, she took a deep breath and punched in the number of his hospital.

"Doctor Lambert?" the receptionist said. "We're referring his patients to the acting head of staff."

Odd. "For any particular reason?"

"Doctor Lambert's taken a post with Doctors Without Borders in the Sudan."

The Sudan? She grabbed the door frame.

"Just like that?"

"An unexpected position came up. Few have Doctor Lambert's qualifications in ophthalmological surgery. There's a desperate need. He decided, overnight."

"*Merci*," Aimée said. She hung up and dropped the envelope on her desk. Tears rimmed her eyes. He'd gone.

"Flee, flee . . ." Hadn't Mallarmé written that? So Guy had run to Africa to save the blind and to escape.

Laure lay in a coma and now all she could do was stand here feeling sorry for herself. She was beyond pathetic.

A news announcement interrupted the broadcast. "Police find links to Corsican Separatist threats to bomb government buildings. Sources in the Ministry of Interior decline to state the targets. More on the top-of-the-hour news."

Corsicans. Instead of this pity party, she needed to do something, quit treading water while she waited for the lab report to surface. Probe deeper, investigate, find proof, a witness. Vindicate Laure. Where to begin?

She remembered the prostitute Zoe Tardou had mentioned. If she was working tonight she'd be on the street.

Aimée smoothed her white shirt, tightened the knot of the black tie under the vintage Saint Laurent "Le Smoking" jacket she'd found at the Porte de Vanves flea market. Over that she donned her black leather coat, winding her scarf tightly against the crisp chill, and headed for the Metro.

Half an hour later, she exited through the verdigris Art Nouveau Metro arch. In the distance, staircases mounted the *butte*, home to small zinc cafés, tiny fifteen-seat theatres. Wind whistled through a broken roof tile along the passage. The burning wood smell of a working chimney wafted past her.

On the steep street, a white-haired man locked his bicycle to the street lamp. *"Ba waoui,"* he said, with the twang of an old-style Parisian, to a man rubbing his arms in the cold. "Have to go down to Paris tomorrow."

That old Montmartrois spirit that grudgingly condescended to Paris "below."

She grinned as she passed him and he tipped his cap to her. *"Bonsoir,* Mademoiselle."

"Et vous aussi, Monsieur!"

She followed the cobblestone street past several small hotels and a prostitute's bar where a miniskirted woman sat in the window petting her dog. A handwritten sign read—RECHERCHÉS HOSTESSES—Hostess Wanted—and the red-lit bar was empty.

She followed the narrow street to the corner. Beyond, it curved and led to a flight of stairs up to Abbesses. The steps glistened in the rays of a single streetlight. Across from the building where Jacques had been shot, she saw a heavily made-up prostitute right where Zoe Tardou had said.

"*Bonsoir*," Aimée said. Her breath came in puffs of mist.

"I don't do women, *chérie*," the woman said, shifting her weight to her other foot. "Try rue Joubert; they work without pimps and do their own thing."

Rue Joubert, near the department store Printemps, was a street of *les Traditionelles*, prostitutes who charged standard prices and used condoms. The categories varied; there was the *marcheuse* who walked the street; the *entraineuse* who worked in a bar; the *caravelle*, at the airport; the *michetonneuse* on a café terrace, and finally, *la call-girl*, at the high end.

"Thanks for the information," Aimée said. How could she get this woman, forty if she was a day, to talk? "A *flic* was murdered here the other night, you've heard about it?"

The woman's eyes darted around the warren of streets and passed over the front of a shuttered plumbing shop. The dark sky cast a gray tint over muffled angular figures bent into the wind, framed by white stone five-story buildings. The scene could have been an Impressionist painting.

"I know you're working, but that night did you see something, or hear something?"

"*Flics* aren't my business."

"Nor mine, but they're accusing my friend, a female *flic*, of shooting her partner."

"Didn't she?" She stared at Aimée for a moment. Of course, the prostitute would have heard all about it in this part of Montmartre.

"She was set up and I owe her a favor," Aimée said. "Were you here Monday night?"

"Every night." The woman shrugged.

"So you heard the shot at around eleven o'clock that night, just before the worst of the snowstorm?"

"What's it worth to you?"

Aimée pulled a hundred-franc note from her pocket.

Just then a middle-aged man wearing a wool overcoat walked by, paused, then looked at Aimée. "It's cold tonight. Like to keep me warm?" he asked.

Aimée shook her head, controlling her shudder.

"*Alors*, this is my corner," said the woman, anger flashing in her eyes.

"Nice to see new blood here, Cloclo. How about a three-way with your friend?" he said, grinning.

Cloclo, whose workname was slang for costume jewelry, stepped from the shadows and took his arm. "You're *my* friend, *chéri*." She guided him along the cobbles. "Special price, eh, you're my last tonight."

"Cloclo!" Aimée called.

Cloclo looked back and laughed.

Aimée held up several hundred-franc notes and pointed to the lighted café-bar sign next to a small hotel on rue Veron. Cloclo nodded, then disappeared around the corner.

She could warm up and nurse a *verre de rouge* until Cloclo turned up, if she did. Given the crow's-feet around the prostitute's eyes that heavy makeup didn't hide, she figured the francs she'd flashed would bring her.

Inside Chez Ammad, the café-bar, a young man behind the counter flashed her a smile. Cropped hair, jagged broken teeth. A street fighter or too many sweets. She figured the latter.

A café of locals, not trendies or *médiathèques*. This might be a good opportunity, while she waited for the prostitute, to ask if anyone here had noticed something odd Monday night. But she couldn't rush it or they'd clam up.

The man stuck a tape in a cassette player. Dalida's voice rose above the conversations in the café. The long brown wood-paneled room resembled a bus. One she wished she hadn't gotten on. Thick cigar smoke hovered like a cloud over a table of middle-aged backgammon players. Bourgeoisie or bureaucrats by the look of their expensive leather shoes.

She wanted a smoke. Tomorrow at 9:37 a.m. it would be four days since she'd quit. And she wished she wasn't counting the minutes. She looked around to see who she could pump for information and pointed to what the man next to her at the counter was drinking.

"The same," she said.

Overhearing her, he said, "You look the active type." With his hooded eyes and splayed workman's hands he could have been the bartender's brother. "Call me Theo."

"I can still do a handstand and cartwheel without splitting my pants," she responded.

His hooded eyes widened and he grinned. "Hear that, Marcus?" he said to the bartender. "We've got an acrobat here!"

"I left the circus," she said, putting three francs on the counter. "Terrible benefits."

She wished the prostitute would walk through the door, hoped she wouldn't have to wait very long. The wet wool smell and cigar fragrance were getting to her.

"Did you hear that, Marcus? Our bricklayers' union's not the only one. The scaffolders' too."

Was this about the scaffolding on the building where Jacques was killed? Interesting.

"So, Theo, you work in construction over there?" She jerked her hand toward the window.

One of the cigar smokers looked up. "Theo's responsible for the noise. It's been six months. The building commission permit was only for two."

"Did I include you *mecs* in my conversation?" Theo frowned.

The oil fumes from the kerosene heater permeated the air. Her nose itched and she sneezed. She caught Theo looking at her legs.

The burgundy, smooth and full bodied, left a tart aftertaste.

"So we should work faster and end up in the quarries?" Theo asked, throwing up his arms.

"Typical union talk," said the cigar smoker. "Always whining."

"Limestone quarry pockets honeycomb the foundation. On this part of the hill it's like you've got to put on velvet gloves just to move a few centimeters of earth."

"He's right," said Marcus, wiping down the counter. "We had to get a special clearance to replace a water pipe!"

A vigorous discussion ensued, reminding her of her grandmother's Auvergnat village, where the café was *the* social scene on winter nights. Familiar, like a worn blanket. But instead of farmers, the café patrons mirrored the face of the *butte*: bricklayers, intellectuals, a reporter from *Le Canard Echaine*, the satirical newspaper, and retired bureaucrats.

The barman, Marcus, refilled her glass and winked. "On Theo."

"*Santé,*" she said, raising her glass, figuring the lull in the conversation was a good time to ask questions. "Theo, wasn't there a shooting where you work?"

"Caused another delay," he said.

"Why's that?"

"Some *flic* offed another *flic*."

"That's not what I heard," she said. The conversation paused. "My neighbor saw men, not cops, shooting on the roof."

"What could your neighbor see in a freak snowstorm? She must enjoy freezing her eyeballs off. Some kind of record, the amount of snow that fell that night."

"I heard that the storm broke right after the shooting," Aimée said.

"To see anything in that weather, she must have laser vision."

Before she could press further, Cloclo walked in, nodded to the regulars, and spied Aimée. Cloclo indicated a table in back underneath a sloping soot-stained glass roof. She remembered her grandfather saying, "Prostitutes are a thousand times more

honorable than actresses. The first sell their bodies; the second, their souls, and more."

"A pastis, if you're buying," Cloclo said, as she passed Aimée
at the counter.

By the time Aimée brought over the drink, Cloclo had
divested herself of her long black coat. Sparkling costume jewelry clinked in her deep cleavage, and pastel pink Diamonique
bracelets encircled her wrists.

"No wonder your nickname is Cloclo," Aimée said.

"I'm on my feet all day," she said. "I like something to
brighten me up."

On her knees, too, Aimée thought, noticing the snags and
a run in her black sheer stockings. Aimée palmed the promised francs under the table into Cloclo's waiting hand.
Cloclo's cheap floral scent mingled with the anise smell of
the pastis.

"We can talk but I don't have much to say," she said.

Great. She'd just slipped her the last of her cash. No taxi-
ride home on a night that promised to freeze the gutter water.

"Listen, Cloclo, think of helping me as helping my friend.
She's in a coma from the blow she got up there. Hard to go
downhill from there."

"This friend . . . your friend, she's the *flic*, right?"

Aimée nodded. "We've been friends since we were ten years
old. Our fathers worked the beat up here. Laure always had an
inferiority complex. Her harelip—"

"I know the one. Young," Cloclo interrupted.

"She treat you right?"

"Left me alone." Cloclo added water to the pastis, stirring
it to a cloudy mixture. She took a long sip, her eyes never
leaving Aimée's face. Aimée tried to ignore the acrid smell
of anise.

For Cloclo, in her line of work, that would be treating someone right.

"Laure wouldn't kill her partner. No matter what."

"I didn't like *him*."

Aimée's ears perked up. "Her partner, Jacques?"

Cloclo shook her head and ran a finger over a black-penciled eyebrow.

"Do you know what Jacques was doing up on the roof?"

"Jacques's not who I meant," she said, glancing at her Diamonique watch.

Startled, Aimée leaned forward. "Who do you mean?"

Something shuttered behind Cloclo's eyes.

"It's getting late," Cloclo said.

Was she afraid? "Sorry, go ahead. I thought you meant her partner, Jacques." Aimée felt the vibration of Cloclo's black stiletto pump tapping the wooden floor.

"That *mec*. He thinks he owns the rue, you know the type I mean?"

Aimée thought back to the musician she'd seen in the doorway, the one Conari had identified as Lucien Sarti.

"Dark skin, eyes, and hair, a musician. You mean him?" Aimée asked.

"Not that good-looker."

"Then I don't know who you mean."

"The guy who gives me a hard time—a crude type," Cloclo said. "Not the one who carries a music case."

Near them a chair scraped over the floor, a voice rang out, "*Adieu, mes amies*."

Cloclo waved to an old man shuffling out.

Aimée had to focus Cloclo on this other *mec*. "Did he know Laure and her partner?"

"How well he knew her partner, that I don't know," Cloclo said, her tone matter-of-fact. "But he flaunted his connections, you know. Wanted freebies."

Something stirred in Aimée's mind. If she could put the details together, some piece would fit.

"Did you see this *mec* and my friend's partner together?"

"I saw them talking in that bar on rue Houdon." Cloclo's eyes flicked across the room.

Finally, a connection. "Zette's? Does this guy have a name?"

She shrugged. "Those Corsicans keep to themselves, eh?"

"He's Corsican, you're sure?"

Cloclo nodded, and her costume jewelry clicked together on her ample chest.

Aimée tried to put it together. Jacques knew Zette and had been seen with this *mec*. Had he killed both of them? Why?

"Where can I find this crude Corsican?"

"Him, you don't want to know. But he goes in and out of the chichi place down the street from my station."

Station...her place on the street.

"You mean opposite the fancy townhouse across the courtyard from number 18?"

"*Oui.*"

"Any idea which apartment he goes into?"

She shrugged again and downed her pastis.

"What does he look like?"

"Like any punk with money. Gold around the neck. Stylish hair and clothes."

Now to the important part.

"Did you hear a shot, Cloclo?"

She shook her head. "I was working, *chérie.*"

"See anything?"

"Like I said." She rolled her mascaraed eyes. "Working. But the good-looker walked up from Pigalle and stood in the doorway, you know where the street divides?" She drained her glass.

Aimée pictured the view from Cloclo's station and the spot where Sarti had stood. If he came from Pigalle, would he have had time to kill Jacques and attack Laure? What about the other *mec*?

"Here's my number," Aimée said, handing Cloclo a card.

"Call me the next time you see the Corsican. Night or day. There are more francs in it for you."

Wednesday Evening

LUCIEN CLIMBED THE WORN stairs leading to avenue Junot, his lungs constricting in the bitter chill. It was a steep staircase dotted by infrequent old-fashioned green metal street lamps, like those in his village. Except for the ice and biting wind, he might have been home. His pulse raced despite disappointment. The recording engineer had greeted him at the studio door with a long face, informing him that he was sorry but the session had been cancelled and telling him to go to 63, rue Lepic, and up the stairs.

Lucien figured Félix was en route to some meeting and would meet him there to break the bad news that SOUNDWERX had reneged on the deal.

Nice! He didn't even have a decent winter coat. And the *flics* were on the prowl for him. And he still didn't have the rent.

Wild aromatic herbs grew out of the old walls, their scent mingling with that of the wet, seeping earth. The stair summit leveled off to worn stones tented by elder, ash, and sycamore branches. A gypsum rock taller than he blocked the path. Fernlike ailanthus branches spread from the crumbling stone wall, their rain-glistening leaves catching the light of the half-moon. He tripped over a raised cobblestone. A rustling in the bushes, and then speckled blackbirds and magpies swooped upward, leaving brown fluttering leaves in their wake.

A wild place in the heart of Paris. He hadn't known one existed.

Ahead, he saw a dark-coated figure under a street lamp, eyes shining under her mauve knitted cap. Slim and lithe, he'd know her anywhere.

"Marie-Dominique!"

Had she been persuaded by Félix to await his arrival to coat the bitter pill?

"Over here, Lucien." She motioned to where wild fig branches and cedar trees interlaced.

"What a spot to meet, Marie-Dominique," he said. Puffs of frost filled the air between them.

"It's the maquis of Montmartre. It reminds me of home." She pointed with her black-leather-gloved finger past the stalks of a garliclike herb. "I discovered it. Wonderful, *non?* An old woman told me her grandmother's farm had been here. There used to be watering troughs for the animals over there."

All Lucien saw were dark stones and underbrush.

"These old walls were part of the mill that ground wheat for flour."

Lucien stepped over the brush and saw the shadowy arms of a windmill looming behind the stone wall. Hidden.

"There were dozens of mills here once," she said. "Now only two remain."

The pinprick lights of Paris below shone like fireflies caught in a net of ferns. In the stillness, the dark, her rose scent drifted toward him. He wanted to fold her in his arms.

"You're in danger, Lucien." Her voice had changed.

"I know. It seems I'm an object of police scrutiny." Longing filled him despite his earlier disappointment. Just seeing her alone made his skin tingle.

"Them, too? I found out that Petru has planted Armata Corsa propaganda at the studio," she said, "and arranged for the police to arrest you!"

"Petru?"

"He works for us, but he's involved in something else. I left Félix a message to warn him that Petru's trying to sabotage you."

"I don't understand."

Marie-Dominique stepped back, doubt showing on her face. "Am I wrong? That group, the one you and your friends joined—?"

Félix. Now Marie-Dominique. He was tired of this. "I signed up and went to *one* meeting with my brother and friends. As I told you. How can you think I'd be part of something that's not even a political movement anymore? They're gangsters! They extort protection money and graffiti the *tête de* Maure all over to make the bombings appear to be political." He kicked a loose, cracked pavement stone that clattered into the bushes. "The true Separatists want to free Corsica, but not like that."

She looked away. He clutched her arm. "I should know. Luca, my little brother, worked construction on the military base until the union went on strike and shut it down."

"Quit that old talk, Lucien. It's always the same!"

"The same?" He had to make her understand. "Luca forgot his tool kit and went back to retrieve it. The gangsters, the so-called "union," thought he'd crossed the picket line. The next day they delivered his body to my mother. What was left of it."

He trembled, trying to forget the bloody image of a mutilated Luca with a *tête de* Maure painted on his chest.

"I'm sorry, I didn't know," she said.

"I had signed up in a drunken moment of idealism. How wrong I was." He kicked a clod of dirt with his toe. "Nothing will stop them or those developers who are gutting the coast, ruining the land—"

"So you're blaming Félix now?" Her eyes flashed.

"I spoke of the developers who are ruining the land." His feet crunched the ice between the cobbles. "What does he have to do with that?"

"As if you didn't know. His military contracts, the development he's involved in . . . why he's there right now. There's been another crisis with the Ministry contract. He's doing the best he can for the island."

The best?

"I didn't know. You've changed, Marie-Dominique. I once thought . . ." He paused. He snapped an elder twig between his fingers. He couldn't bottle it up any longer. "I never understood. Now I've figured it out. Your hotheaded cousin Giano saw us in the cave and made trouble. So your family sent you to Paris to make a match with Félix."

"I prevented the vendetta."

"The vendetta?" She sounded like his mother. "It's changed. Young people don't care; they hate the rivalries and killings. I should have spoken up, explained to your father. Or maybe the vendetta is just an excuse. You agreed to marry a rich man. Maybe you really wanted the good life. But Félix? An old roué?" He wanted to bite his tongue. He hadn't meant to say that.

"How can you attack Félix?" she said, hurt in her eyes. "Someone who's trying to help you . . . your career. But, as always, you lash out with no regard for anyone else's feelings."

Shame and anger filled Lucien. Had he gotten it all wrong? Conflicted, he looked down. His legs didn't seem to work. He was torn, paralyzed. He should go, he knew.

"That's the one thing I miss, the scent of the maquis," he told her.

"'The maquis has no eyes but sees everything,'" Marie-Dominique reminded him.

Did it see inside him? Did she?

"I'm late for my next job," Lucien said, finally making his legs move.

Her face was in shadow.

"You're still a terrible liar, Lucien."

She edged past him. Stopped. Stood on the stairs, her wool coat glistening with drops of rain in the light of the street lamp. Her back to him, her gloved hands shaking. "You don't understand."

And then he finally realized. For her, he'd just been a fling. A flirtation, easily gotten over.

"You have no ears to hear what I'm saying," Marie-Dominique said.

She'd changed. Hardened. Where was his Marie-Dominique with the sand-dusted feet and olive-oil-stained hands?

Her heels clicked down the stone steps and when he looked, she'd already turned the corner.

LUCIEN PULLED his coat collar higher and stared at the fingers of mist floating over the buildings below. He was cold and alone, the murmur of Paris below him. He should be recording right now, but Félix was in Corsica, the *flics* and this Petru were in league against him, and Marie-Dominique had left him again. As they said, a life could fall apart in seconds. And his had.

Bad luck dogged him. His *grand-mère* would call it "the evil eye." Superstition, all superstition. He believed in science, empiricism. Still, the image of the old *mazzera* came to him, "the witch" they called her in the village. She was supposed to know how to lift curses.

He saw the piercing topaz eyes in her lined face, her black shawl redolent of the herbs she used, the tarnished silver cross and amulets she wore around her neck. He'd still been in short pants, sleeping on the platform in the attic under the skylight when he'd visited her. A rash had covered his palms and he'd tried to hide them under his school desk. The older boy he had asked to whittle him a slingshot saw them and ridiculed him: "Leper."

Desperate to rid himself of the rash, he'd walked through the *mazzera's* open door. The one-room stone house smelled of smoke and pork grease. Smoked sausages and cured hams on strings hung in rows from the wood beams. The old crone, huddled by the wood-burning stove with its chipped enamel coffee pot, looked up.

"*Petit*, you've come to buy my *sanglier?*" she asked in a curious high-pitched voice.

She cured and smoked the best wild boar sausages in the village.

"N-not exactly," he stammered.

Her eyes, like a young woman's, penetrated the smoky haze.

"*Non*, of course not. You need my help," she said. "Come here. Show me your hands."

Surprised, he stepped forward, past the sleeping dog curled at her feet.

He lifted his palms, his eyes down, and showed her. "Maman's tried ointments, olive-oil soap, but nothing works."

"You want it to go away and your friends to stop making fun of you."

How did she know? He nodded, shifting his sandaled feet on the uneven wood floorboards.

"It's a sign, *petit*. Ask yourself why."

Perplexed, he backed away. "You're supposed . . ."

"I see things." Her voice crackled and the dog thumped its tail. "You've forgotten a promise, haven't you?"

A promise? Hadn't he fed the chickens this morning?

"I mean forgotten what you know deep inside. So the spirits have sent you a reminder."

She made the sign of the cross over his forehead and chest three times, murmuring words in some language he didn't understand. Latin sounding. "Every night for three nights look into the sky and ask your ancestors' help." She poured herbs and boar fat into a small mortar and ground them with a pestle into a foul-smelling brown paste.

"Smear this on your palms afterward," she said. "Three nights, don't forget."

He reached in his pocket and pulled out a tied clump of sage he'd gathered in the maquis. He handed it to her.

"*Merci*, good boy," she said. "You honor the customs."

For three nights, staring at the glistening stars, he'd crossed himself. Thought hard. The promise he'd made to his grandfather to carry on the family music tradition came back to him. As he applied the awful paste, his dead grandfather's face floated above him.

The fourth day he'd sat at his school desk and had seen that his rash had gone. And so had the older boy. "Moved to Bonifacio," his teacher said. Slingshot and all.

He never knew if the vile paste or his exhortations or both had worked.

But he had no *mazzera* to lift this curse now. He scattered a handful of bread crumbs for the blackbirds perched on a leafless sycamore branch and made his way down the steps.

Late Wednesday Evening

"BONSOIR," AIMÉE SAID. "Lucien Sarti, *s'il vous plaît*."

"Who's calling?" a woman asked.

"Aimée Leduc."

"He's gone. Left a few days ago."

What could she say now? Think fast.

"Doesn't he work at a club? I'm Félix Conari's associate. There is a big snag with his music contract," she said. "I must contact him."

Pause. A sizzling sound came over the phone. Was the woman cooking?

"Give me your number. If he calls . . ."

"06 57 89 42. Please, as soon as possible."

She clicked off. A hungry musician should bite at that. She hoped so.

A moment later her phone vibrated in her pocket. Hungry all right.

"*Allô?*"

"Sorry to call you so late. Yann Marant here," a voice said, loud conversation buzzing in the background. "I just finished work, but I found something, although maybe it's nothing, to do with your investigation."

A break, finally?

"Can we meet? My phone's acting up," she said.

"Café Noctambule," he said. "It's noisy but I'm unfamiliar with the area."

"No problem."

YANN STOOD in the Café Noctambule, a dive with seventies-era smoky mirrors on the walls. On the small stage, a bouffant-haired man crooned *chansons*. The place was packed and couples revolved to the accordion and the beat of the snare drum.

Yann waved. "Over here."

Next to him, two women argued, snarling at each other like cats in an alley. A smallish mild-mannered-looking man grinned at their show.

Yann covered his ears. "I'm sorry, no place to talk here. Hungry?"

Aimée nodded. She couldn't remember when she'd last eaten.

A few doors away, they found a cigarette-box-sized bistro, five tables crowded into a dark room with a coal-burning stove. Warm as toast, but full. Reluctant to leave, Aimée suggested that they stand at the zinc counter and order a *jambon-beurre*.

"I appreciate your calling, Yann. Anything might help."

"Now I feel silly. I read too many suspense thrillers," he said, twisting his hands. "It's probably nothing, but you said . . ."

"Go ahead." She hoped she hadn't made the trip for nothing. Patience, she had to have more patience.

Despite Yann's wrinkled black pants and loosened ponytail, he exuded more appeal than most computer geeks she knew. And was better looking. Had he really recalled some vital detail or was he using this as an excuse to meet? But the warm bistro held more allure than her cold, empty apartment.

"Tonight, after I left Félix's, I threw a water bottle into the construction's Dumpster, the one parked in front of the building being renovated," Yann said. "Everything fell out, a mess. I know it's forbidden but, well, I scooped it up, climbed up to throw . . ." He paused. "Sorry to bore you, you'll think I dive Dumpsters at night but I don't."

"*Bon appétit*," said the white-aproned bistro owner, setting a plate of ham and buttered baguette sandwiches in front of them.

"Please continue," she said, taking a bite. As crumbs from the bread crust fell, she caught them in her palm.

"Trying to make space, that's when I found these." He reached into his pocket, set down several crumpled, blurred black-and-white photocopied papers smelling of plaster dust, and smoothed them out. They showed hand-drawn floor plans with thick arrows and Xs inked in. "I figured these came from the site, and I was about to throw them back when I noticed this."

Curious, she leaned forward, following his finger. A diagram bore a notation: *rue du Mont-Cenis* and *rue Ordener*.

"So there is a building at the intersection of these streets," she said. "But this isn't a blueprint. What is it?"

"That's what I wondered. With all these Separatist bombings . . . well, perhaps I'm reading too much into this." He exhaled. "Sorry, at least I feel better. But stupid. Forgive me? Maybe it was kind of an excuse to meet you again." A small smile played at the edges of his mouth. "I don't know many people here."

She returned his smile but her mind focused on the diagram.

He folded the papers. "Now you'll think I'm a nerd, joined at the hip to my computer. And you're right."

"Wait, Yann," she said, pulling out her pocket map and thumbing it open to the Eighteenth Arrondissement.

"The Mairie is on that corner," she said, her voice rising. The City Hall was the only building at that location. "May I see that diagram again?" Her heart beat faster.

Along the side, in smaller script, was written: (2) 18:00 change (1) 23:00 change. Arrows pointed to the symbols for entrances. She thought back to the newspaper, the article describing bomb threats to an unnamed government building.

She stared closer. "It could mean that two guards man the main entrance until the 18:00 shift change, then one guard takes over."

Yann blinked several times. "Who would leave such incriminating papers in a Dumpster?"

"*Exactement*," she said. "But they could be old plans, outdated, and their implication forgotten."

She chewed on the baguette, thinking.

"I guess it doesn't link to that *flic*'s murder," Yann said, his face reddening. "Real life's not like a thriller where it all connects."

Was he right?

She studied the diagram more closely. Saw Atlas, the name of an alarm company, an X on what appeared to be a service entrance. More Xs on rue du Mont-Cenis. The placement of a car or truck bomb?

She should direct Yann to turn the diagrams over to the authorities. Stay out of it. Not dirty her hands with the Ministry's military wing. They'd clamp down on this so fast. Just thinking of dealing with the security sector made her palms sweat. She should . . . but did she ever do what she should?

Turning over information wasn't her style. Yet information given might earn a favor in return. That's how they operated.

"If this diagram's for real, it would be criminal not to report it," she said, deciding to take a gamble. "Mind if I show this to a contact at DST?"

"The terrorist brigade? Of course not," he said. "You don't think—"

"Yann, did anything strike you about Lucien Sarti?"

Yann smiled. "My first impression? You'll think it . . . well, he seems to be a sort of wandering troubadour, he lives rough, but his music drives him."

"How do you mean?" she asked, surprised.

"Wedded to Corsica, the land and people, an idealist telling stories through his music," Yann said. "Somehow he found Félix and sent him a tape of this entrancing blend of traditional polyphony and techno."

"Would you describe his music as political?"

Yann's brow furrowed. "I'd say it was about freeing Corsica *and* returning to nature. Félix can't say enough about his music but . . . ."

She nodded. Waited. A couple passed them, letting a gust of winter air enter.

"Enthusiastic, that's Félix. A huge heart," Yann said. "Then he discovered that Lucien's a member of the Armata Corsa. That made it difficult for him to push a contract through."

The diagram, this linkage of Lucien Sarti to the Corsican Separatist movement. Did it add up to Jacques's murder? Had she read Jacques wrong? Had he met with Lucien Sarti to discover a plot, or to prevent a terrorist bombing? Was the musician his informer?

She had to find Lucien Sarti. A long night stretched ahead of her.

In the restroom she took a deep breath and called Bordereau, a contact at the DST, on the public phone. Always the public phone with the DST. They could trace calls within three minutes.

Bordereau answered on the first ring. "Unit 813."

"Aimée Leduc," she said. "Got something you might like to see."

"Always interested in your little gifts," Bordereau said. "Twenty on my favorite," he added.

She glanced at her Tintin watch: she would have to hurry. "Make it twenty-five." And hung up.

TWENTY-FIVE minutes later she nodded to Bordereau, who was waiting inside the gate of the offices of the Archdiocese of Paris, a seventeenth-century building a block from the Ministry of Interior where he worked. One day, if she came to know him better, she'd ask him why he didn't work at the DST on rue Nélaton. He looked no more than thirty, but he was well past forty. Bordereau's *en brosse* short hair glittered with beads of rain. She'd first met him at the Reuilly pool during lap swim when his waterproof pager caught on the filter and she'd recovered it for him. The numbers had displayed a ministerial access. She knew at once that he worked intelligence and at a high level if he wore a pager in the pool. A useful man to know. And not bad in a Speedo.

A band of light crossed the pocked stone entrance as the porter, a grizzled, bent man, opened the tall wood door.

"*Entréz,* Monsieur," he said.

Bordereau nodded. Together they stepped inside the bas-relief-lined vestibule permeated with a smell she remembered, the smell particular to a Catholic school at least during the two years she'd attended. An atmosphere she associated with hanging tapestries in high-ceilinged halls, the cattle stampede of students on wooden stairs, and nuns in full habit, their wimples and veils blocking all peripheral vision.

The porter disappeared. She pulled the diagram from her bag, kneeled, unfolded it, and spread it on the waxed parquet floor.

"This was found in a Dumpster," she said. "I can't vouch for authenticity or much else. On a nearby rooftop above the site, a *flic* was murdered Monday night."

"It's dry." Bordereau said, his eyes scanning the diagram. "Was it at the bottom?"

"That's my information," she said. "According to my map, it shows the Mairie in the Eighteenth."

He didn't whistle but she thought he wanted to.

"I think it ties in with the *flic*'s murder and the garroting of a Corsican bar owner, Zette, on rue Ronsard. That was made to look like a vendetta killing, but I think it's connected."

Bordereau was quite still. His economy of movement struck her.

"Your rationale?"

"The dead *flic* moonlighted on and off for Zette," she said. "Too much of a coincidence, I think. Now I have some questions for you, OK?"

He nodded, his eyes still on the diagram.

"Did this attack take place?"

"Almost. Sunday night. It was thwarted; the bombs were defused."

The night before Jacques's murder, a failed bomb threat.

"Was it related to the Armata Corsa?"

"Rumor has it," he said, getting back to his feet, folding the plan, and slipping it into his coat pocket. "But we had no proof. Your source?"

"Yann Marant, a programmer, threw trash into an overloaded Dumpster near 18, rue André Antoine. When the trash fell out he tried to shove it back and found this."

"*Merci.*"

Even if it's outdated, it must have some value, she thought.

"Anything interesting about Corsica I should know?"

His blond eyebrows shot up. "Besides mafiosi under the guise of Armata Corsa using arms from Eastern Europe to rob armored truckloads of sensitive documents? And a data-encryption leak from Big Ears?" He grinned. "No, I don't think so."

She returned the grin. "A data-encryption leak—what do you mean?"

"Keep it coming. And forget I said that." He stood up. "Haven't seen you at lap swim this week."

"Busy."

On the Metro, she tried to make sense of it all: sensitive documents, a data-encryption leak, a failed bomb threat rumored to be connected to Corsicans? The implications gnawed at her. A rooftop murder in a snowstorm, Laure charged and in a coma. Events were spiraling out of control.

Thursday Morning

STREAKS OF THE MORNING'S first light filtered through the mist enveloping Pont Marie. Aimée slid Miles Davis's tartan winter sweater over his hind legs, settled him in her bike's wire basket, and cycled through the mist to Leduc Detective. Feeling guilty about being absent again, she'd arranged for Marcel, the one-armed Algerian war veteran who ran the kiosk on rue du Louvre, to dog-sit Miles for a few days.

In the office, she powered up their espresso machine and made a strong espresso *double*. She hoped for some responses from the three clubs where she'd left messages for Lucien Sarti. With any luck she'd find him and discover his link to Armata Corsa and why he'd left Conari's party before being questioned. Her hunch was that he'd witnessed Jacques's murder and had some connection to it or to the diagram Yann had found. Or worse.

In the meantime, she cranked open the window shutters to let in the damp gray air from rue du Louvre together with the smell of butter emanating from the nearby *boulangerie*. She put on a trance-techno tape she'd bought from a DJ last night. Moody, and with a steady beat. She booted up her computer and searched the Net for information on the data-encryption leaks that Bordereau had mentioned and to find out what she could about Big Ears.

She came up with Big Brother, the nickname for the U.S. and U.K.'s Echelon, the big ears of eavesdropping.

That sounded old-fashioned, dated by the Cold War, she thought, ancient history.

Au contraire, she discovered, as she dug deeper. Echelon, according to NSA, the National Security Agency based in the U.S., was responsible for the interception of international signals; all traffic from telephone links, to e-mails, to faxes, whether sent over land lines or by cell phones.

More than impressive.

Echelon, a network, operated on a filter system that utilized banks of powerful computers programmed to recognize key words in various languages and intercept messages containing those words for recording and subsequent analysis. All from a Helios-1A satellite beaming down to earth to wire and parabola-dish antennas.

She knew Helios-1A took high-definition photos for surveillance: spy stuff. How did that work? Searching further, she found a French military site. What she saw there made her sit up. France had its own version of Echelon: "Big Ears," dubbed "Frenchelon." She searched for twenty minutes until she discovered a short article in the left-leaning *Le Nouvel Observateur* indicating that Frenchelon had the capacity to process two million phone calls, faxes, and e-mails each month. Or more. It was even rumored to be capable of tracking individual bank accounts.

Her phone rang. "Leduc Detective," she said.

"*Bonjour*, I'm calling from Varnet and we're interested in your proposal. Can you answer some questions?"

She switched gears as she shuffled through the pile on her desk. "Of course. Your proposal's right here and I'm delighted to help you."

She spent the next half hour walking the Varnet manager through Leduc's proposal, clarifying information as to the computer-security service they offered. And the next two hours running the programs waiting in her laptop. By the time René appeared, she'd worked three hours and updated all the accounts on their database.

"We're current, René," she said. "Rent paid and twenty-three francs in the bank! How's that for being in the black?"

"At least Saj will work for food," René said, hanging up his camel wool coat on the rack.

Saj, from the Hacktaviste academy where René taught, hacked part-time for them.

"This should help," he said, setting down a check from Cereus.

Wonderful. Thank God, it covered René's paycheck. If their clients paid on time, they'd have six figures to join the twenty-three francs, but that would be a miracle.

"Varnet's interested; I think we've got a new client."

Instead of being relieved, he appeared worried.

"What's the matter, René?"

"No sign of Paul or his mother at their apartment. I checked twice yesterday *and* last night."

A bad feeling came over her.

"Did they do a runner?"

"Hard to say."

"We need his statement. The autopsy found one bullet but your little friend Paul saw another flash. But for him to skip school—"

"Paul's nine years old, he's lonely, and his mother's alcoholic!" he said. "Where would they go?"

"We look until we find them," she said. "Dig up your Toulouse-Lautrec outfit."

"He knows I'm not Toulouse-Lautrec, Aimée."

"Don't give up. We not only have to find them but we must convince his mother to let him talk to Maître Delambre."

"I'll need your help for that, Aimée," he said.

"But our first priority is to review the lab findings on the gun residue found on Laure's hands. Right now I have to corral Maître Delambre. Find out what's holding up the lab report."

René rolled his eyes.

"I need to do this for Laure. You with me, partner?"

"If we do it together," he said.

Her eye fell on the underground Paris map tacked to the office wall. Orange and pink delineated the old quarries and limestone formations in the eighteenth and fourteenth arrondissements. She pulled out her cell phone. Affixed the broken antenna.

René's mouth turned down. "That's the third phone in—"

"I've got a mirror in it."

"Always the fashionista!"

"Listen, last night I spoke to the prostitute on that beat. According to her, a Corsican goes into that building regularly." She pointed to the diagram she'd made. "He's crude and she doesn't like him. She saw this Corsican talking with Jacques in Zette's bar. There's some connection."

"Connection? Most likely she was telling you what she thought you wanted to hear."

She shrugged. "And I think Sarti, the musician, who went to Conari's party and left before being questioned, knows something."

"Suspicions, ideas. That's all you've got," René said.

Aimée stared at the map of the wall, at the limestone

formations of Montmartre, orange and kidney shaped, that spread over the area. "Sarti stood right here, I saw him." She pointed, lost in thought, looking for a link. "Yet the diagram Yann Marant found—"

"Marant, the systems analyst from Conari's party?" René interrupted.

Aimée nodded. "Good memory, René. He is the consultant to Conari's construction firm. He found a diagram, like a floor plan, in a nearby Dumpster."

"Since when do systems analysts work with contractors?" René took out a linen handkerchief with his initials, RF, embroidered on the edge, and blew his nose. "The sure way to catch a cold, coming out of the Metro to a hot office!" He blew his nose again. "Conari's firm must have Ministry contracts."

"Why do you say that?"

"Having a systems analyst is a government requirement. Look in the guidelines. We'd need one, too, if we did Ministry work."

"René! You're not suggesting we angle for Ministry work?"

Before he could answer, she pointed to the piles of paper on her desk. "Look, we *have* work, and will have *more* work from the proposals we've sent out. You know our problem's with negligent clients who take forever to pay." Corporations were notorious for delaying payment to independent contractors.

"It's either collect or do a *créance*," René said. "Which invites another kind of trouble."

She knew all too well that the *créance*, a loan made by a bank against the borrower's pledge of accounts receivable plus a ten percent commission, spelled trouble. When a bank collected, firms would notice and figure it reflected Leduc Detective's financial difficulties.

"True, René, but we're not there yet."

Not quite. She took a deep breath, counted to five. They had to get back on track. She drew a quick sketch, replicating the diagram she'd turned over to Bordereau.

"Look at what Yann's diagram showed. Supposedly, the bombs were set here, in the Mairie, by Corsican Separatists, where there are Xs on this diagram."

René's mouth dropped. "Bombs?"

"Defused before they could go off. My DST contact confirmed it. What if Jacques had an informer who knew about the plan or—"

"Defused when?"

"Sunday night."

"Jacques was murdered Monday night," René said. "Nice try."

Deflated, Aimée stared at the map. Thought hard.

"Correct." She wouldn't give up that quickly. "Suppose Jacques knew of a backup terrorist plan and met an informer to try to discover the next target. My DST connection also mentioned a data-encryption leak," she said. "Suppose there's a connection."

"*Flics* don't buy suppositions," René said.

Aimée nodded.

"I fished around for Big Ears and data-encryption leaks and found Frenchelon. Want to help me?"

"Ask Saj," René said. "Last year, he designed those 'nasty little ciphers,' as the Ministry called them, to retool security in the Bankverein Swiss bank scam. Remember?"

Bankverein Swiss had lost millions of francs to hackers but kept it quiet to avoid customer panic. And covered it with their reserves. A mere dent, financial analysts concluded, in the bank's hefty assets.

She'd call Saj later.

René took the Varnet folder. "Shall I follow up with a visit?"

"Before they change their mind? Good idea. Take this contract form with you and sign them up." She paused. "What happened with your date?"

He looked away. "That's for me to know and you to find out. Meanwhile, here's the refund notice from the tax office. Finally!"

"Bravo, René!"

He surprised her all the time. It had taken a year and René's tenacious determination to wade through paperwork issued by a string of offices to obtain their refund.

"Don't celebrate yet. Now I have to reach the bureaucrat who dispenses refunds. He's been out with gallbladder problems. But then we will be able to afford the new laptops we need."

She stood up and hugged him, caught the pride in his eyes and the pink on his cheeks before he turned away. René blushing?

"Get the refund, partner, and they're yours. And more. You can impress your girlfriend."

"Then I better get going," René said, reaching back for his coat.

"Me, too."

Out in the hallway she realized she'd forgotten to stop at the accounting firm next door for an envelope that had been left there according to the delivery notice.

"Go ahead, René," she told him.

"How are you, Diza?" Aimée said to the receptionist. "Got something for me?"

Diza, wearing a tight green wool skirt, fuchsia floral-print silk shirt, and knockoff agnès b. jacket, balanced a tray of espressos from the café below. Though she was in her forties, she dressed young and carried it off. Most of the time.

"On my desk, Mademoiselle Aimée," she said, grinning. "Coffee time for the boys."

The "boys" she referred to were none of them under sixty.

Aimée slit open a manila envelope with her name printed on it in block letters. Several grainy black-and-white photos fell out. The kind made at night with a long-distance tele-photo lens. They showed two women standing on a street. She looked closer and recognized Cloclo and herself in conversation. Her stomach clenched. Two more photos showed René with a woman with spiky hair. Herself or . . . ?

"Such a nice photo of you and Monsieur René," Diza said, peering over her shoulder. "You two were having fun. That's good. Nice to see Monsieur René smiling."

"*Alors*, Diza, it's not me."

"Looks just like you, Mademoiselle Aimée," Diza said.

"So she does, Diza," Aimée said, nonplussed. Spikey hair, heels and all: René's new girlfriend, Magali, resembled her!

"Diza, how did this envelope arrive?"

"By messenger. You know, the ones who ride like madmen on their bikes. One almost ran me over yesterday."

"Can you describe him?"

Diza grinned. "Let's see, black cap, down jacket, you know the big kind that puffs out, jeans. Like all of them."

"Yellow teeth?"

"Come to think of it," she said, dropping a sugar cube into one of the espressos, "yes."

The *mec* from the phone booth who'd chased her through the Marché Saint Pierre! The photos meant, We know who you are and we're watching you.

Aimée ran down the stairs out onto rain-slicked rue du Louvre. She caught René before he stepped into a waiting taxi at the curb.

"René, look at these photos. We're being watched."

René set his briefcase on the taxi seat and thumbed through them, a tight smile on his face.

"I didn't think stalkers went after men," he said.

AIMÉE PACED in the cavernous marble-floored Tribunal. It was crowded with scurrying lawyers, their black robes trailing, and with defendants knotted in earnest discussion; the smell of cold stone and wet wool lingered in the corners. She peeked through the oval window of the courtroom's oak door. Four robed judges sat on a dais—more oak—one leaned back, her eyes closed.

A minute later, Maître Delambre came through the door. His cheek was swollen and his arms loaded with dossiers. He'd survived the dentist's chair, it seemed.

He pursed his lips when he saw her.

"Those *mecs* are still following me," she said, keeping her voice calm with effort.

"Better mind your own business, Mademoiselle Leduc. A difficult task for you, I'm sure," he said, shifting the pile of dossiers to his other arm. "Laure's case looks open and shut. Guilty."

"What do you mean? You don't even have the lab report."

"It came this morning," he interrupted her, pulling out a sheet. "The report confirms the preliminary finding of gunshot residue on her hands. None on yours, however."

It didn't make sense. How could Laure? Why would she?

"Why the delay?" She thought fast. "Wouldn't that indicate issues as to inaccuracy or as to procedures? May I see this report?"

He handed it to her. "According to the lab, they've experienced an unusually high frequency of cases. A big backlog. But the GSR test results are clear, and damning."

She scanned the report, shaking her head.

"That's all?"

"It's in black and white. What more do you want?"

She looked closer. "It says here the detailed lab analysis will follow. Where is it?"

Maître Delambre expelled a breath of disgust, then rifled in his briefcase. "Hmmm, percentages, element and metal composition. *Voilà*."

Aimée studied the paper. Checked the numbers. Her mind reeled. "Gunshot residue's composed of lead, barium, and antimony."

"So you're an expert on this, too," Maître Delambre said. "Mademoiselle Leduc of the many talents."

"I own a gun—licensed, of course," she said. "All bullets contain lead, barium, and antimony." She pointed to one of the columns of numbers. "Few bullets contain *this*."

He leaned over her shoulder. "The expert found a problem?"

She ignored his sarcasm.

"A very high tin content. Ninety-eight percent. That's unusual," she said. "Do you have another copy of this report?"

He handed her one.

She studied it. "Demand a retest. These lab findings are crucial!"

Maître Delambre ran his fingers through his sparse hair. "Look, I'm sorry. The lab performed its function, which is to show the presence, or absence, of GSR. And from these findings, a GSR presence has been clearly demonstrated. As far as the *flics* are concerned, and I'd have to concur, this indicates she fired the gun that killed her partner. Internal Affairs has an open-and-shut case. I can't help her."

Something was very wrong. "That's not good enough. Nothing makes sense unless she was set up," Aimée said. "The gunshot residue must have come from another gun, one with high tin content in its ammunition."

"You raise an interesting point. But it's moot."

"Ask yourself this: she could have taken care of her partner much more easily and made it seem like an accident, so who set her up and why?"

"As far as I can see it's over," he told her. "She and her partner argued in the presence of a whole barful of witnesses. Internal Affairs gave her the option of working with me, an outside lawyer, an unheard-of courtesy, but in the light of this evidence, they're taking over. As they should have in the beginning. Someone pulled some strings to get her outside representation but this is now internal police business. Not mine."

So Morbier had tried to help Laure.

"Please, demand another lab test to be carried out in your

presence. Ask questions about the high tin content of the residue. I doubt if anyone's been convicted on the evidence of gun residue alone. Find out. You don't want to lose one of your first cases, do you?"

He rocked on the heels of his shiny black shoes.

Aimée persevered. "The ammo from a *flic*'s weapon is composed of three elements. *No* tin. Any *flic* will tell you that. You have to demand another test, compare these results with a bullet fired from a Manhurin."

"I know she's your friend but I'm afraid—"

"Delambre, what a *coup* for you!" she said. "What appeared an open-and-shut case turned upside down by the lawyer who insisted on a thorough ballistics test. You'd make your reputation."

He blinked. She could tell he hadn't thought of that.

"You'd show the old-school types a thing or two," she said. "La Proc's always looking for new go-getters for her team, believe me."

She didn't know that for sure but figured it sounded good.

He was wavering.

"Boris Viard runs the lab. He's good. Talk to him." She'd almost convinced Delambre, she smelled it. "What have you got to lose but a case that no one thinks you'll win anyway? Try Viard."

"Let me think about it," he said.

"Did you use the police reports I found?"

"According to the Code Civil they belonged in my client's dossier," he said. "Article . . . well, that's legalese. You're right. But their appearance caused surprise in several quarters."

She balled her hands in her pockets feeling the absence of Guy's ring. "Which ones?"

"Let's talk over here," he said, gesturing her behind a pillar.

Drafts whipped past her black stockings. She shivered, wishing the cold from the stone floor didn't travel up her legs.

Maître Delambre cocked his head. "Internal Affairs expressed halfhearted dismay, but soon shut up."

"In surprise or dismay?"

He grinned. "Why, since I hadn't noticed these before, as I informed the inspector, I commended the bureau for its efficiency in updating me."

Not so green after all.

"Isn't Ludovic Jubert head of Internal Affairs now?" she said, trying a hunch.

Maître Delambre paused and shook his head. "No, but that name sounds familiar."

She'd checked several branches in the RG and Ministry directory but none listed officers' names. She'd run into a dead end at every turn.

"I'm convinced another gun was fired that night."

A black-robed magistrate clapped Delambre on the shoulder as he walked past.

"We have a witness," she told the lawyer.

"Then this witness needs to come forward." He shook his head. "Still, as the gunshot residue was found on her hands, I don't know how effective such testimony would be in the Internal Affairs investigation."

Panic hit her. "The witness is a boy. He's still in school."

"Minors can be subpoenaed under the law."

"Wait," she said. "He'll come to you of his own accord."

"And finding a second gun would help," Delambre said.

Of course it would. And knowing the identities of the men who had been on the roof, too.

"I'm working on it."

He bundled the files in his briefcase. "Time for my next trial, excuse me."

"Please call the lab to request another test. All it would take is a phone call."

He rubbed his cheek and winced. "I've stuck my neck out far

enough already." He checked his watch. "My next client's waiting. I'm sorry."

Disappointed, she fingered the office keys in her pocket and shook her head. "Me, too."

She'd have to do it all herself.

Late Thursday Afternoon

IF ANOTHER BULLET EXISTED, she had to find it. Back in the office she located her jumpsuit in the armoire and stuffed it into her bag along with a tool kit. By the time she reached the building on rue André Antoine, she'd controlled her apprehension and had a story ready. The photo of her and Cloclo had been taken right outside this building. She had to forget that. There was no sign of Cloclo there now.

"You again," the concierge said, as she swept the cold hallway. Today she wore a housedress with a blue smock over it, but still had on rain boots. "The apartment's been sealed by the police. No access is allowed."

"You're right," Aimée said. She showed the concierge a work order she'd typed up. "It's the skylight this time. Mind letting me get to work? My partner's out sick and I've got three other calls to make."

A dog barked from the concierge loge. "Let me see that." She read the work order. "Men came yesterday for this. I had to vacuum the hall again, double my work. You've wasted a trip. A mistake."

The killers back looking for the bullet? Or the true locksmiths? "Louis and Antoine?" she asked the concierge.

"Eh? I'm not on a first-name basis with all the workers who traipse through here, Mademoiselle."

"A *mec* with bleached white hair?"

The concierge's brow furrowed. She shook her head.

"Aaah, then Antoine. A black cap, down jacket, and bad teeth?"

"I'm not sure," she said. "Check with your dispatch office but I tell you the work's been done."

The dog barked louder, its nails scratching against the closed loge door. "If you don't mind—"

"Madame, you must have heard the skylight break that night."

"I've had enough questions. Like I told the *flics*, there was a storm."

For a nosy concierge she hadn't noticed much.

"It says right here to fix the rear-hall skylight on the third floor," Aimée said, holding out the form. "The least you can do is let me check it out."

The concierge shushed her dog, set the broom against the wall, and put her hands on her ample hips. "Keep your hair on, Mademoiselle, I'm only doing my job."

"Same here," Aimée said. "I take it you have no problem with me going up to see if the rear skylight's secured while you feed your dog, who's jumping out of his skin with hunger?" Blame it on the dog; that might work.

A guilty look crossed the concierge's face. "Since you insist."

Aimée pushed past her. "Excuse me."

She had to work fast. On the third floor she set down the tool kit. What if those guys had already found the bullet? If they were the shooters, it would be gone. But if they were just hired goons, as she hoped, she had a chance. They'd have been searching just as she was. Maybe they hadn't been lucky. Maybe she would be.

One way to find out.

A frieze of carved rosettes and leaves framed the ceiling, thick with years of coats of paint. A table saw and planks of wood stood near the skylight. All the apartments on this floor were being remodeled. The vacant one's door was now barred

by a red-wax police seal. A perfect secret meeting place. Yet
instead, Jacques had been lured up to the roof.

With both hands she dragged the table under the skylight,
climbed on top, reached up, and felt for the hasp.

Downstairs, the dog barked louder. She heard the
concierge's voice speaking to someone on the telephone, then
her footsteps mounting the stairs.

Aimée turned the hasp and pushed with both hands. The
heavy skylight opened a few inches. Wind swirled inside, carrying gravel and grit, spitting at her face. She gave another
heave and the skylight fell back, opening to the sky.

She stretched her arms up, hooked her elbows over the
frame, jumped up, and wiggled her hips through the opening.

She pulled herself onto the roof, now covered in a layer of gray
slush. The flat area of the roof looked much smaller in the late
afternoon light. The slate tiles ascended, angled every which way
like children's blocks. The roof overlooked the street and faced
the building where she figured Paul must live. He would have
had a perfect view. The church's high roof blocked visibility from
all other sides. No wonder no other witnesses had come forward.

Here she was, climbing on a roof, and she'd promised herself, never again. Yet she *had* to find the other bullet. She must
keep her gaze focused ahead of her. And not look down.

Her foot slipped and she grabbed a metal pipe. She closed
her eyes, inhaled, then exhaled. Her fingers scraped against
the cold rough metal and her heart felt ready to jump out of
her chest. Again she inhaled, exhaled, concentrating on her
breathing, imagining a white light as her sessions at the Cao
Dai temple had taught her. Trying to ignore the brisk wind.

She repeated the routine ten times, until her nose tingled
with cold. She opened her eyes, calmer, and tried to visualize
that Monday night: the sleeting wind, drifting snow, and the
flat spot where Jacques's body lay.

She edged across the tiles to the tall chimney that she and

Sebastian had climbed over, reached out, and found the spot she remembered. She ran her hands over the rough pock-marked stucco that flaked between her fingers. Wrong, the place she'd felt was smooth. She slid, leaning against the chimney, to its rear, gripping the ledge with one hand, the other tracing the smooth wall.

Aimée's fingers found an indentation. Circular, the size of her pinkie tip. Her breath came fast as she pulled herself around. Below her feet lay the leaf-clogged gutter, and then, several floors down, the street. Perspiration beaded her forehead. She pulled out her penlight. Saw a charcoal-powder sunburst in the midst of white-gray-caked pigeon droppings.

"Mademoiselle, please come down." The concierge's voice whipped by her in the wind.

Had the concierge climbed up and poked her head out the skylight? Didn't she have anything better to do?

"*Un moment*, my tool bag fell," Aimée shouted back.

Her penlight revealed the copper gold stub end of an embedded bullet.

"You've made a mistake, Mademoiselle," the concierge said. "What are you doing up there?"

Exasperated, Aimée blew air from her mouth and felt the perspiration dripping from her forehead.

"Madame, go back downstairs. I'll join you in a moment."

"The office said—"

"Madame, *attention*, it's dangerous. Don't come up here."

Aimée heard the skylight shut. She had no time to waste. She needed to gouge out the bullet before the concierge returned with the *flics*. She felt her foot sliding and hugged the wall, terror stricken. Bits of gravel fell from the roof and she looked down, hearing horns and shouts.

The gravel rained over a stalled truck in the street.

Big mistake. She shouldn't have looked down. Her stomach felt queasy. Crippling fear overwhelmed her.

Concentrate. She had to push it aside, and concentrate.

She took the miniscrewdriver from her tool kit, chipped at the stone surrounding the bullet, then with a swift turn gouged it out. She caught the bullet, scooped it into a Baggie, and put it into her pocket. Shaking, leaning against the wall, she felt her way down.

By the time she made it back to the skylight, opened it, and slid back into the hall below, her hands had steadied.

She grabbed her bag, shoved the table into its place, and met the concierge on the stairs. "Madame, everything's taken care of here," she said. "I'm leaving now."

"I checked with the locksmith office; the woman has no record."

"Schizophrenic! That new woman's schizophrenic." Aimée rushed past her. "I guess I have the afternoon off."

FROM THE Metro station she called Viard at the Laboratoire Central de la Préfecture de Police and arranged to meet him. Trying to control her excitement, she ran all the way to the police lab situated near Parc Georges Brassens. At the brown-red brick building she caught her breath and showed her police ID, an updated version she'd made from her father's.

She found Viard in the basement firing range. Shredded black figures on white paper hung from a wire. From the starburst shots centered in the figures' stomachs and hearts she figured he practiced every day.

"Not bad," she said. "You know what the customs officials say?"

"Our black-figured targets differ from their white ones, which shows our priorities?"

She grinned. "You said it, not me. I've got a puzzle for you to solve."

"Make it good," Viard said, returning the SIG Sauer automatic to a drawer and pulling off his safety goggles and earmuff headgear. He ran the ballistics lab and he owed Aimée. She'd introduced him to René's apartment neighbor, Michou, a female impersonator who worked in a Les Halles club. Last month Michou and Viard had celebrated six months together, a record for him, and they had invited Aimée and René to their anniversary dinner.

"Can you tell if a bullet's responsible for the GSR in this report?"

She handed him a copy of the lab report she'd gotten from Maître Delambre. "Viard, notice the ninety-eight percent tin content in this column. Anyone who's loaded a Manhurin knows that gun doesn't fire high-tin-content bullets."

"Of course. I also see that residues were found on the subject's hands," he said.

"Let's talk in your office," Aimée suggested.

His office, on the second floor, held a standard-issue metal desk and bookshelves crammed with ballistic and gun manuals; the floor was covered with a nondescript fawn carpet. In contrast, by a curtained window, were shelves crowded with orchid plants. Exquisite and delicate in appearance, they were rooted in fir bark, peat moss, pearlite, and lime. Their petals were colored all hues of purple, from light violet to a deep almost indigo. Others were yellow, some white. They were like butterflies caught in midflight.

"You've gotten more orchids."

He nodded. "Mexican and South American varieties like these Phragmipediums thrive in indirect sunlight," he said, picking up a spray bottle and misting them.

Did Viard tend his orchids to find a beauty absent in his work? She noticed the lines around his mouth were deeper, his brow's crease more pronounced. Did staying in the closet wear on him?

Above his desk hung gun-show posters and a colored spectrum showing the trail of magnified bullets, arced like rainbows.

She took the Baggie out of her pocket and dangled it in front of him. "I'm not a betting person, but a franc says the GSR in this report came from this.

"A franc?"

"I'll throw in a bottle of Château Margaux."

He whistled, incredulous. "Do you know how much these tests cost to run, Aimée?"

She shook her head. "As a taxpayer, I pay for it."

"You and a few others. Listen, my department's budget couldn't absorb this. Or even Internal Affairs'."

Was that why Delambre had rejected her idea? He knew they didn't budget for special tests? And procedure didn't call for it?

"So Internal Affairs covers the costs?"

"Most of it, but only the basic test. Standard procedure, end of story." He shook his head as he kept on misting the orchids. "You know I'd help if I could. It's impossible. I'm sorry."

She had an idea. It might work.

"But, Viard, the Ministry's involved. In tandem with Internal Affairs. Didn't I mention that?" She knew there was a link there somehow. Right now she didn't know where. That could wait. "I just assumed you knew."

"Ministry of the Interior?" He shrugged, set down the spray bottle, and checked his desk. "I haven't received any requisition or paperwork."

"Let's see, what was the name . . . the man responsible?" She ran her fingers through her spiky hair, glanced at the piled-up SIG Sauer pistol manuals. "Starts with a J. Jubert, that's it. Ludovic Jubert."

He nodded. "In that case. Well . . ."

She tried not to show surprise, eager to find out which office Jubert worked in.

"I forget which division he's in."

Viard stared at the lab report. "There's an incompatibility

between a Manhurin bullet's residue and the GSR on the officer's hands?"

"Incompatibility, yes. Also, please test to see if this bullet's tin content is compatible with the GSR on the officer's hands."

She hoped she'd left enough residue traces on the wall from which she'd pried the bullet for the *flics* to find later.

"Well, if the Ministry's paying . . ." His eyes lit up and he pulled out a requisition form. "I suppose, in lieu of the requisition, I could note *approval en route*."

"Wonderful idea," she said.

Despite her eagerness to pinpoint Jubert's location, right now she mustn't deflect Viard from running the test, or raise his suspicions by asking how to reach Jubert.

Viard slipped latex gloves on and took the Baggie from her. She'd hooked him.

"What's the white stuff?"

"A gift from the pigeon gods."

"Aaah *merci* . . . fascinating," he said, pulling goggles from his desk drawer. His voice had changed, it was higher. Excitement vibrated in it. "High tin content is a signature of the Eastern European models hitting the marketplace these days."

Something resonated in the back of her mind. Bordereau's words. Think. "You mean the Eastern European arms used by the Armata Corsa?"

She could swear he almost rubbed his gloved hands in glee. "After the Bucharest conference last year, I've been dying to try this." He stared at the dull copper-nub-nosed bullet. "I'd say it's a Bulgarian make but let me run a test I saw performed on a Sellier-Bellot."

AT LEAST Jubert's department would foot the bill for tests run on a Sellier-Bellot, whatever that was. She liked that it was expensive and that Viard had fairly salivated to carry it out. She felt it in her bones—she'd exonerate Laure. And find the culprit.

Time weighed heavily. It would be hours, maybe a day, before Viard got back to her with the results. In the meantime she had to deal with questions she'd put aside.

She exited the Les Halles station and found an Internet café with cane-bottomed stools and posters advertising the Chatelet ethnic music festival papering the walls. The steady beat of trance music competed with the whoosh of the milk steamer. She slid ten francs to a doe-eyed waitress in flared paisley pants, found a vacant terminal, and logged online. First, she trawled the net for Ludovic Jubert's name in the Ministry system. Once again, she found nothing.

It was time to address the feeling she'd sensed behind Zoe Tardou's hesitant answers, her frightened manner. She'd meant to revisit her earlier—this reclusive medieval scholar who lived in an elegant Deco apartment across from where Jacques was murdered.

The geranium stem. Had Madame Tardou witnessed the murder when she was watering the flowers in her window box and kept silent out of fear? She had mentioned overhearing the names of planets, spoken in another language from the roof. Corsican? And she had let slip that she had spent time in an orphanage. An anomaly struck Aimée. If Zoe was the step-daughter of the well-known Surrealist Max Tardou, why would she have lived in an orphanage? How did that fit?

If something itched, scratch it, her father had said. She had to probe deeper. What better place to start than online.

She searched under Surrealism and Max Tardou, finding an array of Web sites. She plowed through them. Tardou, a well-known painter, had fled the Occupation to Portugal at the onset of World War II. So much for his later claims of fighting in the Résistance. According to a Surrealist Web site, Zoe's mother, Elise, had met him after the war.

She searched further. She found photos of Elise; one in pro-file, taken at a Montmartre Dadaist ball. It showed a crowd in turbans and bowler hats with the Greek letter π painted on their faces. Another showed Elise backlit, her blonde hair pulled high on her head in a halo effect, her mandarin eyes slanted with kohl, draped in a cloak of her own design. A striking woman, renowned for her Dadaist poetry.

Unable to find more current information, Aimée was about to exit, when she noticed a cross-reference. This one listed the name Elise Tardou in a 1980s documentary film about Lebensborn. Strange. Was it the same Elise Tardou? Lebensborn referred to the Nazi stud-farm program to propagate Aryans. It had been established in Norway, Germany, and occupied Europe. Even a member of the seventies group ABBA was listed in the documentary as a child of the Lebensborn. What was the connection here? Was there one?

She downed her espresso and read further. Château Menier, outside Paris in Lamorlaye, bordered the only Lebensborn site in France. Aimée hadn't known one existed. She was shocked. She read further. The article quoted an excerpt from the account of Elise Tardou, identified as a Dadaist poet, about her captivity there in 1944. What Aimée read astounded her.

"There were French women in the château, though not many," Elise was quoted as saying. "Few admit it. The shame. It wasn't our choice, we were captives. Most of the women were prisoners from Poland, and blue-eyed Hungarians. They had a nursery, ran it like a birthing factory."

Nineteen forty-four. Zoe looked to be in her fifties. A terrible idea entered Aimée's mind. She printed out the page. And then located an article on a summer art colony, the haunt of the old Surrealist icons in the sixties. It had been located in Corsica.

Corsica! According to an article she'd read previously, the Tardous had spent their holidays in Corsica every August. For years.

She'd caught Zoe Tardou in a lie. Now she thought she knew why. She had to test her theory.

* * *

"MADAME TARDOU!" she said, knocking on Zoe Tardou's door.

No answer.

After five minutes of knocking, when her knuckles were sore, the door opened a crack.

"I spoke with you the other day, remember? You had a miserable cold," Aimée said. "I hope you're feeling better. I brought you some Ricola cough drops."

"That's very kind."

Aimée put the cough-drop box into Zoe's hands, noticed the blond-gray hair pulled into a bun, her slim figure under the wool sweater. The striking aqua blue eyes.

"May I come in?"

"I answered your questions," Madame Tardou said. "I won't go to the police station."

Again, that fear of the outside. Agoraphobia?

Aimée put her boot into the doorway. "I just need to clarify a detail, to remove it from the inquiry. That's all."

Hesitantly, Zoe opened the door wider. "You're persistent, Mademoiselle," she said, "but I have nothing more to say."

"Please, this won't take any time at all. You'll see." Aimée edged past her and kept walking toward the large room filled with Deco furniture. The room with black blankets hanging over the windows. She felt in her bag for her hairbrush.

Zoe Tardou, reading glasses perched on her chapped nose, stood with a red pencil in her hand. "I'm copyediting proofs on my treatise, you see. I can spare you only a moment."

Aimée paused to look at the photos on the grand piano. Studied them.

"You spent summers in Corsica, Madame Tardou, didn't you?"

"Is that a crime?"

"Corsica, L'Ile de Beauté. Yet you told me you summered in Italy."

"We went to Italy, too."

Aimée nodded. "Your stepfather, Max Tardou, established an art colony in Bonifacio where he tried to resurrect Surrealism. You went there for years while you were growing up."

Aimée ran her palm over the smooth blond wood case of the piano. She pointed to a photo. A black-and-white scene of sunbathers with an awninged café in the background.

"Café Bonifacio. It's still there."

"What does this have to do with anything?"

"You understand Corsican. And you speak it, don't you?"

Zoe Tardou's fingers twisted the red pencil back and forth. "I was only a child."

"Even as a teenager you must have summered in Corsica," Aimée said. "You may even have attended a Corsican school."

"Yes, I did. How does that matter?"

She'd admitted it!

Aimée moved closer to the woman.

The pencil snapped between Zoe's fingers.

"The voices you heard from the roof spoke Corsican, didn't they? You understood them, recognized the names of the planets and constellations."

Fear shone in those compelling blue eyes. She pushed the glasses up on her nose with trembling fingers.

"Maybe . . . yes . . . I'm not sure."

"Think. They spoke Corsican. Exactly what did they say?"

Zoe covered her glasses with her hands, then looked up and nodded. "Yes. But it had been so long ago since I heard that language. From another lifetime."

"Why couldn't you tell me?" Aimée said, controlling her excitement.

"It was so strange to hear Corsican, I thought I was dreaming, I was unsure—"

"You looked out, pretending to be watering your geraniums," Aimée interrupted. "That's natural. You understood what they said. It was quiet, as the storm hadn't erupted yet."

Aimée paused. Waited. "It's all right, we're telling the truth now," Aimée said, her tone soothing, urging. "Accounting for all the details, clearing this up, eh? Most investigative work depends on the tedious details, checking and rechecking."

Zoe watched her. Unmoving. An aroma of *herbes de Provence* and something roasting, Mediterranean style, wafted from the kitchen. Wonderful. Aimée's stomach growled.

Aimée sighed. "Nothing glamorous in this, believe me." She tried for a matter-of-fact voice. "Did you hear the glass break in the skylight?"

Zoe shook her head.

"Yet you recognized the men on the roof."

"But I—" She covered her mouth with her hands, again that little-girl manner, as if she had been caught in a fault.

"—got scared?" Aimée finished for her.

Zoe Tardou nodded.

"Who did you recognize?"

"No trouble, I can't have trouble," Zoe said, putting her hands up like a shield and stepping back. "I can't get involved. Now, I've got something cooking on the stove. . . ."

The smell of thyme was stronger now.

"All I need is a name." Aimée smiled and reached for a notepad in her leather backpack.

"I don't know his name. The one I recognized—anyway, it doesn't mean he shot anyone."

"Of course not, you're right. But he can help us find the one who did, don't you see? We need your help."

Zoe Tardou hesitated.

"Does he live here?"

"I've seen him on the stairs, but I don't know him."

"What does he look like?"

"He had bleached hair the last I saw him. He changes it. I don't really know, I don't think he lives here."

Aimée wrote in her notepad.

"But he could work in the building? Or for someone who does live here?"

Zoe shrugged. "He's too coarse."

Was this the *mec* Cloclo had referred to? Or just a workman, like Theo, who had offended her delicate sensibility?

"Coarse? You mean he was a construction worker? One of the men doing the remodeling?"

"He was not a workman. He made rude comments. But he was dressed in designer black. *Trendy.*"

"A young man?"

"I didn't pay attention."

"What about the other man?"

"Just his back, that's all I saw."

"Did you hear the gunshot or see the flash?"

Madame Tardou shook her head. "When I heard voices talking about constellations . . . what they said was mixed up with words that didn't fit."

"What did you hear?"

"I didn't tell you before because it doesn't make sense." Zoe paused, rubbed her cheek.

"Go on, it's all right," Aimée said, trying to control her impatience.

"They said '*turrente*,' a stream; '*parolle*,' which means 'words,' but it didn't make sense or seem to mean anything. They spoke about planets and streams. No, there was more . . . that's right . . . *cincá*, searching for, searching, they said 'searching.'"

Planets and streams and searching, talking about Corsica, and then murder? "You're sure?"

"Corsicans don't articulate, they swallow the consonants at

the ends of words." Zoe's gaze settled on her piled desk. "They did repeat the old saying, that I recognized."

"Which is?"

"*Corsica audra di male in peglyu.*" She shook her head. "'Corsica will always go wrong,' typical of their pessimism tinged with pride." Zoe shrugged, spent. As if she'd run out of things to say. "My head ached, I felt miserable. I lay down and must have fallen asleep watching the *télé*. That's all."

Aimée believed her, but she had to check.

"What show did you watch?"

"Show? An old Sherlock Holmes film. Too bad I missed the ending. Now I must work," she said, eager for Aimée to leave. "I don't know any more."

"There's something else," Aimée said. How could she phrase this? "I admire your mother. It takes a courageous woman to speak of Lamorlaye, and the Lebensborn. Why did she finally . . . ?"

"Talk about her captivity? The way they used the women?" Zoe asked, all in one breath. And for a moment, Aimée saw the same wistful gaze she'd noted in the photo of Elise.

Aimée nodded.

"The past was too heavy to bear any longer, Maman said. When the filmmaker approached her, she felt it was time. Nothing that horrible was worth all that effort of conceal-ment, my mother said."

"That took such courage."

"And the odd thing was: after that, she wrote poetry again. It was as if the weight of her history had lifted."

"I respect her for speaking out," Aimée said.

Zoe's brows knitted in anger. "My stepfather didn't," she said. "He threw her out and tried to disinherit me, but he died before he could."

"To disinherit you because you were fathered by a German?" Aimée asked.

"Those twenty-fifth-hour Résistants who watched the Occupation from afar turn out the most heroic of all!"

"I'm sorry." Aimée didn't know what else to say.

"Sorry?" She gave a short laugh. "So were the women, so are we, the children. Children of the enemy. Raised in guilt for who we were. Our very existence was the cause of shame. Whether I was too young, or just misplaced in the chaos of the German retreat in 1944 I'll never know, but I wasn't transported to Germany like the others," she continued. "My mother found me in the room with telescopes, an observatory adjacent to the château that had been turned into an orphanage. I was lucky. Others displaced at the war's end were reared in group homes with hardly any food or nurturing, ostracized for their background, and became misfits. Bereft of parents who never searched for them, either dead or lost or wanting to forget, many ended up in mental institutions. At least, I found my biological father, alive after all this time."

Aimée stared, incredulous. "Did you meet him?"

"A sad old gentleman living in Osnabrück. He remembered my mother. After the war, he'd owned a pharmacy," she said, with a small smile. "He'd studied medieval history at university."

Thursday Evening

ONCE OUTSIDE, AIMÉE BELTED her leather coat. Zoe's words haunted her. No wonder she avoided the authorities. Her story didn't seem to help but at least she'd admitted hearing words spoken in Corsican. Aimée scanned the alleylike street. No Cloclo. No *mec* with a down jacket.

How could she warn Cloclo her "station" was being watched?

Aimée climbed the stairs to Place des Abbesses. There, CRS teams in blue jumpsuits cradling Uzis strolled the streets. This signaled a definite terrorist alert. She felt a tightening in her chest. What was going on?

She entered a warm café and picked up a paper to see if she could find out. She sat at the window overlooking the steps leading to the alley, a perfect vantage point from which to watch for Cloclo.

She rubbed her gloved hand over the fogged-up glass. More worries assailed her. Cloclo bore a grudge against the "crude" *mec,* the one Zoe Tardou had just described. She might say something to get rid of him. Yet if Cloclo did speak to him, Aimée would be ready and only seconds away.

Several young men, unemployed judging by the time of day, played at the Fussball machine. Aimée ordered a *croque-monsieur* from a waitress with red rose tattoos up her arm.

Outside, passersby scurried through the gray evening light just sinking behind the eroding stone buildings. Mist lingered over the steps. Aimée tried to avoid the predatory gaze of a man in black denims and a blue turtleneck near the Fussball machine. She tapped her feet to the beat of the radio's techno station and opened the newspaper to the headlines to read: COUNTERTERRORISM POLICE DISCOVER EXPLOSIVES TRACED TO ARMATA CORSA.

Her shoulders tensed. That accounted for the CRS presence outside in the square. And for a moment, she was afraid. Another building mined with explosives?

She read the article: "Today a special counterterrorism unit, acting on a tip, found a cache of detonators and explosives in a government building."

A grainy photo showed a dismantled detonating device.

She read further.

Corsica has been plagued since 1975 by almost daily machine-gun-nings and other attacks by a small but active, nationalist movement. Favored venues for Separatist attacks have been on the island of Corsica, and rarely in France until now. Most bombings have been designed to minimize risk to human life but maximize material dam-age. Explosions occur in the early morning hours when buildings are unoccupied. Corsican terrorists have targeted police stations, French government buildings, and the property of non-Corsicans on the island. They extort funds from outsiders through the imposition of a "revolution tax," and punish those who fail to pay. Sources would not reveal the government building in Paris just targeted, only that the *tête de* Maure—a Separatist symbol picturing a black face with a white bandanna—was discovered. Links to a known Armata Corsa terrorist cell operating in the eighteenth arrondissement are being pursued. Ministry insiders indicate this was an attempt to embarrass the French government and pressure it into negotiations with fratricidal Mafia-style gangs that have jumped on the Separatist bandwagon.

The *tête de* Maure, like the poster she'd seen somewhere. And Yann had said Lucien was a member of the Armata Corsa.

From what she knew, Corsica had to stay French not only for the security of the holiday homes lining its pristine beaches, but also as a convenient military outpost. A strategic sentinel in the Mediterranean, home to the Mirage-4, the jet that carried an atomic bomb.

Her mind raced into high gear. She took her notebook and wrote down what she knew so far. Zoe Tardou had recognized a man on the roof speaking Corsican about the planets and streams, before Jacques, who was half-Corsican, was mur-dered. Jacques had an affiliation with Zette, the murdered Corsican bar owner. Laure's hands had borne traces of gun-powder residue with a high tin content. And she'd found a bullet that she hoped would match the tin content of the residue on Laure's hands. Plans of a foiled plot on the Mairie in the eighteenth had been found near the place where Jacques was murdered.

Nothing fit! And yet it reeked, worse than sour milk. Had Jacques enmeshed Laure, his unknowing partner, with a gang of Corsican Separatists? If only Laure were to regain consciousness. But what answers would she have if she did?

The newspaper article indicated that a Corsican Separatist cell was operating in Montmartre. She pulled the hairbrush, containing a minirecorder in the handle, from her bag. One of René's toys; he loved gadgets.

Had it recorded?

She took a toothpick from the ceramic holder standing on the white paper covering the table and stuck it in the rewind pinhole: a low whirr. Then she stuck the toothpick in *Play*. Zoe Tardou's voice mingled with the shouts of the Fussbol players. Aimée rewound and replayed the conversation: "stream . . . searching," the names of the planets. What did it mean?

She'd copied it all in her notebook by the time her *croque-monsieur* arrived, a frugal bistro invention. Day-old bread was dipped in egg, fried with a slice of ham, melted cheese, and béchamel sauce, a filling meal on a winter day. She set her map of Zoe Tardou's building and the courtyard and scaffolding and rooftop of Paul's on the paper tablecloth. She added in the Dumpster where Yann Marant had found the diagram.

Her cell phone rang.

"*Allô?*"

"That *mec* passed by me," Cloclo said. "Twenty minutes ago." Too late. Aimée hadn't seen her arrive.

"Where are you, Cloclo? I don't see you on the street."

"House call for an old client," she said. "I'm in Goutte d'Or. On rue Custine where it meets rue Doudeauville."

Or, as one politician commented, "where the bourgeois bohemian *bobos* met the *boubous*, colorful African immigrants' robes."

"So he's gone!"

"Not if his kabob's still grilling," she said. "He went into Kabob Afrique. There's a big line trailing out onto the street."

"Cloclo, you're being watched," Aimée said.

"Men pay me for that, you know."

"I'm serious. Be careful. Work another beat for a few days."

"*Vraiment?*" Aimée heard a throaty laugh. "I could use some sun. Cannes, Menton, or do you suggest Cap Ferrat?"

"Can you describe the guy?" She threw some francs onto the table.

Just then the man who'd been ogling her walked over and took Aimée by the elbow.

"Care for a drink?" he asked. "I'm partial to big eyes and long legs."

She knew his type; any encouragement and he'd be all over her like a rash.

"*Desolée*, I feel the same," she smiled. "But I'm partial to a brain between the ears."

She grabbed her coat.

"Oooh, letting the skirt get away?" one of his friends sniggered as she left the café.

She ran, the phone to her ear, into the wet street.

"Like a . . . ," Cloclo said, her voice wavering, ". . . that lizard that changes color."

A chameleon changed to fit its background, she thought.

"Why do you say he's a chameleon, Cloclo?"

". . . black hair, sideburns today, leather jacket . . ."

"Careful, Cloclo, I mean it . . ."

The line went dead.

At least Cloclo was working somewhere else now and she had given Aimée a description. She ran down the Metro stairs, slid in her pass, and joined an older woman reading *Le Figaro*, waiting for the train. If she made a quick train connection she might get to the kabob place in time.

She changed lines once and exited from Château Rouge station in seven minutes.

Under a weak setting sun filtering through a break in the clouds, she saw awning-covered stands selling all types of bananas: short, thick, green, yellow, red, as well as stubby plantains. Men wearing long *djellabas* stood by upturned cardboard boxes on which tapes and "used" VCRs were displayed for sale. Laundry flapped, hanging from chipped metal balcony railings above, suspended from fissured buildings. As she walked by, women in colorful *boubous* shouted "*Iso, iso*," hawking barbecued corn in plastic bags. Several discount travel shops advertised flights—Paris-Mali, for two thousand francs—on hand-lettered signs.

The *quartier* reminded her of an Arab medina with its tangle of threadlike alleys, the perfume of oranges, and the cries of hawkers everywhere. She stood in the Goutte d'Or, "the golden drop" on the other side of Montmartre, named for the vineyards that once covered the slope. North African soldiers recruited for the First World War had found cheap lodgings here overlooking the Gare du Nord train tracks, after 1918. And the tradition continued; it was still cheap and even more rundown, teeming with Africans and Arabs and other segments of the "third world" according to conservative rightists and the encroaching *bobos*.

Aimée scanned the street and spied Kabob Afrique midblock.

Thursday evening

LUCIEN PUSHED OPEN THE corrugated metal siding that had been nailed over the warehouse door, slid out, and hitched the music case onto his back.

Three years in Paris and he had achieved nothing.

Kouros, he figured, had pulled out of the recording deal at the hint that he might be connected to terrorists. And now, instead of a SOUNDWERX contract, the law was after him and, almost worse, a fellow Corse had tried to frame him as a terrorist.

In the damp street, a line of customers trailed out of the door of the kabob place. He noticed a jean-jacketed, spiky-haired woman peering into a shop window with her back to him. Her long black-stockinged legs ended in stiletto heels.

He might as well call the Chatelet ethnic music organizer and make an appointment. Since his DJ jobs were in alternative clubs the *flics* didn't police, he'd survive.

He passed Kabob Afrique, its faded green shutters latched open. Right now, he'd prefer a *canastrelli* biscuit, the traditional late-afternoon Corsican treat, with wine. And to be near sun-drenched, rose-yellow stone houses, basking in the last copper rays of the sun. Instead, he stood in a densely packed lane of silvery gray nineteenth-century buildings, in the wan wintry light.

The woman wearing the jean jacket was asking him something. "Pardon, Monsieur . . ." Her bag dropped on the cobblestones in front of him.

He bent down to retrieve it at the same time she did. They knocked heads as their hands touched. "My fault, sorry," she said.

Her flushed cheeks, huge eyes, and striking face put him off balance. He'd forgotten other women, stunning women, existed.

And then he saw fear in her eyes. She clutched her bag, stood, and retreated. She edged around the street corner into a narrow lane, getting away.

Women! He readjusted his *cetera* case. Then he glanced down the lane. He was aghast to see the glint of a knife being wielded by a man who had cornered the woman against a pile of broken furniture.

Thursday

LAURE HEARD THE VOICES. Faraway voices, punctuated with beeps, and shuffling footsteps. Cold, she was so cold. And her head so heavy and cotton filled. She tried to speak but her dry, thick tongue got in the way.

"What's that?" said a young voice in her ear. "Good. I know you're trying."

What were those noises? The sounds, the moaning. They came from her. She felt a searing pain in her side. A flash of white passed by her. Then a smiling face was looking at her, a warm damp washcloth stroked her brow. The monitor tinkled beside her.

"Hello, Laure. You're back with us now, aren't you?"

She nodded and felt a dull throb behind her eyes.

"Try this."

Ice chips traced her lips, her fat tongue licked them greedily.

"Slowly, Laure. You're thirsty, *non*? Take it nice and slow."

She sensed heated blankets laid over her feet, hot-water bottles shoring up her side. The licks of ice were chilly and invigorating. Drops of water trickled down her eager, parched throat.

She grew aware of shadows on the row of beds, the bustle of nurses, and the low monotone of a loudspeaker system somewhere in the background.

"Someone's here to see you, Laure," the voice said. "Says he's an old friend. A family friend."

Drooping eyes were watching her; a man sat in the chair next to her bed. His head nodded. "You had us worried, Laure. You look much better. Remember me, Laure?"

The retirement party, the café, and Jacques. It all flooded back. This was Morbier, her father's old colleague.

"You don't have to speak," he told her. "Squeeze my hand if you understand."

She *had* to speak, to tell him about the roof, the scaffolding . . . she had to talk. About coming to, and the men, the snow in her face. And how they laughed. Those men. And their gun, the other gun. Someone had taken hers. They'd kicked her when she reached for it. The glint of metal from his pocket. How everything went black again.

She spoke, but no sound came out.

Thursday, Late Evening

AIMÉE CURSED HER BAD luck. The *mec* who'd chased her after Zette's murder was holding a knife to her face.

"You don't pay attention, do you?" the *mec* said. He'd backed her against rain-soaked broken chairs and old tables piled up in the alley, evidence of an eviction. This street lay off the beaten track and was deserted.

"I don't know what you mean. You must be confusing me with someone else."

She wanted to know whom he worked for. Why threaten her . . . *here*. But first things first.

She grinned. "I get it now, big boy. If you like me, just ask." She pointed to the Hôtel Luxe, a run-down, soot-blackened sagging hotel across the street. "For you, a five hundred franc special treatment."

A flutter of doubt appeared in his eyes. She was not the kind of hooker he was familiar with.

"I don't have to pay for it," he boasted, advancing closer. "You're the curious type." He eyes traveled her legs. "Poking your nose in everywhere."

His leather pants glistened with beaded rain mist. Just let him take one step closer.

"Respect is a two-way street, big boy." She smiled and licked her lips. "Put that knife away and come here."

In his nanosecond of indecision, she kicked with all her might at his kneecap. He doubled over in pain, clutching his knee, and howled. The knife clattered on the cobblestones. Thank God for pointed stiletto heels.

She scooped the knife up and took off. Tripped on a chair leg, scrambled, and pulled herself up the moss-embedded stone wall. At the corner she skidded into him again, the *mec* from the doorway whom she'd just bumped heads with. Deep-set, intense black eyes, chiseled features, black curly hair, sideburns: a good-looker, as Cloclo had said.

"Looks like you can handle yourself," he said.

Lucky this time, she slipped the knife into her pocket.

"You're Lucien Sarti, right?" she asked.

His concerned gaze changed to suspicion. "Who are you?"

And then trouble walked up the street. The limping *mec* had a cell phone to his ear. Was he calling for reinforcements? He swung the thick leg of a broken chair at her.

"Keep walking," she said.

From the frying pan into the fire. Why was Lucien Sarti here? And the *mec*? Had Cloclo set her up?

"Quick," she said, gesturing Lucien to a half-open gate. She hoped it led to another street, to escape.

"Look, I don't know who you are or how you know my name," he began.

"Explanations later. Hurry," she said.

He hesitated. She pulled him by the arm and they ran past filled Dumpsters beneath a row of rose bushes sheeted, ghostlike, against the frost with clear plastic. Two-story townhouses bordered the quiet *impasse*. A dead end. Aimée's pulse quickened. Where could they go?

Behind them, footsteps pounded. She turned left, up an unevenly paved passage, and ducked behind a wet hedge, pulling him by the arm to join her. They crouched in a gutter. His denim thigh rubbed hers. His look was intense and his breath was warm against her ear.

"Why's that *mec* chasing you?" he asked.

She put her finger to her lips. From his backpack peeked an instrument case. On the right stood a Louis Philippe-style townhouse; *oeil-de-boeuf* round windows in its facade were like eyes watching them. She couldn't see any doors leading from the courtyard to another street.

She felt a prickling on her skin, gasped for air. The footsteps stopped. Receded. And then it was quiet.

He stared at her as the water in the gutter gurgled over his feet. "He's gone," he said. "Let's go."

Sarti's long black lashes were so close she could see how they curled.

She stood, brushing off the sodden, dead leaves. Grime streaks and grease soiled her stockings. She had to collect herself, and try to get information from him.

"You're looking for me. Why?" he asked.

"I saw you in Montmartre the night the *flic* was shot."

"Wait a minute," he said, his eyes narrowing. "How did you find me? I don't like *flics*. Like you."

"Did you shoot him?"

His jaw dropped. "What kind of *flic* are you?"

Why did he have to look vulnerable and fierce at the same time?

"My friend was framed for the murder," she told him. "And I'm not a *flic*, I'm a private detective."

Before she could ask more questions, an automatic garage door rolled up, revealing a late-model Mercedes driven by a frowning mustached man. "*Allez-y!* You're trespassing on private property," he said.

With quick steps they walked back the way they had come. She peered into the street. All clear. She took a deep breath. And froze.

The man who'd threatened her, along with two others with black caps, emerged grinning from the doorways. Reinforcements had arrived.

"So you like foreigners, too," the *mec* she had kicked said. "Looks like a Corsican, my specialty."

She glanced around the passage, recognized it for the kind of place where street hawkers had once stored their carts at night. A fire-alarm box was affixed to the stone wall. No time for anything else. She elbowed it hard, breaking the glass, and pulled the handle. Only a loud whir resulted. Weren't these things supposed to send off an air raid-siren-like whoop?

Another *mec* with black curly hair, wearing a leather jacket and boots, was just visible in a doorway. The hair on her neck rose. He could have been the musician's brother. A twin brother. Her heart raced. If he was the one Cloclo meant, could they all be in league together?

The musician took the knife from her and pushed her behind him.

He spit and said something in Corsican. Her shoulders tensed, expectant.

"Look, there are four of them . . ." she began. Her palms were damp. Where could they go?

A siren bleated nearby. Talk about high alert and quick response from the local fire department. Had the Mercedes owner called the *flics*?

The sirens wailed closer. Louder. And the gang scattered, including the musician's double.

She couldn't control the shaking of her hands. But she didn't want to be there when the fire brigade blocked the street looking for the fire. Or the *flics* appeared.

"Let's go. We need to talk, somewhere safe," Lucien Sarti said, palming the knife. "Whoever you are."

RENÉ PACED ON THE uneven floorboards outside Paul's apartment. Plaster crumbled in a fine dust from the wall, moldy mildew smells hovered by the skylight. At least he didn't have to wear the Toulouse-Lautrec guise. Right now, he wished he had a hot rum to give him courage.

He'd left another message on Aimée's phone. Just her voice-mail message answered him. The stairs creaked and a woman in her thirties ascended, her red-hennaed hair knotted in a green clip. She had eyes that reminded him of Paul's. She wore a long black skirt and a poncho, and carried a string shopping bag filled with nestled wine bottles.

"Can I help you?" she asked in a brisk tone.

"Madame, I met Paul—"

"Ah, you're the actor. Paul told me about you," she interrupted. "He wrote a wonderful essay, thanks to you."

René hesitated. He wished Aimée were here.

"Actually, I hoped to speak with you and Paul."

"Perhaps another evening," she replied.

What should he do? She was struggling with her key and the heavy string bag.

"Let me help you," he said.

"*Non, merci*, I can manage."

"Mind if I wait for Paul?"

"Why?" Suspicion clouded her eyes.

René stepped back. "There's an important matter. . . ."

A sudden panic showed in her face. "You're checking up on us, aren't you? From social services."

"Not at all," René said, taken aback.

"I know your kind. Worming your way into our life. You want to take Paul away!"

"Relax, Madame," he said desperately. "Look at me. I don't know about social services or anything like that. I do know Paul's a bright boy. Intelligent, talented, but shy."

A flicker of shame crossed her face. "Shy, *oui*. My fault, right? That's what you're saying."

"There's something we need to discuss. Please, let's talk inside, not in the hallway."

"Discuss? My place is a mess." She hesitated.

"You should see mine," he told her.

With more prodding, he coaxed her inside. By the time he'd helped her clear the small table of dishes, reached up, and rinsed two glasses clean and set them on the table, his hip throbbed from the cold. There was no heater in the slant-roofed one-room apartment. But it was neat despite the sofa bed, desk, and mismatched period chairs that filled the cramped space.

"Chilly, eh?" he said.

She gestured to the stove and unpacked her string bag.

On his tiptoes he turned the knob of the small gas oven. The blue pilot light flickered, hissed, and caught. He opened the door and a trickle of heat radiated out.

"Establish rapport, appear nonthreatening," said the last chapter in the detective manual. Anxious to disarm her, René made conversation. "Those stairs are quite a hike," he said. "I mean for someone like me," he added, watching her pour wine from an unlabeled bottle. It looked like generic rotgut with viscous sediment in the bottom. "In my former apartment I had quite a climb. Have you lived here long, Madame?"

"Isabelle," she said. "You can cut the small talk."

Easy on the page, harder in real life. René realized the detective manual's advice had limitations.

"Paul's father left after he was born." She drained her glass. "We've moved around. Always in Montmartre."

"You're lucky, great view." He gestured to the large window with lace curtains.

She rested her elbows on the worn table, seemed to relax. "I don't know what you want to 'discuss,' but I suggest you tell me."

"It's better if we all talk together—you, me, and Paul," he said, trying to stall.

"What's this about?" she asked.

Might as well get to the point. "Paul told me he saw the shooting the other night on the roof," René said.

"You're crazy! Paul makes up stories. He has a vivid imagination."

"Let's find out. I'll ask him again, in your presence. Everything will remain confidential."

She poured herself another glass and noticed René hadn't touched his. "Too good to drink with me at my table?"

He preferred wine at meals, not on an empty stomach, but he knew his duty.

"Not at all, Isabelle." He took a sip. A toasted walnutlike aroma. Not a bad way to warm up. "An aged Merlot?"

She nodded.

"Isabelle, I'm sure you're concerned." He handed her a card; thank God, he had one with him. "Paul says there were two gun flashes. If he gives this evidence to her lawyer, an innocent police officer will be cleared."

"Innocent policeman? You're joking."

About to say "policewoman," René paused. "What do you mean?"

"That one demanded protection money."

"Jacques Gagnard, the man who was murdered on the rooftop?"

"Look, it's not my business," she said. "Forget I said anything."

"How do you know the *flic* was bent?" he asked, easing his dangling leg onto a chair rung to relieve his aching hip.

She shrugged. "No big secret if you work the street or have a café with machines."

Like Zette's bar on rue Houdon, René thought. Maybe Aimée had hit the mark after all.

"I need more than that. It's vital; a policewoman is suspected of killing her partner."

Isabelle's short laugh took him aback. "Ask me if I'm surprised."

Her speech had cleared. After the wine she appeared more lucid. Some drinkers were like that. Then, a blackout.

"Your son saw a man murdered. It happened *right across from you*."

She drained her glass.

"Those were real gunshots, not the *télé*. Have you realized your son could have been hit by a stray bullet?"

She looked away.

How could he reach her? He took another sip of wine, wishing his hip didn't hurt so much. Poured more in her glass. "Isabelle, say this *flic* was corrupt and an angry contact shot him. We need your help to find the guilty man."

"You're undercover, right? Some special detective unit."

René took a big sip. Let her think that. He nodded.

Isabelle stared straight ahead, then locked eyes with his. She pushed a strand of red hair behind her ear and took a deep breath. "There were *three* shots. I saw it all."

"Three?" René's stomach flip-flopped. Whether from the wine or her words, he didn't know. It didn't matter. "Paul said . . ."

She shook her head. "Paul didn't see the third one. The last shot."

"Did you see who fired?"

"I don't want Paul involved, you understand," Isabelle said.

Negotiate, like it said in chapter eight, page eighty-seven. Reluctant witnesses would try to negotiate. Agree, but obtain your objective.

René nodded. "If you agree to meet the lawyer and give evidence, Paul can be kept out of it."

"Then it's a deal, little man?"

No one had ever called him that in his life and gotten away with it.

"Count on it. And my name's René."

She pushed aside her half-full wineglass. "*Et donc*, René, I was sitting right here, writing my uncle for help. Paul was asleep in his alcove behind the curtain. Or so I thought. That's why I noticed. It was black outside, like coal; a storm was brewing. Then, all of a sudden, something flashed right across my line of sight from that roof. I heard a bark like a gunshot. It startled me so much I spilled the ink." She pointed to a splotch on the table's surface.

"Go on," he prompted.

"Dark figures were moving on the roof. I turned down the radio. In five minutes, maybe more, I saw another flash."

It could make sense. Had they ambushed Laure, used her gun on Jacques, then put their gun in her hand and fired again?

"How much of that had you drunk, Isabelle?" He gestured to the empty green bottles on the floor by the fridge.

"I got my check Tuesday."

"What does that have to do with—"

"No money on Monday, René. I ran short. Paul had to have food," she said. "But I stock up on food when I get my check. Always. Then I can't spend it on my friends."

He stared at the bottles. To a lonely woman, wine was a friend.

"My boy's a monkey. He goes up on the roof all the time. I blame that old fool downstairs who lets Paul help him," she said. "I heard the door creak open and then I saw the third flash. Paul set his schoolbag on the table and crept into the sleeping alcove. Eh, you can be sure I gave him a talking-to. Told him we'd have trouble if he opened his mouth. He promised, after I put the fear of God in him."

Something bothered René.

"Peering out into the dark from your window, how could you see figures?"

"Before the storm came in full force, I could make out shapes. There were two dark figures."

"Isabelle, think of how it looked from the other side. If you had a light on, wouldn't they have seen you?"

"I keep the light on over the sink so as not to disturb Paul," she said. "Low, like this."

Isabelle stood and turned off the overhead light. A soft pink glow bathed the corner. "I could see out but, sitting here, they wouldn't see me."

René glanced at his watch and stiffened. "It's late, shouldn't Paul be in bed? Where is he?"

"Hiding, as usual. But he always comes home, sooner or later."

"Isabelle, he could be in danger. Have you thought of that? Was the light on when he put the bookbag on the table?"

Something registered in her eyes. She'd had a new thought.

"What is it, Isabelle?"

Whether it was the wine or the warmth dribbling from the oven or both, she rubbed her cheek and volunteered more information.

"This *mec* asked my neighbor where Paul was. He's rough, arrogant, pushes his way around the *quartier*. Why did he want Paul?"

René's heart sank. "Maybe Paul's hiding from someone. Maybe that's why he's so late."

Or maybe he'd been caught. Where the hell was Aimée?

She grabbed the wineglass. Her hand trembled, sloshing red driblets on the tabletop. Like blood, René thought.

"We'll have to move," she said.

"You can't run away," he told her. "Call the police."

"Police? No."

"If he's in danger, you have to. After he's found, and you can tell the lawyer what you know, you'll both be safe. I promise." At least he hoped so.

She hesitated. "I stay away from the *flics*. I have a record."

"What happened in the past doesn't matter," he said. "Think of Paul."

He saw the struggle in her face.

"He could come home any minute."

René hoped so. Otherwise he'd have to look for him.

"Now, tell me where he might be hiding."

Thursday Night

"SO, MUSICIAN, WHY'S THE *mec* following you, or is it the other way round?" Aimée said. Her breath, a vapor trail, dissipated in the night air over the lighted outdoor ice rink at Rotonde de la Villette. "I need to know."

"You and me both," Lucien Sarti said, leaning on the rail, looking down.

A few skaters, mostly couples at this time of night, crossed the ice. The music almost drowned out the distant screeching of brakes from the overhead Metro line at Stalingrad.

"He's the one trying to frame me."

"For terrorism?" she asked. "Is he part of your Separatist cell, gone rogue?"

He shook his head.

Behind them loomed the domed rotunda of La Villette, a circular arcade fronted by Doric columns, a barracks during the Commune, later a salt depot. Ahead lay the wide dark-water basin that funneled below them and narrowed into Canal Saint Martin.

They were in an open public place at least, although only a few figures, huddled against the bone-chilling cold, waited in line at the crêperie stall.

Her cold thigh still felt the warmth of his pressing against her. Instinct screamed that it must be the other *mec* who Cloclo had meant. Hadn't Lucien Sarti defended her? But "Never assume," had been her father's dictum.

He pulled the knife from his pocket, holding it low. A worn wooden hilt, a serated blade. "A fish gutter," he said. "The weapon of choice on the Bastia docks."

She knew they were also used in restaurant kitchens. Then her cell phone trilled. René? She pressed *Answer.*

"Aimée, forgive the late notice." The husky voice of Martine, her best friend since the *lycée*, boomed over the line. "Gilles shot more pheasant than we can eat in a lifetime. They're plucked, herbed, and roasting. And there's a perfect Brillat-Savarin for after dinner. Say you and Guy will come, please."

These days, Martine inhabited the world of the Sixteenth Arrondissement. Soirées and châteaux on the weekend. Courtesy of her boyfriend, Gilles. But that milieu was staid and lifeless to Aimée.

"Martine, I can't talk," she whispered, turning toward the canal.

"Did you and Guy fight again?"

"Eh, what's that?"

"You heard me, Aimée."

No use pretending. Might as well come clean. She could never keep the truth from Martine for long.

She cupped her hand over her mouth. "Guy moved out, Martine," she whispered. "This is not a good time." She squirmed, embarrassed that Lucien Sarti might overhear her.

"Then, of course, you must come!" Martine said, her husky voice rising. "Gilles's colleague from *Le Point*'s here. You'd like him."

The conservative right-leaning journal, known for nostalgic articles on the de Gaulle era? Not likely.

"Look, this *mec's* chasing me. . . ." Aimée whispered.

"Lust often, love always, as they say. You sure don't let the grass grow under your heels!" Martine said. "A bad boy?"

"Bad-bad."

"Tiens! You mean . . . nom de Dieu! *Not this again . . . you're not getting involved!"*

"Later, Martine." She clicked her phone off and turned back.

"Your man moved out, eh?" Lucien said.

She wanted the metal sewer lid under her feet to open up.

Sarti leaned his long legs against the skating-rink fence. The glittering quayside lights reflected in his eyes. Faraway eyes. "My woman . . . once she was my woman . . . belongs to someone else now."

"I'm sorry." Caught off balance, she didn't know what else to say. These things happened. As she well knew.

"Life's like a train," he said, his voice low. "I got off too soon."

Maybe she had, too. Not tried hard enough with Guy. Now, in some way, she felt that she and Sarti shared something, as if they paddled in the same boat.

She had to get back to the point.

"Let's discuss that guy, the one framing you. Your doppel-gänger? How do you know him?"

"Petru?"

"If he's the one who looks so much like you."

"He's from another clan," Lucien Sarti told her. "He's different from me."

Clan? Sounded old-fashioned, insular.

"What do you mean?" she asked. She kept her eye on the sparse crowd at the crêpe stall under the arcade. A kerosene lantern hung from the cart. She heard the scraping of ice skates, scattered laughter of couples, and the strains of a Strauss waltz wavering on the wind.

He should have been fearful, but Lucien Sarti appeared sad and wistful. He didn't seem like a killer.

"I miss the rhythm of village life," he said. "Here the horns beep at a red light, one runs from one Metro stop to the next. Rushing, always rushing. In Corsica the pace of life is human."

"Petru appears to have adapted pretty well," she said. "Who does he work for?"

"You should know," he said.

She thought quickly. Of course. Yann Marant had said Lucien Sarti had arrived at the party later. "You were at Monsieur Conari's party. How do Petru and his goons fit in?"

"Goons? All I know is that she . . . someone warned me Petru had planted terrorist pamphlets in the recording studio and arranged for the *flics* to arrest me."

"Do you believe this woman?"

His eyebrows rose. "Why should I doubt her?"

Why frame him as a terrorist? How did that connect to Jacques's murder? Too many pieces—odd, disparate ones. How to connect them?

"Why would Petru implicate you, then follow you?"

"Like I said, he's not from my village." Lucien paused with a tight smile. "Who knows? My great-uncle could have stolen his father's mule. Eh, it's just like you Parisians characterize us."

"Interesting angle, musician. You're the one stereotyping."

"So, you willing to hang out with an alleged Corsican Separatist?" He interrupted, shooting her a look.

Cut the sarcasm, she wanted to say.

"Not if I can help it." No reason for him to know she made a beeline for bad boys, once even a Neo-Nazi who'd turned out to be a good guy in disguise. "Convince me you're not one."

"To you, we're goatherds with shotguns, taking care of vendettas, savage and wild like our island, eh?"

"Let's get back to the point. What did you see the night Jacques Gagnard was killed?"

"You, handcuffed, being herded into the police van," he said, not skipping a beat.

There was more, she sensed it.

"Did you hear shots?"

His hand trembled for an instant on the ice-coated railing.

"I think you saw something," she said.

"You're not a *flic*."

"I told you, I'm a private detective," she said. "Someone framed my friend but I'm going to get her off."

"That's what this is about?" His fingers relaxed.

She nodded. "I found Jacques Gagnard, dying, on the snow-covered roof. His heart still responded, his eyes blinked." She looked down at a hole in a patch of gray snow. "He tried to tell me something. His eyes communicated. It's hard to describe."

The *flics* had dismissed it as a dying person's involuntary response. Why was she telling him this? She should shut up, ask the questions.

Lucien rubbed his arms and leaned on the railing. "They gunned down my grandfather in the village. He bled to death under a chestnut tree," he said, his voice low. "It took a long time. I sat with him as the shadows lengthened. A dragonfly fluttered, attracted to the blood on his chest. His three fingers moved . . . and moved . . . my brother told me I imagined it. I was young." He paused, rubbed the growth of stubble on his cheek. "A week later my uncle found the murderers, three of them, hiding in a lemon grove."

He shrugged. "I still see the branches swollen with fruit, lemons fallen split and pulped on the dirt, their citrus scent mingled with the metallic tang of blood. Revenge, that I would have taken, an obligation to my grandfather. . . ."

His eyes seemed faraway. He spoke hesitantly yet he was confiding something deeply felt. No stranger had ever spoken to her like this—by turns intimate, sarcastic, then sad.

She was sure he knew more than he was telling about Jacques Gagnard.

"Let's try again. Tell me what happened. Why weren't you questioned at the party?"

He turned away, his face in shadow.

"You need my help, musician. Assuming you've told me the truth."

"Revenge, that's in my culture. I helped you, didn't I? Let it go. I'll get by on my own."

"With the CRS roaming everywhere? There's probably an alert out on you already if you're a member of Armata Corsa."

"Not me. Not anymore. You are misinformed. I play music. That's what I do."

"How do I know you weren't working with Petru? You could have killed Jacques Gagnard, and set another *flic* up, then double-crossed Petru. And maybe that's why he's after you."

Was that hurt in his eyes?

"I'm sick of this," he said. "I've never fired a gun in my life. You've got the wrong person."

"Convince me."

"Few have a code. Honor." He leaned close to her; his breath touched her face. "Should I trust you?"

"Why not? Who else can you trust?" she said. "I'm interested in neither your political nor nonpolitical views. My friend's in a coma. She'd never shoot her partner. All I care about is clearing her."

He studied her. Deciding.

Bon, she'd say it the way he'd understand. "That's *my* code, Lucien."

So he told her what happened: Félix, the party, the woman, and how he'd forgotten his ID and had to sneak away. She remembered the list of party participants who had been interviewed. There were no Corsican names.

She nodded. "Now try again. Tell me everything you saw. Tell me what you left out."

"Left out?" He closed his eyes. Thought. "An old man came out to walk his dog. And I saw light," he said. "A flickering light, escaping from holes in the ground."

"You mean the construction site? Here?" she asked, excited. She pulled out her diagram.

She pointed and he nodded.

"After the shot, I heard breaking glass."

The skylight. Their escape.

"The fence around the construction is low there. I saw the lights."

It made sense. She remembered seeing the glowing tip of a cigarette on the ground. She'd wondered where those damp footprints had led. Now she knew; they hadn't gone out into the street, but down somewhere in the construction site.

"What's in your backpack?"

He blinked in surprise. Then gave her a wide smile and leaned his leather-clad elbows on the railing. "Search it. Be my guest. I have nothing to hide."

She ignored his mocking gaze, his long legs. "Why don't you show me?"

He pulled out his wooden music case, unlatched it.

"My *cetera*," he said lifting out the wooden instrument. The bowed wood face was smooth and worn from playing, the strings new. "A traditional instrument, our variation of a lute."

From his case rose the scent of bergamot and was that currant? *Non*, deep and dense, more like a dark fig.

"Our tradition makes music out of everyday life; it's music with its feet on the ground."

She'd heard a Corsican polyphonic chorus coming from the church around her corner one evening, and stood, transfixed. Ancient, yet timeless, resonating somewhere deep within.

He plucked his *cetera*. The high melodic notes carried on the crisp air, evoking another world, another time.

A couple, arm in arm on the ice, paused and listened.

He laid the instrument back in the case with care.

"You don't trust me, do you?" he said. "Because I'm Corsican."

"As long as we help each other, I do," Aimée said.

"More Corsicans live in France than in all of Corsica. It's a diaspora. There are villages with only twenty people left, old people. Mountains cover eighty-five percent of the island. Rich Parisians come for vacation eager to imbibe nature, wine, and organic honey." Sarcasm layered his voice. "But haven't you heard, we're integrated now? Pasqua is the Minister of the Interior; that model, the one for Marianne, is Corsican; even the quay by the Préfecture's named after Corsica."

"Did Petru know Jacques Gagnard? Or did you?" she asked, keeping her voice even with effort.

He shook his head, but he turned away and she couldn't read his face. There was a thick roll of paper in the back pocket of his backpack.

Plans, copies of blueprints for targeted buildings?

"What's that?" she asked warily.

"My once-brilliant career," he said. "Ruined by the Separatists."

He unfolded the thick sheets. SOUNDWERX was engraved on the top of the pages.

"They forgot the Isadore after Lucien," he said. "Close enough; Lucien Sarti. A contract that will never be executed."

Her cold hands dropped her penlight and the contents of her bag spilled out in the slushlike snow: sand from the Brittany beach, her kohl eye pencil, Nicorette patches, worn Vuitton wallet, dated Hôtel Dieu pass to Laure's ward, well-thumbed cryptography manual, the holy card from her father's funeral, a black leather neck cord with a knotted silver teardrop pendant, a worn Indian take-out menu, and her cell phone. She dried the items off with her gloves and scooped them back inside.

Lucien had picked up the penlight. "You're one of those

career types, live for your work? Don't clean house, eh. Bet you don't even cook."

Aimée felt her cheeks burn. Was it so obvious? As Guy had observed, making espresso was her only culinary skill?

"Restos were invented to eat in, weren't they?" she said, taking the penlight, shining it on the thick document.

"'Multipackaging,' 'tape and vinyl,' 'promotional materials,' 'SOUNDWERX label,' 'large venues,'" she read from the contract. "Impressive. Talk about hitting the big time."

"Not anymore," he said. "Petru put a spoke in that wheel."

"Why?"

"Who knows? I met him once, then the second time with you."

"It doesn't make sense. You must be hiding something."

He stared, his dark eyes plumbing her.

"The *flics* want to talk with you about the bomb planted near the Mairie of the eighteenth arrondissement," she said, taking a guess.

He flinched. She figured her comment had hit home. She backed away from him, hitching her damp bag onto her shoulder.

"Are you going to inform on me?"

"I've got a better idea, musician. We're going to find Petru."

Thursday Night

NATHALIE GAGNARD'S DAMP SWEATER clung to her. Her hand came back wet from touching her cheeks. She was crying, and she hadn't even realized it.

Light from the streetlamp slanted through her half-closed shutters and checkered the sisal mat under her bare feet. In her apartment, once a ballroom—a quarter of it, anyway—clung the dense odor of white chrysanthemums for Jacques's funeral service. They lay in the sink, needing water, still wrapped in green paper. The body of the man she ached for would repose in a steel morgue drawer until the ground dried out enough for a grave to be dug. The flowers could wait.

The phone rang next to her.

"Madame Gagnard, Officer Rassac calling," said a voice she recognized. "Please accept our condolences. We've taken up a collection for the funeral. The way we think Jacques would like it." Pause. "We hope you'll agree."

Had they made arrangements for Jacques's funeral without consulting her? As the ex-wife, she wasn't even a proper widow nor would she be entitled to his pension. She scrabbled for her cigarettes, found the packet, and lit one.

"Madame Gagnard?"

She exhaled; a gray wisp of smoke trailed into the room.

"So you've managed everything." She bit back the rest.

There was a pause. "We wanted to make things easier, you know. The men . . . ," he paused again, cleared his throat. "We wanted to relieve you of this unexpected burden."

Her tears flowed, accompanied by sobs she couldn't control.

"Do whatever you want." She hung up, ashamed. They knew she had no money.

If only Jacques had been able to keep his hands off the machines. The gambling fever was a curse. Their debts mounted, they'd pay off one loan shark, then Jacques would gamble again and get in debt to another.

She ground out her cigarette in the full ashtray. A few months ago he'd joined a program on his own, tried to quit, surprising her. He'd told her he was quitting for himself, it was something he had to do. She hadn't asked him why, just thanked the stars. And then, last week, those telltale shining eyes, that fevered look. Right away she knew. He'd gone back to the machines.

Mounting excitement, pills, big plans, a coup, he said, that would make all their debts disappear. Like every big idea he'd had, it backfired. And this time, it took him with it.

Her heart heaved. Jacques's tousled hair, the way he'd tickled her under her knees, how he'd made her purr beneath the sheets. Life with him had been a joy—on good days.

She grabbed the half-empty bottle of Ambien pills and curled her legs under her on the couch. She longed for oblivion. To forget. She thumbed open the horoscope page in *Marie Claire*, as she did every month, and scanned the advice under her sign, a Scorpion, drawn biting its lethal tail.

Jacques had said she embodied Scorpio's dark, jealous nature and secretiveness. And despite his free spirit, he'd seemed to like it during their five years of marriage. Opposites attract, wasn't that the saying?

Under Scorpio's Feelings Forecast she read: Venus rising indicates time for reflection. The same for dreams. Take time, ponder, the answers will come. A warm-colored sun illuminates your journey.

Answers will come? Already, as she'd told the reporter, that bitch was in custody. The little harpy with her cleft lip, like the upper lip of a hare, a sign still regarded in her Breton village as the malicious act of an elf or fairy. Old sayings and beliefs still held sway in the countryside. Hadn't her mother refused to let her pregnant sister cross in front of a rabbit for fear of miscarriage?

That Laure was cursed and transmitted the curse to others around her. Nathalie known it the moment she'd laid on eyes on her.

Nathalie's fist balled, knocking the pills over, sprinkling them across the floor. How many had she taken tonight? The doctor said two would dull the edge of anxiety. Two?

She'd vowed to Jacques she'd never go back on the street. She'd given her word. Did it matter now?

Jacques, fresh from the military in Corsica, and new to the police force, had found her. She would never forget that bitter February evening. The *flics* were making a routine sweep of rue Joubert; she was just a few months into The Life. At the Commissariat he'd grinned, handing her hot coffee and offering her a seat in his warm cubicle. He'd treated her like a human being and winked, offering her a "*cousine*'s" job, which was what they called informers. He'd promised her better things and, to his credit, later he had made an honest woman of her. She owed her life to him.

And it had been sweet, especially those last few days. Talking with him every day, sometimes twice, his saying he needed her, that only she could help him, and it would all work out. He'd leave the force, they'd settle in Saint Raphael, buy that little bistro. But now, it was all over, all due to that jealous whiner.

Proof? Why did they need more than Laure's smoking gun? Those *juges d'instructions* got more fussy every day; soon, as Jacques had said, they'd need to video a crime before anyone got nailed.

What had Jacques put away, the night she came home early? Groggy, she reached down for the pills, picked them up one by one, put some back in the bottle, and took two more. Or was it three more?

Little was left to comfort her. Most days her only interactions were at work or with the cashier at Casino, the market, who lived downstairs. Her life had been mechanical and soulless since Jacques had left. And now he was gone for good.

The *Marie Claire* fell to the floor. Her muscles had relaxed. The walls glazed before her eyes, a hazy aura of vanilla light came through the window from the street. Hadn't her horoscope indicated a colored sun . . .?

"I'M SORRY, I'M THE only one here," said Félix Conari's housekeeper. "Petru? I haven't seen him. Madame and Monsieur are out."

"Please," Aimée said. "I must reach Monsieur Conari."

"Monsieur Conari?" said the flustered housekeeper. "He's gone straight from the airport to services at Eglise Saint-Pierre de Montmartre. That's all I know."

"*Merci*," Aimée said, clicking off her cell phone.

"I have a gig," Lucien said.

"First, let's go to church," she said.

THE TAXI stopped on rue Saint-Rustique, the oldest street in Montmartre, wide enough, she imagined, for a twelfth-century cart. She handed the driver thirty francs. "Keep the change," she said, hoping to earn late-night taxi karma, and he grinned.

A gutter ran down the middle of the street, like an inverted seam, leading to Eglise Saint-Pierre, a church built on the site of Roman temples to Mars and Mercury. In the fifth century, an abbey, later the birthplace of the Jesuit order, had stood here. Now it was the oldest chapel in Paris. During the Revolution, it had been a telegraph station. In the Franco-Prussian War, a Prussian munitions depot. At the time of the Commune, a fortress against the Communards and starving masses who were reduced to hunting rats.

The bronze sculpted Italian doors stood open, revealing a candle-lit medieval stone chapel. A small crowd was leaving the mass. The courtyard, usually crowded with tourists, lay deserted this winter night.

The musk of incense made her nose itch. Their footsteps

echoed as they passed the statue of Marie Thérèse of Montmartre and walked toward the columns crowned by sculpted leaves.

Félix Conari was shaking hands with the priest, clasping them within his own. A gray-haired man wearing a dark suit, red tie, and blue shirt, the uniform of Ministry types, stood next to him. His was a face she'd seen often in the paper next to that of the Minister of the Interior.

Church and state. Bad partners. She didn't like it.

She caught Conari's eye. If he was surprised, he didn't show it. A few moments later, he excused himself and joined them.

"Forgive me, Monsieur Conari, but your housekeeper—"

"My wife didn't tell you? Aaah, I forgot she's at a reception, but it's good you found me." Conari put his arm around Lucien. "*Ça va*, Lucien?"

Lucien gave a hesitant nod.

"We celebrated the annual memorial mass for my sister. Come, let's talk outside," Conari said. His silk tie was rumpled, his eyes tired and red. Near the pillar, he picked up his brown overcoat, which was resting on a folded suitbag with an Air France luggage tag.

Outside the church, which was overshadowed by Sacré Coeur, he buttoned his coat and steered them to the adjacent cemetery gate. Mist topped the summit of rue du Mont-Cenis, the street that was once the ancient pilgrim route.

"We must clear up this misunderstanding, Lucien," said Félix.

The dark cemetery, with a sign saying it was open once a year, revealed sinking sarcophagi pitched at drunken angles. Druids, Romans, medieval men, they were all under here, somewhere.

"How can we reach Petru?" Aimée asked.

"He was supposed to meet me at the airport."

"Two hours ago he threatened us."

"I haven't seen him since Monday," Conari said. "I don't understand."

He seemed as lost as she felt. She'd thought Conari would have answers. She'd been clutching at connections, grasping at straws driven by a feeling in her gut, unsubstantiated by anything more than an overheard conversation in Corsican, Zette's body hanging from the WC door, a nine-year-old's observations from the roof, lights in a construction site at night, and a sour taste in her mouth about Ludovic Jubert.

"Félix, what's going on?" Lucien asked.

Conari gave a deep sigh. "I'm concerned, too," he said. "Petru hasn't returned my calls."

"Petru tried to incriminate me. And he's been following me."

"You're serious? He threatened you, Lucien?" Conari shook his head. "Petru's a hothead, he gets out of line sometimes. But this sickens me."

"Out of line, Félix?" Lucien said. "He planted information at the recording studio to tie me to the terrorists and then alerted the police."

"So Marie-Dominique told me," Conari said. "On the outside she's a sparrow; inside, a protective hawk, like all the Vescovatis women."

A vein pulsed in Lucien's forehead, just visible under a black curl. So Conari's wife had warned Lucien.

"Why, Félix?"

"Ask him," he said. "Ever since Marie-Dominique phoned, I've tried to find him. There's some misunderstanding. But don't worry, I'm going to salvage the deal with SOUNDWERX."

"I thought Kouros pulled out." Lucien's mouth tightened.

"Lucien, my boy, we signed the contract!" Félix said. "Look on the bright side."

Lucien shook his head. "But Kouros didn't sign it."

"His handshake's his word, remember, Lucien?"

"Not if there's any taint of the Armata Corsa. He made that clear."

"*We* have a contract, Lucien," Conari said. "I'll get you into the recording studio as soon as I can. Right now, I have to concentrate on my construction contract."

"How long has Petru worked for you?" Aimée asked.

"Six months or so. He does odd jobs," Félix Conari said. "His cousin married my sister. He's from a different clan than Marie-Dominique."

"Does that explain him turning on Lucien and sabotaging his recording deal?"

"Corsican hotheads make no sense to me, Mademoiselle," Conari said. "I married into a family and I try to help people like Lucien when I can. But ancient wrongs don't interest me."

"Was one of his little jobs to cover up the shooting of a *flic* on the rooftop opposite yours during your party?"

Conari's eyes widened. "Petru? You think he shot someone? No, he was serving at dinner. At the table. You saw him, Lucien. We all did."

"A witness heard men speaking Corsican on the roof," she said.

Félix Conari shook his head. "In that howling storm?"

"I think the police will be interested, Monsieur Conari. Especially if they learn you've employed a suspected Corsican terrorist."

Lucien's hands twisted on the grip of his music case.

"Terrorist? Petru? There's a mistake. Maybe some macho posturing. . . ." Conari pulled his lower eyelid down with a fingertip, an old-fashioned gesture meaning, Who are you trying to kid? "I want to help but I have no idea why he'd plant false information. My wife could have misheard."

"Yet you said he's disappeared."

"We have to straighten this out." Conari took his cell phone, hit the speed dial. "Petru, I'm back, we must speak," he said. Then Conari snapped his cell phone shut. "I got his voice mail. The moment he calls me, I'll let you know."

"His number?" she said. She was programming the number into her cell phone as Conari showed it to her.

"Does he live in your apartment?"

Conari shook his head. "Petru lives somewhere in the *quartier*."

"Don't you know where he lives?"

"He just moved, but he has been secretive about a lot of things," Conari said. "When I think about it, it is odd."

"Where did he live before?"

"Near Place Froment, above a Turkish grocery," Conari said.

"Something more specific, Monsieur Conari?"

"We picked him up there once," he said. "I waited in the car by the cemetery wall. Let's see, I remember my driver fetched him. The shop had everything—food, hookahs, even Turkish videos."

Lucien hitched the backpack onto his other shoulder. "I've got to go. I've got a gig, Félix."

"Lucien, believe me. Mademoiselle Leduc, I'm sorry for what happened. Petru's got a temper. But to fly off like this? I don't understand."

"Where were you, Monsieur Conari?"

"I'm negotiating with the Ministry. It's difficult with these Separatist attacks aggravating the situation."

Wasn't everything blamed on the Separatists? And he still hadn't answered her.

"Where were you, Monsieur Conari?"

"The isle of beauty," he said. "Corsica." He let out a sigh.

The priest beckoned to Conari.

"Excuse me, I must thank the padre."

"LUCIEN, WHERE exactly did you see those lights?"

Aimée stood shivering before the building on whose roof Jacques had been shot.

Lucien pointed. "The lights came from over the railing. You can see the hole from here."

"Where?"

He put his hands around her waist. Strong hands. And lifted her up. Only an inky black hole fringed with frost met her gaze.

"Dots of moving lights," he said.

A tunnel?

He set her down. His hands rested on her hips a moment too long.

"Tomorrow, I'll sniff around Petru's old place if I can find it. Meanwhile, if he reappears, call me." She handed him her number. "Don't you have a cell phone?"

"Against my principles," Lucien said.

Annoying, and it made him difficult to reach.

"If Petru gets in my way, I'll take care of him." Lucien shouldered his bag. "I'm really late for a job."

"Look . . ."

"Leave a message with Anna at Strago."

"I already did."

"Just a word of advice." He paused, his face in shadow. "A girl like you ought to stay away from types like that *mec*."

Angered, she stepped back. Her heels sank into the slush.

"The *mec* with the knife? You think I invited it? He chased me," she said. "And threatened me, after I found Zette, the bar owner, garroted. *Another* Corsican."

The crash of a can and the screeching of a cat came from over a wall. She paused. "Your type's the one I should watch out for."

And then his hands encircled her waist and he was kissing her on both cheeks. Soft kisses. Warm and lingering. She took a deep breath, enveloped in his warmth and the wet tang of his leather jacket. There was the cold promise of snow in the air.

"Especially *my* type, detective," he breathed in her ear.

She watched until the shadows swallowed him and the echo of his footsteps faded, still feeling his warmth on her face.

Thursday night

LAURE TRIED TO SCREAM. Only garbled sounds came from her mouth. The green walls looked different, they'd moved her.

"Nurse, the patient's agitated. Monitor the EKG. Now!"

A white-coated doctor stood over her, his prominent nose and plastic-coated badge catching the light from the blinking machines. "Laure, take it easy. Don't struggle. Do you feel this?"

A pinprick. Cold.

She shook her head. Thought she shook her head. Only her thumb and index finger moved. She concentrated.

"Blink, Laure," he said. "Once for yes, two times for no. Can you do that?"

Laure blinked twice.

"What's that? You're trying to say you didn't feel it?"

She blinked two times again. Felt her eyes bulging from her head. Couldn't he see her fingers moving on the white sheet. Look, she wanted to scream, my *fingers*. The doctor leaned forward, his stethoscope swinging over her chest under the white sheets.

Do it. Touch it. Show him.

But her hand didn't respond. Her eyes followed the path where her fingers would go; she could almost feel how smooth the steel disk would feel. How cold to her touch. But like a stalled engine, trying to kick over, coughing, choking, sputtering to a stop, the rest of her didn't cooperate.

"Give her two milligrams of Valium," the doctor said. "We've got to control the tremors or the tubes will pop out."

Look at my eyes . . . my eyes! She blinked twice in rapid succession. No more drugs, no more slowing my mind and words. She had to communicate. To tell them.

Find Aimée.

"Doctor, she's trying to tell you something," said the nurse. "That dose will knock her out."

"Just do it, nurse."

Laure pinched his stethoscope so hard it popped off his neck.

Thursday Night

AIMÉE DIDN'T NEED LUCIEN Sarti's kind of trouble. Why couldn't she get the way his eyelashes curled out of her head?

At the bookstore on Place des Abbesses that had stayed open late for a poetry reading, she found an edition of that morning's *Corse-Matin*, the Corsican daily newspaper.

At least the bookstore had a heater, so she could get the chill out of her bones. On the third page she found two articles datelined Bastia. One reported a bomb threat to the central Bastia post office, discovered to be a hoax. A shorter article described vandalism of a fighter jet on the runway at a military installation, blaming workers from the nearby construction site. The construction company, Conari Ltd., declined to comment. Félix Conari's firm.

Flights had been canceled, and the airspace over Corsica declared a no-fly zone. Overreaction? That was a precaution the military enforced when national security was at stake. Even at an outpost on the tip of Corsica, far from the French mainland? Yet Conari had flown back.

Her eyes fell on another stack of newspapers.

IN COLD BLOOD, MY HUSBAND'S PARTNER SHOT HIM! The headlines stared back at her from *Le Parisien*. Next to a photo of Jacques Gagnard in uniform, a sidebar said: "as told by Nathalie Gagnard."

Sick to her stomach, her anger simmering, Aimée stuck her metal nail file into the antenna slot of her cell phone, wiggled it, and called 12 for information. She requested the number of Nathalie Gagnard and was connected.

"*Allô*, Nathalie?"

"Why ask me for ideas? You've already planned Jacques's funeral," said Nathalie, her voice slurred.

Drunk?

"Nathalie, you're going to retract those lies in the newspaper article," she said, controlling her tone. "Taking vengeance on Laure won't bring Jacques back."

"What? You *salauds*. I have n-n-no money to pay . . . Jacques . . . gambled it all."

Aimée caught her breath.

"Gambled?"

A sob answered her. "Debts. I can't even pay to bury him."

It began to fall into place. Jacques gambled yet he had a new car. He was in debt. But something on that snow-covered roof was supposed to make him a rich man.

"Nathalie, it's Aimée Leduc. I'm coming over."

The line went dead.

On her map, she found the nearest station—Lamarck-Caulincourt, one of the deepest stations, carved out of the old gypsum mines.

Ten minutes later she emerged in the drizzling mist under the curving Art Nouveau arch of the Metro. An inviting yellow glow came from the bistro by the steps. Dark stairs like parentheses ran up both sides of the hill. Then another flight of stairs, a street, and more stairs. They looked like rows of sagging accordion keys. At the top, the frosted white dome of Sacré Coeur resembled a pastry made of spun snow.

Plastic bags tossed by the wind fluttered and caught on a metal grille. Like her progress in this investigation, she thought, every step impeded and whipped about by the wind, ending nowhere. Laure's innocence was still in doubt. She'd have to make Nathalie admit Jacques's gambling habit to the authorities. Aimée wouldn't leave until she did.

Deep inside, Aimée felt that a larger conspiracy existed, and that Laure was enmeshed in it, like the fly in a spider's web. If only Laure were to recover and could talk!

The green metal lamppost illuminated the little-trafficked side of Montmartre where the occasional café still sold charcoal. A chic pocket of *intellos*, bourgeoisie, and the occasional Socialist bookshop in which Trotskyite pamphlets still filled the shelves. This was where the Surrealists had invented the "kissographe." To most, it meant a flight of stairs instead of a street; a climb of several flights, hauling groceries after a long day, rewarded by a breathtaking view.

Out of breath, she paused, noticing the walled Saint-Vincent's cemetery entrance with placards illustrating various plans for coffin burial. Three-deep coffin burials were the most economical. She turned left on rue Saint Vincent, passed the rose-walled Lapin Agile cabaret, and the last vineyard in Paris, its bare stalks of vines coated by a rim of frost.

Nathalie Gagnard's building adjoined the rue du Mont-Cenis stairs. Not thirty minutes ago, she'd stood at the top with Félix Conari and Lucien, overlooking another cemetery.

Circles . . . she'd gone in circles all night.

She pushed Lucien out of her mind.

The building was once a *hôtel particulier*, now chopped into apartments. Aimée saw the worn digicode numbers and letters. Too bad she'd left her plasticine back at the office. Frustrated, she pulled out her miniscrewdriver, unscrewed the plate, and connected the red and blue wires. The door clicked open. She stuck her boot in the opening, screwed the plate back on, and entered a dark hall.

After hitting the light switch, she scanned the mailboxes, found "Gagnard," and hurried up the spiral staircase before the timed switch could cut off.

"Nathalie?" She knocked on the door. "Nathalie! It's Aimée Leduc!"

Silence, except for the measured ticks of the timed light.

She pounded on the door. "Are you there, Nathalie?"

A man wearing chunky black motorcycle boots peered from behind a neighboring door on the landing.

"Mind keeping it down?" he said. "We're conducting a séance in here!"

A séance?

"Sorry, I'm worried about Nathalie. . . ."

"I feed her parakeet. Nathalie was fine the last time I saw her."

"Her voice sounded slurred over the phone. Do you have her door key? Would you mind opening the door for me?" She flashed her detective badge.

His eyes crinkled in interest. "A detective in kitten heels?"

"Let's forget the fashion commentary."

"I bet you ride a scooter, too."

He meant Aimée didn't look like a professional. What should a detective look like?

"Should I wear some kind of uniform to look official and stand out in a crowd?"

If René were here, he would have shot her a warning look. A ripple of chimes came from inside the neighbor's apartment.

"*Désolé*," he said and slammed the door.

Her feet hurt, the cold air chilled her legs, and her patience was exhausted. She pounded on his door until he opened it.

"Look, I'm on official inquiry. You must cooperate with me."

His eyes widened and he stepped back. "Bossy, aren't you?"

"Nathalie's in trouble," she said. Deep trouble from the sound of her voice.

"The spirits won't like that."

"The spirits? Ask me if I care!" Too bad she hadn't kept the fish-gutter knife. She stepped closer and glared at him.

He read the message in her eyes.

A moment later, he held out a key chain around the frame of the door. She took it, tried the keys until one fit, turned it, and opened the door.

"*Merci*," she said, delivering the keys back to him. Then at Nathalie's door she called, "*Allô?*"

She found Nathalie sprawled in her vomit on the parquet floor. Labored breaths whistled from her open mouth. The phone and pill bottle lay next to her.

She panicked, then reached under Nathalie's shoulders, dragged her to the small bathroom, and put Nathalie's head over the toilet.

"Come on, Nathalie, get the rest out!" she urged.

Nathalie's head rolled, her black hair clumped to her thin cheekbones.

Aimée grabbed the rubber gloves by the bottle of CIF cleanser near the shower, pulled them on, and stuck her finger down Nathalie's throat. A loud heave was followed by a spew. All over Aimée's leopard-print heels and the floor, missing the bowl.

And for fifteen francs more she could have waterproofed them.

Then Nathalie heaved again, this time on target.

"Nathalie. Nathalie, can you hear me?"

Her head lay on the toilet-bowl rim.

So much for relentlessly questioning her about Jacques's gambling.

Aimée stepped out of her shoes, put them in the sink, and toweled off. In the other room, she picked up Nathalie's phone and dialed 17 for SAMU, the ambulance corps, and gave the address.

"I found Nathalie Gagnard unconscious with a half-bottle of Ambien, I got her to throw up—"

Clicks and a sound like waves in the background.

"You've got to hurry."

"We're sending an ambulance that's already in the area," said a calm-sounding dispatcher. "It should arrive in three to five minutes."

"There are several flights of stairs," Aimée said.

"Aah, a Montmartre special," the dispatcher said. "So no ballerina medics on this call. Thanks for letting us know."

"Any advice?"

"Check for other pills."

Aimée rooted around on the floor and found some pills in the cracks between the wood slats. "I just scooped up more Ambien from the floor."

"Make sure her mouth stays clear and she can breathe, that there's no obstruction," said the dispatcher without missing a beat.

THE STRETCHER carrying Nathalie bumped the wall, and one of the buff paramedics, a Hôpital Bichat armband straining around his arm, swore. Aimée shut Nathalie's apartment door behind them, used the rest of the CIF to clean up the mess on the floor, and set her shoes to dry by the heating vent. That done, she located coffee beans in the freezer of Nathalie's trunk-sized refrigerator, ground them, and found a beat-up metal Alessi all-in-one espresso maker. She lit the gas burner, which flared to life with a blue flame.

She wouldn't leave this apartment until she found some evidence documenting Jacques's gambling. The two rooms, wrapped around the corner of the building, remained quasi-intact with a high recessed sculpted ceiling, and she realized this had once been part of a ballroom. A faded charm remained despite its crude conversion into living room and sleeping nook.

While the espresso maker dripped and hissed, she searched the apartment. No desk, no files, no books. Nothing. Just a pile of well-thumbed *Marie Claire* magazines and a parakeet, asleep in a covered birdcage, a box of bird seed below. Where did Nathalie keep her bills, paychecks, records?

She checked the kitchen cabinets, under the sisal rug, unzipped the sofa cover, checked the lamp shades, and felt for anything taped under the table. Again, nothing. In Nathalie's armoire, she found a selection of skirts, white shirts, several jackets, and one black dress. And an array of colorful scarves to dress up her basic wardrobe.

Didn't she ever wear jeans?

Aimée got on her knees and struck gold. Under Nathalie's bed she found a squat olive green file cabinet. Nicked, old—and locked. She levered it out and pushed it across the floor to the kitchen where she swiveled her nail file inside the lock. Instead of popping open, the lock jammed and broke. *Just her luck!* Par for the course, she thought, a perfect accompaniment to an eventful evening: a knife held to her throat; an encounter with a moody, sarcastic *artiste* whose touch she wanted to forget; Félix Conari's reminder of his affiliation with church and state; and only a garbled reference to Jacques's gambling from a pilled-out Nathalie. And then Nathalie's special addition, vomit on her good heels!

Bound and determined to find something while her shoes dried, she rooted through the kitchen drawers, found a meat-tenderizer mallet, summoned her energy, and whacked the lock, over and over, until it cracked.

Feeling better, she tried jimmying the top drawer open, only to end up using a can opener to open its side. Inside lay financial statements in folders going back some years. The second drawer held letters, and the third, mostly receipts and clippings.

She stirred two brown-sugar cubes into the chipped espresso cup and sipped, yawning while scanning the files. Statements from the last five years, requiring tedious checking. She opened the window a crack, trying to keep her head clear. Below lay the frosted, skeletal grape vines that produced a harvest each fall. The pride of Montmartre, but acidic. An acquired taste. She found a crocheted blue blanket and wrapped it around her feet.

Bankruptcy papers, the divorce decree. She leaned forward and got to work. The plaintive strains of someone practicing the cello accompanied the drip of melting ice outside Nathalie's window.

Boring, routine checking of handwritten financial notes and printed bank documents. After half an hour she discovered the discrepancies. Big discrepancies. And easy to track after she'd discovered the pattern.

The large deposits had started three months ago, coinciding with the Gagnards' divorce decree and bankruptcy. No moonlighting *flic* made fifty thousand francs a month working part-time! No wonder Jacques had convinced Nathalie to keep the driving school. It was a perfect place to stow the infusion of francs that had been deposited every month for three months. A simple way to hide blackmail?

Looking around the clean, utilitarian kitchen and IKEA assemble-it-yourself apartment furnishings, she doubted whether he had shared the largesse with Nathalie. Simple greed, always demanding more . . . had that been his downfall?

But this didn't dispel the possibility that it was something Jacques knew that had killed him.

With the few rigged machines she'd seen, she doubted Zette could afford a fifty-thousand-francs-a-month payoff. Jacques could have collected from other small bar owners and mined the district. A pattern?

Zette's murder might have been a warning to others of what

lay in store if they neglected to pay up. Yet, Jacques had been murdered two days before Zette's death.

She opened another file and glanced at a water-stained Monoprix flyer advertising a men's coat sale, a torn typed page inside. Why keep something like that? She put it back with the other papers.

Stymied, she sipped more espresso, pulling the blanket up over her lap. Had Jacques worked with others? She found several deposit slips with J. Gagnard written both as payee and payor.

So far, she'd only found answers that raised more questions. Opened a can of worms. Jacques could have been killed by any of his "clients" eager to stop the payoffs. That gave her a whole slew of possible suspects. She doubted that the authorities would be eager to investigate extortion charges against a slain, respected officer. After all, they had Laure and her smoking gun.

She looked at the twisted mess she'd made of the file cabinet drawer and was about to kick it when an idea stopped her. She bent down and, avoiding the rough, sharp edges, felt under each drawer for something taped. Nothing.

She'd found evidence of Jacques's extortion and knew that he gambled. But on a deeper level, she suspected there was more.

Whoever had killed him would have trashed Nathalie's place by now if they suspected he'd hidden something valuable here. But they were divorced; Nathalie could have brushed off anyone who questioned her, denying that she remained in his confidence. Yet the newspaper article that had appeared in today's paper would connect her to him. If they hadn't known about Nathalie before, they would now.

Something bothered her. What was it? She stared at the moonlight on the rimmed frosted window, then back into Nathalie's apartment, scanning it afresh. No computer. She scrutinized the apartment again. No printer.

She took out the Monoprix flyer, found the torn typed paper inside: a half page of computerese: //_e738:Ñ followed by more hash marks, numbers, strings of letters. She stared at it. Hadn't Oscar Wilde said that the true mystery in the world is the visible, not the invisible.

A pattern repeated. Of course, part of an encryption key! Bordereau's words about the data-encryption leak echoed in her mind. Did this fit? Had she finally found the link?

To piece the puzzle together she had to get onto a computer. Excited, she stuck the page in her pocket, put the files back, pushed the cabinet back under Nathalie's bed, donned her now-dried shoes, killed the lights, and was just about to close the apartment door when she heard footsteps coming up.

She shut the door without a sound, slipped off her shoes, and padded barefoot up to the next floor, crouched down, and listened. A Wagnerian opera came from the neighbor's flat, masking the sound of knocking on Nathalie's door. What kind of séance were they having?

She peered down through the metal railing, saw knitted caps on men's heads, and their down-jacketed shoulders. Then one of them looked up.

Her heart pounded. She'd seen the *mec*'s profile; it was the one with bad teeth and the knife. Her hands shook.

The timed lights clicked off. She backed up the steps. Don't come up here, she prayed. Then light flooded the landing and stairs again. She heard shuffling, a grunt, and the impact of a crowbar as the *mec* wedged the door open.

"Quick," one of them said, ". . . waiting outside."

She'd have to hurry, silently descend, and slip past the broken door, evading whoever was waiting. Pulling on a woolen cap, she said another prayer as she tiptoed past the half-open door and downstairs to the vestibule.

An older woman wearing a winter white wool cape was

checking her mailbox. "Cold, eh? Are you the new tenant on the top floor?"

Aimée was in no mood for conversation. She wanted to leave. Now. She put her finger over her lips, then whispered, "I'm worried. The door of number six has been broken open. And I heard noises inside as I walked by."

Thumps sounded above. Alarm showed on the woman's face.

Aimée nodded, pulling the woman close. "Don't go up there. I forgot my cell phone. Do you have one?"

The woman nodded.

"Punch in 18, call the *flics*," Aimée said.

As the woman pulled out her cell phone, Aimée slipped on her shoes, and left.

On the glistening outer steps she hesitated. Up or down? She heard the thrum of an idling engine and, looking down, saw the yellow lighted tip of a cigarette held by someone in the driver's seat of a car. She kept to the darkened border of the stairs, climbing fast, and had almost reached the top when a figure stepped out of a doorway and blocked her path.

Thursday Night

THE OVERHEAD LIGHT POOLED on the table. René stared at a worried Isabelle.

"It's your fault," Isabelle said. "You! We were fine until you appeared, asking questions, pretending to be . . ."

"Blaming me won't help find Paul," René said.

Inside he felt sick and full of guilt. If the killer was on to Paul, no place he'd hidden could keep him safe.

René saw himself out of the apartment where Isabelle kept vigil. Above him, a lone brown leaf from a plane tree drifted in a slow dance on the breeze. He watched it, feeling as lost as the leaf. He had already checked the rooftops and the cave where Isabelle said Paul sometimes hid. No trace. Where would a frightened boy hide? He tried to think the way Paul would.

The darkened Montmartre street lay deserted at this time of night. René walked, the ache in his hip exacerbated by the freezing temperature. Around the corner, past the building where Jacques was murdered, he saw the construction site. Frost laced the corrugated metal fencing the courtyard.

Could Paul have hidden here? He searched the fence for holes or loose siding. Nothing.

He tried Aimée's phone again. There was no answer, so he left a message that was cut off by static. Why was she always breaking her phone?

Further on, he found a padlocked Cyclone fence. The thin timber slats blocked any view from the street. He retraced his steps, running his hands along the fencing, with no better result.

He tried to ignore the terrible feeling in the pit of his stomach that Paul had been kidnapped before he'd had a chance to hide.

As he was about to give up, he heard scraping sounds from a doorway. The hair on the back of his neck rose. He thought back to the photos that had been delivered to their office. Had someone followed him?

Perspiration beaded René's forehead. He smelled mildew, old earth, and gypsum. Then he heard a creaking, followed by a louder cracking sound. Vandals, stray cats, or—?

"You lied," a young voice accused him.

"Paul?" he said, with relief.

Paul's white face shone in the streetlight. The faint mewling of a cat and running footsteps sounded from somewhere down the street.

"Your mother's worried to death," René said. "It's freezing. Where's your coat?"

"More lies! Maman knows I take care of us," he said, defiance in his eyes though his lip trembled. "I'm the man of our house."

René didn't know what to say to this shivering "man of the house" with smudged dirt on his face and mismatched space-invader socks, one blue and one yellow, showing over his rain shoes.

"Come upstairs, Paul," he said. "If you mean I lied about Toulouse-Lautrec—"

"You're not a detective," Paul said.

"I'm a *computer* detective," René said.

"Prove it."

Footsteps echoed in the distance.

"Here's my card," René said, looking around nervously, trying to herd Paul forward. "Be happy I didn't tell your mother about those model airplanes! Now get inside before you freeze."

Thursday Night

AIMÉE SWERVED ON THE icy steps in time to avoid the old woman and her pet schnauzer. She hiked up the cascading series of stairways and stuck her nail file in her cell phone again. One message. Why hadn't it rung? Bad reception on the *butte*? Or her missing antenna? If René had deposited Varnet's money in the bank, she'd buy another cell phone.

She listened to her message.

Static, then René's voice. "Aimée." Short gasps came over the phone. "The building site off rue André . . . ."

The line fuzzed and the message ended. Had René tried to investigate without her and gotten into trouble?

She looped the long wool scarf twice around her neck and

knotted it as she ran into the cold night. Forget the infrequent late night Metro, she'd make it there faster on foot.

Worried, Aimée ran up the steep rue des Saules, past the pearly dome of Sacré Coeur looming over the dark rooftops. She sprinted down winding rue Lepic with its shuttered windows. Music and a crowd spilled out of Le Jungle, the Senegalese club on rue Gabrielle. "What's your hurry? We've got a table. Join us," a man called to her.

"*Non, merci*," she said, swerving away from his laughing figure, her footsteps pounding on the uneven cobbles.

In Place Émile-Goudeau, she slipped on the water overflowing from the gutter and almost lost her footing. She passed the squat Bateau-Lavoir washhouse, Picasso and Modigliani's former studio, now an art gallery. Out of breath, she paused by the green metal Wallace fountain, wishing her feet didn't hurt and that sweat hadn't drenched her shirt. Then she ran down the steps. Not far now, a few streets more, if she could just keep running.

Her lungs heaving, she crossed windswept Place des Abbesses and kept left. Down the staircase, clutching the double railing, past Cloclo's station in the doorway of a building adorned with stone medallions. No Cloclo, just darkness.

Rue André Antoine was deserted except for the whipping wind. Then she saw two figures, short figures, just visible in a doorway.

"René!"

As she got closer, she saw his companion was a little boy with defiant eyes, who was shivering. She pulled off her coat.

"You must be Paul," she said, draping the coat around him.

"Where's your computer?"

Catching her breath, she grinned. "At the office."

"About time, Aimée," René said.

"I found Nathalie Gagnard, overdosed on pills," she said. "Poor thing's getting her stomach pumped but I found

Jacques's bank statements and something else that makes for interesting reading."

He inhaled. "Sorry, maybe I overreacted. Varnet coughed up, that's the good news. We're solvent." He paused.

Should she read between the lines to try and figure out what he couldn't say in front of Paul?

Paul shoved her coat back at her and ran into the apartment building without a word, slamming the door.

"What was that about, René?" she asked. "Didn't you convince Paul's mother to let him give evidence?"

"His mother's our witness. *She* saw three flashes."

"Three? But she drinks, doesn't she? I thought Paul—"

"I'll explain on the way back," René said.

Friday Morning

AIMÉE TWISTED THE WHITE porcelain knob of her claw-footed tub. The water heater had fired up, thank God. She poured in lavender essence. Steam rose as she sank her cold legs and aching feet into the hot water.

As she inhaled the citron-tinged lavender, her mind wandered. René's recounting of Paul's mother's story, the names of planets, the phrase "searching the stream," Bordereau's mention of a data-encryption leak, and the computer printout in Nathalie's files whirled in her head. Five minutes later, with the water still only up to her hips, the gas flame sputtered and died.

Great.

She toweled herself dry, pulled on her father's worn flannel robe and woollen socks. With the printout, she worked on her laptop in bed, searching and culling encryption sites. Without success. She needed Saj.

As orange dawn streaked the sky, she curled up under the duvet and slept, exhausted. She was awakened by the phone ringing in her ear and opened her eyes to see the cursor on the laptop screen blinking by her face.

"*Allô?*"

"Aimée, big problem," René said. "Maître Delambre's gone to a hearing in Fontainebleau. Isabelle's having second thoughts. She says she can't give evidence. What should I do?"

She couldn't let their witness get away.

"Meet me at 36, Quai des Orfèvres," she said. "Bring her with you, any way you can."

She filled the sink with ice cubes and stuck her face in, to wake up. Holding her breath, she kept her face immersed until her cheekbones went numb. She pulled on black tights, a woolen skirt, and a black cashmere sweater and zipped up her knee-high boots. At the door she grabbed her coat and ran down the worn marble stairs, swiping Stop Traffic red lipstick across her lips.

She called La Proc as she ran along the quay. She was their only hope. Eight minutes later she met René and Isabelle huddled by the guard post. Gunmetal gray snow-filled clouds threatened above. Around her ankles, a flurry of wet leaves gusted from the gutter.

"*Bonjour,* we have an appointment," she said, showing her ID to the two blue-uniformed guards.

She herded René and a hesitant Isabelle inside the courtyard of the Préfecture, turning left under the arcade to the wide brown wooden doors.

"Where's Paul?" Aimée asked.

"At school." Isabelle glanced at René. "Where's her computer? You said she works on a computer."

"Sometimes we have to do things the old-fashioned way," René said.

They climbed several flights of the brown-tiled stairway.

Aimée remembered counting them as a little girl. Five hundred
and thirty-two steps, still the same. When she got to the top, if
she'd counted right, her father would give her a Carambar. At
the Enforcement Section, she showed her ID again.

Isabelle pulled back, staring at the group of policemen
standing by the head of the stairs.

A uniformed *flic* ushered them along a high-ceilinged corridor, past open-doored offices. Their footsteps echoed on the
polished wooden floor. A few heads looked up as they entered
the long arched corridor of the *procureur général's* wing.
Aimée heard laughter, a snatch of conversation—"Barring
the miracle of the loaves and fishes, her sighting puts the *mec*
in the *boulangerie* at the time of the murder"—and smelled the
aroma of coffee.

She paused. Isabelle had come to a halt and was buttoning
her coat, her mouth tight. "I'm leaving."

"What's the matter, Isabelle?"

Isabelle shook her head. "Forget it."

Dread hit Aimée. Too late now, she wanted to say. So much
depends on you. Instead, she nodded. "This place makes me
nervous, too."

"*Stupide*, I'm leaving, I can't get involved."

"It's a lot to ask of you, I know," Aimée said, perspiring. "We
wouldn't impose, René wouldn't be so persistent, unless we
had to. Remember, it's not *about* you and Paul."

"Easy for you to say!" Isabelle turned away.

Frightened, nervous probably, needing a drink. Aimée had
to reach her, to convince her. She put her arm around
Isabelle's thin shoulders. "You're right, Isabelle, easy for me to
say. You can walk away right now, go down the stairs, and
leave. However, a man was murdered and you were the
unlucky one who witnessed the shots. And if you don't speak
up, the killers will get away with it. They'll probably do it
again. And then someone's looking for Paul—"

She paused. Isabelle wouldn't meet her gaze. So close, and yet . . .

"I'll pick Paul up," Isabelle said. "I'll take him to my sisters in Belleville."

"Can you tell me this won't go through your mind when you're out on the quay, or taking Paul to a new school? Won't you constantly wonder if the *mec* who was looking for Paul will turn up at your door? And worry that this time he'll find him?"

Isabelle's eyes clouded. "I did time in prison. Years ago, but still, they won't take what I say seriously."

"That's past. You know how prison feels. My friend will go there if you don't help us," she said. "René's arranged a place for you and Paul to stay. A safe place. Please."

"Mademoiselle Leduc." The *flic* cleared his throat, beckoning to them. "May I remind you, La Proc's got a tight schedule."

The lines at the corner of Isabelle's mouth had relaxed a fraction. "Today?" she asked Aimée. "We can go today?"

"Right after you speak with La Proc. You'll do fine, just tell her the truth. La Proc's fair. Remember that."

After a single sharp rap, a woman's voice called, "*Entréz.*"

The *flic* opened the door and gestured them inside. Tall ceilings, windows overlooking the Seine, a framed photo of Mitterrand wearing the blue, white and red ribbon of Le Président. A coveted corner office indicated Edith Mésard's status.

La Proc wore her blond hair coiffed sleekly behind her ears. In her tailored dark green Rodier suit, holding a dossier, she looked formidable. It was the word Morbier had used to describe Mésard's prosecutorial skills. A white-haired man sat next to her desk.

"*Bon*, make it good, Mademoiselle Leduc. You've got fifteen minutes," La Proc said.

"Thank you for making the time, Madame La Proc," Aimée began.

"You won't mind if a consultant to Internal Affairs stays?" Edith Mésard asked. "He's interested in what might transpire."

The white-haired, ruddy complected man filled out his double-breasted navy blue suit. His eyes flicked over them, calculating. Who was he?

Aimée cleared her throat. "All the better. This is my partner, René Friant; Isabelle Moinier, and you are Monsieur . . . ?"

"Ludovic Jubert," he said. His eyes locked on hers.

She felt the color drain from her face and a leaden sensation in her feet. She'd finally flushed him out. Yet she was filled with fear.

"Monsieur Jubert, you worked with my father, didn't you?" She paused, searching for the words. "I've been wanting to speak with you."

"So I gather, Mademoiselle Leduc."

Concentrate! She had to concentrate on his reactions as well as to make sense to La Proc.

"You can catch up later, I'm sure," Edith Mésard told her in a calm tone underlaid with steel. "You indicated urgency, Mademoiselle Leduc? I'm listening."

"On the night of Jacques Gagnard's murder, Mademoiselle Moinier, who lives on rue André Antoine in the adjacent building, saw three flashes. I think that means there were three shots fired. I believe that a high-tin-content bullet, presently undergoing tests in the police lab, was responsible for the gunshot residue on Laure Rousseau's hands, not her Manhurin."

"So you're saying what?"

"Laure didn't shoot her partner."

"I don't understand," Edith Mésard said. "Where did this 'bullet' that's being tested come from?"

"The rooftop. I dug the bullet out of the chimney."

Ludovic Jubert hadn't said a word. His eyes hadn't even blinked. Behind him, flecks of snow fluttered outside the window, drifting over traffic moving at a snail's pace along the quai. And disappeared into the sluggish pewter Seine below.

"Who do you suggest shot Jacques Gagnard?"

"Another apartment resident heard men speaking Corsican on the scaffold that encircles the roof."

Edith Mésard looked at Ludovic Jubert. Aimée saw his shoulders move in a slight shrug.

"If you and your partner would wait outside, please," Edith Mésard said.

"YOU LOOK like you saw a ghost," René said.

She nodded and sat beside him on the wooden bench. The hall radiator sputtered, emitting ripples of heat. "I did. In the flesh."

A metal trolley with several coffees stood by a potted palm.

"Tell me about it over coffee?"

She nodded.

He edged off the high bench, slipped some francs into the tin with "two francs s'il vous plaît" pasted on it, filled two plastic cups with espresso, and handed her one.

"It's about my father. And Jubert."

"Your father?"

"And a cover-up." She sighed, leaned back, and told him about Laure's hint that her father had been involved in some cover-up and Jubert's supposed connection to the Place Vendôme explosion that had killed Aimée's father.

"You could have told me before." René's large green eyes flashed in anger. "But, Aimée, Laure's disjointed ramblings don't prove anything."

She rubbed her eyes. "Jubert knows I broke into STIC. That's why he's here. He probably found out I used his name to request an expensive ballistics test. He wants to see what I've discovered."

René shook his head. "How can he prove it? You covered your tracks, right?"

"Jubert's not a good adversary to box with. But if I'm going down, he's joining me."

René took her hand. "You've found the eyewitness you needed to clear Laure, and the lab report. Hell, you've even found the bullet."

"If they'll accept it as evidence and credit Isabelle's account."

"How can they not?"

"I hope so," she said. Looking down at her wet boots, she told him, "You won't like this, but it's better you work at home. Don't go to the office."

He rolled his eyes. "Giving it to me piecemeal, eh. What else haven't you told me?"

"I can't pin it down but there is a thug named Petru mixed up in this, too. He's Corsican, but he doesn't fit in with the Separatist movement. And he—or his friends—were on my tail."

René handed her a box from his briefcase. "This arrived this morning."

The return address was Dr. Guy Lambert, Hôpital Quinze-Vingts, Opthamaligie Department.

Something she'd forgotten at his office? She slit the tape with her keys.

Inside lay a six-month supply of her eye medication, a referral to an eye specialist, and several lines of Lord Byron's poem "Fare Thee Well":

> And life is thorny; and youth is vain;
> And to be wroth with one we love,
> Doth work like madness in the brain.

She crumpled the paper.

René stared at her.

"Guy's parting gift. Conscientious, as always."

"What do you mean?"

"He's gone to Sudan to work with Doctors Without Borders."

"Sudan?"

"To save the blind of Africa," she said. "To get as far away from me as he can, and still work medical wonders."

René kept staring. "He saved your vision, Aimée."

Her lip trembled. If René didn't shut up she'd burst into tears. She lowered her gaze.

"Like I didn't know that, René!"

"Another thing you didn't tell me," René said, hurt and something else mingling in his voice.

"Isn't it enough that I burden you with my love life . . . or my nonexistent love life, most of the time?" she asked. "It would be selfish. You've found someone and seem so happy; it's not fair to dump on you."

Instead of the acknowledgment she expected, more anger flashed in his eyes. "I thought we were closer, Aimée."

"You're my best friend! But do I have to reveal the squalid details of how I let Guy down?"

Pride, yes, her pride prevented her from revealing that Guy had left her. Left her because of who she wasn't.

René shook his head in disgust.

All wrong, she got everything wrong with René whichever way she turned.

"Didn't you throw yourself into this investigation to fill the void, Aimée? As usual?"

She slumped in the chair. Was he right?

He stood up, brushed off his black wool jacket, and handed her a card with the address of the Convent des Recollets. "Paul and Isabelle's accommodation. The convent offers assistance to families in transition."

He took his briefcase and walked down the hall.

What had she done now?

She called after him, "René, you're so happy, I didn't want to—"

He turned. "So I gather."

How could it all go so wrong and all at the same time? René upset, Laure in a coma, Guy on another continent leaving Byron to console her: three thin lines. And Jubert with his gray snake eyes, now high up in Internal Affairs. The list grew. And the gnawing fear that Jacques's murder was part of something bigger. The tape in her head replayed Lucien Sarti's voice, the sensation of his thigh brushing hers, and his warm lips' imprint on her cheek.

The door opened, and the floor creaked under Isabelle's feet.

"*Ça va?*" Aimée managed a small smile, handing her the convent's address. "They're expecting you. Ask a friend to bring your things over. Stay until things get sorted out."

"*Merci*," she said.

"Mademoiselle Leduc, a moment please." Edith Mésard spoke from her office.

Aimée crunched her plastic espresso cup and tossed it into the wire trash bin.

Edith Mésard and Jubert stood by a grouping of wingback chairs. A cigarette butt smoldered in an otherwise clean ashtray on the windowsill.

"No need to sit down, Mademoiselle. I'll make it brief and to the point," Edith Mésard said. She buttoned her tailored jacket. "Besides the municipal code infractions I could charge you with, not to mention a misdemeanor charge of evidence tampering and some hijinks with the police intranet system—" she paused. "You're compromising a joint *Renseignements Généraux* and *Direction de la Surveillance du Territoire* undercover operation."

Aimée was startled. She hadn't expected this.

"What do you mean?"

"As Monsieur Jubert pointed out, it's too late in the game.

The covert operation is too far advanced for us to switch directions."

"You're asking me to cease trying to clear Laure Rousseau? I won't. I've handed you exculpatory evidence on a plate. Heaping full. There's no way to ignore it."

"I'd suggest you listen, Mademoiselle," La Proc said. "For a change."

Aimée felt as if she were back at school being reprimanded for talking out of turn. Jubert watched her without a word.

"If Laure's off the hook," she said. "I'm all ears."

"Do you forget, Mademoiselle, we operate in the real world according to regulations, Le Code Civil, and the judicial system?"

"So you're saying you won't—"

Jubert spoke for the first time, his voice calm and even. "She's saying, Mademoiselle, all pertinent and legally obtained evidence will be presented at the hearing of the charges against Officer Rousseau."

Right. She trusted him no further than she could spit.

"Do you agree that the bullet I obtained will be accepted into evidence?"

Jubert pulled at his chin with his thumb and forefinger.

"Mademoiselle, I see you don't mince words," he said. "Refreshing, I'm sure, in your line of work."

Her line of work? Like she strong-armed witnesses? While he worked the old-boy network of favors asked and granted, shrouded by payoffs, implied and unspoken.

"We'd like your assistance," he went on.

"My assistance?" She blinked.

"Your persistence has been noted. Instead of compromising our operation, which you seem bent on doing, we want you to work with us."

Right. Her father had worked for the RG and it got him killed. She hated their everyday world of lies, deceit, and cover-ups.

"My report card said, 'Doesn't play well with others.' I haven't changed," she told him.

But she had the sinking feeling that working with "them" was the price for Laure's vindication. A complex RG and DST sting operation, orchestrated by the Ministry, was the last thing she wanted to be involved in. Her dealings with the secret world had blown up, literally in her face, in Place Vendôme and taken her father's life.

"You're thinking of your father. A tragedy, yes," Jubert said. "Nothing to do with this operation or this branch. The circumstances were totally different."

"I'd like to know who was responsible," Aimée said, her gaze fixed on Jubert.

"That branch closed down. If any files exist, they're classified," Jubert said. "Live in the present; think of this as your contribution to guarding and preserving the security of France."

Appealing to the patriot in her with their hollow jingoism? Think again, she wanted to say. Their offer smelled, but they didn't leave her many options.

"Will you guarantee that Laure Rousseau's suspension will be lifted and she'll be cleared of all charges?"

"Under the law, in Internal Affairs investigations, officers charged with a crime remain suspended until the hearing officer reaches a decision."

They would do nothing for Laure.

"You can't ignore the witness who saw figures on the roof, the three flashes, the high-tin GSR content."

"Duly noted, Mademoiselle," Jubert said. "Of course, by using my name you prioritized a test—a fancy, expensive one, I believe—but I will authorize it after the fact, given your cooperation."

Aimée stared at Edith Mésard with her perfectly applied makeup, a hint of blush, not too much.

"That's all you can say?"

Edith Mésard returned her stare, reaching for her overcoat. "I will see justice done, Mademoiselle. Count on it. My record speaks for me. It's why I serve."

Edith Mésard clutched her Lancel briefcase. "I believe, in the Sentier case, our dealings proved that?"

In that case, Mésard had gotten parole for Stefan, an old German radical who'd known Aimée's mother.

"Now, do I need to charge you with infractions of the code and a serious misdemeanor? Under the Security Services Protective Act, a consultant under contract in an ongoing investigation is exempt from prosecution." She paused, clipping her cell phone to her side pocket. "But you tell me."

Mésard was good. Still, she'd revealed how much they needed Aimée. Needed her like the country needed butter if Mésard was willing to invoke the Security Services Protective Act on her behalf.

Could she work with people who had links to the surveillance that had killed her father? Once she got involved with them, there would be no walking out. On the other hand, connections meant everything, and the closer she edged to the secret world, the more opportunities existed to find out about her father's contract with the RG, and why he had died.

And maybe it would explain why Jacques was killed, too.

Doing business with the devil she knew seemed better than doing it with the one she couldn't identify. And it was the only way she'd get Laure off. She nodded.

"Good," Edith Mésard said, as if it was all in a busy morning's work. "Monsieur Jubert will give you the details."

Her heels clicked across the floor and the door shut behind her with a whoosh of cold air.

"Sit down, Mademoiselle," Ludovic Jubert said. "I know you're quick so this won't take long."

She sat down in the wingback chair, crossed her legs, and prayed she could do this.

"Before we start I need to know about the report," she said.

"Report, Mademoiselle?" Jubert raised a thick white eyebrow.

She pulled out the photo of the four of them—Morbier, Georges Rousseau, her father, and Jubert—on the steps by Zette's place and set it on the windowsill. The snow was still falling outside, like scattered feathers.

"Aaah, I had a flat stomach then," Jubert said.

"I think you know what I want," she said.

"I am clueless, Mademoiselle. Mind if I smoke?" he asked, as if they were in a café instead of La Proc's office.

She pulled a Nicorette patch from her bag, then threw it back in. "Not if you offer me one."

He handed her a pack of filtered Murati Ambassador, a Swiss brand. She took one and he lit it with a silver lighter. She inhaled, and the smooth kick slid to the back of her throat.

"Now try not to think of this as the dentist's chair, Mademoiselle," he said. "Enjoy this little guilty pleasure and let's get started."

"You'll have my full cooperation," she said, leaning back and savoring the Murati. "But first I need to know if you, or all of you, and my father were involved with a gambling scam in Montmartre. One Georges Rousseau took credit for stopping it though it's still going on in Zette's bar. And all over the *quartier*, I imagine."

"That's what you're worried about? This secret?" He seemed genuinely surprised.

"Tell me and it will go no further than this room."

His gray eyes flickered as he weighed his answer.

"Corruption's a serious charge," he said.

"I don't believe Papa was involved in a cover-up of corruption. I think you were and saddled him with your crime. You stigmatized the rest of his life."

"Your mother did that, Mademoiselle," Ludovic Jubert said without missing a beat. "She tainted his career prospects."

Her American mother who had left them and joined a group of radicals in the seventies. "That's *your* opinion." She took a drag to cover the jolt Jubert's words had given her.

"Jean-Claude paid for that many times over," he said, looking out the window. "A good *flic*. He had a nose, as they say, for the odor of crime. No getting past that. And I see you do, too." He sighed. "Georges Rousseau liked the odor. He didn't mind running informers and giving them too much leeway."

"Are you saying Georges Rousseau was the corrupt one? He died a decorated—"

"And valorous commissaire," Ludovic Jubert interrupted. "We had to cover for him. He'd compromised too much in Montmartre."

Was that what Morbier was hiding? Why did Laure think it was Aimée's father who was implicated?

"Some of Rousseau's informers played by the rules," Jubert continued. "Still do. We turn a blind eye to their little operations and they reciprocate with information on more serious matters. Matters affecting national security. All *flics* depend on informers; we wouldn't get far without insider information." He ground out his cigarette, impatient. "But you know this. You know how the system operates."

She'd been raised on it. Her father hated it and left to join her grandfather at Leduc Detective. One doesn't touch pitch, he'd said, without being blackened.

"Then you're saying Georges Rousseau took bribes and became corrupt," she said, "but was decorated and promoted because his network of informers was needed? Then why does Laure believe *my* father was corrupt and the proof's in a report?"

"Use your imagination," he said.

"You're implying Laure's father fingered mine, shifted his own guilt onto my father?"

"Close."

"Where's the police file?"

"The RG deep-froze most of them."

She shook her head. "I don't believe you."

"Mademoiselle, it's in your interest to do so." He stood. "Still the little firebrand, I see," he said. "Daddy's little girl. Your father wanted a boy, you know."

Bastard! That stung. How would he know?

She clutched the edge of the chair, white knuckled. She wouldn't let him see how his words had rocked her. She recalled Laure's mumblings and Morbier's comments scrawled on the newspaper.

"This all ties to the investigation of Corsican Separatists six years ago, doesn't it? The question of where they were getting arms. *That's* the secret report. My father worked on it, didn't he? With you?"

Ludovic Jubert stabbed out his cigarette and nodded.

"Your father always said you were sharp," he said.

"Did this involve the explosion in Place Vendôme that killed him?"

"Not at all. It is as I told you. Let's move to the present, shall we?" He opened a drawer in the desk and took out a file.

"We believe this man's running a Separatist network in Montmartre. We count on you to find him."

He handed it to her. "Look inside. He's a Corsican terrorist, a member of the Armata Corsa, responsible for bomb threats to the Mairie and for holdups using the arms that were stolen six years ago."

"Eastern European arms—?"

"Taken from Croatia, stockpiled by our military in Solenzara, at least until they disappeared six years ago. This past year they've been turning up in Paris with disturbing regularity."

"How do you know this?"

"We have big ears, Mademoiselle."

Big Ears . . . Frenchelon?

She opened the file. Lucien Sarti's image stared back at her.

Friday Morning

LAURE SAT UP IN the hospital bed, the computer keypad propped lecternlike on her hospital tray table. A hospital phone stood on the night table next to the violets Aimée had brought.

"*Très bon*, wonderful progress, the commissaire's so pleased you can use this special equipment," said the young therapist, beaming at her. "Each time you tap a key, I copy down a letter. So far, you've said, 'I remember' and what looks like a name and phone number, *oui?*"

Laure blinked. If only she would stop running off at the mouth and hurry up. Why didn't this saccharine-voiced woman call Aimée?

"I'll inform the officer on duty and we'll take it from there." She patted Laure's arm. "He wants to hear right away about anything you know that may help with their investigation." Laure blinked twice for no.

She slid her finger onto the letters n . . . o . . . w.

"Now?"

Laure blinked. Cold saliva drooled down her chin and she felt her shoulders sliding down the damn pillow.

"Excuse me, Laure," the therapist said, "I must check with the officer first."

The therapist stepped out of the ward. Laure slid further down, her head sinking into the pillow. And then she saw the pencil. She gripped it between her thumb and index finger. If only she could knock the telephone receiver off its cradle. With all her might, she swatted at it with the pencil. The smudged receiver wavered but held.

She tried again, this time wedging the pencil under it and levering it up. As the receiver fell she heard the dial tone. Quick, she had to do it fast, before the therapist returned or the recorded message came on and said, "If you'd like to make a call . . ."

She tapped Aimée's eight numbers. Where was the connect button?

She heard footsteps, saw the blue uniform.

"What's she doing?"

Friday Morning

AIMÉE HANDED THE FRANCS to Pascalou, her local butcher, who wiped his hands on the red-smeared apron straining around his rotund figure.

"I threw in a little treat," he said and grinned. "Something Miles Davis likes."

"You spoil him, Pascalou," she said.

"Time for him to have a special friend, Aimée," he said, wagging his finger.

And what about me? She just smiled.

"*Merci.*" She pocketed her change and hefted the white waxed-paper packet of Miles Davis's lamb shanks. The bells tinkled on the butcher-shop door as she shut it.

Not thirty minutes ago, she'd listened to Jubert's description of the terrorist cell concealing arms somewhere in Montmartre. She had kept quiet regarding Lucien Sarti. She couldn't figure him out. Suspicion of Jubert still nagged her. Would he keep his end of the bargain concerning Laure?

She had to find Petru, more and more convinced was she that he, rather than Lucien, was the key. There was no reason to inform Jubert yet. She would deliver a terrorist to him, but it wouldn't be whom he expected.

First, she had to work on Frenchelon to find out how they'd traced the terrorist network back to Lucien Sarti.

She called Saj, ordered Indian takeout from Passage Brady, and booted up her laptop at home. By the time Saj arrived, in a flowing Afghan embroidered shearling coat, the pakoras and vegetarian thali sat on the fireplace mantel, the steam escaping and fogging the tarnished mirror behind it. Cumin and the scent of coconut curry filled the salon that doubled as her home office.

"Smells wonderful," he said.

"Ready for overtime?" she asked. "I think you'll like this project."

Saj eyed the laptop screen. "Frenchelon, hmmm. So we're working on satellite netspionage?" he asked.

"Netspionage? I like that," she said, her fingers clicking over the keys. "Digital dead-letter drop, heard of that?"

He nodded, hung his coat behind the chair, and kicked off his sandals. "Do it all the time. Where's René?"

"At his place," she said, leaning back in her chair. "Working."

"So they're watching your office like last time, eh?"

Saj was quick.

"Who is it this time?"

"Supposedly Corsican Separatists, or else the local mafia under the guise of the Armata Corsa. Charming *mecs*, either way."

Saj paused, holding a garlic naan midair. "Talk about a bad-boy magnet! I don't get it. You and René do computer security. How come you keep getting involved with thugs?"

"Nice segue," she said. "It's all related. And something smells way off. That's why I called you."

"I need to center, Aimée," Saj said, wiping his hands and settling cross-legged on her threadbare Savonnerie carpet.

She groaned inside. Why couldn't he center before he came?

"Why don't you join me? It's been a while for you, *non?*"

She'd made a stab at meditation at the Cao Dai temple in November and failed at mindful breaths. Her legs had cramped, her mind run rampant, yet she had experienced one brief shining moment when the world fell away and somehow she'd breathed with the universe.

"Right now I can use all the help I can get."

She sat cross-legged beside him, touched her thumbs to her middle fingers. Tried to clear her mind.

"Deep asana," Saj said. "Breathe in through the nostrils, hold it, good, now a long exhale."

Conscious of the leafless tree branch slapping her window, the crackle of the logs in the fire, and the hardness of the wood floor, she waited. The other "state" remained elusive. Yet after ten minutes her mind had cleared.

Saj stood up and helped himself to the Indian food.

Bordereau of the DST had mentioned a data-encryption leak in the same sentence with Corsican Separatists. "Look at this," she said. "Data-encryption leaks and one link relating to Frenchelon. What do you know about a connection to the satellite Helios-1A?"

"The satellite has a stowaway on board, the Eurocom, an interception cartridge that picks up Inmarsat and Intelsat signals so it can read microwave and mobile phone communications. My friend at Dassault Systèmes worked on the Eurocom's manufacture."

"Impressive," she said. "A great tool with which to find terrorists."

"They call it searching the Bitstream; it's like sifting sand to find a coin most of the time."

"Say that again," she said, drumming her chipped nails on the space bar.

"Eh, searching the Bitstream . . . ."

"That's it!" Hadn't Zoe Tardou heard "searching the stream" from the men on the roof speaking in Corsican to cloak their meaning? She'd found the connection at last.

Saj grinned, pushed a dark blond dreadlock behind his shoulder. "All things to all people, I'd say. One juicy intercept was Brezhnev's phone call to his mistress from his limo. Another, the *Rainbow Warrior* scandal with Greenpeace, via ARABSAT and Gadhafi's conflict with Chad. But NATO's the prime target for Echelon and a real sieve. Of course, it's also used for rampant corporate espionage."

Her ears perked up. She sat forward in her chair. "Can you crack it?"

"Now why would I do that?"

"To show you can," she said. "How difficult would it be for you or anyone else?"

"Get real, Aimée. We're talking big boys with big toys."

"Say someone hired you to intercept a satellite feed."

He shrugged. "It doesn't work like that," he said. "I'd need special equipment."

"Like what?"

She could tell she'd sparked his interest by the way he'd already clicked on the Net and brought up some sites.

"Like a satellite," he said. "And say I had a satellite, the Faraday cage poses a problem."

"Like a cage for tigers?"

"That's one way of putting it," he said.

"Where's this Faraday cage?"

Saj tied back his dreadlocks with an elastic band. "Far as I know, it's at the same facility as the parabola satellite dishes. Would have to be to access the feed." He pointed to his screen. "See, e-mails, land lines, cell-phone conversations, and faxes are beamed in a stream of data. Satellites in a geosynchronous and a polar orbit receive this data, then transmit it back in a continuous sequence of bits, downlinking the raw stream of data to a dish or to antennas on land. This data feed's piped from the antenna into the Faraday cage for deciphering. Inside the cage, a program picks out key and sensitive words and encrypts them, then sends the encrypted info on, via fiber optics, a protected radio network, or a disc."

"Why not by e-mail?"

"Not safe, unless you use a cipher and have a key at the other end."

Plucking words out of the ether, then sorting them and making sense of them. She stood and paced in the room. A suffused weak winter light shrouded the pear tree below in the courtyard.

"Rumor has it Frenchelon processes two million phone calls, faxes, and e-mails worldwide each month," she said. "Maybe more. It even tracks individual bank accounts. Or so they say."

Saj nodded. "The genius lies in the Faraday cage's banks of computers that are programmed to recognize key words." He rolled his neck from side to side.

"Like addresses, phone numbers surveilled by the *Direction Générale de la Sécurité Extérieure*; embassies, foreign ministers, multinational corporations, and suspected agents?"

Saj nodded. "The system records and transmits them for analysis. *La routine*, they call it. What doesn't turn out to be relevant is thrown into the information garbage can."

"So Frenchelon transmits encrypted data of these e-mails, faxes, and phone conversations, filtered and sorted by key words, to where?"

He shrugged. "The analysis hub could exist anywhere."

She leaned forward, deep in thought. His explanation made her determined to get an Inmarsat satellite phone, which would be harder to intercept since it used its own three satellites. She had known about the *Central d'Écoute Téléphonique* central listening center under Les Invalides where tapped phone lines were monitored by the judiciare and military. But only under authorization by the president at Matignon Palace. Or so the story went. This was far more all-encompassing.

"How would a criminal get into Big Ears?" she asked.

He paused. "Easiest thing would be to get the cipher key, depends how often they change it—once a day, once a week on Thursday, or whatever—tap into the microwaves, and—"

"Sell the feed and the key to the highest bidder," she said, her eyes lighting up, "like a renegade terrorist group."

What if Jacques had stumbled onto the cipher key involving the Corsican Separatists? But how would Jacques, a *flic* in the eighteenth, have access to a high-security agency leak?

Thoughts whirled through her head: Jacques gambled, he moonlighted for Zette—who operated illegal gambling machines in his bar—escorting "VIPs". Maybe VIPs did slum in Montmartre at Zette's. Maybe Zette had told her the truth and it was some security dweeb whom Jacques had squired around who had info to share. But why would he spill his guts to Jacques, a *flic*? Correction, a bent *flic*. But selling classified encrypted data to Corsican Separatists was another league altogether, a whole other division. The connection to Jacques remained muddled at best.

She opened the file on her laptop that she'd copied from STIC and combed through Jacques Gagnard's data. Two minutes later she'd found it. Stupid. She should have checked before. He'd served in the military at Solenzara and been discharged for misconduct. Gambling? It had been six years ago. Selling the missing arms? But those infusions of cash to his bank account were recent.

"What's going on in that spiky-haired head of yours?"

"Illegal thoughts." She gave him a big smile. "Finish up the pakoras and show me the Frenchelon sites."

"Look, I hack and crack, do encryption. What kind of job is this?"

"A big one. Can you highlight the possible hubs in France or, better still, refine the target to the Paris area?"

"Check this out," Saj said. "Outside Paris, in the suburb of Alluets-le-Roi, the DGSE have a big installation of parabolas and antennas," Saj said, pulling up an e-mail. "But according to my friend, they handle intercepted communications right here in Paris, too."

"Where?" Aimée stood up.

"*La piscine*," he said.

"At a pool?"

"That's what they call it. It's on Boulevard Mortier, right behind the public pool." He meant the military caserne in Belleville bordering the Périphérique ring road, a nineteenth-century barracks once, the home of the 104th corps of Le Mâns.

"So, in theory, a data-encryption leak would come from there?"

Saj gave a small smile. "Bound and determined to connect this, eh?"

They were getting closer, she sensed it. Smelled it. Not just smoke, but sparks she could fan into a fire.

"Put it this way," she said. "What would you do, Saj, if you had skills and access to this encrypted data and a hidden agenda, say, selling military and ministerial documents, plans for Corsica? Or stolen arms?"

"The best plans, the ones that work, are real simple," he said.

"Simple? So tell me simple."

An idea formed in her mind as he spoke. Had Jacques known who was furnishing the arms? Or how?

"The ideal? A hardware guy, probably an outside consultant, since the military hasn't trained enough of them yet. Or maybe he's part of the team that set up the system, or installed a satellite communication fiber optic line, for example. He knows the hardware since he's installed it or designed it. He knows the vulnerabilities. One day something fizzes and, doing repairs or system analysis, he realizes this whatever is a back-door access to valuable data. Maybe for only so many hours, or period of time, or maybe he can engineer an open door for an hour once a week. And he sells this stream."

A genius, Saj was a genius!

"A back door, of course! What about the cipher key?"

"Good point. No one can read the data without the key. That's the money part, reading it. Say he provides the cipher key for a price, but it's only good once. They change them constantly."

If Saj could think like this, chances were someone else had, too.

She handed Saj the printout from Nathalie's file.

"Like this?"

Saj scanned the printout, gave a low whistle. "Let me work on this. You've got a devious little mind, Aimée," he said, clicking away nonstop.

"As they say, 'Takes one to know one.'" She picked up her bag. Time to do the footwork. "Call me when you find something."

AIMÉE TOOK the Metro to station Guy Moquet, named for a seventeen-year-old Communist Résistance fighter. She paused on the platform and saw the copy of his last letter, dated 1943, from prison, behind a glass plaque. Seventeen years old. The lines that stuck in her head were his only worry being that he might have died in vain. What would he think now, if he'd lived?

She tried Cloclo. No answer. She climbed the Metro steps into the bone-chilling air. She bent against the wind climbing rue Lamarck, passed a parking garage, a funeral parlor, a small instrument shop from which a man was carrying a violin case, a shoemaker with miniature porcelain shoes filling his tall window. Reaching Place Froment, she confronted six small streets intersected by a kidney-shaped island facing a café under a red sign reading TABAC. Opposite nestled a motorcycle riding school, a bakery, its glass panels painted with fading *belle époque* threshing scenes, a hip resto, and a pharmacy with a lighted green neon cross above its window. A bourgeois enclave. Had Conari been wrong? Had she wasted a trip?

She walked by a small Arab grocer's with bins of fruit and vegetables outside under a canopy. Across the way stood Hôpital Bretonneau, once a children's hospital, now inhabited by squatters, judging from the graffitied LIBRE ART, LIBRE ARTISTES sign. Huge and taking up most of the block.

She turned on rue Carpeaux. Entered the corner café with its smell of wet dog. A spaniel lay behind the counter next to the owner, who had a cell phone cupping his ear. From the look of it, the café had last been decorated in the fifties.

The owner nodded to her, the phone still cradled on his shoulder.

"Monsieur, I'm looking for the Turkish grocery store," she said.

He jerked his thumb out the window toward the blackened stone hospital wall bordering Montmartre cemetery.

"*Merci.*"

How had patients felt about the view from their windows, a tree-speckled cemetery bordered by a high wall containing the final resting place of Émile Zola, among others?

Aside from the vineyard, and the cemeteries, the hospital occupied one of the largest sites in the area. A demolition and renovation approval sign dated 1989 was posted on the wall but the place still hadn't been rebuilt.

Then she spied the Turkish grocery, a storefront with bins of fruit, packaged Parmalat tomato sauce, and a dusty hookah in the window. Inside, Turkish music whined and two men played cards on the counter by the cash register. The narrow store was crammed to the old roof beams with canned food, rubber sandals, oddments, Turkish tapes and videos.

"*Bonjour, Messieurs,*" she said, picking up a bottle of Vittel and laying a few francs on the counter. "*Salaam Aleikoum.*"

"*Aleikoum salaam,*" said the older of the two men, returning her greeting.

"If I may interrupt you for a moment," she said, "my friend Petru used to live upstairs, but he's moved. Any idea where I can find him?"

"Petru?"

"A Corsican. He changes his hair color more often than I do," she grinned. "You know who I mean, eh?"

"Haven't seen him for a while," the man said. His companion said something in Arabic. "I'm sorry, my friend said since yesterday."

She thanked him and went through the open door to a small apartment foyer that smelled of pine soap. A young woman in a blue smock, her hair in a thick black bun, mopped the cracked tiles.

"Pardon, Madame, I'm looking for Petru, a Corsican. Did he leave a forwarding address?"

The woman set her mop in the metal pail. "Gone." She paused and wiped her brow. "Here people don't leave addresses when they move," she said. Her accent was Portuguese. "Clean, all clean, the place is vacant."

A glittering earring hung from the woman's pocket. It seemed familiar. Aimée stared at it. "How beautiful. It's pink Diamonique, *non?*"

The woman clutched the earring and backed away.

"Madame, did you find this on the steps, or in Petru's apartment?"

The woman shook her head.

"A prostitute came here looking for Petru, didn't she? She wore costume jewelry like this," Aimée said.

"I do my job, clean the halls, mop down the stairs and—"

"When was she here? Yesterday, last night?"

The woman made the sign of the cross. "I don't steal."

"Of course not. But did you see—"

"She's saying I stole it?" The Portuguese woman's eyes blinked in fear. She repeated, "I clean good. *Verra*, see. No lose my job. She's hurt. Black eye, big, swollen. She come after me?"

"Bruised, you mean she'd been beaten up?"

The woman nodded.

"I tell her God will forgive her this life," the woman said. "Tell her, go to Bus des Femmes. Get rest. They help women like her. She laugh at me. Then I find it this morning."

She put it in Aimée's hands. "Take it to her. No trouble. I make no trouble."

Worried, Aimée wondered if she'd get there in time.

AIMÉE FOUND the Bus des Femmes, the mobile unit offering medical, legal, social, and practical support to working prostitutes, parked near Porte de St. Ouen. A long motor home, painted purple, emitting steam and the fragrance of coffee from its open door. Inside, a coffeemaker and leaflets covered a small table. A straw basket of rainbow-colored condoms hung from a window with "Take me, I'm Yours" printed on it. Lists of clinics were pasted on the windows. Two women chatted as they sat on long benches drinking coffee. Another woman was doing a crossword puzzle.

From their heavy makeup, miniskirts, and bustiers, Aimée figured most of the women were just taking a break from work. The close, warm air, filled with cheap scent, made for a relaxed atmosphere, the feeling of a safe haven.

"Like some coffee?"

Aimée paused before a young woman in a tracksuit with a folder under her arm.

"No thanks," she said. "I thought Cloclo might be here."

"I'm Odile, on-site legal aid." She smiled and extended her hand. "Cloclo's your friend?"

"In a manner of speaking," she said. "I think Cloclo was beaten up."

Odile nodded. "We see it more and more. Many have moved off the main boulevards into more secluded spots: car parks, massage parlors, trying to avoid the Brigade des Moeurs, the morals squad. Or they work late nights, from 3 a.m. to 7 a.m., when most people are at home, sleeping. But driving them underground makes them an easier target for violence."

Of course.

"Is she Eastern European?" Odile asked. "Those girls do twenty to thirty clients a day to avoid a beating from their pimps." Aimée hoped Odile hadn't seen her wince.

"She's older and works on rue André Antoine," Aimée said. "She's a *chandelle*," she said, a prostitute who waits under a lamppost. "Have you seen her?"

"You understand we respect a woman's right to privacy. No johns, no *flics*, or anyone else gets information. If you don't see her here, I'm sorry, I can't help you."

"If she's with the doctor, could you tell her I'm here? She's in danger."

Odile shrugged. "That's true for all of our women."

Aimée saw the pamphlets on sex trafficking and hostels for women in crisis, the worn platform heels of the woman doing the crossword puzzle and the purple bruises on her legs that makeup didn't hide.

"I haven't seen her," Odile disclosed.

Disappointed, Aimée crossed the boulevard toward the Metro. She figured Cloclo had been looking for Petru, too. Maybe she'd found out where his new place was but she'd disappeared. Probably she'd given Aimée the runaround.

She peered in several fogged-up café windows, hoping to find Cloclo, but didn't see her. At Café le Rotonde, the last one before she reached the Metro station, she looked inside. No Cloclo at the counter. But as she was about to give up,

Aimée saw Cloclo, huddled in a black coat, her feet up, at a far back table standing flush against the tobacco-stained wall.

Aimée ordered and paid for a brandy. "You look like you could use something strong," she said, setting it down in front of Cloclo. The café decor looked unchanged from the thirties except for the *télé* blaring above the bar.

"Not you again," Cloclo said. Yet her hand shot out and took the small balloon-shaped snifter.

"Did Petru do this?"

Cloclo snorted. "Him?"

"Weren't you on the way to the Bus des Femmes?"

"They don't have this," Cloclo said, downing the brandy.

"Bus des Femmes has a doctor, Cloclo. You should be examined," she said. "Where's Petru?"

"Why?"

And then the centime dropped. Hurt and anger flared inside. "Petru's your pimp, right? You lied, even after I warned you of the danger."

Cloclo waved Aimée away with her costume-jewelry-be-ringed hand.

"My head's splitting. Listen, he paid me to tell him when I saw you," she said, rubbing her temple.

Paid her? "I'll double it. Where the hell is he?"

And for the first time Aimée saw fear on Cloclo's made-up face. "I have to go," she said and scrabbled for her purse.

Aimée reached over and clamped her hands on Cloclo's shoulders. "Not until you tell me where I can find Petru."

Cloclo's eyes darted around the café. "It's not safe. And he's not my pimp."

"You're not leaving until you tell me."

Cloclo downed the brandy.

"*They* took him."

Aimée stiffened. "Who?"

"A van pulled up; some *mecs* grabbed him and drove off."

"*Mecs* with black caps and down jackets, one with bad teeth?"
Cloclo nodded.

"Where?"

"They sped off, I don't know where."

Aimée noticed the red welts on Cloclo's neck, pictured Cloclo's bleak future. She threw the earring and fifty francs on the water-stained table. "Go see the doctor, Cloclo."

Friday Evening

DARKNESS HAD FALLEN OVER the wet street filled with buses and taxis. Passersby gripped shopping bags and hurried, their coat collars raised against the frigid air.

Aimée was stumped, didn't know where to turn, where to look. She called Strago. No answer. Then she had an idea.

Sebastian, her cousin, knew the club scene. She reached him at his framing shop in Belleville. The pounding of hammers in the background told her that her little cousin was working late.

"Sebastian?"

The pounding ceased, replaced by the slow whir of a table saw.

"Rush order, Aimée," he said. "Twenty prints to frame and hang for a resto opening tomorrow. No time to climb roofs tonight."

His business had taken off. She felt proud of him. And he'd been clean, drug free, for four years now.

"One question, I'm looking for a DJ spinning vinyl, Lucien Sarti. Got an idea where I could find him?"

"What's his moniker?"

"DJ moniker? No clue. He's a Corsican musician, plays a blend of techno and polyphony."

In the pause, she heard grinding and the punch of metal.

"He could spin in a style totally different from his own music."

"What do you mean?"

"Trad, cyber, synth, eighties industrial, trance. You name it," he said.

She didn't have all night. How could she ever find him?

"Sebastian, please narrow it down."

"DJs cater to the club crowd, that's how they make a living. The good ones create a style and guard it. Lead double lives. I know a *flic* who spins vinyl near République, but you'd never know it. A down and dirty place full of goths, punks, metalheads, and transients."

Hadn't Yann said Lucien slept rough?

"What's it called?"

"Gibus on rue du Faubourg du Temple," he said.

"Gibus . . . argot for a flip-flop cap?"

"The same. Everyone spins there at one time or other."

She could start there. And with a little work, she had the perfect outfit.

DOWN A PASSAGE under the railway lines she found Gibus. There was no name outside, only a scuffed graffitied door, where a few goths stood smoking. She heard the flutter of wings as pigeons swooped from the rusted rafters above.

The roofed passage once had been occupied by depots and warehouses for goods arriving by train. Now freshly painted signs proclaimed it to be a future site for an Internet and software hub dubbed "Silicon Alley," sponsored by the government. Judging by the peeling walls and dilapidated buildings, they had a long road ahead of them.

Aimée walked through the door, passing twenty francs to a skinhead with several gold teeth.

"DJ tonight?" she asked.

He nodded and unlatched the worn velvet entry rope, leading to a corridor with fluorescent pink walls. "It's goth night, mind the stairs."

Goth. She wouldn't look too out of place with her long black net dress and matted black hair extensions. If Sebastian had steered her right, someone in the DJ network would know Lucien. She descended in the dark, holding the metal banister of a thin spiral staircase, and felt her way along the damp wall of the stone vaulted underground passage that was vibrating to the thrum of heavy metal. Her hands came back moist with an oily patina.

The passage widened into a cavern redolent of *papier d'arménie*, the old-fashioned dark rose strips, folded accordion style, burned to freshen rooms, which left a distinctive aroma behind. A smell she associated with her piano teacher, an old Russian woman who burned it to hide the fact that she cooked on a hot plate and lived in the same single room she taught in.

Aimée sniffed something else. Cats, she figured, to keep down the rodent population. Fine by her.

Her eyes grew accustomed to the dim light given off by black candles burning in niches in the walls and lining the bar. The goth crowd, male and female, wore black lipstick and nail polish. They congregated against the moisture-laden walls or sat on what looked like prayer benches, presenting a tableau reminiscent of a medieval tapestry, updated with a twentieth-century twist. Several goths clustered deep in conversation, over a leather-bound volume whose cover bore a gold-embossed cross. Some *après*-club Black Mass negotiation?

She heard voices raised in an argument. Someone was being sick in the corner. In this kind of place, one kept moving to avoid a fight. She lifted her trailing hem and headed toward the bar.

Her second dive that night.

She ordered a Belgian beer laced with *framboise*—raspberries—from the barman. A row of silver rings curved up his ear and glow-in-the-dark bracelets shone up his arm like twisting fluorescent green snakes. She paid but stopped him from pouring the beer into a tall glass as she noticed the sink filled with scummy water. She took the bottle. Hygiene, she realized, was not a priority here.

State-of-the-art speakers blared from niches in stone coves. A woman leaning on the pewlike benches nodded to the beat, her black-ringed eyes like dark holes in her face, her chains clinking against the spiked dog collar on her neck.

"Who's spinning?" Aimée asked, sidling next to her.

"MC Gotha, my boyfriend," the woman said, pride in her voice. "Grooves, *non?* Zero le Crèche, he calls it."

At least that's what Aimée deciphered; the woman's tongue stud garbled her words. The DJ bent over a turntable, big hair and tight black tank top, his silver-ringed fingers catching the reflection of the flickering black candles.

"I thought he'd show tonight," Aimée said, as if to herself. "I promised to return his mix."

The woman shrugged, shifting on her chunky platform boots.

"That other DJ, you know, the Corsican musician?"

The woman's black eyes narrowed. "Tonight's goth."

Aimée scanned the crowd. "He spins all over. I really have to find him." She paused. "Bet your boyfriend knows him. Introduce me?" Unacquainted with the protocol, she figured it was wise to ask for an introduction, after noticing the pointed black nails and vial of garnet liquid, like blood, hanging from the woman's neck.

"He's busy," she said. "Can't you see?"

"Trouble, I've got trouble, if I don't find the Corsican," Aimée said. The Stella Artois bottle the goth held was empty. "Ask him for me, eh? I'll get you a beer while you do."

Hesitation painted the woman's face as the DJ announced a break. By the time Aimée returned, they were standing together.

Aimée handed her the beer and the woman rewarded her with another shrug and passed it to her boyfriend.

"Corsican? I know the one you mean," the DJ said, reaching out his ringed hand. "He's not here. I'll give him the mix."

She didn't know what to do. She hesitated. What if she gave him a disc and he played it? Though she doubted one DJ would handle another's mix—wasn't it their signature, their stock in trade—? There was something about a man with black nail polish and a better manicure than hers that she didn't trust. The only things in her bag were empty floppy discs.

"Dark hair and eyes, a musician who mixes polyphony and techno. We're talking about the same one?"

"You're the second one tonight." The DJ made a face.

Second one?

"What do you mean?"

"I mean it's goth time, not laid-back time," he said, "That one's a lightweight." He looked bored, gave a dismissive sigh. "Better luck in the chill room."

So she wasn't the only one looking for Sarti.

Chill room . . . was that here or at another club? She made her way back toward the bar and followed a couple into the dark cavern behind, crowded with milling goths. Their black attire was like a uniform. The smoke and the rotting smell from the walls not masked by the *papier d'arménie* was getting to her. And in the humid, swamplike air her hair extensions had begun to droop. Already the temporary adhesive had melted into telltale glop on her neck. If she didn't leave soon they'd come off in big clumps. She pulled a net scarf over her head and hoped they'd stay attached.

Drum and bass with a few sampled jazz riffs drifted from somewhere. She followed the beat into another cavern where a mixed crowd lay sprawled on sofas or danced with closed eyes.

The man unpacking his coffin box—a hard plastic carry

case for turntables—nodded at her question. "DJ Ketlogic, a chill-room man for sure," he said. "Good trance mix."

She smiled, as if she understood what he meant. "Where is he?"

"You missed him."

BACK IN MONTMARTRE she found a third club. At least she could take off the fake hair and stuff it in her bag now. Anything that didn't kill you made you stronger. Wasn't that what they said?

She entered the smoke-filled club now pulsing with techno located in a once elegant *hotel particulier* with high ceilings. The yawning marble fireplace was piled with alternative newspapers. There was a tarnished fin de siècle mirror above it and a theatre space up the stone stairs, so worn they had almost melted.

"DJ Ketlogic spinning tonight?" she asked.

"Check the bar," said a man with a shaved head and dead brown eyes.

Lucien himself stood there by the brass-handled beer pulls. Her cell phone vibrated in her pocket. *Just* when she'd found Lucien.

"*Allô?*" she said, impatient.

"Aimée," Saj said. "You had a good idea. I burrowed around and discovered a connection between the central listening center at Les Invalides and the Big Ears."

"You did?" Never mind how—Saj had taken her idea and run with it. And found a connection! "Go on, Saj," she said, watching Lucien gather up his music case.

"They're monitoring Montmartre from a flat in the *quartier*, right there! Sounds like a sweet setup. Cozy, they just ordered Chinese takeout. Bet they'll hear us tomorrow or whenever when they decrypt this."

"Where?" she asked.

"Sixteen, rue Nicollet. Watch out."

"*Superbe*, Saj."

She'd better get there before they shut it down. But, having finally found Lucien, she couldn't just leave empty-handed. As if he sensed her presence, he turned. His black eyes glittered in the dim light of the bar as he looked her up and down.

"Your usual attire?"

She'd forgotten her goth outfit. No wonder people had given her a wide berth in the Metro.

"Makes life interesting," she said. She moved toward him and took his arm.

"Like to live on the edge, don't you?" he said.

"They've mounted an operation and you're it," she said in his ear. "I'm supposed to turn you in. I'll have to unless you guide me to Petru or help me find him."

"You just don't give up, do you?"

"If I do they'll land you like a fat fish. Tonight, tomorrow, or the next day. Your choice."

He shrugged. "I don't know where the *salaud* went."

"Right now, I believe you. But you can help me find him. Let's catch a taxi."

THE STEEP stairs of rue Nicollet, a dark narrow seam on the less fashionable side of Sacré Coeur, loomed overhead. Strains of African music floated from an open window. Green plastic garbage containers stood by a gate on the steps; tree branches cast sticklike shadows over number 16's small walled courtyard. Before Aimée could ask Lucien to wait, she heard groaning in the shadows. Human moans. Embarrassed, she wondered if they'd stumbled on an amorous couple. Or . . . the groaning escalated . . . were they the sounds of some-one in pain?

She skirted the garbage containers and stood on the dark wet pavement leading to a back building. A figure huddled against the rear wall. She shone her penlight on it to reveal a man, his black leather coat torn, bleeding onto the brown, sodden leaves. Petru.

"*Salaud, bastardo*," Lucien swore, followed by more words in Corsican she couldn't understand. He'd pulled out a knife and thrust it at the shaking Petru.

"Stop!" She never thought she'd protect this *mec* but now she pulled at Lucien's arm. "Wait, I have to talk to him."

"It's going down now," gasped a white-faced Petru. "The guns, the rocket launchers. I have to tell them. . . ."

"Tell the DST?"

He nodded, slumping further. His face creased in pain.

So Petru was an informer for the DST.

"Liar, you framed me," Lucien accused, shaking Aimée off.

"Why did you pay Cloclo?" Aimée asked.

"To keep tabs on you," Petru gasped. "What you found out. I played along, trying to find the real villain, but the DST thinks it's you, Lucien. I have to tell them. . . ."

"Who's behind it?" She knelt, ripped off the hem of her black net dress, and used it to stanch Petru's leg wound. Lights blazed in an upstairs flat. Her cell phone vibrated in her pocket once again but she ignored it. She heard doors slam, footsteps. The DST. Not the folks she'd care to meet on these dark stairs.

"Who, Petru?"

His eyelids fluttered. "Conari's site . . . the hospital . . . tunnel."

Conari . . . the hospital. Think, she had to think. She pulled Lucien back.

"Give me half an hour before you tell them, do you understand?" But Petru's eyes had closed, his head slumped forward.

"I'll take care of him," Lucien said, elbowing her aside.

"The DST will take care of you if we don't leave now," she said, alarmed.

Comprehension dawned in his eyes.

"Quick!" She ran up the steps two at a time, panting and

wishing to God she hadn't gained that kilo. When she reached the summit by an *école maternelle*, she heard Lucien behind her.

Her cell phone vibrated again. She caught her breath and hit *Voice Mail*. Two calls, both of them just static, then someone breathing. A heavy breather. Then the sound of the phone crashing on the floor and "Nurse, the patient . . .," then a buzz.

Her heart jumped. Was Laure trying to phone her? She steadied her shaking hands and hit *Call Back*.

"*Oui?*" said a low voice.

"It's Aimée Leduc, I have several messages on my phone."

"Our patient, Laure Rousseau, is agitated. It seems she's trying to get a message to you. She's able to use a keyboard."

Was Laure OK? Trying to communicate with her?

In the background Aimée heard a garbled noise.

"She can't speak, but she can tap letters and numbers on a keyboard."

"What has she said—I mean, tapped?" Aimée asked, wishing the nurse would hurry.

"Your name, number, and what looks like, 'Remember . . . men saying Breton.' That's all."

"Men on the roof? Ask her if it was the men on the roof. Please, nurse."

Aimée heard the nurse ask.

"She blinked yes."

Laure had remembered something from the roof.

"Does she mean Bretonneau, the hospital?"

"She looks tired—"

"Please, it's vital. Ask her," Aimée said, trying not to shout.

"Yes. She tapped yes."

"Tell Laure I'm en route."

She stuck her cell phone in her pocket.

"Is Conari behind it?" Lucien asked.

"Things point to him but I'm not sure." She had doubts. Yet

he could use Lucien's music contract to launder arms money. He had Corsican contacts and a construction company. But his ties to the government, evidenced by the man from the Ministry they'd seen with him at the church, confused her.

"Let's find out."

TOO BAD she hadn't looked closer at the construction trucks parked inside the Hôpital Bretonneau courtyard. "Conari Ltd." was painted on them. It all fit together. The place had been vacant for six years, since 1989, according to the demolition permit on the wall. The year Jubert said her father had been given a contract to work on the stolen arms case.

She had been careless and now it would cost her. Again. No time to think of that. She had to get inside. They climbed over the locked gate, past the squat, which was dark and partly boarded up. She punched in Morbier's number.

Busy.

She had to reach him. Tried again. Gravel crunched from a side building.

She tried another number.

"René? No secrets, right? I need your help."

"Aimée?" he said, his voice sleepy.

"Call Morbier, keep trying to get him to alert the *flics*, not the DST. . . . Only *flics*, you understand?"

"What? Why?"

"I'm at the Hôpital Bretonneau in Montmartre, by the cemetery," she said, breathing fast. "There's an Armata Corsa arms cache underneath it, somewhere in the tunnel past the squat. No DST or RG. Make sure Morbier understands. Just the *flics*."

"*Mon Dieu*," René said. "Don't tell me you're there!"

She heard a clinking, like keys, over the phone.

"Hold on," he said, awake now. "Wait right where you are until I get hold of Morbier, Aimée."

"I can't. I have to settle some business."

"Business. You're crazy! Does it have anything to do with clearing Laure?"

"Everything. Jacques's killers are inside. I promised her I'd nail them. One more thing. Call Chez Ammad, the bar on rue Veron, and ask for the bricklayer, Theo. Find out from him which day Dumpsters by his building site on rue André Antoine are emptied."

"Eh, a Theo . . .?"

"Please, René, *right now!*"

She clicked off before he could protest further.

In the shadows, Lucien pulled her close. She could see the mist of his breath in the cold air. He cupped her chin with his warm hands. A silhouette of black curls ringed his face.

"What did you mean? Is Conari inside?" he asked.

"He'll use your contract as a way to launder money from gun sales," she said. "He's been providing arms, for a price, to those who made bomb threats under the guise of the Corsican Separatist movement."

Lucien's grip stiffened. "How can you be sure?"

"It's a theory; you have to test it, eh, like a scientist? Use the empirical method and find out."

In this instance, barge right in and hope to God her hunch was right. At least partly right. Whoever handled the stolen arms had to be stopped. She figured Jacques had been trying to do so. Otherwise, he wouldn't have involved Laure.

Clouds obscured the moon; a single street lamp glowed over the cemetery wall. Cold air cloaked her legs. In the rafters above them, a nest of pigeons fluttered and cooed, disturbed by their noise.

"I need a sign," he said.

"What? You're worried about the evil eye?"

Before he could answer, she kissed him hard. Long. Her lips melting on his. Responding, his arms crushed her to him.

She pulled back and caught her breath. "Will that do?"

Silence except for the backfire of a car.

"For now."

Did she hear amusement in his voice?

"Over there," Lucien said, pointing to a crumbling brick building, a diffused light now radiating through the barred windows. "Careful, there's someone there."

She saw the orange tip of a cigarette and nodded. They crept toward the building's sagging brick pavilion, careful to step around the gravel and wood piled by the trucks. Lucien had hitched his music case onto his back. He edged ahead. She heard a loud thump and an *ouf*, as someone expelled air and crumpled.

Lucien had caught the *mec* from behind, sat him down, and ground out his cigarette.

"Nice touch," she said. Testing a hunch with a strong guy at her side wasn't a bad idea, though she'd never admit it to him.

Only one guard? Why not more? Unless the rest . . . .

"You have a plan?" he asked.

She nodded. "We take them by surprise. Figure out where the arms shipments leave from and barricade it."

Lucien shifted the scuffed metal door, slid it open, and she followed him inside the half-gutted building, past concrete mixers and old hospital gurneys turned on their sides. She flashed her penlight around them. No holes or openings leading to a tunnel. Just broken light fixtures, piles of crumbled lath and plaster, an old crucifix tilted against the remnant of a sagging green wall. Had she got it wrong?

She kept going, past exposed brick and arched iron beams. Saw a yellowish glow ahead. Plastic construction tape labeled DANGER WORK SITE UNSAFE STRUCTURE hung from wooden sawhorses.

She reached for her spray can of Mace and with her other hand picked up a metal rod. And felt herself sinking.

"Lucien!" she called. But the only answer was the cracking of floor boards and the swoosh of shifting grains of sand. Under her feet, the floor was tilting, crumbling, throwing her off balance. Petrified, she grabbed for something, anything, as the floor gave way under her. Her hands came back covered with grit and tangled in an electric cord. And then she was dangling in cold air, swinging, her knees hitting against heaps of dull white stones. She heard the loud rumbling of a generator and saw the hewed-gypsum-walled cavern floor far below.

Terror paralysed her. Her hands slid; she couldn't hold on. She smacked against a conical mound and grabbed at plaster that flaked under her fingernails.

Bumping and clutching at rough ridges and crumbling, gouged surfaces, she slid several meters to a subterranean dirt floor. Scattered gypsum mounds gave it a lunar-landscape look. Dizzied, she gazed up to see the layers of Fontainebleau sand and glistening travertine, packed sandwichlike over the compressed off-white and yellowish pinnacle of gypsum she'd slid down.

She'd landed in an old quarry under the hospital, part of the galleries webbing the underground that had been mined to build Sacré Coeur. There was not much to commend the sturdiness of their foundations to those living overhead in buildings resting on them. Amazing that Sacré Coeur didn't tumble on its head.

Pounding came from the other side of the huge white flaky mound.

Where was Lucien?

Earsplitting blasts from a generator had masked her descent. On all fours, covered in caked white gypsum, she crawled around the mound, crouched behind rolls of abandoned chainlink fence and hollow metal poles, and then gasped.

A stone's throw away, men in camouflage fatigues, Eastern European by the look of them, stacked ammunition and dull

gray machine guns in metal boxes emblazoned with the slogan
ARIEL, SPARKLING LAVAGE POUR TOUTES LES VÊTEMENTS!

Like the washing-machine detergent box on Zette's table.
The killers' calling card? Worry about that later. She had to
stop them. But how?

To the side of the cratered gypsum quarry were split, rotted
wood coffins, hoes, shovels, and a forklift. A storage area for
grave diggers and their equipment from the adjoining Montmartre cemetery. Gruesome. The men, intent on loading the
boxes, ignored them.

A small open-platform train car sat on tracks leading to a
tunnel. She figured the tunnel snaked under the street and
went to the cemetery. If she could short out the wires connected to the generator's battery she'd plunge the cavern into
darkness. That would stop the men and allow her to escape
through the tunnel. At least, she'd have a shot.

Fear coursed through her. Several feet away from her stood
the throbbing industrial generator with rusted wires protruding
from it. Cans with funnels were lined up next to it; it ran on
gasoline. Even with the men engrossed in their work, she'd have
little time to play with the wires. Or to flip the circuit breaker
she saw, protected in black housing on the control panel.

She felt in her pocket for a lighter. In the worst-case scenario, she'd knock the gasoline cans over and . . . no, that
would be stupid. Live ammunition boxes were stacked by the
Ariel cartons!

What could she do? She eyed the corroded metal sprockets
and debris in her escape path, memorizing her route. If she got
that far!

The generator had a revolving fan, its blades encased in a
rusted tan metal frame to cool the exposed motor. She had an
idea. She scrabbled her hands around to find something, anything, long enough for what she needed. Found it.

The generator's noise muffled shouts and swearing in

Corsican. She saw Lucien, his arms behind him, thrown to the ground, then shoved behind large metal cable spools. She peered around the side of the generator. Conari, his shirt bloodstained, sat behind the forklift, tied up. She couldn't make out another figure partially obscured by Lucien. Wait! His shoes. She knew those shoes.

Someone walked toward the generator. A hand leaned down to pick up a gas can. She had to do it *now*.

With all her might, she shoved a long metal pipe across the dirt, cramming it into the revolving fan. There was a deafening squealing of shredding metal jamming the motor. Then a grinding and crunching, emitting a shower of sparks and spitting shards of metal as the motor ate the pipe. A hail of metal shrapnel rained off the rail car. The man was screaming.

The light wavered. The generator coughed and screeched to a halt, plunging the cavern into darkness. Her whole body tingled and shook. There were shouts and more screams of pain. Twenty seconds had passed but it felt like twenty minutes. Then, a sickening odor of burning oil from the generator. So rank she could taste it. A voice whimpered in pain.

"What happened? Idiots, go to the backup generator!"

Beams of flashlights swept the grayish white smoke-filled haze. She heard an echoing loudspeaker, incomprehensible words. The *flics*? Morbier? Then short staccato bursts, the thuds of bullets. *Mon Dieu.* Lucien was exposed to a rain of bullets! She ducked and saw the shoes, running over the gravel toward the tunnel.

He was getting away! She struggled to her feet, coughing, her ears ringing, as she grasped the rolled-up chain-link fence for support.

She caught herself, then ran, hoping she'd memorized a clear path, and took off down the tunnel, following the train tracks. Footsteps pounding ahead guided her. The frigid tunnel narrowed. And then there were no more footsteps.

She stopped, gasping, leaning against the earth wall. She was in the cemetery, its mausoleums silhouetted against the now clear sky, with just a thin tissue of cloud skirting the pearly white fingernail of a moon.

How could she find him in this necropolis?

Crunching sounds of broken glass came from her right.

She tripped on tree roots snaking over a gravestone, tried to still her shaking hands, wipe the damp vegetal humus from her face. She made her legs move but had no clue as to where they were taking her.

Center, she told herself. Focus on the sensations surrounding her, as she had done when she'd been blind: sounds, currents of air, the feel of disturbed earth. The jade bangle on her wrist, an opalescent green, glinted in the thin moonlight.

Her thoughts cleared. A stillness came over her. She guided her feet around the uneven graves without tripping. Then she paused.

She sensed him, hovering. She smelled the sweat of his fear. The scent Laure had caught on the scaffolding.

"Yann, I know you're there," Aimée said. "Your jogging shoes gave you away."

A covey of startled night birds erupted, flapping their wings.

"But you're brilliant, Yann," she said. "From me, that's high praise."

Ahead, an elongated shadow moved through the damp air.

"The bricklayer from the construction site confirmed that the Dumpster's emptied on Wednesday. It was impossible for it to have spilled over the night you 'found' the diagram. But that's minutiae, a minuscule detail. Maybe your military service was in Corsica."

"You knew that?"

She hadn't. Guessed. Like she had about the Dumpster.

"No wonder you spoke Corsican and discovered the arms

cache. My father was hired to find the stolen armaments six years ago."

"You're like a ghost," he told her. He stepped into view.

She realized she was covered in white powdery plaster. A ghost, at home here, with all the others.

"Conari got involved. You threatened him, so he went along. Jacques demanded more money, and Zette knew too much."

"Jacques wanted to pull out, the fool," Yann said.

The cold metal of an automatic was pressed against her temple. His breath panted in her ear; her arms were grabbed and twisted behind her. He pushed her forward.

Keep him talking. Anything. Hadn't René said the Ministry required construction firms with Ministry contracts to use systems analysts? "So ingenious. You'd worked on Ministry contracts. Was that how you tapped into Big Ears?"

"Tap into them?" He rolled his eyes. His ponytail hung over his shoulder. His suit jacket was studded with irregular bits of metal. The tang of burnt oil clung to him. "As it turned out, after all my preparation, I didn't need to. I installed the communications in Solenzara where I worked with those guys. I just shared a bottle of Courvoisier with them and caught up. Easy."

And simple. That's how it worked with old comrades in the military. No wonder she'd kept running into dead ends.

"So you listened in on Conari's line at the DST flat and knew they were monitoring your 'operation.'"

"Just like the old times." Yann's breath frosted and faded into vapor trails over the uneven headstones. "Even then, in Corsica, Jacques gambled. He blackmailed me, until I had no choice."

"Jacques threatened to inform after he'd discovered the cipher key? The cipher key only you could access. The one thing proving you were involved. So you quieted him for good?"

She heard the trigger pulled back. Where were the *flics?* Her hands trembled. Get him talking.

"Didn't it go like that? You realized Petru was working undercover for the DST. You knew they were closing in," she said, her words coming out in a rush. "I got too close, so you threw suspicion onto Lucien."

He twisted her arms so tight her circulation was cut off. "A little late Wonder Girl."

Perspiration beaded her upper lip. Had the *flics* missed Yann's escape in the confusion?

"Why now? Why move so many guns now?"

"Conari and his construction trucks. A little here, more there, he didn't care to know as long as he got paid." Yann's eyes gleamed. "Amazing how it all comes down to money. No one ever has enough."

He pressed her down to her knees over a sagging iron-fenced grave. She gasped as the rusted iron bit into her ribs. She forced herself to go on. "But you're a perfectionist. The snowstorm, the party, luring Jacques up to the roof, knowing he'd bring backup. Everything worked until you got to the skylight. You'd forgotten to arrange for gunshot residue on Laure's hands." She panted, the blood rushing to her head. "In your hurry, you put *your* gun in her hands and fired. Your one mistake."

"I liked you," he said, leaning down, his hot breath in her ear. He stroked her cheek with the gun's cold muzzle. "Didn't you get it? That night in the café? But I was nothing to you; you weren't interested. If only . . ."

His words made her skin crawl. "You're not my type."

He whacked her with the back of his hand, slamming her against something pointed. A cross? She grabbed at the ground, her hands filled with dirt.

"Give up, Yann, it's over."

Then he kicked her and she crumpled onto a flat, smooth slab. Her eyes registered the letters: François Truffaut 1932–1984, carved in granite in front of her nose. Was she going to be shot on the gravestone of Truffaut, the Montmartrois who had immortalized the *quartier* in his films? Not if she could help it.

"You're like all the rest!"

"Second mistake." She kicked, connecting with his thigh, and he yelped. Somehow she got to her feet, then he pulled her down.

"Bitch!"

She swung, throwing dirt in his face. A shot pumped by her ear, deafening her. A burning sensation creased her arm. She rammed into him with all her might and his head landed with a crack on the granite next to her. Scrabbling and raking her fingers through the wet leaves, she found the gun as Yann, stunned, lay beside her, groaning.

She felt a spray of pebbles on her hand, looked up, and saw René. The ringing in her ears hadn't stopped.

He reached down and helped her up, then took rope from his pocket and bound Yann's hands.

"Thanks, partner," she said, clutching her bleeding arm and the gun.

He dusted off his jacket, eyeing her outfit, plastered with mud and wet leaves. "A new look?"

"Eh? Look at me when you talk until I can hear again."

"Fashionista all the way." René rolled his eyes. "You said you wanted the *flics* to wrap this up."

She sagged against a tree, saw a blue uniform rounding the gravestone. "About time."

Saturday Afternoon

THE DARK, HYPNOTIC PULSE vibrated from the stage,

which was washed by red-, orange-, and pink-hued lights. Lucien's song, layered with hip-hop and the rippling chords of his *cetera*, took Aimée to a faraway place swept by the southern sirocco. Even on painkillers, the music thrilled her, evoking the maquis-scented air, the flapping of silver-scaled fish caught in nets, and a sun-drenched granite island. Under a dull black ceiling, Lucien's music transported his audience.

Applause. People milling, and then Aimée grew aware of Lucien's hand—large, warm, and on her shoulder. She tried not to wince.

"You have a gift," she said, looking up into his deep-set eyes.

"Can I show you something?"

She nodded.

They left the Conservatoire National de Paris and climbed the hilly streets. Beside a glass-fronted building, an old workshop, Lucien pulled aside the wire fence.

"Make it good, musician."

"Go ahead. I know the owner," he said.

She crossed the weeds and picked a path through the brush, thankful for her leather pants. A deserted terrace with many round tables met her eyes. "It's a restaurant."

"How about a one-of-a-kind view?"

He led her to the back and unlocked a door with a long black key. She followed him up the musty winding stairs. He opened a creaking window. The view took her breath away. The wooden arms of a windmill framed a sea of zinc-covered roofs and chimney pots stretching below. They stood in the windmill of the Moulin de la Galette.

"It's still a village here," she said. "Untamed by Paris."

"I've been invited to the World Music Festival in London," Lucien told her.

"Congratulations! Wonderful for you." She glanced at her Tintin watch. "Before you go, I have a view to show you."

HER LEGS touched Lucien's under the sheets. His warmth enveloped her. She sighed and nudged him. In answer, he wrapped his arms around her, kissed her neck, and continued what they'd been doing.

Some time later, she blinked her eyes open. Miles Davis nestled, spooned between her and Lucien. Weak winter light shone on Lucien's cracked leather jacket hanging over the door of her armoire. The train ticket to London stuck out of its pocket. His denims were on the floor. His *cetera* case was silhouetted against the window overlooking the Seine.

"Hey, musician," she said, peering at the clock on the dresser. "I'm late."

In answer, he pulled the pillow over his head.

She stood up, slipped on her black leather pants, eased her bandaged arm into the sleeves of her turtleneck, and stepped into her boots.

SHE FOUND Morbier in the hospital at Laure's bedside, a lopsided grin on his face.

"Nice of you to show up, Leduc," he said. "I gave Laure the rundown, but I'm sure you'll spice it up with the details."

She kissed Laure on both cheeks. Yellow bruises, a sign of healing, framed Laure's temples.

"Without your help, Laure, the *flics* couldn't have caught him."

"*Bibiche* . . ." Aimée could make out that much; the rest came out garbled. Laure tapped furiously on the computer keyboard.

Morbier read out loud: "I've been reinstated, Jacques cleared. Get me a new speech therapist, this one's slow and *stupid!*"

Aimée smiled, then turned away. Half an hour later, she walked arm in arm with Morbier over the tiled floor. They paused at the glass windows overlooking the dry fountain in the courtyard. A coating of ice sparkled the basin's lip.

"You won't tell her, Leduc," Morbier said.

"Is that a question or a statement?"

He sighed. "A little of both."

"Ludovic Jubert told me you made a pact in the police academy. A one-for-all, all-for-one kind of thing. Right?"

Morbier averted his eyes and shifted his worn brown shoes.

"So Papa didn't inform on Rousseau despite his corruption, bound by that promise. Neither did you or Jubert. After Papa died . . . ," she paused, taking a deep breath, "Rousseau's report said Papa took the bribes and knew of the arms shipment. It was easier that way, so you two kept your mouths shut as long as Rousseau agreed to retire."

Morbier stood still. So still she could hear the gurney's rubber wheels gliding on the floor, the muted sobs of a woman rocking on the bench, covering her face in her hands.

"Life and death hold secrets, Leduc," he said. "Some are best kept."

Her papa was clean. She knew, they all knew. Except Laure. But she wouldn't tell her. Couldn't.

Out on the quay, they paused, the lighted facade of the Hôtel de Ville before them, Notre Dame illuminated on their right. All in her backyard.

She smoothed down the tweed lapel of Morbier's jacket and stared at the slow-moving Seine. Pinpricks of ice glinted on the iron rungs once used to anchor barges. And at this moment, in the lingering shadows of dusk, with the whine of sirens in the distance, a child's laughter from a passing stroller, and the Seine lapping below her, she felt at ease with her ghosts. For now.

"Hungry?" she asked.